PUMPKIN SPICE, KNOTTY NIGHTS

A WHISPERING GROVE NOVEL

OMEGAVERSE ROMANCE

HARLEY KNIGHT

CONTENTS

PUMPKIN SPICE, KNOTTY NIGHTS
A WHISPERING GROVE NOVEL

I vowed never to belong to anyone again... Some promises are meant to be broken.

At twenty-two, I've already had my share of hell with being forced into an arranged marriage with an abusive man by parents, who couldn't care less. But Whispering Grove is my fresh start. My own apartment. My brewery job. My life, finally.

So when my bestie drags me to the town's Halloween festival, I'm trying to enjoy the pumpkin spice and haunted hayrides like a normal person. I even laugh when I think I see my ex in the house of horrors. Just my anxiety playing tricks, right?

Until he walks into the Harvest Dance. Very real. Very angry.

Pure panic sends me straight to the biggest, scariest Alpha in the room. "Just pretend you know me," I whisper to the glowering stranger. He growls something about why I would pick him, and I'm honest: "Because you look like no one would dare mess with you."

What I don't expect is his two equally intimidating friends

appearing at our side, or the way all three men look at me like they've found something they've been hunting for.

Now I have a choice: keep running from my nightmare… or stand my ground with men who promise protection.

The problem is, accepting their help might save me from one Alpha's obsession, but can I protect my heart from three more?

1

CINDY

alloween in Whispering Grove is like watching your grandmother get a tattoo… unexpected, slightly disturbing, and impossible to look away from. Our sweet Christmas-obsessed town transforms into something unrecognizable every October, trading the music on the overhead outdoor speakers from "Silent Night" to "Thriller" and replacing the year-round twinkle lights with fake cobwebs that will absolutely still be there come December.

"If I die in there, I want it on record that I *knew* it was a death trap." I cross my arms, glaring at the House of Horrors squatting at the edge of the festival like it personally offended me. It leans slightly to the left, draped in fake cobwebs and flickering red lights that scream tetanus and poor life choices. The plywood façade is painted to look like rotting bricks, but it mostly looks like someone lost a bet and went wild with a staple gun and two dollars' worth of spirit store clearance items. Somewhere inside, a chainsaw revs. I flinch. "See? It's already claiming victims."

Harper bounces beside me, practically vibrating with Halloween enthusiasm. She's gone all out tonight with purple-tipped black hair styled in elaborate victory rolls, dramatic winged eyeliner that could cut glass, and a vintage horror movie T-shirt tucked into a tulle skirt that shouldn't work but absolutely does on her. The combat boots with spiderweb laces are just the cherry on top of her spooky sundae.

"Don't be dramatic," she says, which is rich coming from someone wearing earrings shaped like tiny chainsaws.

"I'm not. That haunted house looks like it was designed by someone whose therapist gave up."

"My therapist thinks I'm making excellent progress, thank you very much." Harper grabs my arm, her collection of silver rings cold against my skin. "Besides, you promised. No take-backsies now."

"I promised to attend the festival. I said nothing about voluntarily entering buildings specifically designed to trigger fight-or-flight responses."

Harper bellows out a laugh, still tugging me closer to the entrance.

The Whispering Grove Halloween Festival sprawls around us in chaos, with people everywhere.

Harper loves all of this with an intensity that borders on religious. She grew up here, but her Mexican grandmother always celebrated *Día de los*

Muertos, teaching her that October wasn't about fear but about honoring what came before, dancing with death instead of running from it. When her abuela passed five years ago, Halloween became Harper's way of keeping that connection alive. She throws herself into it with the same passion her grandmother brought to her *ofrendas*, just with more fake blood.

"Come on," Harper wheedles, pulling me past a booth selling candy apples. "We need to get our adrenaline up before the Harvest Dance. That's where all the hotties are going to be."

"According to what source?"

"Jeff told me."

"Jeff being the guy who disappears for days without responding to messages?"

Harper's grin turns defensive. "He lives three hours away in Wild Falls. He can't always—"

"He can't text from Wild Falls? Did they not get cell towers yet?"

"He's busy with work—"

"Doing what, exactly?"

"Investment banking."

I stop walking. "In the town whose main exports are disappointment and that weird cheese that tastes like feet?"

"Don't be a cheese snob." Harper tugs me forward. "Besides, when he is here..." She fans herself dramatically. "That man knows exactly how to make me smile."

"And we're entering the murder house now!" I

announce loudly as a family with small children passes.

The bored teenager at the entrance doesn't look up from his phone as we pay. His zombie makeup is already smearing, and it's only eight o'clock.

"Welcome to your doom," he drones. "Don't touch the actors. They won't touch you unless you sign the waiver for the extreme experience."

"There's an extreme experience?" My voice climbs an octave.

Harper's eyes light up like someone just offered her a puppy made of nightmares. "Should we—"

"Absolutely not."

We push through hanging chains that immediately tangle in my hair, and the temperature drops like we've entered a meat locker. The festival sounds fade, replaced by speakers playing what I can only describe as ambient suffering.

"This is fun!" Harper shouts, then immediately shrieks as something brushes her shoulder.

"Super fun," I mutter, grabbing her arm. "I'm having so much fun I might actually die."

We shuffle forward through strobing lights that make everything look like a horror movie directed by someone having a seizure. The corridor opens into a maze of mirrors, each one reflecting distorted versions of ourselves. Harper makes faces at her stretched reflection while I try not to think about how accurate the funhouse effect feels—warped, wrong, like I'm still that girl from two years ago who didn't know who she was.

"So, Jeff's coming to the dance tonight," Harper admits, apparently immune to the creepy dolls now surrounding us, their heads turning to follow our movement.

"How nice for Jeff."

"He's bringing friends."

"How nice for Jeff's friends," I say sarcastically and stick my tongue out at her.

She hip-checks me, nearly sending me into a mannequin dressed as a bloody bride. The white dress makes my stomach clench... too close to memories I've buried, to the girl who ran through the woods in torn lace and fear.

"Sorry!" Harper catches me. "I didn't think—"

"It's fine." The laugh that escapes me is too bright, too sharp. "Just wasn't expecting the wedding theme in a Halloween house." I push back the thoughts because it's been almost two years since I ran away from my family, from the man I was meant to marry, leaving him at the altar.

We round another corner into fake cobwebs that stick to everything. A child's voice sings off-key from hidden speakers, which is infinitely worse than screaming.

"Jeff's really sweet," Harper continues, determined to distract me. "He brought me flowers last time. Roses. They were black roses."

"Okay, that's actually pretty good."

Something lunges from the shadows. We scream, clutching each other like we're trying to become one person with twice the anxiety. The actor cackles before disappearing back into the darkness.

"I hate this," I gasp. "I hate this so much."

"You love it," Harper insists, though she's breathing just as hard. "When was the last time you felt this alive?"

She's not wrong, which is annoying. The adrenaline feels refreshing and nothing like the constant terror I lived with before. This is fear I can walk away from.

We navigate through a medical scene that appears too realistic for comfort, then a tilted room that makes me nauseous.

"Oh, look, angry clown. Revolutionary," Harper continues.

"Is that supposed to be blood, or did someone spill their fruit punch?"

"That skeleton is wearing Crocs. I refuse to be scared of someone in Crocs."

I'm actually starting to relax, letting myself lean into the ridiculousness, when we round another corner.

A figure stands at the end of the narrow hallway. Black suit. Tall frame. Blond hair slicked back in a way that speaks of money and control. Backlit by red lights that turn him into a nightmare.

Van. The man I was supposed to marry. The man I

ran from in a wedding dress nearly two years ago. The man whose cigarette burn still marks my arm.

Every muscle in my body locks. The scream building in my throat isn't fun or controlled. It's the one I've been swallowing for two years, the one that tastes like smoke and desperation.

"Cindy?" Harper's voice sounds like it's underwater.

The figure starts walking toward us, and I can't move. My vision tunnels, and suddenly I'm not here—

I'm in his mansion, his hand around my throat, his voice calm as he explains how I'll learn to be silent.

I'm at the ceremonial hall, counting the seconds until my life ends.

I'm running through woods, branches tearing at white lace—

"MOVE!" Someone shoves past us, the group behind us, breaking the spell. The lights flicker brighter, revealing the truth. It's just an actor, maybe twenty, with theatrical makeup and a cheap suit. Nothing like Van except in my panic-broken brain.

"I thought—" I gasp to Harper, unable to finish. "For a second, I thought that was Van."

"Shit." Harper's face goes pale. "Let's get some air."

She doesn't wait for agreement, just drags me through the rest of the house like we're being chased by actual demons. We burst into the October night, and I immediately bend over, hands on knees, gulping air like I've been underwater.

"Breathe," Harper soothes, rubbing my back. "You're safe. He's not here."

Except I've been seeing him everywhere lately. Two weeks ago on the sidewalk, and I hid in a local bakery cafe, but it turned out to be some tourist. Last week at the gas station, just another tall blond guy. My paranoia has been in overdrive all month, and I hate it. I hate that after almost two years, he still has this power over me.

"Come on," Harper says, steering me toward the food vendors. "Pumpkin spice fixes everything."

"That's your solution to all things."

"And when have I been wrong?"

We find a table near the beer garden, which is just picnic tables with string lights and paper butterflies that look more like mutant moths. Harper returns with two steaming cups and a concerned expression.

"We don't have to go to the dance," she offers. "We can go home, watch horror movies, eat our weight in candy—"

"No." The word comes out harder than intended. "No, I'm not letting a panic attack ruin tonight. I'm not letting him, even the memory of him, control me anymore."

Harper studies me for a long moment, then nods. "Okay. But if you change your mind—"

"I won't." I take a sip of the pumpkin spice latte, letting the sweetness ground me. "Besides, you promised me hot guys to judge. I demand eye candy as compensation for emotional trauma."

Her grin could power the entire festival. "That's my girl! Come on, let's go see what Whispering Grove's finest have to offer."

The walk to the barn takes us through the rest of the festival, where we pass the ring toss game, a pumpkin carving contest, and a haunted hayride that's just a tractor pulling a wagon while someone half-heartedly waves a plastic knife.

"Two stars," I tell Harper. "The mask is crooked, and he's clearly texting."

"Harsh but fair."

The barn glows against the dark field, wrapped in so many string lights it's probably visible from space. Orange and black balloons gather at the entrance like a craft store exploded. Music pours out that, surprisingly, isn't that loud.

Inside the barn, it's packed. The back half holds benches where groups cluster with drinks, the middle is cleared for dancing, and a stage at the far end hosts a live band doing decent covers of classic rock with Halloween twists.

"Drinks!" Harper states, and she's already weaving through the crowd.

I watch her trajectory change when she spots someone near the bar... Jeff. He's handsome with perfectly styled dark hair. When Harper literally throws herself at him, he catches her easily, laughing in a way that makes me soften toward him slightly. The way he looks at her, like she's the only person in this packed barn, okay, maybe I get it.

Which means I'll be waiting a while for that drink.

I drift deeper into the barn, following the edge of the crowd. Despite everything, I love the energy, the music, the freedom to just exist without anyone watching to make sure I'm being properly demure. I even start to relax, letting the music wash over me, the bass thrumming through my chest like a second heartbeat.

Then I lift my gaze and freeze. And I see him.

Not a maybe. Not my paranoia. Not a look-alike.

Van Stone, in the flesh, standing near the entrance I just came through.

I'm going to be sick. He looks exactly the same, devastating in that cold, calculated way. His suit is perfectly tailored to his athletic frame. His blond hair is styled as I remember, without a strand out of place.

He's alone, which somehow makes it worse. No handlers, no family, just him with those ice-blue eyes scanning the crowd with methodical intent.

Then those eyes land on me.

The fury that transforms his face makes my blood turn to ice. His jaw clenches, hands flexing at his sides in that way that always preceded pain. Close to two years of running, of hiding, of becoming someone else, and he's found me.

My brain screams at me to run, but my legs won't cooperate. Where would I go? He's blocking the main exit. Harper is lost in the crowd. I don't recognize anyone else I know to run to. Panic flares over me, and I frantically scan the room. That's when I spot salvation, or at least a delay of doom.

There's a man sitting on one of the benches that line the wall, and sweet Jesus, he's enormous. He makes the bench look like dollhouse furniture. Six foot five at least, built like someone who bench-presses cars for fun, he's maybe in his late twenties, early thirties, and extremely handsome. His black hair is short but longer in front, falling across his forehead in a way that should look boyish but doesn't, not with that jaw, those shoulders, that presence that seems to push against the air around him.

When he turns to look at something, I catch his profile of harsh angles softened only by surprisingly full lips and long, dark lashes that seem at odds with the rest of him.

I don't think. I just move toward him in a hurried walk, my heart thundering in my chest.

"Please, just pretend you know me," I whisper, dropping onto the bench beside him.

He turns fully toward me, and my brain short-circuits. His eyes are amber, but that description does them no justice. They're the color of threads of gold that catch the light, deep-set under dark brows that are currently raised in question. This close, I can see the faint stubble along his jaw, the way his throat works as he swallows, the fact that his shoulders are literally twice the width of mine.

"Interesting opening line," he says, and his voice, God, his voice is low, rumbly, and something dangerous. "You always approach strangers with requests for improv?"

"Only when—" I glance at Van, who's pushing through the crowd, getting closer. My voice cracks. "Please. There's a man. He—I need—"

Mountain Man follows my gaze, then looks back at me. Something shifts in his expression, a sharpening that transforms him from casually intimidating to lethal.

"Ex-boyfriend?" he asks quietly.

"Ex-fiancé." The word tastes like ash. "The kind that doesn't understand 'ex' means 'over.'"

I can't stop looking between them, Van getting closer, this stranger beside me who smells like spiced caramel and toasted marshmallow with notes of vanilla that make no sense because men who look like him should smell like motor oil and violence, not comfort and warmth. My brain is spinning, overwhelmed by fear and this unexpected scent that makes something in my chest unclench for the first time in years.

"Why me?" he asks.

I glance up at him, trying to stop myself from trembling. "Because you look like no one would dare mess with you." I'm honest, desperately needing his help.

Van is maybe twenty feet away now, his expression promising retribution.

"What's your name?" Mountain Man asks, leaning close enough that his breath tickles my ear.

"Cindy," I whisper back.

"I'm Holt. Let me handle this." He slides an arm around my shoulders, the weight of it grounding and terrifying in equal measure. Then, louder, with a laugh that's all dark edges: "There you are, sweetheart. Been looking everywhere for you."

The endearment should make me flinch, as Van used to call me that while hurting me, but from Holt's mouth, it sounds different. Protective. A shield instead of a cage.

Van stops several feet in front of us, and I feel Holt inhale slowly. His arm tightens around me.

"Can we help you?" His voice drops to something deadly.

"You're with my Omega." Van's tone could freeze hell, each word precise and cold.

"Funny," Holt says, and I feel the rumble of his voice through his chest. "She doesn't smell like yours."

The territorial words should terrify me. This kind of primitive Alpha posturing is exactly what I've been avoiding. But something about the way Holt says it, protective rather than possessive, makes me lean into him instead of away.

"She's been promised to me." Van's composure is cracking, his voice rising slightly. "She belongs—"

"To herself," Holt interrupts, and the authority in his voice has even Van stepping back slightly. "See, that's your problem, thinking people belong to anyone but themselves."

"Problem, Holt?" A deep, male voice comes from our left. I twist to see two men who definitely weren't there before, and my heart stops because, for a second, I think they might be with Van. Then I notice how they're positioned, flanking us protectively rather than aggressively, and the way one of them grins at Holt with familiar ease.

They're both devastating in completely different ways. One has auburn hair, gray-green eyes that seem to shift color as he moves, and is built like a boxer. He smells as sweet as candied apples and spiced cider with undertones of leather that shouldn't work together but do.

The other's moves captivate my attention. Dark blond hair falls past his collar, and his brown eyes are so dark that they're almost black in the barn's dim lighting. The scent of buttery toast with cinnamon and sugar wafts from him. I almost drool at the smell.

"This fucker seems confused about basic consent," Holt tells them, never taking his eyes off Van.

"Hate when that happens," Auburn states cheerfully, dropping onto the bench to my left.

"Really ruins the vibe," Dark Blond agrees, settling on the other side of Holt.

Neither touches me, but their presence is overwhelming. Three massive Alphas surround me, their combined scents causing my head to spin. I should be terrified. Instead, I feel safer than I have in two years.

"Three against one?" Van sneers, but I can see him calculating odds.

"Three protecting one," Holt corrects. "Big difference."

Van's gaze finds mine, and the hatred there makes me shrink back instinctively. "You think you can just disappear, Cynthia?"

There it is. My real name. The one I buried along with that wedding dress when I ran from him less than two years ago. The one only he uses now, wielding it like a weapon.

"She did disappear," Holt says, standing slowly. When he reaches his full height, Van has to tilt his head back to maintain eye contact, and the power shift is beautiful. "Seems like you're the one who doesn't understand how disappearing works."

"She has obligations—"

"Had." I find my voice, though it shakes. "Past tense. As in done. Over. Filed under 'mistakes I ran from.'"

Auburn makes a sound that might be a laugh. Dark Blond shifts slightly, further blocking Van's view of me.

Holt takes two slow steps forward, closing the distance between him and Van. His hand runs through his hair, biceps flexing in a way that's both casual and threatening. When he speaks, his voice is low enough that only our small group can hear.

"Here's what's going to happen. You're going to turn around. You're going to walk out of this barn. You're going to leave this town tonight. And if I see you near her again, if I even hear you've been asking about her, I'll introduce you to some friends of mine who specialize in making problems disappear. The permanent kind of disappearing. We clear?"

Van's jaw clenches. His gaze flicks to me once more, a promise of violence that covers me in goose bumps.

"I'll see you around, Cynthia," he barks out softly, and somehow that's worse than shouting.

Then he turns and strolls away, shouldering through the crowd hard enough to knock drinks from hands. The moment he's out of sight, my whole body starts shaking.

"Breathe," Holt says, turning back to me. He crouches in front of the bench, putting us at eye level. "You're safe."

"He found me. I'm not safe," I whisper. "After almost two years, he found me. How did he—what if he—"

"Hey." Holt's voice is gentle now, all that dangerous edge gone. "Look at me."

I do, and the concern in those eyes draws me to him.

"You need us to be your security?" Auburn asks, and I can't tell if he's joking. "Because we're very good at it. Ask anyone."

"Well, don't ask the people we've secured against," Dark Blond adds. "They might be biased."

"Guys," Holt says mildly, though his lips twitch like he's fighting a smile.

"Cindy!" Harper calls out, appearing like an avenging angel, Jeff trailing behind her. She takes in the scene, me shaking, three enormous strangers surrounding me.

"What happened? Are you okay? Who are—"

"Van was here," I interrupt. "He found me."

The color drains from Harper's face, then floods back red. "Are you sure? Where is he? I'll kill him. Jeff, hold my earrings—"

"He left," I assure her quickly. "These guys... helped."

Harper's gaze rakes over them. "And you are?"

"Holt," Mountain Man introduces himself, standing. "These guys are Luke and Arrow."

Luke (Auburn) gives a little wave. Arrow (Dark Blond) nods solemnly.

"They made Van leave," I tell Harper. "Made sure he knew I wasn't alone."

Something in Harper's expression softens slightly. "Thank you. We should go, though. In case he comes back."

"If you need anything," Holt says, pulling out his phone, "day or night—"

"I don't—" I start to protest.

Holt immediately nods. "Okay, then. Just so you know, we're usually at Savor, at least one of us, and mostly in the evenings, if you need anything. Please don't be afraid to ask for help."

"Savor?" I ask, trying to calm my racing heart.

"Restaurant on Main," Arrow says. "I opened it recently. These two just mooch."

"We provide security," Luke protests. "Very important security."

"You provide commentary on my menu choices," Holt adds with a smirk.

"Very important commentary," Arrow adds.

Despite everything, I find myself almost smiling. "Thank you. Really. I don't know what would have happened if—"

"Nothing would have happened," Holt says firmly. "Not while we're around."

The possessive edge should scare me, but it doesn't. Maybe because I can still smell them, all three distinct scents tingling in my senses, and butterflies burst in my stomach. Or maybe because, for the first time in two years, someone stood between me and Van without wanting something in return. Or I'm just high on adrenaline and not sure what I'm smelling.

"Come on," Harper says, linking her arm through mine. "Let's get you home."

As we leave, I glance back. All three men are watching us go, and there's something in their expressions that tells me they care. Like they're seeing something they've been looking for, which is insane.

"Those were not normal good Samaritans," Harper says once we're outside.

"Nothing about tonight was normal." I'm still trembling, Van's face burned into my mind—his rage, his fury.

He found me.

He found me.

"Three stupidly hot Alphas protecting you from your psycho ex? That's not normal. That's romance-novel territory."

"Hell, it's horror-novel territory for me."

"Are you smiling?" Harper stares at me.

I am a bit. And that scares me too much.

Because despite the fact that my worst nightmare just walked into my safe haven...

Despite the fact that I'm still shaking from it...

I'm smiling about three strangers I shouldn't trust.

Because safety isn't real.

Not for me. Not anymore.

My heart won't slow down.

Van's threat echoes in my head.

I'm not safe.

Not here. Not anywhere.

Tomorrow, I'll figure out what to do.

Tonight... I just want to disappear.

I just want to be free.

But freedom doesn't come for Omegas like me. And just like that, Mother's words dance in my thoughts: "Omegas don't get to run. We survive by standing still and taking what is expected of us."

2

HOLT

"Think she's safe?" Luke's question hangs in the air as we watch Cindy move through the crowd with her friend, Harper, and some guy in designer jeans who probably has a trust fund and calls it investing.

I can't take my eyes off her. The way she moves carefully but not defeated, cautious but still laughing at something Harper says. Her honey-blonde curls shine in the barn lights, and every few seconds, she checks for threats. She's wearing tight, dark jeans that hug her curves and a soft green sweater with tiny black cats all over it. When she turns to glance back at the barn entrance, the light catches her face, and something primal in me roars to life.

Mine. The word pounds through my blood like a drum. Her scent clings to my nostrils as though it's taken up permanent residence. Clove-studded orange, sugar brittle, and pumpkin spice loaf fills my senses, and I fucking adore the smell already. Fuck!

"I doubt that prick Van will take the hint," Arrow states, his voice deceptively calm as he watches the crowd. "Guys like that? They don't hear 'no.' They hear 'try harder.'"

"She came out of nowhere," Luke muses, still tracking her movement. "One minute, we're suffering through another Halloween festival because Arrow wanted to check out the competition's food trucks, and the next, this honey-haired goddess drops into our lives. Or more like almost on your lap, Holt."

"With a psycho ex who clearly can't handle rejection," Arrow adds. "Did you see his expression? Like someone took away his favorite toy. Fuck, I want to punch that look off his face."

"She's not his fucking toy," I snap.

They both stare at me, and Luke grins. "Oh, he's got it bad already."

"Doubt that douche came alone either," I continue, ignoring Luke's comment. "You know how those types operate. Vindictive to a fault. Probably has backup waiting outside."

I'm still watching Cindy, the way the green of her sweater makes her skin glow, how she tucks a strand of hair behind her ear. It's nothing like any Omega I've ever been with, and I've been with plenty. Betas too. Meaningless encounters, mutual satisfaction, nothing more. But this... this feels different.

"Think she might be my scent match," I say.

The confession hangs between us. I've never had one, never thought I would. Heard about them my whole life, that scent that calls to your very DNA, that one person whose pheromones align with yours so perfectly it's like finding the missing piece of yourself. Always thought it was bullshit romanticism. Propaganda to make Alphas settle down.

But standing here, her scent still wrapped around me like a blanket, I know it's real. Something inside me that's been locked for thirty-two years just opened, and she's holding the key.

Both their heads whip toward me. I brace for the mockery, the jokes about the big bad Alpha going soft over one tiny Omega. Instead, Luke lets out a long breath.

"Thank fuck you said it first," he mutters. "Thought I was having a stroke or something. Did you catch that scent? Like every good thing I've ever wanted wrapped up in one person."

Arrow sets down his beer, and the expression on his face is something I've never seen in our fifteen years of friendship. "When we sat down with her, something in my chest just... shifted. Like the world tilted and suddenly made sense."

"Scent matches aren't that uncommon," I admit, though I'm trying to convince myself as much as them. "Happens, I'm sure. Just never thought it would happen to me."

"To all of us," Luke corrects. "With the same woman. What are the odds?"

"Better question," Arrow adds quietly. "What do we do about it?"

We've always planned to share an Omega if we found one. Made a pact years ago when we first formed our own pack after leaving the Savage Reapers MC. We'd been through hell together, refused to let anything, even an Omega, come between us. But planning for something theoretical and having her right there, smelling like everything we never knew we needed, are two different things.

"Could be we're imagining things," I force myself to say. "She was terrified, pumping out distress pheromones. Maybe we're just responding to an Omega in danger."

Luke snorts. "Right. Because we're known for our white-knight tendencies. Remember that Omega last month at the bar who kept rubbing against you? You literally peeled her off and walked away mid-conversation."

"She was drunk," I defend.

"She was interested," Arrow counters. "And you felt nothing. No pull, no protectiveness, no sudden urge to murder everyone who looked at her wrong."

He's right. The way my blood boiled when Van stood there, when he dared to call her his... I haven't felt such rage since our enforcer days. Since the really dark times when we did things that would make normal people run screaming.

"Look," I say, rolling my shoulders. "Whether she's our scent match or just an Omega who needs help, we're not letting her out of our sight while that prick is lurking around. Agreed?"

"Agreed," they say in unison.

We move through the barn, keeping our distance but maintaining a visual. I watch how she laughs with Harper, her hair cascading down her back. Watch how she touches Harper's arm when she talks. Watch how she keeps checking over her shoulders and around her.

She's perfect. And she has no idea three ex-enforcers are watching her like she's the answer to every question we never thought to ask. Then they reach a parked car in the parking area.

"They're leaving," Arrow notes as he joins me.

We follow in the shadows, Luke somehow managing to look casual despite being six feet, two inches of coiled energy. Arrow moves like smoke from my side, there and gone before anyone notices. And me? I'm trying not to look like what I am, a predator who's found something worth hunting.

The parking lot is darker than it should be, half the lights out or flickering. October fog rolls in from the mountains, giving everything that small-town Halloween vibe—fake cobwebs on every light pole, plastic skeletons hanging from trees, even the parking lot attendant booth is decorated with those gel window clings that look like bloody handprints.

I spot two shadows, nine o'clock. They're following Cindy's group, staying just far enough back to seem coincidental. But not with the way they move, the way they mirror every turn.

Luke joins me. "Want to introduce ourselves?"

"Not yet," I decide out loud. "Let her get safe first. Then we play."

Cindy climbs into a silver Honda, with Harper driving and the trust fund boyfriend in the back. The two shadows immediately jog to a black BMW parked three rows over. Subtle as a sledgehammer.

We pile into my truck, a massive black Silverado with a lift kit and huge wheels. It's obnoxious and exactly what suits us.

"Why do you always get to drive?" Luke complains from the back.

"Because it's my truck," I remind him, firing up the engine. The rumble probably wakes half the neighborhood, but I've never been good at subtlety.

"Technically, we all paid for it," Arrow points out from the passenger seat.

"Technically, you can both walk," I counter, pulling out fast enough to make Luke grab the door handle.

"Jesus, Holt, she's not gonna disappear. You can follow at normal speeds."

"This is normal. For me."

The Honda turns onto a main street, heading toward the residential area. Every house is decorated for Halloween with orange lights strung along rooflines, inflatable creatures on lawns, those motion-activated monsters that scream when you walk by. Whispering Grove goes all out for Halloween, trying to compete with their Christmas reputation. Even the street signs have little witch hats on them.

The BMW follows Harper's Honda at a distance that would seem reasonable to anyone not looking for it. We hang back farther, using my knowledge of the town's layout to parallel their route.

"Think Harper knows she's being followed?" Arrow asks.

"Maybe. She seems sharp. Protective of our girl too."

"*Our* girl," Luke repeats with satisfaction. "I like the sound of that. Hey, remember when Brick found his Omega?"

"Brick, who used to run some errands for us?" Arrow laughs. "That man was the size of a small building and turned into a puddle the first time she smiled at him."

"Complete personality change," Luke agrees. "Went from breaking legs for the club to baking fucking cupcakes for her book club."

"They're happy, though," I point out, remembering the last time we saw them. "Disgustingly happy."

"'Three kids in four years' happy," Arrow adds. "Man's living his best life."

"And he said the same thing we're saying now," Luke continues. "That he knew the second he scented her. That everything before her was just marking time."

I can't remember the last time these two were buzzing with this much energy. Usually Luke's flirting is surface-level—all charm, no substance. And Arrow hasn't shown real interest in anyone since we left the club. But now they're both practically vibrating with anticipation.

"She's turning," I note, watching the Honda's tail-lights disappear down Maple Street, deeper into the residential section.

The BMW slows, clearly trying to figure out how to follow without being obvious. That's our opening. These streets are narrower, lined with big oaks that create a canopy overhead. Jack-o'-lanterns glow on every porch, and someone has gone all out with a full graveyard setup on their lawn, complete with a fog machine.

"Arrow, let's give them some guidance," I suggest, and he's already reaching for the megaphone we keep under the seat. Sometimes you need to yell at people from a distance. Old habits from the enforcer days.

I floor it, engine roaring as we close the distance. The BMW driver sees us coming in his rearview and tries to speed up, but I'm already swinging around, cutting him off at the next intersection so he can't follow Cindy. He has two choices: stop or ram my truck. Given that my truck would destroy his BMW, he stops.

"You know what to do," I tell Arrow.

He's already hanging out the window, mega-phone in hand. "Good evening, gentlemen! Seems you're lost. This road? It doesn't go where you think it does."

The BMW's window rolls down. I can't see clearly, but I hear the voice, some entitled prick who sounds like he was born with a silver spoon surgically attached.

"We're just driving—"

"Wrong answer!" Arrow cheerfully interrupts through the megaphone, the sound echoing off the houses. "See, you were following that Honda. We were following you following that Honda. It's like a really boring parade where everyone's invited except you."

Luke laughs from the back seat. "Arrow's having too much fun with that thing."

"Here's what's gonna happen," Arrow continues, still using the megaphone even though we're maybe ten feet away. "You're gonna follow us. We're gonna show you the scenic route out of town. The one that ends with you nowhere near here."

The passenger door of the BMW opens. A guy built like a refrigerator starts to get out.

I'm out of my truck before he's fully standing, and the look on his face when I tower over him is almost worth the entire night.

"Get back in the car," I say quietly.

"You can't just—"

"I can. I am. I will continue to. Get. Back. In. The car."

Luke is out now too, casually tossing his keys in the air and catching them, each toss making the heavy keychain, weighted with a brass knuckle attachment, glint in the streetlight. "Man, I love it when they think about fighting. Makes the whole thing more fun when they realize they can't win."

Arrow is still hanging out the window with the megaphone. "Folks, we're experiencing technical difficulties with our guests' ability to follow simple directions. Please stand by."

"Do we really need the megaphone?" Luke asks.

"Oh, we definitely do," Arrow answers, grinning as he raises it again. "IT REALLY ADDS TO THE AMBIENCE."

Refrigerator Guy glances between us, clearly doing the math, and when he gets back into the car, it's obvious he doesn't like the outcome.

"Smart man!" Arrow calls out through the megaphone. "Now follow us. Don't think about turning off. Don't think about running. Just follow like good little ducklings."

We climb into the truck, and I lead them through town at exactly the speed limit. We pass the elementary school, which is covered in paper bats, the library with a massive spider on the roof, and the fire station, where one of the trucks has its ladder raised like a dragon's neck, with a painted dragon head at the top.

Arrow provides commentary the entire way. "Take a left here. Oh, look, you're following! Good boys. Now a right. Still with us? Excellent."

"You're enjoying this too much," Luke adds.

"Fuck yeah, I am," Arrow corrects, lowering the megaphone from his mouth. "We haven't had fun like this in months. Remember that dealer who tried to set up shop behind our restaurant? This is way better than that."

"That ended with him in the hospital," I point out.

"Yeah, but he walked again. Eventually. I think," Luke says.

The backstreets of Whispering Grove are our territory. Every shortcut, every dead end, every road that looks like it goes somewhere but doesn't, we know them all. The BMW follows because what else can they do? They're strangers in our town, and we've made it clear that leaving is their only option.

Finally, we reach the river port. It's not much—a boat launch that's seen better days, a parking area covered in gravel, and the river itself, dark and swift and about forty feet wide. Someone has even put up Halloween decorations here of a skeleton sitting on the dock with a fishing pole.

I stop the truck. The BMW pauses behind us.

"This is the best part," Luke says, practically bouncing.

We all climb out. The BMW guys do too, and now I can see them clearly. Refrigerator and Van, who's trying to look tough but failing.

Arrow raises the megaphone one more time. "Welcome to the Whispering Grove Port Authority. Population: You're leaving."

"This is fucking kidnapping," Van protests.

"Nope, these are directions," I correct. "You wanted to know where our friend lives. Well, she lives in a town where you're not welcome. This river? It goes all the way to Wild Falls. You can follow it, find your way back to wherever you crawled out from."

"I wasn't paid for this bullshit," Refrigerator mutters, eyes flicking between Van and us.

Van's face is glowing red, jaw tight enough to crack bone. "Shut the fuck up," he snaps, lifting his chin toward me like I'm something he already owns. "She belongs to me. My family paid—*invested*—for her. The arrangements, the contracts—"

"I don't give a fuck about your blood money," Arrow cuts in, his voice low now, lethal. He finally lowers the megaphone and takes a step closer. "She belongs to herself. And if you've got a problem with that, say the word. Let's settle it right here."

He cracks his neck like he hopes Van says yes.

Van opens his mouth, but Refrigerator holds out an arm, trying to contain the explosion. "You don't know who you're messing with. The Stone family has connections—"

"So do we," I say, stepping forward. My voice is calm, too calm. Because for a moment, I let them all see the man I used to be.

The one who bled for the Savage Reapers that I ran.

The one who made monsters flinch.

The one Van has no idea how to handle.

"We built our connections with fists and blood and fear," I say. "You want to know what happened to the last guy who threatened someone under our protection?"

Silence.

"Exactly," Luke chimes in with a cheerful smile.

"Because no one ever found him. Funny how that works."

The Savage Reapers might be behind us, but the instincts never left. We walked away from the violence.

But for Cindy? An Omega in trouble.

For *our* scent match?

We'll drag hell up by its throat if we have to.

Van's lip curls. "You think this ends here?"

"I think you should start moving before it does," Arrow adds.

For a beat, no one moves. Just the rush of the river behind them and the heavy breathing of too many men itching to draw blood.

Then Van finally steps back, slow and reluctant, eyes burning into me like he's carving a promise into my skin. "You can't be serious about swimming out of here?"

"Oh, I'm dead serious." Luke grins. "Hope you stretched first. The current's a bitch this time of night."

Refrigerator takes a step forward. "You can't make us—"

Arrow moves fast, not violently, but with purpose. He doesn't touch Refrigerator, just steps into his space, crowding him. Something in Arrow's eyes remains calm, calculating, *deadly,* and has the bigger man stumbling backward.

"We used to do this professionally," Arrow explains, voice almost friendly. "Hurt people, I mean. Got real good at it. Bones, nerves, pressure points. All that fun anatomy stuff."

He smiles like they're swapping recipes, not threats.

"Been trying to retire. Live quiet lives. But you? You're making us nostalgic for the old days when problems got solved once... permanently."

Refrigerator swallows hard, his face paling as he flicks a nervous glance at Van, who has Luke staring him down.

"So what's it gonna be?" I ask, stepping up beside Arrow. "You take the river voluntarily, or we send you back in pieces with a message carved into your back for the Stone family."

Van's nostrils flare, fury simmering just beneath the surface. He doesn't move, but the way his jaw clenches says everything.

"This is insane," Refrigerator mutters, staring at the river. "It's October. That water is freezing."

"Better cold than dead," Arrow says, cracking his knuckles.

"You wouldn't actually—" Refrigerator starts.

I take three slow steps forward, Luke following suit, driving Van closer to his buddy, closer to the pier's edge. That's all. Three steps, and both men start backing up like the ground has shifted beneath them.

"You touch me," Van growls, "and I swear to God—"

"You'll *what*?" Luke cuts in, stepping out of the shadows with a grin that doesn't reach his eyes. "Call your daddy? Cry about it to your contract lawyer?"

Refrigerator shifts uncomfortably. "Van... we're outnumbered."

Van's glare burns into each of us, jaw clenched, body coiled like he's one second away from snapping. "Fuck you," he spits, voice low and venomous. "All of you. This isn't over."

"We're counting on that," Arrow says coolly.

Refrigerator exhales through his nose, clearly not thrilled with the situation. "Seriously?" he mutters to Van, barely audible. "We're *swimming*?"

Van growls, then jerks his head toward the river. "Move."

Refrigerator mutters something under his breath but follows. They both stomp into the water, splashing and cursing as the cold hits them.

"Shit! This is freezing!" Refrigerator barks. "My balls are gonna sue."

"Ten bucks says Van drowns just to spite us," Luke says, filming with one hand, grinning like it's a nature documentary.

"I give them five minutes before the river decides to do us a favor," Arrow adds.

We stand at the edge, watching as the current takes them.

Van doesn't look back.

Refrigerator slips once, swears loudly, and keeps going.

They vanish around the bend, two dark shapes pulled into the black water, swallowed by the current and the night.

They're gone.

Cold. Humiliated. Furious.

Van won't forget.

But neither will we.

We stand there, silence stretching as the river swallows the last of Van and his hired muscle.

Then I laugh.

It catches me off guard, a sharp, unfiltered, and real chuckle. It bubbles up from somewhere buried, the kind of laugh I haven't had in years.

Luke glances over. "What?"

I shake my head, still grinning. "We just ran two guys out of town like something out of an old Western. For a girl we met *less than an hour ago*."

"A girl who most likely is our scent match," Arrow corrects, his voice quieter now. More certain. "That's worth a little river enforcement."

"A little?" I raise a brow. "We just made them *swim* to another jurisdiction."

"Yeah, well." Luke shrugs. "Wait until Van shows up again. That's when things will get *really* interesting."

"He'll definitely come back," I add, the weight of that settling into my chest. "Guys like him always do."

Arrow doesn't flinch. "Good. Been too long since we had a real problem to solve," Arrow mutters like he's looking forward to it.

"No killing," I say, half joking, half praying.

Luke chuckles, finally lowering his phone. "You

know we can't help it. You put wolves in the wild, they *act* wild."

Arrow glances behind us. "What do we do about the car?"

I follow his gaze to the sleek BMW Van rolled up in. Expensive. Flashy. Loud in every way a predator shouldn't be.

"Shove it into the river," I say.

Arrow doesn't hesitate. "On it."

Luke grins.

They move like they've done this before, because we have. Arrow yanks the driver's door open, leans in just far enough to throw it into neutral, and then plants a shoulder against the side to push, while Luke lines up at the rear bumper and does the same. Their muscles strain as tires crunch over gravel and roots. I just stand there and watch, arms crossed, the wind tugging at my shirt, the river still churning from its last offering.

The front wheels hit the slope, and the car picks up speed. Gravity takes over. The river doesn't resist but welcomes the offering with a hungry splash as the car plunges in nose-first, water rushing in like blood to an open wound.

It rocks once. Twice. Then starts to drift, the headlights flickering beneath the surface like dying stars before they give out, and the whole thing starts to sink.

The car vanishes beneath the surface. No splash. No drama. Just... gone.

Like it never existed.

Like we didn't just start a war.

Luke claps his hands. "Well, I'm starving. We just committed at least three misdemeanors and a probable felony. That calls for snacks."

Arrow snorts. "What's that make us? Grand Theft Auto and Chill?"

"Illegal dumping," Luke corrects and chuckles. "Very romantic."

I ignore them as my eyes sweep the dock one last time.

No cameras. No dockmaster. No late-night fishermen. Just a sagging boathouse, peeling signs, and weeds cracking through the asphalt.

Nothing but shadows and silence.

I glance behind us again. Empty. Not even a stray cat.

Perfect.

"So what now?" Arrow asks. "We find her?"

"I already got her friend's license plate," I say. "Old sedan, cracked taillight. Won't be hard."

Luke raises a brow. "You memorized that in the middle of everything?"

"I was busy," I mutter. "But not blind."

I step away from the water, the cold finally starting to sink into my bones.

"We find her. Keep watch. Quietly. She doesn't need more fear in her life right now. And she sure as hell doesn't need us barreling in like monsters."

"And when Van comes back?" Luke asks, voice darkening.

Arrow nods. "Then we meet him. And this time, we don't ask nicely."

The wind shifts. The current pulls. The river hides our crimes like it was made for us.

"She doesn't know what's coming," Luke says after a moment.

I look toward the road ahead. Toward the town where the girl who walked into our lives like a warning is.

"No," I say quietly. "But we'll make damn sure she survives it."

3

CINDY

I'm in the barn, but everyone else has vanished like smoke. Just me and Holt, and somehow I'm strad-dling his lap on the bench, my thighs pressed against his, feeling every solid inch of him beneath me. The fairy lights above us blur into stars, or maybe that's just what happens when he looks at me like I'm the only thing in his universe.

"We've been waiting so long," he says in his deep, rough voice I already love. His massive hands slide up my thighs. "Centuries. Lifetimes. And here you are, smelling like everything we've been missing."

"I don't understand," I whisper, but my body does.

"You will." His nose finds that spot where my neck meets my shoulder, and I gasp as he inhales deeply. "You were made for us. Three pieces of the same soul, and you're the missing center."

The barn shifts, melts, re-forms. We're still there but

not there. Luke appears behind me, his hands sliding into my hair, tilting my head back.

"Finally," he breathes against my temple. "Do you know what it's like? Searching every face, every scent, knowing you're out there somewhere?"

Arrow materializes at our side, his dark eyes intense as he traces a finger along my jaw. "We would have burned cities to find you. Would have torn apart anyone who kept you from us."

I'm surrounded, overwhelmed, drowning in their combined scents, and it should terrify me, but instead I'm melting, dissolving into sensation. Holt's mouth traces my collarbone while Luke's fingers stroke my shoulder, and Arrow's thumb brushes my bottom lip.

"Too much," I gasp, but my body arches into their touches, betraying how much I want this. "I don't know how to—"

"We'll teach you," Holt growls against my throat. "Everything. Anything. We've got time now. All the time in the world."

His teeth graze the curve of my neck, and I shudder, heat curling low in my belly and pooling between my thighs.

"Sensitive," Luke breathes against my ear, his voice velvet and sin. "You feel that? Right here?" His fingers trail down my ribs, dragging slow, teasing circles along my skin. "That's mine now."

He chuckles when I arch into him, the sound rich and full of hunger. "God, you're perfect. We're going to worship *every inch of you... kiss you until you forget what it felt like to be alone."*

Arrow still watches me like he's already claimed me. His stare burns through me, dark and possessive, jaw tight like he's holding back something feral.

"Do you have any idea what you look like right now?" he rasps, stepping closer. "Soft. Ready. Fucking beautiful."

My breath stutters in my chest. I can't move. I don't want to.

"When I touch you," he continues, "it won't be careful. It'll be reverent. And if you think reverence means gentle..."

His gaze drops to my lips.

"...you're in for a surprise."

Luke hums against my skin, nosing just beneath my jaw. "You want to be touched like that, don't you?" he whispers. "You want us to take our time. To make it last."

His fingers skim beneath the edge of my shirt, and I gasp. The heat of their attention settles heavily on me, inescapable and intoxicating.

"I'll take that as a yes," he murmurs, kissing the place where my pulse flutters.

They're not just looking at me like I belong to them.

They're acting like it.

Speaking in promises and possession, like it's already decided.

And maybe it is.

Maybe I was always meant to end up here—

Between them.

For them.

My fingers are digging into Holt's shoulders as my body

arches, caught somewhere between fear and unbearable pleasure. "Be gentle. I've never... I haven't been with anyone. Not really. Not like this."

Everything stops.

Three powerful bodies go still around me, breaths catching like they've been struck.

Holt's hand stills at my waist. Luke lifts his head from where his lips had been tracing fire along my collarbone. Arrow curses under his breath, low and sharp.

Then Holt pulls back just enough to see me. His gaze locks on to mine, amber gone molten, something feral barely contained in the depths.

"No one's touched you?" he asks softly.

I shake my head, too overwhelmed to speak.

Holt exhales gradually, like he's trying to leash himself. "Then no one ever will. Not after this. We'll be the first. We'll be the last."

Luke's voice brushes against my ear like velvet laced with danger. "We'll take you apart, sweetheart. Slowly. Carefully. Until there's not a single inch of you we haven't claimed."

"You won't even remember what it felt like to be untouched," Arrow murmurs, his hands gliding down my thighs like a vow.

They move with new intention. Worshipful. Possessive. Every caress is reverent and darkly addictive, as if my admission flipped some invisible switch. They don't rush. They savor. Every inch of skin they touch feels like it's being branded—theirs.

Holt leans down, his lips barely brushing mine. "We'll make it perfect for you. But perfect doesn't mean soft."

My breath catches.

"It means unforgettable."

I wake with a gasp, my entire body *lit*. Sheets twisted, thighs damp, breath ragged. My skin feels sunburned from the inside out, and I swear I can still feel the imprint of Holt's body pressed against mine, Luke's voice in my ear, Arrow's hands on my thigh.

There's no sound but my own ragged breathing, the creak of the house settling around me.

I sit up, dazed, heart pounding.

I've never had a dream like that before. Not like this.

Not with the sense that something had shifted.

That something was coming.

My lips still taste like caramel.

My skin tingles like it's been claimed.

"What the hell was that?" I whisper to the morning silence.

But deep down, I already know. I meet drop-dead gorgeous Alphas, and my body betrays me.

I stumble to the bathroom on wobbly legs, splash cold water on my face until the burning recedes to a manageable simmer. In the mirror, my reflection looks wrecked—pupils overtaking the hazel irises, cheeks blushing, lips swollen like I've actually been kissed.

A cold shower helps, barely. I have to bite my lip to keep from making any sounds as the water hits my oversensitized skin. Every drop feels like a spark against raw nerves. By the time I step out, I'm flushed, shaky, and deeply annoyed with my body for betraying me.

I wrap a towel around myself and move to the small mirror above the sink. My hair is a tousled mess, naturally wavy and always a little too wild to behave. It falls just past my shoulders, a soft, mousy honey blonde. I rake a wide-tooth comb through the tangles, grimacing when it snags. Blow-drying is fast and aggressive, more function than finesse, and I smooth it with my fingers, scrunching the ends to keep the wave.

Makeup is quick. Concealer under the eyes, a swipe of mascara, tinted balm. Just enough to fake energy. Just enough to pretend I didn't wake up panting from a dream that felt more like a memory.

Then I pull on my favorite work clothes of black fitted pants that have survived at least a hundred brewery spills, a tight black T-shirt with our logo across the chest, and worn-in boots. They're nothing special, but they've molded perfectly to my feet. It's my armor. Familiar. Functional. I sometimes wear a skirt on those days that warm up.

And for a moment, I almost feel human again.

Almost.

The knock on my door makes me jump.

"Cindy! Dear! Are you awake?"

Mrs. Meadow. I check the time. Just after seven o'clock. She must have heard me moving around.

I open the door to find my neighbor in her signature housecoat, this one covered in dancing pumpkins, holding a plate of what smells like cinnamon rolls.

"Morning, Mrs. Meadow," I manage, hoping I don't look as thoroughly debauched as I feel.

"Oh, good, you're dressed. I worry about you, dear, a young, unmated Omega living alone. It's not proper, not safe. You really should consider moving back with family, or at least finding a nice Alpha to protect you."

If she only knew why I can't go back to my family.

"I appreciate the concern," I say gently, taking a cinnamon roll. It's still warm, probably fresh from her oven. "But I'm doing okay on my own. In truth, I love living... independently."

She gives me a look. The kind that says she's heard that before. But I mean it.

Because the truth is that I've *had enough* of being smothered under the weight of *concern*.

Omegas are coddled, overprotected, told it's for our security, when really, it's about control. We're expected to be soft, pliable, obedient. We're rarely trusted to decide for ourselves, but we're constantly told what's best for us. I grew up behind glass, trapped in a house that treated me like a fragile possession. I couldn't step outside alone. Couldn't go to the store without an escort. Couldn't *breathe* without someone making sure I did it properly.

They said it was love. Safety. Family.

But love shouldn't feel like prison bars.

And I went along with it because I didn't know any better. Maybe I was scared. Maybe I didn't have a voice strong enough to fight back. My only real example of freedom was my aunt, who taught me what independence looked like in stolen afternoons and whispered phone calls.

My mother hated it. Tried to keep us apart. Said she was reckless, dangerous, a bad influence.

But when my aunt died... something in me cracked wide open. Like all the air had been sucked from my world, and suddenly I realized what I'd been missing.

That was the day I started looking. Digging. Researching the rare places in the country where Omegas weren't silenced or owned. Where they could *live*—run businesses, vote on local councils, go on dates or to bars or to *nowhere at all*—alone.

Whispering Grove was one of maybe a handful of small towns that didn't just tolerate Omegas, but welcomed them. Protected them *without ownership*. Encouraged them to be part of the community. To be whole. They even had heat clinics, which were discreet, well run, and staffed with actual medical professionals. Resources designed to help Omegas manage their cycles without shame or fear. So we weren't at the mercy of biology. So we could have options. Control.

In Whispering Grove, being an Omega doesn't mean surrendering your life. It means finally getting to *live* it.

That's why I came to hide here.

Why I'm not leaving. Even if that asshole Van found me. I won't let him drive me from my home, no matter what I have to do.

"Hmm." My neighbor purses her lips in that way that means she disagrees but won't argue. "Well, you be careful. Town's full of strangers for Halloween. Some of them…" She trails off as a truck pulls up outside, music blaring. "Oh! That's my grandson. Family's here. Must go!"

She bustles off, and I watch through the window as three generations of Meadows pile out of vehicles. The kind of family gathering that happens because people want to be together, not because they're calculating what they can gain from it.

I grab my backpack, step outside, and lock the front door. A quick glance around and no one watching me, then I'm strolling toward the bakery on the main street. The October morning takes my breath away. Whispering Grove has transformed itself into a Halloween wonderland that would make movie studios jealous. Every single house on Cottage Lane has embraced the season. Porches draped in synthetic cobwebs that glitter with morning dew, skeletons arranged in funny poses, inflatable witches swaying in the breeze. And carved pumpkins in front of every home I pass. I love it here.

Even the air smells like October, with woodsmoke from fireplaces, cinnamon from someone's baking, that crisp leaf scent that only comes this time of year. Mr. Shouz is out adjusting his lawn display, which has evolved into an entire zombie apocalypse scene, complete with a survivor camp made of cardboard.

"Morning, Cindy!" he calls, waving a plastic severed arm at me.

"Morning! The zombies are looking extra deceased today!"

"Thank you! I added more blood splatter last night. The wife says it's too much, but I say go big or go home!"

This is what I love about Whispering Grove. People here are unapologetically themselves, throwing their whole hearts into whatever brings them joy.

Main Street continues the theme but amplified. Every storefront window is painted with Halloween scenes—the hardware store has tool-wielding jack-o'-lanterns, the pharmacy has vampire pharmacists dispensing blood prescriptions. The vintage shop has dressed all its mannequins as famous movie monsters, and I swear the *Creature from the Black Lagoon* mannequin waves at me.

Orange and black bunting zigzags across the street like a Halloween crown.

Flour & Fable Bakery has outdone itself, but that's no surprise. The window display is a gingerbread haunted house that's actually haunted. I watched the owner, Lily, rig up tiny motors so miniature gingerbread ghosts fly around it. The entrance door to the cafe has been framed with autumn leaves that smell like cinnamon when you brush past them, and inside, the paper bats hanging from the ceiling each have tiny LED eyes that blink at random.

Harper is already at our corner table, wearing a

sweater with a zombie that says "I'm Dead Inside" but somehow making it appear cheerful.

"You look like you either didn't sleep or slept too well," she observes as I collapse into my chair across from her.

"Both? Neither?" I slouch. "I still can't believe Van found me," I say, the words tumbling out. "That fucking asshole. Almost two years I've been free, and he just shows up like he has any right—"

"I know, honey. I know." Harper reaches across to squeeze my hand. "Did you get any sleep at all?"

"Some. Had every lock on and propped a chair under the door handle. Watched the street for an hour before I could even try to close my eyes." I laugh, but it's shaky. "Between the fear and a seriously heated dream about Mr. Hot Mountain Man, I'm a complete mess. I might need three coffees. Minimum."

"Steamy dream?" Harper's eyebrows shoot up. "About Holt?"

"And the others showed up too, and—" I bury my face in my hands. "My brain is broken. Absolutely broken."

"Morning, lovelies!" Lily appears like a caffeinated whirlwind, her golden-brown eyes sparkling with excitement. "Oh my, someone needs emergency coffee. I'm on it. The usual but make it extra?"

"Make it a triple," I plead.

"I totally get it. And it's been chaotic here all morning! We ran out of oat milk by nine, someone knocked over the pumpkin spice syrup, and the espresso machine started making a noise like a dying possum, but we're pushing through!"

"Lily, you're rambling," Harper says fondly.

"I ramble when I'm overworked!" She giggles and it's adorable. "Halloween brings out the weirdos *and* the caffeine fiends. Oh! And Mr. Finley came in earlier dressed as a bat, forgetting he had a meeting with the town council. He just flapped in like it was normal." She leans in with a grin. "They made him keep the wings on. Said it added 'seasonal whimsy' to the zoning discussion."

Harper laughs.

"Anyway, we've got new Halloween flavors on rotation. There's a caramel-pumpkin cold brew that tastes like a sugar high, and something experimental with black cocoa that might be cursed. I haven't decided."

"Sounds great. Bring us one of each to try them out," I say, then wink at Harper. "We'll have the themed drinks instead of the usual."

"Coming right up! Extra sugar, extra caffeine, extra chaos!" Lily chirps, spinning on her heel and practically skipping back to the counter.

"Okay," Harper says once Lily disappears behind the counter. She leans in, lowering her voice. "About those guys. I didn't want to dump this on you last night after everything, but, girl... you picked the absolute *best* bodyguards."

"Well, yeah," I say, grabbing a napkin and fiddling with it. "Did you *see* the size of them? It's why I picked

Holt to help me. Dude looks like he could bench-press a truck."

Harper gives me a look. "No. Not just that. Cindy. Do you *have any idea* who you sat next to? Who they are?"

I blink. "What do you mean?" I shake my head, frowning. "I've only been in town for less than two years. It's small, sure, but a lot of people live here. I haven't met everyone."

"Well, turns out you met *them*." She leans in further. "They're not just hot, scary-looking dudes with protective instincts. They're ex-Savage Reapers."

My brain blanks. "They're... what?"

"Savage Reapers Motorcycle Club," Harper says, voice hushed but urgent. "And not like the friendly weekend bikers who drink at Mason's Pub. These guys were the real thing. Organized. Armed. Feared. Their club wasn't anywhere near here. They were based halfway across the country. No one knows why they came here exactly, but word is they left the life a few years ago and decided to disappear into something quieter."

My mouth goes dry. "And people just... let them?"

Harper shrugs. "Most folks don't *know*. They kept their heads down, opened real businesses. But someone found out—maybe a background check, maybe someone recognized them—and it got around. Quietly. The locals don't talk about it much, because honestly? No one wants to piss them off."

I stare down at the napkin in my hands, now torn to pieces. "What did they *do* for the club?"

"That's the part no one really wants to say out loud," Harper says. "But the most popular theory? Enforcement. The kind of men you call when you want a problem to disappear without questions."

A shiver moves down my spine, but it's not from fear. It's more like... realization. Understanding. Holt, Arrow, and Luke hadn't *hesitated* last night. They'd moved like they were used to danger. Like they were *built* for it.

I laugh, but it's brittle and tired. "Of course. Of *course* I'd accidentally recruit a trio of ex-biker enforcers. My track record with men is a goddamn horror movie."

Harper tilts her head. "Or maybe... maybe it's the best luck you've had in years."

I look up, startled.

She shrugs. "Think about it. You're terrified of Van, right? You said it yourself—he's dangerous, obsessive. So who better to stand between you and him than men who *used* to be dangerous but now put that danger to use by protecting people?"

"I just..." I shake my head, still trying to catch up. "They're bikers."

"*Ex*-bikers," she corrects. "I did my research this morning. Holt and Luke run that high-end security company, Blackline Forge & Security. They only take on top-tier clients. And Arrow's restaurant? Booked solid for three months for dinners. These aren't thugs hiding out. They built something here."

I exhale hard, letting that sink in. I should feel scared. I should be questioning my instincts. But I don't. Not really.

Because last night, when Van showed up… Holt stood in front of me like he'd already decided I was his to protect. Arrow's eyes had dared anyone to touch me. Luke had laughed like violence was a game and I was the prize.

"They're not after me," I say quietly.

Harper leans back, studying me. "No. I don't think they are. But they stood up for you."

I nod slowly. "Which should terrify me."

"But it doesn't," she finishes.

"Nope." I look out the café window, heart thudding like it's keeping time with something coming closer. "It doesn't at all."

Lily returns with our drinks. One mocha with what appears to be edible glitter, tiny fondant bats, and actual dry ice making them smoke, and one caramel-pumpkin cold brew drink. The treats are even more elaborate. A cemetery of brownies with cookie tombstones, cream puffs shaped like ghosts with chocolate chip eyes, and tiny pumpkin cakes with gold leaf.

"Lily, this is incredible," I breathe.

"Halloween is my art festival! Oh, and the bookstore is doing a horror reading tonight if you want to come. Local authors reading their scariest stories. I'm providing themed snacks, obviously. Bloody velvet cupcakes, monster cookies, maybe some witch fingers if I can get the almonds to look right for fingernails."

"Sounds amazing and you're a genius," Harper tells her. "Feed them sweets, then sell them books while they're on a sugar high."

"That's the plan! Though, honestly, I just love seeing people happy. And nothing does that more than unexpected cookies." She glances at the growing line. "Gotta go! Mrs. Kim wants her usual, and if I make her wait, she gets cranky!"

After we finish our breakfast, every incredible bite of it, Harper walks me to the door. Lily catches us there, pressing small paper bags into our hands.

"Morning tea treats." She winks. "Halloween macarons. They have Pop Rocks in the filling."

"Lily, I would die for you," Harper says seriously.

"No dying! It's bad for business!" Lily laughs, shooing us out.

Harper hugs me on the sidewalk, tight and fierce. "You're going to be okay. And if Van shows up at the brewery, I'm right there."

"I know you are, thanks."

"And maybe... maybe think about those bikers. I know they're not what you planned, but plans change."

"My plan was to stay invisible and alone forever," I remind her.

"Terrible plan. Your new plan should involve hot men who want to protect you."

The brewery warehouse looms ahead, all exposed

brick and industrial windows, *Whispering Grove Brewing Company* painted in elegant script above the main entrance. That's where Harper and I part ways, as she works in the marketing department.

Inside smells like heaven for beer lovers. All malty and rich with hints of citrus from the IPA we're brewing. The exposed copper tanks gleam behind glass walls, and the taproom up front is already being set up for the lunch crowd.

"Cindy! Thank God you're here!"

Garrett, the owner, emerges from his office looking frazzled, his flannel shirt untucked, dark hair sticking up where he's probably been running his hands through it. At six foot two with broad shoulders from years of hauling equipment, he cuts an imposing figure, but his deep green eyes are as kind as ever.

"Morning to you too, boss," I say fondly.

"Sorry, sorry. Morning. You look nice. Is that a new shirt? Doesn't matter. Listen—" He's already grabbing his notebook from his back pocket, flipping through it as he walks backward toward the door. "The ad agency completely screwed up. Half the flyers for the Halloween tasting never went out, and then they lost all the files in some kind of data breach. Long story short—they had to remake everything from scratch and just got the new batch printed. But now it all needs to go out. Can you handle distribution? The marketing team is tied up with something else urgent. The stack is on your desk."

"How far do you need them to go?"

"Around town for sure. Maybe all the tourist places on the outskirts of town if you have time? I know it's a lot, but the festival starts tomorrow and we want everyone to come visit our booth. The first batch we ordered went out last week—surrounding towns, regional partners, and a few of the highway stops. But this set just arrived, and they're for the *local* crowd. Main Street, shops, hotels, all of it. They need to go out today."

"I've got it," I promise.

"You're an angel! A saint! I'm naming a beer after you!" He's already out the door, presumably late for some supplier meeting.

I head to my desk, still smiling at Garrett's chaotic energy. The brewery office is cozy with exposed brick, vintage brewing posters, and a few plants I've managed to keep alive. My desk faces the window overlooking a small field and the city in the distance. I can spot the Halloween decorations from here.

The stack of flyers sits in the center of my desk, glossy and professional. I pick up the top one, admiring the design of the copper tanks looking mysterious in moody lighting, the taproom full of happy customers, the Halloween beer names in Gothic font. It turned out fantastic.

Garrett's brewery has exploded over the past year, tripling in business, expanding the staff, and somehow still managing to keep its cozy charm. It's been nonstop, but the kind of busy that feels like momentum.

Then I see it.

In the background of the main photo on the brochure, barely noticeable unless you're looking, but clear enough if you know what to look for.

Me.

I'm laughing at something, holding a flight of samples, looking happier than I ever did. My hair catches the light, and my face is turned just enough to be recognizable.

"Oh, fuck," I breathe, sinking into my chair. "Fuck, fuck, fuck."

This must be how Van found me. He must have seen a brochure, recognized me.

The photo was from our summer event. I remember that day, the first time I felt truly free, truly like myself. And now it's the thing that brought my past crashing back.

My stomach churns like I'm going to be sick at thinking of him again, and I'm convinced he's not going to leave me alone.

Maybe I should move in with Harper for a while. Safety in numbers. Her apartment is above the vintage shop, has good locks, a fire escape. She'd let me stay as long as I needed.

I slump forward, head on my desk, and sigh loud enough to rattle the flyers.

"Why is my life like this?" I ask the universe.

The universe, as usual, doesn't answer.

But I know one thing for certain... Van is in my

town, in my safe space, and he won't stop until he gets what he came for.

Me.

The question is whether I keep running or finally turn and fight.

I think about the dream again, about being surrounded by them, protected by them. About how my body recognized them even if my brain was screaming *Danger!* How their scents were so warming that it scares me to think my attraction to them is more than physical.

Maybe Harper is right. Maybe there's dangerous, and then there's *dangerous*.

But right now, I need to distribute these flyers and pretend everything is normal. Pretend I'm just Cindy Young, brewery assistant, miniature enthusiast, definitely not a runaway Omega with an Alpha stalker and inappropriate dreams about bikers.

Just another October day in Whispering Grove.

If only that were true.

4

ARROW

"**G**uess who just scored us five grand for one fucking table?"

I stride out from the kitchen into the main dining room, grinning like I just pulled off the heist of the century. Holt and Luke have taken over the corner booth as though they own the place. Which, technically, they part own—but that's not the point. They're demolishing what looks like an entire tiffin tower of food meant for four people. The copper tins are stacked like little treasure chests, each one holding something ridiculously delicious. I swear I only left the tower with the two of them for ten minutes, and they've already turned it into a crime scene.

"You finally sell that weird painting in the back?" Luke barely looks up from the bottom tier, where he's fishing out pieces of honey-glazed pork belly with his fingers like the savage he is.

"That's worth more than your bike," I say automatically, sliding into the booth and grabbing a piece of the Korean fried chicken from the middle tier before Luke can claim it all. "No, I just got the most beautiful fucking call."

I glance around my restaurant and love how it turned out. Savor doesn't look like the typical high-end restaurant, and that's exactly how we wanted it. When we designed this place, we went for a "we could kill you but we'd rather feed you" aesthetic. Black steel beams cross the ceiling, not that industrial bullshit everyone does, but actual salvaged beams from an old factory we may or may not have used for less legal purposes back in the day. The tables are live-edge walnut that Holt and I hauled from a lumberyard ourselves, each one unique, surrounded by leather chairs or booths that look vintage but are fucking expensive.

The walls showcase rotating art from local artists who've done time. Currently, it's Jackson's series; the guy did five years for grand theft auto and apparently learned to paint. His pieces are of traditional land-scapes that are on fire. They're dark as fuck, and I love them.

"So this call," Holt prompts, because he knows me well enough to recognize when I'm winding up to something good.

"This woman calls, right? Sounds like money. Not new money either, that old-establishment type who says 'supper' instead of 'dinner.'" I snag another piece of chicken, this one with the gochujang glaze that makes grown men weep. "She wants a table for twelve."

"That's good money," Holt says through a mouthful of food.

"For Saturday night."

"Fuck no," Luke immediately says. "Saturday is booked solid. We've got the anniversary, that weird book club that drinks too much wine, and half the town trying to impress their dates."

"That's what I told her. Very politely said we were fully committed for Saturday but would be happy to accommodate another evening."

"Let me guess." Luke grins, sauce on his chin like a fucking toddler. "She didn't take no for an answer."

"She offered double our banquet price. Four hundred per head."

They both stop eating, staring at me.

"What's the catch?" Holt asks, because there's always a catch.

"None. She just wants our full tiffin banquet experience. Seven courses, wine pairings, the whole production. And I couldn't say no."

"So where the fuck are we putting them?" Luke asks. "Unless you're planning to kick out the book club, and those ladies scare me more than any enforcer we ever faced."

"The back courtyard." I recline in the booth, already visualizing it. "We set up a marquee, one of those fancy clear-sided ones so they can see the gardens. String lights, heaters, make it look intentional instead of improvised."

"In three days?" Holt raises an eyebrow.

"We've done more with less. Remember that time we had to move three bikes and enough hardware to arm a small country with six hours' notice because the feds were sniffing around?"

"That was different." Luke laughs. "That just required balls and a complete disregard for speed limits."

"This requires that plus aesthetic sense." I lift my gaze to them. "Holt, you're sourcing the marquee. Luke, furniture. I want it to look like we've always had a private dining space out there."

"Fuck me," Luke mutters, but he's grinning. "Arrow's going full Martha Stewart again."

"Martha Stewart with a body count," I correct. "Speaking of which, we need to prep for tomorrow's festival. The food truck ready?"

"Delivered to the festival grounds this morning," Luke says proudly. "That beautiful bastard is parked and ready to cook. Full kitchen, serving window, the works. Even has those heat lamps that don't make food look like it's been under a nuclear reactor."

Tim, our head chef, emerges from the kitchen with a pot of fresh coffee, the Colombian stuff that costs a fortune but tastes like heaven had a baby with cocaine. His sleeves are pushed up, tattoos on full display, and he's grinning like a man who knows he just outdid God.

He sets the coffeepot and tray of miniature tiffin boxes on the table with a dramatic flourish. "Bosses, your preview of tomorrow's food porn. Try not to moan too loudly. I don't need the health inspector asking questions."

He pops the latches on one of the tins, steam curling up like a promise. "Bottom's duck confit street tacos. Middle's loaded fries, truffle and bone marrow. And the crown jewel"—he opens the top tier with a wink—"bourbon cake bites. You're welcome, assholes."

"You outdid yourself," I state, to which Tim smiles proudly and heads back into the kitchen.

Luke doesn't wait. He's already digging in, grabbing a cake bite. "Jesus fucking Christ," he moans around a mouthful. "This is almost as sweet as *she* is."

And there it is. We all know exactly who he means.

"Speaking of *our girl*," Holt says casually, as though he hasn't spent the last twenty-four hours in a quiet, spiraling obsession. "I did some recon."

"You mean you stalked her like a fucking creep," I translate, grinning.

"I gathered intelligence," Holt corrects with mock dignity. "She's in a townhouse on Cottage Lane. Works at the brewery. Keeps a routine but changes it up just enough to avoid patterns."

"Or she's just smart," I say, stealing one of the mini tiffins. "Girl who changes her name and skips town to run from an ex knows how to stay off the radar."

"Van called her Cynthia the other day at the

Harvest Dance," Holt adds. "She told me her name was *Cindy*. And digging at her work, she goes by Cindy Young. So yeah, she definitely changed her name to hide in town. I doubt that's her parents' surname."

Luke lets out a low whistle. "Of course she did."

"I don't care what name she's using," Holt mutters. "I'd recognize her by scent alone."

"Fuck me sideways, that scent. It's like Christmas morning had a baby with everything good in the world. Clove-studded orange. That brittle sugar snap. Pumpkin spice loaf, warm and fresh out of the oven."

"We need to get closer to her," Holt states, and there's something dark and hungry in his eyes that matches what I'm feeling. "Really scent her properly. Our first meet was fast, chaotic, adrenaline filled. We need to know for sure."

"What, you want to walk up and take a big sniff?" Luke laughs. "Hey, sweetheart, mind if I smell you? Promise we're not weird, just three ex-bikers who think you might be our mate?"

"Done worse," I admit.

"Yep, it *is* creepy as fuck," Holt says. "Doesn't mean we're not doing it."

The rest of the day flies by with prep work, readying for tomorrow's event. I'm in my element, coordinating with Tim and the kitchen crew, finalizing the ingredients, making sure we have enough product for both the truck and regular service. This is what I love—creating something from nothing, feeding people, watching their faces when they taste something that changes their whole day.

By the time evening rolls around, we're ready for phase two of Operation Protect Our Girl. Yeah, Luke named it. He's terrible with names.

We pile into Holt's truck. Me in the passenger seat, Luke in the back, and Holt driving. The truck is ridiculous, lifted with wheels that could crush a small car, but it blends into Whispering Grove's mix of practical and excessive.

"Got the supplies?" I ask.

Luke holds up a bag. "Coffee, those little cream puff things you made, beef jerky, and those nuts roasted with the maple and cayenne. Plus, two pizzas here next to me."

Holt pulls into a shadowed spot not far down the street from Cindy's place. "That pizza smells so fucking good. I need a piece now."

He throws the truck in park and reaches blindly for one of the boxes. Luke is already tearing into the jerky with one hand while prying open the pizza box in Holt's hand with the other.

"Meat lovers," Holt announces like it's sacred scripture. "Heavy on the pepperoni, sausage, and whatever ungodly thing Tim added that makes it perfect."

I grab a slice and burn my fingers on the cheese. Worth it. "That's brisket," I say. "Tim doesn't play fair."

Holt grabs the second box and opens it, inhaling the delicious aroma. "Barbecue chicken with jalapeños and crispy bacon. Sweet, smoky, and spicy. Like someone we know."

Her townhouse is cute as fuck, painted a soft blue with white trim, little flowers in window boxes even though it's October. The kind of place that says *I'm making a life here,* not *I'm ready to run at any moment.*

"Top floor," Holt points out unnecessarily. We can all see the warm light behind her curtains. "She's home."

"No shit, Detective Obvious," Luke says, licking grease from his fingers. "The question is whether Van's gonna try something."

"If he's dumb enough to return to town," I confirm, reaching for another slice.

"He thinks she belongs to him," Holt says, voice low, and that edge is there, the one that used to come right before blood. "Probably can't compute that she ran. In his mind, she's property that's been misplaced."

"I want to misplace his fucking teeth," I mutter, tearing off a bite of crust like it's his face.

A Honda sedan pulls up outside her building, and I instantly recognize it as Harper's from when we followed her and Cindy after the Harvest Dance. Harper gets out, purple-tipped black hair glinting in the streetlight, overnight bag in hand.

"Smart," Holt approves. "Numbers are good. Harder to grab someone when there's a witness."

"Think they're having a girls' night?" Luke asks. "Doing each other's nails, talking about feelings and shit?"

"I think they're probably figuring out how to deal with a stalker ex-fiancé who won't take no for an answer," I say, eyeing the lights still glowing from Cindy's place. One of the shadows moves—nothing distinct. Just enough to make my jaw tighten.

"We could get closer," Luke suggests, already reaching for the door handle like that's a normal thing to say. "Make sure they're actually safe."

"And what, peek in their windows?" Holt says. "That crosses from protective to restraining order real fucking quick."

"When did you become the voice of reason?" Luke mutters.

"When you started thinking with your knot instead of your brain."

Luke snorts but doesn't deny it.

We all go quiet again, chewing through the last of the pizzas, eyes fixed on the soft light behind those second-floor curtains. No movement now. Just the hum of the streetlamp and the low rumble of Holt's engine.

Then my phone rings.

The screen lights up with a name that turns my good mood to ash.

Mack.

I sigh like I've just been handed a live grenade. "What?" I answer, already bracing for chaos.

"Big brother!" Mack crows. "How's my favorite Alpha doing?"

His voice has that manic edge, the one that usually

means he's high, drunk, or standing on the edge of a very bad idea. With Mack, it's usually all three, plus a flare gun and a questionable tattoo artist.

"I'm your *only* Alpha brother," I remind him, because God forbid he ever forget it. "What do you want?"

"Can't a Beta check in on his successful, restaurant-owning, uptight older brother without wanting something?"

"Not in this lifetime," I mutter, already checking the time and wondering if I'm about to have to post bail. Again.

Luke leans over to read the name on my screen and grins. "Oh, good, it's the family disaster."

"I heard that!" Mack yells through the phone like he's on speaker. He's not. His volume just comes with the personality.

"You could, but you don't. It's been almost a year since you called, and that was because you needed bail money after that bar fight where you nearly killed someone."

Luke and Holt exchange glances. They know my family history, know how fucked up it all is. Parents who tried to *pray the Alpha out of me,* literally. Starvation, isolation, conversion therapy that was basically torture with a religious soundtrack. And Mack, my baby brother, who stayed even after I begged him to run with me. He was barely thirteen when I left. Just a kid. And he stayed.

"That was a misunderstanding," Mack says, and I

can practically hear his shrug through the phone. "Guy shouldn't have looked at me like that."

"The guy was the bartender. He looked at you because you were destroying his bar."

"Details," he says, like we're talking about a parking ticket. "Anyway, I'm back in town. Staying at the motel by the highway. Thought maybe we could grab a beer, catch up. I miss my big brother."

He doesn't miss me. He misses having someone to bail him out. Someone to absorb the blame like a sponge for his craziness. In Mack's world, everything wrong in his life is somehow my fault—for leaving, for being born an Alpha, for not dragging him out when I escaped that goddamn house.

"I'm busy. Halloween festival, restaurant stuff."

"Right. Your fancy place." His voice sharpens, just a little. "Heard you're doing real well. Making bank. Good for you, Arrow. Real good."

Here it comes. The ask. It always does. It's like he physically can't help himself.

"I gotta go," I say. "Maybe we can meet up in a few weeks."

"Few weeks. Sure. Whatever, man." He pauses for just long enough to twist the knife. "Room twelve, if you change your mind. You know... if you remember you've got a brother who spent three years in trauma recovery therapy after I left home."

The guilt hits like it always does. Sharp, familiar, useless. A punch to the gut I've already taken a thousand times.

He hangs up before I can respond, which is probably for the best. Nothing I say ever helps anyway. Not where Mack is concerned. There's no fixing a wound when the person keeps picking it open just to feel something.

"You good?" Luke asks, real concern cutting through the usual sarcasm.

"Peachy." I let the phone drop into the cup holder like it burned me and drag a hand through my hair. "My psycho brother is back, probably broke, definitely about to cause problems."

Luke doesn't say anything. Just offers me one of the last cream puff things Tim made, like sugar might soften the edges of old wounds.

I take it and eat it in one bite.

"Want us to handle it?" Holt offers, and by *handle*, he means everything from a talking-to to making him disappear.

There's no smile on his face when he says it.

Just the calm, bone-deep loyalty of someone who's already decided *who matters* and what he's willing to do about it.

"No. He's still my brother. Despite everything, he's family."

"Family is who you choose," Luke says. "We're your family. That guy is just someone you share DNA with."

He's right, but it doesn't make the guilt easier.

"Can we talk about something else?" I ask. "Like… are we really doing this?"

Luke pauses mid-chew. "Doing *what* exactly?"

"This," I say, gesturing toward Cindy's apartment. "Sitting out here like guard dogs with snack packs. Talking about scent matches and bonds and, hell, *Omega shit*. Are we really ready for what comes next?"

Holt glances over, one hand draped casually over the wheel. "You mean the part where claiming her changes everything?"

"Yeah," I admit. "The part where it's not just instinct anymore. It's a *life*."

Luke makes a face when I glance over my shoulder at him. "Don't say it like that. You sound like you're about to buy a minivan and wear a tool belt."

"I'm serious," I state. "You bond an Omega, you don't just get heat and sex and domestic bliss. You get *need*. You get *responsibility*. You get... babies."

Luke chokes on a pecan. "Jesus, say that again but slower."

"*Babies*," I repeat, watching him gag dramatically. "Tiny, screaming, half-feral versions of us. Covered in drool and teeth."

"I'd be the fun one," Luke says, recovering. "I'd teach 'em to cuss in four languages and throw knives."

"You're not helping your case," Holt mutters.

But I see the flicker in his expression. The stillness. Because he's thinking it too—what it would mean to really settle down. To be *chosen* and not just taken seriously... but completely.

"I always thought we'd burn out before we got this far," I admit. "Either the law would catch up, or someone would put a bullet between our eyes. But now we've got a legitimate business. A town that doesn't hate us. And... her."

Luke shifts in his seat, quieter now. "You think she wants that? The white-picket-fence shit? With us?"

"She wants safety. Stability. A future," Holt says. "Things we never had. Things we've never really been good at offering."

"Doesn't mean we can't try," I add. "But we don't get to go at this half-assed. Not with her. If she chooses us, we owe her everything."

The silence that follows isn't heavy—it's *solid.* Like something slotting into place.

The lights in her townhouse start going off one by one. Bedroom last.

"She's in for the night," Holt says, adjusting his seat.

Luke yawns. "Do we get to sleep, or is this a twenty-four-seven babysitting gig?"

"We watch a little longer," I say. "Just in case."

And we do. We stay. We wait. Not just for danger.

But for her.

Because for once, that's something we don't want to steal.

We want to *deserve* it.

5

CINDY

I'm already dressed in the comfy work polo, but I've done my best to fight the beige with Halloween flair by adding bat pins on the collar, orange-and-black-striped tights under my skirt, and spider earrings that jingle when I move. Professional, technically. Festive, definitely. According to Harper, I'm serving corporate goth lite. According to me, I'm just trying not to scream into a pumpkin bucket.

The brewery booth at the festival is always packed the first night, everyone wanting to try our seasonal Halloween brews. There's the Vampire's Kiss stout, the Witch's Brew IPA, and my personal favorite, the Pumpkin Massacre ale that tastes like autumn decided to fight cinnamon and everyone won.

Harper is picking me up in an hour, which gives me just enough time to add some orange eyeshadow and maybe that spiderweb bracelet she got me last year.

I'm debating whether temporary tattoos are too much when my phone rings.

No caller ID.

I usually ignore those. They're either telemarketers or wrong numbers or someone trying to reach me about my car's extended warranty on a car I don't own. But something in my gut, that same instinct that told me to run two years ago, that whispered *danger* when Van's hand first tightened on my arm, makes me answer.

"Hello?"

Silence for a heartbeat. Then: "Cynthia."

The world tilts. My knees buckle, and I have to grab the dresser to stay upright, my fingers white-knuckled against the wood. That voice. Perfectly modulated, never too loud or too soft, with just the right amount of disappointment permanently woven through it like a thread of poison through silk.

My mother.

My chest constricts. I can't breathe. The room spins, and I'm not in Whispering Grove anymore. I'm back in Greyridge; I'm seventeen and being told my opinions don't matter. I'm nineteen and watching my sister get married to a man she met twice. I'm twenty and my mother is putting pins in my hair for my wedding while telling me to be still, always still, never moving, never speaking, never being anything but what they need me to be.

"How..." My voice cracks like glass. I clear my

throat, try again, but my mouth is desert dry. "How did you get this number?"

"You changed your name to Cindy," she accuses, and she says it like I'm a child who put on Mommy's makeup and called herself Princess Sparkles. Like my new identity, my freedom, my entire life here is just a silly game. "We have ways of finding things, darling. Your father has connections everywhere. And Van heard enough when he found you. Did you really think you could just disappear?"

My father's connections. The same ones that found Van a loophole in every law, that made bruises disappear from medical records, that turned a forced marriage into a romantic fairy tale for anyone watching from the outside.

"Where have you been?" she continues, and I can picture her perfectly. Sitting in her pristine living room with the white furniture no one's allowed to actually sit on, not a hair out of place in her steel-gray chignon, probably wearing the pearls my father gave her after Juliette's wedding. The successful daughter's wedding. "We've been sick with worry."

Right! Not "I was worried" or "I missed you" or even "I wondered if you were alive." But "we." Always the collective, always the unit, never the individual. Never just my mother merely caring about me.

"You just ran out like that on your wedding day." Her voice rises slightly, the only sign of emotion she'll allow herself. "Who does that, Cynthia? Who leaves their family in such embarrassment, in such a predicament?"

I sink onto my couch, my legs liquid, useless. The memories crash over me like a wave I've been running from for two years, finally catching up, finally pulling me under.

Her hands in my hair, placing rhinestone pins in. Each one pressed in hard enough to hurt, little pricks of pain I wasn't allowed to flinch from. "Stop fidgeting. An Omega must always be still, always perfect. We are not like Alphas, who can afford to be rough, or Betas, who can afford to be forgotten. We must be porcelain dolls, beautiful and break-able, worth protecting."

But who protects us from our protectors?

"Your sister never had these issues," she said that morn-ing, comparing me to Juliette even on my wedding day. "She understood her role. Smiled when told, spoke when asked, spread her legs when required."

She didn't use those exact words, of course. Mother would never be so crude. But the meaning had been clear in every lesson, every lecture, every look of disap-pointment when I'd asked why, when I'd suggested maybe, when I'd dared to think.

I remember the weight of the dress, how it dragged at me like hands pulling me down, down into a life I didn't choose. The corset so tight I could barely breathe, and wasn't that perfect? An Omega who can't breathe can't scream.

"That's my past," I manage, my voice stronger than I feel. Each word is a fight, pushing through years of conditioning that tells me not to talk back, not to disagree, not to be anything but grateful for whatever scraps of autonomy they allow me. "I'm no longer that person. The daughter you had is dead."

She laughs. The laugh that used to make me feel two inches tall and incorrectly shaped, like I was a puzzle piece hammered into the wrong spot.

"Oh, you were always so dramatic. You get it from your Aunt Alina's side, I suppose. That woman filled your head with such ridiculous notions."

Aunt Alina. Even her name has my chest aching with missing. She was the one who'd told me stories about Omegas who were warriors, healers, leaders. Not just wombs with decorations. She was the one who'd taught me to cook not because it was my duty but because creation was power. She was the one who'd whispered, "You can run, you know. When the time comes, you can just run."

And I did.

My hands are shaking now, violent tremors that start in my fingers and work their way up my arms. But anger is mixing with the fear, turning it into something else.

"What do you want, Mother?" The word tastes bitter. "I'm not coming back. I'm not marrying Van. Nothing you say will change my mind."

"Tsk." I can hear her shifting, probably smoothing her skirt even though no one's watching. Or maybe Father is. Maybe he's sitting right there, listening, judging, calculating how much this phone call is worth. "I finally find out where you are, call to see if you're okay, and you treat me like this? The world doesn't revolve around you, though you seem to think it does."

"No," I say, surprising myself. "I thought it revolved around you. Around Father. Around what the family needed. I was just a spinning cog, wasn't I? Until I stopped spinning."

"You left our family with such a huge debt," she continues as if I hadn't spoken. They always did that, talked over me, through me, around me.

"A debt?" I laugh, but it's fake. "You mean the money you got paid for selling me? How much was I worth, Mother? What's the going rate for an Omega daughter these days?"

I remember finding the papers. The contract. My bride price listed like I was cattle. Half a million to clear their debts.

She sighs like I'm being deliberately obtuse, like I'm five years old and refusing to understand why I can't have candy for dinner. "An Omega's job is to strengthen family bonds, create alliances. I did it. Your grandmother did it. Your sister did it beautifully, I might add."

"And look how happy Juliette is," I snap. "Two smiling children, never leaves the house without permission."

"Your sister is fulfilled. She has purpose."

"She's miserable."

"She's an Omega who knows her place."

The words hang between us.

"Even your cousins understood their duty," she continues, relentless. "Every Omega in our family has done what's necessary. Except you. And your Aunt Alina, of course."

"At least Aunt Alina was happy," I say firmly.

Another sigh, heavier this time, theatrical in its disappointment. "And look how that ended. Alone, no children, died with her cats for company. Is that what you want? No family around you when you're old?"

I think about Aunt Alina's funeral. How packed it was. Friends, neighbors, people she'd helped over the years. The library she volunteered at closed for the day in her honor. The community garden planted a tree with her name on it. She had more family than my mother ever will, just not the kind that shares DNA.

"Yes," I say immediately. "That sounds perfect, actually. Cats don't try to sell you to pay off their gambling debts."

"Cynthia," she says sternly. "Your father had some unfortunate investments—"

Silence.

"Cynthia, darling," her tone shifts to what she thinks is warmth but feels like a Venus flytrap opening its petals. "I don't want to argue. I've cried many nights worrying about you."

Cried. My mother, who didn't shed a tear at her own mother's funeral because public displays of emotion were common. Who told me when Whiskers died when I was eight that tears didn't bring back guinea pigs or change facts. Who watched my father backhand me for speaking out of turn at dinner and merely reminded me to ice my face before the swelling started.

"Van finally found you and told me, putting me out of my misery," she continues, and my blood goes ice-cold. They've been talking. Coordinating. Of course. "And then you speak to me so rudely when I only care for you, love you."

"I'm fine," I say flatly, staring at my miniature Whispering Grove street I put together, the tiny perfect world where tiny perfect people live tiny perfect lives. "Please leave me alone and tell Van to stay away. It's over. I'm not going back."

"Well," she says. "Van mentioned you have another Alpha. Is that true?"

My mind flashes to the barn. Holt's arm around me, solid and safe, nothing like Van's possessive grip. His voice in my ear: "Let me handle this." The scent of spiced caramel, toasted marshmallow, and warm vanilla had my whole body recognizing home in a stranger. Luke and Arrow flanking me like guards, like protectors, like they'd burn the whole barn down before letting Van touch me.

"Yes," I hear myself say. The lie falls out so easily, self-preservation dressed as truth. "I'm taken. And he treats me wonderfully. The way it should be."

"Then," she says slowly, "the least you can do is let your mother meet this man who will be your Alpha."

My shoulders flinch back. Oh, no. No, no, no. The

room spins again. I've just made everything so much worse.

"That's... that's not necessary."

"I insist." Her voice has that steel underneath the silk now. "Your father won't let this go. He's on my back daily about the embarrassment, the financial situation. The Stones are... upset about the arrangement falling through."

The Stones. Van's family. Old money, older values, the kind of people who still think Omegas should be seen and not heard, bred and not educated.

"Let me meet this Alpha, Cynthia," she continues. "So I can tell your father something to make him leave it alone. Will you do that for me?"

Everything she does is for her. Not for me. Never for me.

I look around my little townhouse, my safe space with its mismatched furniture I picked myself, my miniature worlds I built with my own hands, my life I created from nothing but determination and terror. She'll critique everything, from the secondhand couch to the lack of proper Omega decorations, whatever those are. The books on my shelves are too many, too varied, too obviously read. The art on my walls is too modern, too abstract, too much opinion for an Omega to have.

But mostly she'll notice what's missing. An Alpha. A protector. A keeper. Someone to tell me what to think, what to wear, when to speak, when to spread my legs and be grateful for the privilege. She will never accept me living alone.

"Cynthia, I'll be in Whispering Grove this Saturday," she says without waiting for an answer, because my agreement was never required, only my compliance. "I'll message you once I arrive to catch up, okay?"

Saturday. Two days away. Two days to produce an Alpha from thin air or face my mother's disappointment and interrogation. If I don't have someone by my side who has *claimed* me, she'll never let it go. Not until I give in, move home, and let her marry me off. And if she senses weakness? If she suspects I'm still unbonded? She'll call Van. Or maybe she already has. One little failure, and I'll be right back in the cage I barely escaped.

My mind spirals back to another moment of decision.

Standing in front of those massive, closed double doors, gold-trimmed, glossy, heavy enough to seal a tomb. Behind them, the ceremonial hall buzzed with anticipation. Guests settling into rows. Soft music playing. Van waiting at the altar like he was entitled to me.

I was alone. My father had stormed off down the corridor, barking into his phone about investments and reputations and some deal that suddenly mattered more than walking his daughter down the aisle. His voice echoed and faded, and for a few stolen seconds, there was no one left to watch me.

This is the moment. I remembered Aunt Alina whispering once, years ago, eyes sharp and knowing, *If you ever decide to run—don't wait. Don't warn anyone. Just find your exit and go.*

So I'd memorized the floor plans, studied the routes the staff used to slip in and out without notice. I'd even stolen a key from the head housekeeper's ring, palmed it on a day I was supposed to be picking out floral arrangements.

Now, with my father's voice disappearing around the corner, that key was burning in my pocket, the one I had promised myself to take everywhere since I stole it.

My hands trembled as I reached for the edge of my skirt, lifting layers of silk, lace, and tulle. I kicked off the heels that had been forced onto my feet that morning.

Now, I thought.

And I turned.

Not toward the room. Not toward the life they'd chosen for me.

I turned and ran.

Through the back hallway, into the workers' quarters that smelled like starch and lemon oil, down the narrow stairwell that led to the back door with no guards. The stolen key slid into the lock with a click that sounded like thunder.

I ran for my life, barefoot and breathless, into the woods that surrounded our mansion. I ran for *freedom* even though I had no idea what that would look like.

I only knew what it *wouldn't* look like.

Like Van's hands on me.

Like my mother's disappointed sighs.

And it sure as hell wouldn't look like my father's calculated indifference.

"If you want closure," my mother says, interrupting my spiral, "this is the way to start it."

"Fine," I whisper, hating myself for the word, for the weakness, for the twenty years of conditioning that makes me still, *still*, want her approval.

"Wonderful! I'll see you then, darling."

The line goes dead.

The phone slips from my numb fingers, clattering on the coffee table. For a moment, I just stare at it like it's a snake that might strike again. Then the tears come. Not pretty, delicate tears like Omegas are supposed to cry. Huge, ugly sobs that shake my whole body, that come from somewhere so deep I didn't know it existed. Almost two years of freedom, of building a life, of becoming myself, and one phone call reduces me to that scared girl in a wedding dress who didn't know if she'd survive the night.

What have I agreed to?

My legs move without my permission, carrying me to the door. I don't even bother with shoes, my tights-covered feet silent on the cold concrete. I knock on Mrs. Meadow's door with shaking hands, probably too hard, probably too desperate, but I can't stop myself.

She opens immediately, takes one look at my face, and pulls me into a hug encompassing all the things mothers are supposed to be.

"Oh, honey," she murmurs, guiding me inside. "What happened? Come, come. Sit."

Her townhouse is the mirror of mine architecturally but completely different in every way that matters. Where mine is sparse, hers is lived-in and loved. Photos cover every surface, children and grandchildren smiling from frames that probably have stories she tells anyone who'll listen. Doilies protect furniture that's older than me. It smells like she's been baking again, probably for another church function where she'll pretend she didn't make the best cookies and everyone will pretend to believe her.

She doesn't ask questions, just puts cookies on a plate and pours milk like I'm five and skinned my knee. The chocolate chips are still melty. She must have just pulled them from the oven. Sometimes that's exactly what you need—someone to mother you the way mothers should, with cookies and patience and no agenda beyond making you feel better.

"My mother called," I finally manage between hiccuping breaths.

Mrs. Meadow's mouth curls downward at the corners. She knows I ran from something. She's never pushed for details, but she knows it was bad enough that I don't talk about family, that I sometimes have nightmares that make me scream. She's probably put together more pieces than I realize. She's sharp like that, notices things but doesn't pry.

"Families can be complicated," she says carefully,

patting my hand. Her skin is paper-soft, marked with age spots.

That's when I notice the boxes. Cardboard boxes stacked along the walls, labeled in her careful handwriting. Kitchen. Photos. Books. Charlie's drawings.

"You're moving?" The words come out accusatory, like she's betraying me, which isn't fair, but feelings aren't fair.

She sighs, suddenly looking all of her seventy-three years. The lines around her eyes deepen. "My daughter-in-law just had twins. Surprise babies at forty-two, can you believe it? They need help, and honestly, dear, living alone at my age is getting harder. The stairs, the maintenance, the quiet."

I understand that. The kind of silence that presses against your ears, that makes you talk to yourself just to hear a voice.

"I'll miss you," I say. "When are you moving?"

"Me too, dear, and it will be soon. I wanted to tell you properly, and was baking cookies to come over and let you know. It's all happened so fast."

Another loss. Another person leaving. Another safe thing becoming unsafe. I know it's not about me, but it feels slightly personal to lose her as my neighbor.

"You'll be fine," she says firmly, reading my face like the large-print books she favors. "You're stronger than you think. Whatever that phone call was about, whatever your mother wants, you are your own person, and you will do what is right for you, not her."

"She wants to meet my Alpha," I confess. "On Saturday."

Her eyebrows rise. "Oh."

"Yep. I don't have one. I lied. Said I did because she was pushing me, and now she's coming here Saturday and expects to meet this imaginary Alpha."

Mrs. Meadow tilts her head, studying me. Her lips press together as she thinks, fingers brushing crumbs from the plate beside her.

"Well now," she finally says, soft and slow. "That's a bit of a predicament."

She leans back in her chair with a quiet sigh. "All I can suggest is… if you have any male friends who could stand in. Just for the visit. If you feel you can't be honest with your mother."

"I really can't," I murmur. "It'll be worse for me if I try."

Mrs. Meadow pats my arm gently, her hand warm and papery. She picks up another cookie and places it into my palm without asking.

"Yes, I think a male friend might be your solution," she says, more thoughtful now than certain. "Someone you trust. Not a stranger. It could be very obvious if it feels… well, staged."

I sigh, my thoughts instantly going to Holt, yet he's a stranger, and it will be so obvious that we barely know each other.

She frowns a little. "Oh, such a tangle. I do wish I had a better answer for you."

"It's okay. The cookies are helping." I smile and eat another one.

My phone buzzes. Harper: *On my way! Wear something cute* • •

Normal life is calling. I have to go pour beer for drunk people in costumes and pretend everything is fine. Pretend my mother isn't coming. Pretend I have an Alpha. Pretend I'm not completely fucked.

"Thank you," I tell Mrs. Meadow, hugging her carefully. She feels fragile but strong. "For the cookies and the advice. And I'm going to miss you when you're gone."

"Anytime, dear. I will miss you too." She hugs me, then I head back to my place.

I wait for Harper, adding those bat tattoos because if my world is ending, I might as well look good for the coming apocalypse.

6

CINDY

The Whispering Grove Halloween Festival sprawls across Miller's Field like a Gothic carnival that escaped from someone's fever dream and decided to throw a party. The enormous field, which was once farmland owned by the Miller family, the original founders of Whispering Grove, has been transformed into zones, with the food section, where we're stationed; the games area, where screams of delight mix with actual screams from the haunted maze; and the main stage, where a band dressed as zombie Beatles is playing "Here Comes the Sun" in a minor key.

Our brewery booth sits between Mrs. Lessie's Severed Fingers, spring rolls arranged to look disturbingly realistic, and Clayton's candy apple stand, where each apple is a work of art. I just served a sample to someone whose apple was decorated to look like

Pennywise, and honestly, it was too good to eat but too creepy to look at.

"Stop catastrophizing," Harper blurts, adjusting the plastic Viking horns she added to her outfit because, in her words, *Vikings are scary and I'm scary cute.* She's been documenting everything for our social media, adding filters that make our beer look like it's glowing with supernatural power. "Your face is doing that thing where you look constipated but emotional."

"That's just my face," I protest, arranging sample cups for the millionth time.

"No, your regular face is cute with a side of sass. This is your 'my mother called and now I want to die' face." Harper snaps another photo, this time of the Vampire's Kiss stout with dry-ice smoke for effect. "Which, valid, but also, you're scaring customers."

The field around us pulses with Halloween energy. There's a zombie-walk competition happening near the corn maze, a pumpkin carving contest, and approximately seventeen different versions of Harley Quinn wandering around. The air smells of kettle corn and cotton candy.

"I can't stop thinking about Saturday," I admit, serving a witch who ordered with a perfect cackle. "Two days to produce an Alpha from thin air."

"Or," Harper says, wiggling her eyebrows, "from that gorgeous food truck two spots down where those absolutely edible ex-bikers are currently making everyone in a fifty-foot radius swoon."

I risk a glance at the Savor truck. It's a sleek black

and has orange Halloween decals of skeletons doing a waltz on the sides. There's already a line, probably because Arrow and Luke look like they stepped out of a bad-boys-of-cooking calendar.

"We need to discuss this strategically," Harper continues, pulling out her phone. "I did some research."

"You stalked them online."

"Of course. Any respectful girl would. Anyway, Luke Brennan, co-owner of Blackline Forge & Security, no official social media but appears in the background of Arrow's restaurant photos looking like a whole meal. Arrow Castellan, owns Savor, has a food blog that's just photos. And Holt Madison, security expert, no online presence, which is either super mysterious or super serial killer. And is the other half of their Blackline security company."

"Geez, don't say 'serial killer.'"

"I'm just saying, the man has zero digital footprint. So, is that intentional or concerning? The point is, these guys went from enforcement to legitimate businessmen. And they gotta have lots of money too."

"And you think I should ask one of them to fake-date me for my mother?"

"Ask all three and let them fight it out. Sell tickets. We could make bank."

I roll my eyes dramatically.

"But seriously," she continues. "You need backup. From what you've told me, your mom's a shark and will smell weakness before she goes for the kill.

Remember when you mentioned about your sister's wedding?"

I do. Juliette tried to back out once. Just once. Said she wasn't sure, that maybe she needed more time. Our mother smiled, told her to take all the time she needed. Then two hours later, she leaked the engagement to the local papers and booked the venue under Juliette's name. By the time the poor girl realized what had happened, the guest list had doubled and backing out would've been a public scandal.

"These guys protected you from Van," Harper points out. "That's already more than your family ever did."

"I hate to bring someone else into my chaotic mess and family."

Harper snorts. "Girl, *these guys* are the epitome of crazy. They've probably seen it all. Hell, *done* worse. So meeting your mom? How bad could it be?"

I cringe internally, because yeah, it could be bad. She has a talent for turning even the smallest get-togethers into full-blown disasters.

Harper waves her hand like it's no big deal. "She pops over, you make her tea and cookies, and one of your terrifyingly hot biker boyfriends sits beside you, looking dangerous but devoted. You think she's gonna try her usual mind games while Captain Murderglare is watching her butter a scone? Please. She'll back off so fast she'll leave scorch marks on the doormat."

Before I can respond, movement catches my eye.

Luke is heading our way, and my brain immediately forgets how to function.

He's dressed for the festival but somehow manages to make *casual devil* look like a fashion ad. The black jeans cling to him like sin itself, and that vintage Metallica tee has been cut just enough to show flashes of skin when he moves, all taut muscle and effortless heat. The leather jacket he wears does nothing to soften him. If anything, it makes him look even more dangerous, as though he walked out of a dream designed to ruin lives.

And then there's everything else, the long auburn hair falling in waves that brush past his cheekbones and shoulders, just messy enough to look natural but not unkempt. A few strands fall over one eye, refusing to be tamed by the black devil-horn headband resting casually against his forehead. The horns don't push the hair back; they accent it, drawing attention to the sharp lines of his face and that infuriating three-day stubble dusting his jaw. He looks like trouble. Beautiful, unfair, Alpha-coded trouble.

"Incoming hotness, three o'clock," Harper mutters under her breath. "I'm going to check our backup kegs that definitely need checking right now immediately."

"Harper, don't you dare—"

She's gone. I shoot her a betrayed look, but she doesn't even turn around.

Luke reaches the booth, hands shoved into his jacket pockets, the devil horns tilting slightly as he grins. "Hey, trouble," he says, and his voice is pure sin wrapped in charm.

"Busy night?"

"It's..." I gesture vaguely at everything, because my brain has gone into standby mode. "Halloween."

"Noticed that," he says, nudging one of the coffin-shaped drink trays on the counter. "The horns gave it away. That and Arrow's insistence we serve everything in tiny boxes. Man's obsessed with theme commitment."

The breeze shifts. His scent hits me. Candied apples and spiced cider, and leather, the kind of smell that gets under your skin and makes you forget your own name. My knees wobble. *Actually* wobble. I have to grip the counter like I'm bracing for impact.

His eyes flick to my hand. "You okay?" he asks, tone shifting as he leans in. "You look like you're about to pass out. Or commit murder. Possibly both."

"Family stuff, I guess," I manage to say, because apparently his presence annihilates my filter.

"Ah." He nods like he's heard this exact tone before. "The kind of family stuff that requires alcohol, or the kind that ends in a court summons?"

I huff a laugh, grateful for the distraction. "Somewhere between wine and witness protection."

"Oof. That's the spicy kind."

His grin is lethal and warm all at once. I should not be looking at his mouth. I definitely shouldn't be wondering what it would feel like to kiss that smirk right off his face. Or how he'd taste. Or if he'd keep the devil horns on.

I force myself to focus on stacking napkins that do not need stacking. "You here for a cider, or just to harass the staff?"

"For the company. The cider is just an excuse."

He winks and reaches for one of the coffin-shaped drink trays. His fingers brush mine, and my entire nervous system short-circuits like it's been hit with a cattle prod. The scent of him rolls in again, and my pulse flares so hard I nearly knock over the tray.

This is not normal. This is full-body chemical warfare. I'm sweating and freezing at the same time, and all he's done is *exist* in my general area.

"You good?" he asks, eyes narrowing slightly like he already knows the answer.

"Yeah. Just busy. Lots of beer. Costumes. Small-town havoc."

He lifts a brow. "So you're telling me you're not overwhelmed at all by the sheer volume of drunk pirates and cornstalks?"

I blink. "Sorry, what now?"

"There's a girl dressed as corn," he says. "Just corn. With fishnets. It's a lot."

I snort and cover it with a cough. "How are you even noticing anyone else in this crowd?"

"Because I already found the best view." His eyes slide back to mine, and it's not even a line. He *means* it.

Oh, no.

I glance away, but it's too late. My face is on fire. I

pretend to read the side of a cider box that I've definitely already unpacked.

Maybe Harper is right, my brain whispers treacherously. *Maybe he could pull it off. If anyone could fake being your Alpha, it's this man with cheekbones sharp enough to ruin you and a voice like bourbon lit on fire.*

Just one day. That's all I'd need.

He would sit beside me, play along, maybe wrap an arm around my shoulders like it meant something. Say all the right things. Smell like he does. Look like he does. My mother wouldn't stand a chance.

I open my mouth. I get as far as "Hey, Luke, can I ask you something completely insane?" before I chicken out.

Abort. Abort.

"Actually, never mind," I say instead. "I don't trust you not to laugh at me."

"I would never," he says, all fake offense. "Unless it's really dumb. Then I absolutely would."

"You're a menace."

He leans against the counter, tilting his head. "A charming menace."

"Debatable."

"Admit it," he says, reaching for one of the cookies Harper made and biting into it with zero shame. "You missed me since the Harvest Dance."

I roll my eyes, but it's weak. My body is still buzzing. My thoughts are a mess. I keep staring at his mouth when I think he won't notice. And I absolutely cannot ask him to be my fake boyfriend. I might faint in his company.

And because I think if he said yes, I might actually want it to be real.

He pulls back but produces a small tiffin box from his back. "Here. Arrow's latest experiment that he got our chef to make up. Pumpkin spice brownies with candied bacon and a maple whiskey glaze."

I open it, and the smell has me grinning. "Are you trying to seduce me with delicious goods?"

"Is it working?"

"Maybe."

"Then yes, absolutely that's what I'm doing," he says, watching me intently take a bite.

I groan before I can stop myself. It's involuntary. Carnal. Possibly audible in the next zip code.

"Good?" he asks, eyes gleaming.

"I'm pretty sure this is drugs," I murmur, licking maple glaze off my thumb.

His gaze follows my movement. "Butter, sugar, and lust," he says. "Triple threat. Arrow believes butter is a love language."

I laugh, mostly to stop myself from combusting. My face is hot. My thighs are hotter. I'm going to need to dunk myself in the beer cooler if this continues. He's not even doing anything. Just standing there, being all smirky and sinful with his tousled devil hair and that little scruff shadow like he forgot to shave and somehow made it sexy.

Of course, that's when a customer saunters up.

Soccer mom in a half-hearted sexy cat costume. Plastic ears. Mesh bodysuit. Clearly regrets every decision that led her here but is now committing to the bit with claws and cleavage.

"What's good here?" she purrs, aiming her entire body at Luke like she thinks he's on tap.

"Everything," I say, stepping in with my most helpful, totally-not-jealous smile. "Would you like to try the Witch's Brew IPA?"

She doesn't even blink at me. Just leans closer to Luke with a giggle. "What do you recommend, handsome?"

Luke doesn't even look at her. "I recommend you listen to the woman who actually knows what she's talking about."

The woman blinks, stunned by the rejection. Luke casually gestures behind her. "Also, your tail's on fire."

She shrieks and spins, flailing to extinguish the tip of her costume now smoldering from a nearby jack-o'-lantern.

While she's preoccupied with not becoming a cautionary tale, Luke slips behind the counter beside me, like he belongs there. Like he belongs next to me. Close enough to smell. Close enough that my body becomes a live wire.

"That was mean," I whisper, trying to focus on literally anything but his mouth.

He leans in as though he has no understanding of personal space. "She was rude. You get my best behavior. For now."

I glance up at him, caught in that devil-may-care smirk and the very real heat in his eyes.

"That supposed to impress me?" I ask, pretending my heart isn't galloping like it's being chased.

"No," he says, low and unapologetic. "Supposed to make you think about what it's like when I'm not on my best behavior."

Oh, no.

Oh, no, no, no.

My brain short-circuits. My tongue forgets English. I nod at a keg that definitely doesn't need checking.

"I'm just gonna... check on that thing... over there."

He grins like he knows exactly what he's doing.

Because I bet he does.

I duck my head and pretend to inspect the tap like it holds the answers to my moral collapse.

Luke leans on the counter, arms folded, watching me with entircly too much amusement. "That keg tell you anything interesting?"

"Only that I'm in danger."

"Immediate or slow burn?"

"Death by embarrassment."

He grins, all sinful delight. "Shame. I was hoping for something more dramatic. I brought a knife just in case things got interesting."

I glance over. "You carry a knife?"

"I carry two. Depends on the outfit." He quirks an eyebrow.

I laugh despite myself. "You planned your accessories around murder?"

"No, I planned them around brunch. But murder was the backup."

He steps closer. I don't move. Can't. His scent slides under my skin like warm syrup. My stomach does a cartwheel. My brain forgets the alphabet. He's not even touching me yet, and I swear my knees write a resignation letter.

Luke's gaze drops to my lips, then flicks back up. He taps the counter between us.

"I could be a gentleman and step back," he says. "But I'm not really built for disappointment."

"That's your line?"

"Would you prefer something with pirates? I've been workshopping one that involves treasure maps and well-timed winks."

I shake my head, biting back a smile. "You're dangerous."

He leans in like he's going to whisper something salacious. "Yeah. I'm a menace with banana bread too. Tell no one."

I burst out laughing.

That's when Harper reappears, completely empty-handed and radiating mischief from the way she grins and eyes us.

"Oh, look, you're still here," she says to Luke. "How convenient."

"Your friend is subtle," Luke says.

"So subtle. Like a glitter cannon in a church," Harper mutters, poking her tongue out at us.

Luke smiles at Harper. "I like you," he says, then turns his attention to me. "But I'd marry *you*."

I choke on air. "Excuse me?"

"You heard me. I'm excellent at impulsive decisions. Got the tattoos and the arrest record to prove it."

Harper whistles. "That might be the most unhinged proposal I've ever witnessed. I'm kind of impressed."

Luke shrugs one shoulder, gaze still locked on me. "I don't do halfway. If I want something, I take it."

My throat goes dry. My brain is all fluttery and *Do not swoon, you absolute idiot*. "You don't even know me."

He smiles, slow, dark, and dangerous. "Not yet."

Harper fans herself dramatically. "Okay, that's it. I'm gonna need a helmet. Or a priest."

"You always look like that when you eat something good?" he asks me, voice low.

I raise a brow. "Like what?"

"Like you're one bad decision away from letting someone wreck you."

My stomach flips. I take another bite of the brownie just to avoid answering, but it doesn't help. His eyes are still on me, tracking, testing. Like I'm already his and he's just waiting for me to figure it out.

Harper breaks the moment with a groan. "Oh my God. Can you two not eye-fuck in public? It's giving off unresolved tension, and I didn't bring popcorn."

"That obvious?" Luke asks.

I manage to swallow and mutter, "A little."

He leans closer, and the air between us grows heavy, electric. "What would it take?"

"For what?"

"For you to stop pretending you're not tempted."

I choke on a laugh. "I'm not pretending."

Harper fans herself. "Someone pour cold water on me. Or her. Or both."

Still, Luke doesn't glance away. Doesn't blink. "I'd risk a lot more than a burned tongue for a bite."

"Flattery from a man who smells like burnt sugar, sweat, and fire-roasted heat."

His grin deepens, dangerous now. "And yet you're still standing here."

A sharp whistle slices through the tension. We both glance toward the food truck.

Arrow is leaning halfway out the service window, arms crossed. A line of people snakes down the field, a few shouting orders and waving cash.

Luke sighs, straightening up like it physically hurts to leave. "Duty calls."

"Go," I say, trying not to sound breathless. "Before your adoring public revolts."

He backs away with a grin that promises unfinished business. "Try not to miss me."

Too late.

Harper doesn't wait. She picks up the tiffin and lifts the last murder brownie like it's a holy relic. "Sorry, not sorry," she says and takes a bite so sinful that her eyes flutter shut.

A beat passes. Then she moans loudly—inappropriate for daylight hours.

"Okay, I'm mad," she declares through a mouthful. "That's the best thing I've ever eaten. I'd sell a kidney to taste that again."

I snort. "Just the one?"

She licks her finger. "Depends how big the batch is."

We both dissolve into laughter, but it doesn't last. Her gaze flicks toward me, sharp with intent. "Sooo…"

"No."

"You don't even know what I was going to say."

"Yes, I do." I rub at my temple. "No, I did not ask him to be my fake boyfriend."

"Cindy!"

"I can't just ask that! It's weird!"

"It's not. It's direct."

"I'd rather crawl into a mossy hole and die alone."

Harper sighs and sits beside me, wrapping the tiffin shut like she's closing a deal. "You know you're gonna have to do it eventually."

I glance sideways toward the food truck. I can't see Luke or Arrow. Just the hum of their truck, alive with heat and spice and him. And the huge lineup.

"I know," I mumble. "It's just… he flirts, sure, but that doesn't mean he'd actually do it."

"He will. All three of them will."

"You don't know that."

"I do," Harper says. "I've seen how they look at you. They're not just messing around."

I shake my head. "It's not even about that. It's about... what if one of them says yes, and then meets my family? What if he sees how broken they are, how they look at me like I'm a stain they can't scrub out? What if he decides it's not worth the hassle?"

Harper doesn't answer right away. She scoots closer, resting her chin on my shoulder.

"I'm not scared of them judging me," I say, softer now. "I'm scared of feeling special for five minutes... and then watching it get taken away."

Harper wraps her arms around me. She smells like cinnamon sugar. "You're special. Not because some guy flirts with you. Not because of whatever they did to you. You just are."

I let myself lean into her for a breath. Maybe two.

And all I can think is *What if I ask... and one of them says yes?*

CINDY

Harper's car smells like pumpkin spice coffee and the vanilla air freshener she bought in bulk, which basically captures her entire personality—caffeinated and extra. We're driving through Whispering Grove's streets mid-morning, the Halloween decorations looking slightly disheveled in daylight, like they partied too hard and have regrets.

"So, Jeff and I are done," Harper announces, taking a corner sharp enough that the cases of seasonal beer in the back shift and clink ominously.

"Oh no! What happened?" I grab the door handle as she narrowly misses a plastic skeleton that migrated into the road overnight. "Wait, is this another one of those 'we're taking a break but we'll make up next week' situations?"

"Nah, this is it. Series finale. No renewal, no spin-off, not even a reunion special." She adjusts her purple-tinted sunglasses even though it's cloudy. "After I dropped you off the other night, I caught up with him and told him I was going back to check on you, make sure you were okay after the whole Van situation. He got all pissy, said I was being dramatic and overprotective."

"But you are dramatic and overprotective. It's part of your charm."

"Exactly! But apparently, when those Alphas circled you like protective wolves, that was fine. When I want to make sure my best friend doesn't get kidnapped by her psycho ex, suddenly I'm too involved."

"Oh, Harper, I'm sorry you fought about me—"

"Don't you dare apologize. It just showed his true colors. We argued for, like, three hours. I may have used the phrase *emotionally stunted walrus* at one point."

"Walrus?"

"I was going for *manatee*, but *walrus* came out. Anyway, after our fight, I drove to your place, but you must have been completely unconscious. Knocked for five minutes, nothing."

"You could have used your spare key—"

"But then I thought, what if Van shows up? What if he tries something? So I stayed in my car outside your place. You know, casual surveillance. Very normal Friday night activity. I had snacks and everything."

I nearly choke on air. "Are you serious? You slept in your car, watching my place? Harper, that's—"

"What best friends do. Plus, no one really notices

what we Betas do. Anyway, I'm pretty sure your hot bikers were doing the same thing from a different angle. We probably could have carpooled, saved gas."

I lean over to hug her while she's driving, which results in us swerving toward a mailbox decorated to look like a monster's mouth. She swings away at the last minute, both of us jostling about.

I blink at her. "Wait—are you *sure* they were watching my place? Like... is that protective or creepy?"

She lifts a brow. "Depends. Do you want it to be creepy?"

"Nope."

"Then it's protective," she says, grinning. "You've got angels watching over you."

I snort. "More like devils in leather jackets and very confusing halos."

Harper pats my thigh. "Then lucky you."

I slide my arm back around her and squeeze tight. "Yeah. Lucky me."

"Okay, no emotional assault while I'm operating a vehicle!" Harper laughs, straightening the wheel. "Save the feelings for when we're parked, or we'll end up as actual Halloween decorations."

The sun breaks through the clouds as we drive through downtown, and I realize Harper isn't taking our usual route to the brewery.

"Uh, Harp? The brewery is back that way."

"I know."

"So where are we—"

She pulls into an alley, and my stomach drops as I spot the name on the building. "Harper. No."

"Harper, yes."

"This is Savor. The restaurant. Their restaurant."

"Oh my God, really? I had no idea!" She parks, grinning like the Cheshire Cat. "What a crazy coincidence! We have an order from them."

"You brought me here and didn't tell me!"

"How else was I going to get you to talk to them about your mom situation? You certainly weren't going to do it yourself."

"You're evil. Pure evil."

"I prefer 'proactive best friend.' Now grab a case. We're already late for delivery."

The back door of Savor is propped open, and the smell that wafts out and through Harper's open window should probably be classified as a controlled substance. Fresh bread, herbs, and something savory that makes my mouth water instantly.

"Delivery for the fancy-pants establishment!" Harper calls out cheerfully.

Holt appears in the doorway, and my brain temporarily shorts out.

He's... a lot. Six feet, five inches of pure muscle wrapped in dark jeans that fit perfectly and a black T-shirt that clings to his chest in ways that should require a warning label. His short black hair is slightly damp, as if he just showered, with the front pieces falling across his forehead. When he moves to help with the cases, every motion is on purpose.

"Morning, ladies," he says, and that voice, deep and rumbling like distant thunder, has my knees considering filing for early retirement.

"Morning yourself, Tall, Dark, and Intimidating," Harper replies cheerfully, popping the trunk. "Got your beer order plus some extras Arrow requested. Something about pairing them with his new autumn menu."

I get out of the car and join them, my cheeks already on fire.

Holt lifts two cases at once, and I definitely don't stare at how his forearms flex, the veins standing out against his skin. He catches me looking, and one corner of his mouth lifts slightly, not quite a smile but acknowledgment that he knows exactly what I'm thinking.

"Need help?" he asks, and I realize I've been standing there holding a single six-pack like it's a lifeline.

"I'm good! Totally good. Just, you know, admiring the... alley. Great alley. Very... alley-like."

Harper snorts. "Smooth."

We're unloading cases, creating a rhythm, with Harper chattering about beer varieties, Holt moving quickly, and me trying not to trip over my own feet every time he gets close enough that I inhale his scent, which drives me crazy with need.

Harper catches my eye and makes an exaggerated gesture toward Holt, mouthing, "ASK HIM."

When I shake my head, she rolls her eyes dramatically.

"So," Harper says loudly. "Cindy might need some help. Boyfriend help. The fake kind. For Saturday. With her mother. Who's visiting. Saturday. Did I mention Saturday?"

Holt pauses mid-lift, those amber eyes focusing on me with an intensity that leaves me forgetting my own name.

"Keep talking," he says simply, not appearing put off.

"How about," Harper says with fake brightness, "you and Cindy discuss the details while I finish organizing these cases? I'm suddenly very passionate about proper beer storage temperature."

Before I can grab her and force her to stay as my social buffer, Arrow appears in the doorway like some kind of culinary summoning. And my heart is racing faster.

He's wearing a chef's coat that should look professional but somehow appears rebellious on him, probably because he's added Halloween pins all over it and what appears to be "Kiss the Cook or I'll Poison Your Food" written in fake blood across the chest. His dark blond hair is pulled back, over his shoulders, revealing the sharp angles of his face, those brown eyes that look like he's planning something delightfully chaotic. How can these men be so deliciously handsome?

"You came!" He beams at me, and the transformation of his face from brooding chef to excited puppy is jarring. I'm flushing all over at his stare. "And not just for delivery! This is perfect. You have to let me cook for you."

"Oh, no, it's really okay. We should probably get back to—"

"I insist. Both of you. When was the last time you had a proper brunch? And I don't mean that sad bowl-of-cereal-standing-over-the-sink situation."

"How? What?"

"Holt, take her inside. Show her around. Harper and I will finish here."

Harper winks at me. "Go. I'll be right behind you. Arrow can tell me about his seasonal menu while we organize."

"Traitor," I mutter.

She chuckles.

Holt gestures toward the door, and I follow him through the kitchen, where stations are set up and perfectly organized, ingredients grouped, pots bubbling, and something sizzling that smells like heaven decided to become food.

"Tim," Holt says to a younger man chopping vegetables with frightening speed, "we'll be at table six."

"Got it, boss," Tim replies without looking up.

The main dining area leaves me gasping. It's incredible. The black steel beams overhead, the morning light streaming through windows, making everything glow warmly despite the industrial edges. The art on the walls that seems less ominous and more passionate.

"This is amazing," I say, running my hand along one of the live-edge tables, feeling the grain of the wood. "It's like... original and a bit dark and inviting. Like it could hug you or stab you and you'd thank it either way."

Holt actually chuckles, a low sound that I love hearing. "That's pretty close to what Arrow was going for. His words were 'approachable intimidation.'"

We slide into a booth, and immediately our feet bump under the table. Instead of pulling away like normal people would, he just adjusts so our ankles are touching.

"So," he says, those intense eyes focused entirely on me. "Tell me what you need?"

"That's a very open-ended question."

"Start with the mother situation."

"Right. That. Okay, so..." I take a breath, trying to organize my thoughts. "My mother is coming to visit, and, well, until she called, I hadn't spoken to her in almost two years. Not since I ran away..."

"From Van."

"From Van, my family, an entire life they had planned out for me." My fingers find a groove in the table's surface, tracing it nervously. "I was supposed to marry him. It was all arranged. My parents owed his family money. And I was the solution. Marry me off to their son, debt cleared, everyone's happy except the person being traded like a baseball card."

Holt's jaw tightens slightly, but he doesn't interrupt.

"The wedding day, I ran. Literally ran in my wedding dress through the woods behind the mansion. Changed my name, came here, started over. And for almost two years, it worked. Until Van found me at the festival the other night."

"And now your mother is coming to try to convince you to return?"

I nod. "Apparently, Van told her where I was, probably hoping to use family pressure to get me back. And he told her I had another Alpha, after meeting you at the Harvest Dance."

He grins, nodding. "So you need me to play boyfriend again?"

"It sounds so stupid when you say it out loud."

"More like survival," he corrects. "You're protecting yourself the best way you know how."

Our feet are still touching under the table, and I'm hyperaware of every point of contact, ankle against ankle, the warmth through our clothes, the way he shifts slightly to maintain the connection.

"The thing is," I continue, "she's expecting to meet the Alpha who has claimed me so there is no question that I am available."

"That's doable. So on Saturday? What time?"

I shake my head and nibble on my lower lip before saying, "Saturday is all she said. She'll turn up and message me so I can give her my address. I figure Van will probably find out where I live, considering my mother found my cell number. But if she sees me happy with a strong, scary kind of guy, she may let it be."

"Saturday is our busiest day at the restaurant, but Luke and Arrow can handle it." His arm stretches across the top of the bench behind him, fingers brushing the leather. My pulse flutters.

"I'm in," he says.

"Just like that?"

"Just like that."

"You don't want to know more details?"

His gaze fixes on me like I'm something fragile and flammable. "We'll go over what we need to. Ground rules, the story of how we met, how long we've been together. I'll come by tonight, and you can show me around. I'll bring a few things, make it look like I stay there."

I blink. "Yes. Toothbrush, maybe some clothes... guy stuff. Whatever makes it believable."

His mouth curves just slightly, not a full smile, more like a warning. "Trust me, sweetheart, I know how to play the part."

"I have a bit of money. Not much, but I can pay you for this. For the protection. For the help."

His face darkens, not in anger but in something unreadable and intense. "No. This one's on the house."

"But—"

"This isn't business for me."

The words hang there, low and final.

Something twists in my chest. It's not just that he said it—it's how he said it. Like there's more he's not letting me see. I open my mouth to say something, to ask what that means exactly, but then I catch the look in his eyes.

He's watching me too closely. Like he already knows I'm unraveling.

"Hey," he says, his voice soft but steady. "I know this isn't just some fake date to you. I can see it in your hands. You're shaking."

I clench them in my lap, trying to hide it. "It's just... I haven't seen my mom since I left. Not since everything. I don't even know what I'd say. What she'll say. And part of me doesn't care, but the other part, the part she broke, still wants her to look at me like I'm not... a failure."

I don't know when my voice started to shake. But it is. Holt just leans in a little, like the gravity between us is enough.

"She doesn't get to decide your worth," he says. "Not anymore."

I look down, overwhelmed. Then I feel his sharp scent, curling around me like smoke. My skin prickles, chest tight. I don't know why it hits so hard. Why my whole body feels hot and restless and hungry. It's not heat. It can't be. But there's something about the way he smells that leaves me feeling dizzy.

I shift in my seat, rubbing my thighs together subtly under the table, trying to ignore the way I'm burning up and reacting to *him*.

"You okay?" he asks.

"I'm fine," I lie, voice thin.

Holt tilts his head. "If we want this to look real… maybe we should lean in harder. Most parents aren't thrilled about their Omega daughters living alone."

I blink at him. "So you're saying… what?"

"I'm saying serious relationship. Maybe even bonded. Gets your mom off your back and sells the story."

There's a gleam in his eye—like this is a game he knows he'll win.

"And let me guess," I say, trying to act unaffected. "You're *very* convincing."

His smile is slow, crooked. Dangerous. "Oh, sweetheart. I can be *sweet* when I want to be."

Heat flushes down my neck. I want to roll my eyes but end up blushing instead. "I believe it."

"Good. Then let's call it a plan."

I exhale hard, heart racing. "It's probably… a good idea."

"Great," he says, standing. "I'll come by around six and bring dinner. We can practice."

Practice.

Alone. In my house. With *him*.

"Okay," I manage. "I'll… see you then."

He gives me one last look. A look that says he sees *everything*. Every ache, every crack, every secret.

And somehow, that makes me feel safer than I've ever felt in my whole life.

The moment Harper pushes through the restaurant doors, she zeroes in on us already seated at a corner booth. Her hair is half wild, and her grin wide. Without even asking, she slides in next to me, jostling me over with her hip like we're in high school and the last fry is up for grabs.

"I'm starving," she declares.

As if summoned by divine timing, Arrow strides out from the kitchen, holding a towering stack of polished-metal tiffins in one hand and a pile of empty plates balanced on his forearm like he was born doing this. His sleeves are pushed up, revealing forearms that could get their own fan club—a dusting of flour, tattoos, flourishes of muscle and tendon.

He sets the containers and plates down with an artful clatter, then clicks each open like he's performing a magic trick. Heat and rich scents bloom in the air. My stomach actually growls.

"We're starting with stuffed French toast soaked in bourbon syrup. Eggs Benedict with lemony hollandaise. Candied bacon for the people who like their breakfast with a side of danger. And hash browns so crispy they filed for a restraining order against soggy potatoes."

Arrow glances my way as he lifts a lid, revealing golden slabs of French toast. "Everything is seasonal, house-made, and morally questionable."

"I'd risk my soul for this toast," I mutter.

Arrow looks entirely too pleased by that. "Then I've done my job."

Harper doesn't wait. She's already serving both of us like she's feeding wolves. She slaps a heap of bacon on her plate and winks at Holt across the table. "You all always feed Cindy like this? Because I'm going to be attending all meals at this rate."

Holt arches a brow, glancing my way. "If she thinks you could handle all three of us?"

Arrow's gaze flicks to me at that. I try not to combust on the spot.

It's getting hard to breathe. They're flirting. This is actual flirting. *With me.*

"You boys always this charming?" I ask, reaching for the bacon to distract myself. "Or is this just how you win over your regulars?"

"We don't feed just anyone," Arrow adds quietly, slicing into his eggs. "We cook for people who matter."

That does something to me. Right in the soft place I try to ignore.

I pretend to focus on my plate, but my body is already misbehaving. Everything feels... heightened. Both their scents crash over me again, deeper, coiling like an inferno between my thighs.

I shift in my seat. I'm not in heat. That's still weeks away. But the air feels charged, thick, as if it's sticking to my skin. My stomach flips, and it's like every nerve I own is tuned specifically to him.

Harper catches on instantly. Of course she does.

"You're awfully quiet, Cindy."

"Just thinking about licking the plate," I mumble.

"Sure you are." And she's already filling my plate again. "Anyway, where's the third musketeer?"

Arrow leans back slightly, arm draped behind Holt. "Luke's getting supplies for the event tomorrow. Said he'd be back in an hour, but I give it twenty minutes before he texts asking where to get the vanilla beans from."

Harper points her fork like it's a weapon. "And here I thought the three of you never left each other's sides. Like cursed, themed triplets."

"We do separate," Holt says mildly. "Occasionally."

"Okay, but for real," Harper continues, clearly on a roll. "Savage Reapers? That's a hell of a past. I mean, going from crime to candied bacon? That's not a pivot. It's a pirouette."

I nearly choke on my hash brown.

My fork pauses in midair, and I give Harper a slow, sideways look. One that screams *What. Did. You. Just. Say?*

"Jesus, Harper," I mutter under my breath. "Maybe lead with literally anything else?"

"What?" she says innocently, already licking syrup off her finger. "It's public record."

"Yes, and so is grand theft auto, but you don't bring it up at brunch."

Arrow just laughs, the sound dark and amused. "She's not wrong, though. It *was* a pirouette. Graceful landing and everything."

"More like a nosedive," Holt mutters, finally speaking up, his voice deep and steady. "We hit bottom first. The food came later."

I glance between them. "So you didn't wake up one day and decide to trade switchblades for spatulas?"

Arrow smirks. "No, but the sharp edges still come in handy. Kitchen's just a different kind of battlefield."

Harper makes a low whistle. "That's unnecessarily hot. Stop that."

I stab another bite of potato, only half paying attention to the food now. "And here I thought you were just overly enthusiastic about seasoning."

"I am," Arrow says. "I just used to apply it to a different kind of meat."

"Okay," I say quickly. "We're moving on before I accidentally find that attractive."

Arrow grins and flicks his fingers along the side of the table like a metronome.

We laugh, and it's surprisingly easy. The four of us. No tension, whether we meant for that to happen or not.

Still, I keep glancing at Holt.

Not because he's loud. He's the opposite of that. But the man takes up space without trying, with those broad shoulders under a dark T-shirt that hugs his arms a little too well. He's solid in a way that says *Nothing moves me unless I let it.*

And he's coming to my place tonight. I can't get that out of my head.

To talk.

And I have absolutely nothing ready. My clothes are all over the floor, my couch is half covered in unfolded laundry, and I'm pretty sure my kitchen sink is filled with dishes.

Arrow catches me staring and winks. A jolt of excitement races up my spine.

Not a quick twitch. Not innocent.

Slow. Intentional. Criminal.

What the hell am I getting into?

"Cindy," Holt says, his voice low and direct. "You okay?"

"Yep," I say quickly, popping a piece of candied bacon into my mouth and immediately regretting how obscene that probably looked. "Totally fine. Just... planning."

"Planning what?" Harper asks, narrowing her eyes in that *I'm about to expose you* way she has.

"My funeral," I mumble. "You know, when I die of embarrassment tonight and have to be buried in the laundry I forgot to put away."

Arrow chuckles again and taps the table with two fingers. "I volunteer to do the catering."

Holt finally leans forward, forearms on the table, gaze locked on mine. "You don't need to clean up for me, darlin'," he says quietly. "I'm not coming to judge your laundry. I just want to talk. Face-to-face. No noise."

My pulse stutters.

Easy for him to say.

He *is* the noise.

"What the fuck?" a voice calls across the restaurant. "You're having a party without me? This is betrayal of the highest order!"

My head snaps up—too fast—and I nearly choke on a piece of bacon.

Luke strides in like a king. He's wearing ripped jeans that were destroyed by artistic intent, not wear. A faded band shirt reads *Funeral for a Viking*, and his boots are scuffed and muddy as if he just walked out of a bar brawl. His long auburn hair catches the light streaming through the front windows, glinting like fire given shape.

And then he grins. Right at me.

That same devil-may-care grin he flashed last night when we chatted at the festival booth. He'd just joined me, all casual swagger, and melted my heart.

Now he's here. With *them*.

All three of them.

God. These men are going to be the death of me.

Luke's expression morphs into mock outrage as he marches toward our table. "You *started eating*? Without me? I disappear for two hours, and you replace me with Purple Hair and Brewery Girl?"

"Purple Hair?" Harper lifts a brow.

Luke gestures vaguely. "It's giving off violet vengeance. Or heartbreak. Scoot over, Violet Violence."

Harper snorts. "That's actually kind of perfect." She slides over, pushing me closer to Holt as she makes space for Luke to squeeze in next to her.

Holt's thigh bumps mine under the table, and his arm brushes close.

"Tim!" Luke yells toward the kitchen. "Emergency! They left me to starve! Need more food, please."

"You were gone for two hours," Holt says calmly.

Luke gasps dramatically. "Two hours of tragic starvation while you're all here feasting like royalty. Look at me. I'm wasting away. I have cheekbones now. This is serious."

"You're literally eating the bacon from my plate," Arrow mutters, unbothered.

"Stealing food doesn't count. It's the principle."

Arrow laughs and leans back.

Tim is there in no time, sliding a fresh tiffin stack onto the table like this happens every day. "Figured you'd want more. You guys eat like wolves."

"You bet," Luke states, shoving half a piece of French toast into his mouth.

I try not to stare. I *try*. But he licks syrup off his thumb like it's a goddamn sin and then grins at me again as if he knows exactly what he's doing.

"You gonna eat that?" he asks, nodding toward the last hash brown on my plate.

I blink. "I was."

He shrugs. "You hesitated. Rookie mistake." He swipes it before I can stab him with my fork.

"You're unbelievable," I mutter.

"I get that a lot," he says, still chewing.

"Usually with more swearing," Arrow adds dryly.

"You've got fight," Luke declares, gesturing at me with his fork.

"She also has pepper spray," Harper supplies helpfully.

"Even better." Luke grins, full wattage. "Nothing says 'romance' like mild chemical warfare."

Holt snorts. His gaze drifts over me slowly, but there's something softer around the edges now. "You okay?"

I nod even though I have no idea what I'm agreeing to. The air at this table is thick enough to bottle. And drink. And then die from.

It's not fair how they're all looking at me.

Holt, with that unreadable stare that feels like he's already halfway into my apartment, checking if the sheets are clean. Arrow, smug and knowing, like he's already picturing how fast he could get me flustered again. And Luke, brand new to this mess and already acting like he belongs in the middle of it.

Too much.

I shove a bite of warm French toast in my mouth to give myself something to do besides spiral.

"You always get this quiet when you're over-whelmed?" Arrow asks, voice low.

I point at him with my fork. "Do you always act like excitement is a love language?"

He smiles. "Only when it's working."

"She's outnumbered," Harper chimes in. "You three are basically an Alpha sandwich."

My eyes bulge, and I give her the death stare, to which she only blows me a kiss.

Luke perks up. "Do I get to be the top bun?"

"You're the sweet pickle," I mutter, regardless.

He grins widely, clearly delighted. "You calling me sweet?"

"I'm calling you unexpected."

Arrow snorts into his food. Holt just studies me and keeps on eating. "I could give you space," he offers, not sounding like he means it.

"That sounds fake," I say, then instantly regret it when his mouth twitches, just the faintest curl at the edge.

Luke props his chin on his hand and gives me a slow once-over that somehow feels more curious than cocky. "You always this quick on your feet?"

"Only when I'm surrounded by beautiful men and one of them might be showing up at my door tonight."

Luke's mouth drops open. "What?"

Harper exhales. "God, I love it here."

"So," Holt starts, nudging his empty plate away. "Just so you two aren't blindsided, Cindy's mom is coming into town Saturday. I'll be at Cindy's place, playing the doting boyfriend."

My pulse skips. I reach for my glass of water I haven't touched, suddenly parched.

Arrow leans forward. "What's your mom like?"

I groan. "Think Martha Stewart meets Cersei Lannister. Everything has to be perfect, or she'll assume I've failed at life. She'll judge my hair, my fridge, the way I answer the door."

"She sounds like someone who needs a reality check," Luke says.

"I'm hoping Holt's general vibe takes the edge off," I mutter.

"She'll either melt or implode," Luke says, grinning. "Honestly? I support both outcomes."

"You're not coming," I remind him, needing this catch-up to go as smoothly and low-key as possible.

"Not planning to." He winks at me again, melting me in my seat. "Just emotionally invested in the drama."

Arrow nods. "We're not saying we'll be there, but if you need anything, reinforcements, a distraction, a last-minute escape plan…"

"I can handle her," Holt says, eyes on me again.

It's supposed to be pretend. But the way he looks at me? The way I feel when he does? None of that feels fake. And that's what terrifies me most.

8

CINDY

I've scrubbed things that shouldn't need scrubbing. Who cleans the underside of kitchen drawers? Me, apparently. The laundry situation in my bedroom closet is reaching critical mass. If that door opens while Holt is here, it'll be like an avalanche of dirty clothes.

The fridge actually has food in it instead of my usual collection of condiments that expired during the last presidential administration. I bought juice—orange, apple, and something called Tropical Sunrise because I panicked at the grocery store and grabbed things randomly. Harper let me raid the brewery's stock, so at least the beer situation is handled. There's even fresh fruit in a bowl on the counter, though I'm not entirely sure what to do with it. Do people just… eat fruit? Raw? Like animals?

I check the clock. 5:47 p.m.

"Okay, thirteen minutes. That's enough time to have another nervous breakdown, maybe two."

And I smell like I've been wrestling furniture in a Pine-Sol factory. Not exactly the sophisticated Omega pheromones romance novels promised me. I lift my arm for a tentative sniff and immediately regret everything. It's sweet desperation mixed with industrial cleaner and a hint of yeast from the brewery.

"Fantastic. I smell like a bakery that's having a panic attack."

No time for another shower. I rush to the bathroom and apply enough deodorant to damage the ozone layer, then spray perfume strategically—wrists, neck, that spot behind my ears Harper swears drives Alphas crazy.

I stare at myself in the bathroom mirror.

"Okay, Cindy. Deep breaths. You're a confident, independent Omega who definitely has her life together and absolutely did not eat cereal for dinner three nights this week. A gorgeous Alpha is coming over to help you lie to your mother. This is normal. This is fine. Sure, he's built like a Greek god, and his voice melts you, but that's irrelevant. You're just two adults preparing an elaborate deception. Nothing weird about that. Totally casual-Friday-night activity."

I study my outfit, a sage green sundress that seemed like a good idea an hour ago. It brings out my eyes, and it's comfortable, which is important because my body temperature is approximately one thousand degrees from anxiety. My feet are bare because putting on shoes in my own house felt like trying too hard, but now I'm wondering if bare feet are too casual? Too intimate? Do feet send messages?

"God, I'm losing my mind. Feet don't send messages. Feet are just feet."

My hair is in a messy bun. Down felt too romantic, like I was expecting something. Up felt too severe, like I was about to conduct a business meeting. This is the compromise, casual but cute, approachable but not desperate.

I catch myself reaching for mascara and freeze.

"No. Bad Cindy. This is not a date. He's not here to admire your eyelashes. He's here to help you deceive your emotionally manipulative mother. Mascara is not required for deception."

I apply it anyway because apparently I have no self-control.

A knock at the door makes me jump so hard I nearly stab myself in the eye with the mascara wand.

"Oh God. He's here. I'm not ready. I'll never be ready. I need at least three more years of therapy before I'm ready for this."

I wipe my sweaty palms on my dress—very classy, very sophisticated—and head to the door. My hand hovers over the handle.

"You're cool. You're collected. You're definitely not having heart palpitations. Just open the door like a normal person."

I do just that and immediately forget every word in the English language.

Holt fills the doorway as if he's sculpted to fit it perfectly. He's changed from this morning to dark blue jeans that hang low enough to be dangerous for my concentration, brown boots, and a charcoal button-up shirt with the top two buttons undone because apparently he wants me to die. The sleeves are rolled up to his elbows, revealing forearms that should require a permit. His black hair is tousled from the wind, the longer pieces on top falling across his forehead.

But it's his face that really gets me. Strong jaw with just enough stubble to scream danger. Those amber eyes that seem to see through all my defenses. The slight crook in his nose that suggests he's been in fights. His lips are both stern and soft, though right now they're curved in the slightest smile as he watches me stare at him as if he's a particularly attractive math problem I can't solve.

He's carrying two large paper bags that smell like heaven and has a duffel bag over his shoulder.

"Hi," I manage, though it comes out more like a mouse being stepped on.

"Hi," he says, and that rumble has my entire body waking up and paying attention.

I watch him take in my appearance, his gaze traveling from my bare feet, up my legs, lingering on the way the dress clings to my curves, and up to my face, where I'm probably blushing like a tomato with social anxiety.

"You look beautiful," he says simply, like it's a fact rather than an opinion.

"I... you... thanks? Come in! Please, before the neighbors see and start gossiping."

I step aside and he enters, bringing the scent of October wind and his own unique smell that makes me want to lick him.

"Is that from Arrow's restaurant?" I ask, gesturing at the bags. "Please tell me that's from Arrow's restaurant, because it smells divine."

He chuckles, setting the bags on my entry table. "Arrow insisted on sending enough food to feed a small army. Said he couldn't let you face your mother on an empty stomach or with subpar food in your system."

The duffel bag catches my attention. "That's... a lot of stuff for one day."

"Want to make sure it looks authentic," he answers. "Your mother needs to believe I spend time here regularly or maybe that I'm moved in."

"Right. Of course. Smart thinking. Very strategic." I'm babbling. "Come in properly! Welcome to Casa de Cindy, where the furniture is secondhand and the anxiety is brand new."

He looks around my living room, and I try to see it through his eyes. The couch I rescued from a yard sale but reupholstered in soft gray fabric. My collection of throw pillows. The coffee table I painted myself during a wine-and-crafts night that got out of hand.

"It's perfect," he says, and he seems to mean it. "Warm. Comfortable. Very you."

"You can tell that from my living room?"

He points to my bookshelf. "The miniature neighborhood you built, complete with tiny Halloween decorations. The five different blankets on one couch. The fact that you have a decorative-beer-opener collection but also use them as wall art. Yeah, I can tell."

He noticed my miniatures. This man pays attention to details, and that's both thrilling and terrifying.

"How about I serve us dinner and learn my way around your kitchen?" he suggests.

"Perfect. I'll grab drinks."

In the kitchen, we move around each other in the small space. Every time we almost touch, my skin lights up like someone is running electricity through it. He brushes past me to reach a cabinet, and I swear my soul briefly leaves my body. I open the fridge, and his hand lands on my lower back to steady me when I wobble, and that point of contact burns through my dress.

"You okay?" he asks, voice closer to my ear than expected.

"Perfect! Great! Just temporarily forgot how legs work!"

His laugh is low and tempting. "Breathe, Cindy. I don't bite." A pause. "Unless you want me to."

I make a sound that's half laugh, half wheeze and escape to the living room with our beers like the coward I am. My hands are shaking as I open them, grateful for my decorative opener that actually works.

"So," he calls from the kitchen, his voice carrying easily. "How was work at the brewery today?"

"Oh, you know, the typical. Had one very persistent delivery driver who thought that my having a boyfriend meant he should try harder, and Mrs. Carp brought in her new boyfriend, who's half her age and with twice her enthusiasm for day drinking."

"Give me names," he says, and there's something sharp in his tone that makes me shiver.

"For the driver or Mrs. Carp's boy toy?"

"The ones who bothered you."

"Easy there, caveman. I handled it. I'm tougher than I look. I once made a man cry using only sarcasm and a raised eyebrow."

"Never doubted it for a second."

I turn on the TV to my favorite YouTube channel of a fireplace in what looks like a Victorian mansion decorated for Halloween. The orange glow flickers across the screen, fake but somehow comforting. The sound of crackling wood fills the silence while I try not to think about the fact that there's a dangerously attractive man in my kitchen serving me dinner like this is normal, like this is my life.

Holt emerges carrying enough food for a small wedding, and I jump up to help.

"Wow, did Arrow cook for the whole town?"

"He gets enthusiastic," Holt replies, setting down containers on the coffee table in front of the couch. "Also, I think he's trying to impress you."

"By putting me into a food coma?"

"By showing you what our pack can provide."

Pack. My stomach flutters at the word.

He opens containers, revealing treasures that leave me drooling. "Maple-glazed pork belly that Arrow literally torched at the table before packing. Roasted vegetables with some sauce he refuses to name but I think involves seventeen different spices and possibly witchcraft. Garlic mashed potatoes that are essentially butter with potato as a suggestion. And chocolate lava cakes for dessert."

He hands me an empty plate and starts serving me before I can protest, which is oddly touching. It's as though he wants to make sure I'm fed. It's such an Alpha thing, but from him it doesn't feel controlling, just... caring.

We settle on the couch, not quite at opposite ends but with a safe distance between us. I curl my legs under me, dress riding up slightly, and I catch him noticing. The light outside is starting to dim, casting everything in that golden October glow that I adore.

"So," I say after my first bite of pork belly has me questioning everything I thought I knew about food. "What does my fake boyfriend need to know about my darling mother?"

"Everything. The good, the bad, the weird."

"Oh, there's no good. Let's start with the weird. She alphabetizes her tea collection but thinks organizing books by color is the devil's work. She only drinks herbal tea or black coffee, never adds milk because that's what poor people do. She genuinely believes that eating with your fingers is a moral failing unless it's specifically designated finger food, and even then she uses those tiny forks."

"She sounds delightful," he adds dryly, taking a drink of his beer.

"Oh, she's a treasure. She also has this thing about posture. I spent half my childhood with books balanced on my head because 'an Omega's spine should be straight enough to hold up society's expectations.' Direct quote."

"That explains why you sit so straight even when you're relaxing."

"And my deep hatred of encyclopedias. Volumes K through M gave me neck problems."

I watch him eat, and it's unfair how attractive he makes basic human functions. The way his jaw moves, the way his throat works when he swallows, how he licks a drop of sauce off his thumb—it's pornographic.

"You're staring," he says without looking up.

"No, I'm... inspecting." The word falls out. Great. Now I sound like a creeper doing a home appraisal.

He finally glances up, the corner of his mouth already tugged in amusement. His eyes don't just look at me; they know me. Or they're trying to. And I'm not sure which is more deadly.

Then he laughs, low and a little rough. "You should come with a warning label in that dress."

I nearly choke on my potato. "This old thing? I just threw it on."

He doesn't answer right away, just tips his head. "You didn't. You chose it for a reason."

I grab my fork like it's a weapon, but it's my heartbeat that's under attack.

"You picked green because it makes your eyes look even more sinful. The hem is short enough to make me wonder what else you've planned, but long enough to keep it classy. You're barefoot, which means you're comfortable around me now. Or you want me to think you are."

"Is this... is this what you do? Weaponize compliments?"

He shrugs, utterly unbothered. "I told you. I pay attention to things that matter."

I stare at him, at the quiet confidence he wears like a second skin. Holt isn't flashy. He's not charming the way Luke is, or smooth like Arrow. He's steel wrapped in silence, sharp when you least expect it.

And he's here. In my house. Sitting on my couch like he belongs here.

I take a shaky breath, trying to reel myself back in. "Right. Okay. Fake-boyfriend prep. We should figure out what kind of story we're telling my mother before she arrives and decides you're secretly running a cult."

He raises an eyebrow. "Would that be so bad?"

"Yes," I say, stabbing at my food. "Though she'd probably find that less concerning than me dating a mechanic."

His smile curves slowly. "Good thing I'm not a mechanic."

"God help me," I mutter, half under my breath.

He leans back on the couch, stretching like he's perfectly at ease while I try not to disintegrate on the spot. "You okay?" he asks softly.

I nod too fast. "Totally. I'm just... wondering what the hell I got myself into."

His eyes hold mine for a beat longer than is necessary. "Something good."

I clear my throat. "So. Our story," I say, shooting for brisk and businesslike, which is laughable given the state of my insides. "How did we meet?"

"What would you tell your mother that she'd believe?"

"Honestly? She'd expect something traditional. Meeting at a coffee shop or through mutual friends."

"Too boring. Halloween dance last year at the community center. You were dressed as a witch—"

"Predictable."

"—a sexy librarian witch, and I couldn't take my eyes off you."

I arch a brow. "What were you dressed as?"

"Myself. I don't do costumes."

"That's such a guy answer."

"But believable. We danced, you spilled your drink on me—"

"I did not!"

"It's our fake history. You definitely did. You were embarrassed. I thought it was adorable, asked for your number to replace my ruined shirt."

"And I gave it to you?"

"After making me work for it. You made me guess your number. Took me seventeen tries."

I laugh despite myself, even as something warm uncurls low in my belly. "That's actually kind of cute."

As if anything about the way he's watching me right now is cute. His gaze is reading everything I'm trying not to say out loud. My skin buzzes under his attention.

"First date?" he continues. "Where would you want me to take you if this were real?"

The question hangs between us, heavier than it should be. Loaded. Too close to something that feels like hope.

I glance down at my plate and then back at him. "I don't know, somewhere nice? Dinner with a view?"

He shakes his head like he's already rewritten the scene in his mind. "Too public. I'd take you up to Mountain Ridge, that spot where you can see the whole valley. Private picnic, good wine, no interruptions."

I swallow. Hard. "Why private?"

"So I could have all your attention. No distractions, no other people trying to steal glances at you in that dress. Just us."

Just us.

Two words that have no right to make my heart slam the way it does. My breath hitches, and I don't even bother to hide it. Not when he's watching me like that.

I'm staring at him, imagining this scenario that

will never happen, feeling things I shouldn't feel. Wanting things I can't want.

"Whatever girl ends up with you for real is going to be the luckiest woman alive," I say softly.

His smile is slow, predatory. Not sweet. Not safe. Like he knows exactly what he's doing to me and wants more. "I'll make sure she knows it every single day."

The way he stares at me has me squirming on the couch. My cheeks burn up, my pulse thuds wildly at the base of my throat. I shove a bite of food into my mouth before I say something I can't take back.

We continue eating, trading information.

Favorite foods. His: anything involving meat and carbs. Mine: carbs in all forms but especially when cheese is involved.

Allergies. None for either of us, unless you count my sudden and irrational reaction to hot guys sitting in my home.

Pet peeves. He hates small talk. I hate mouth breathers.

And somewhere in the middle of it all, I forget this is supposed to be pretend.

"What's our relationship like?" he asks. "Sex life."

I nearly drop my fork. My heart slams against my ribs, and heat creeps up the back of my neck. "Do we have to discuss that?"

"Your mother might ask questions. We should be prepared."

"She won't ask about our sex life!"

"She might ask me. When you're not around. Whether I've claimed you, marked you."

"Marked?" I squeak, the word catching in my throat.

"Bitten," he clarifies, voice dropping low and dark like smoke curling through my bloodstream. "Alphas bite to mark their territory. Shows ownership."

"Yeah, I know, and it's a bit barbaric."

"That's biology. And your mother will want to know you're properly claimed. Protected."

The room feels smaller all of a sudden. Warmer. His scent wraps around me, sharp and masculine. I shift in my seat and instantly regret it. Every nerve is lit up, humming with awareness. I set my plate on the coffee table in front of us, and Holt does the same.

"Fine," I manage, trying to sound unaffected even as my thighs clench. "Tell her you bit me somewhere she can't see."

"Where?" He leans forward slightly, eyes locked on mine like a predator circling. "I need specifics in case she pushes."

"I don't know, my shoulder?"

"Too visible. She might ask to see."

"My... hip?"

"Better. But I think inner thigh. High up, where only I would see. Where my mouth would have to travel up your soft skin, kissing every inch until you're begging—"

"Wow." I jump up, a cushion tumbling to the floor. My face is on fire, skin flushed and tight like it doesn't fit right. "Is it hot in here? It's definitely hot. I'm opening a window."

I fumble with the latch, desperate for air that doesn't smell like him. But even the breeze doesn't help. He's still in the room. Still watching me like he's already won. Then I collapse back on the couch.

"We should also discuss pet names," he continues, calm as anything while I'm one wrong move from combusting. "What do I call you?"

"My name?"

"Boring. I need something more intimate."

"Like what?"

"Duchess. Princess. Sweet girl. Baby girl. Little one."

I snort before I can stop myself. "What, are you trying to start your own fairy-tale harem?"

He grins. "You could be my temptation."

I blink. "That's not a pet name. That's a sin."

"Exactly."

I shake my head, laughing despite myself.

He leans in a little more, that dangerous gleam in his eye. "Fine. 'Good girl,' then."

I make a sound that's definitely not human. "You can't call me that in front of my mother!"

"Why not? If we're as serious as you want her to believe, I'd be possessive. Protective. Making sure she knows exactly who you belong to."

"I don't belong to anyone," I say automatically.

"I know that. But she doesn't believe that. So we play her game, by her rules, and win."

There's logic there, but my brain is too fuzzy from his proximity to process it.

"Tell me about your pack," I say, desperate for safer ground. "How did you three end up together?"

He leans back, considering. "Met Luke first. Bar fight that turned into a job offer. Arrow came later, needed help with some trouble. We just fit. Like we'd been waiting to find each other."

"That's sweet, actually."

We've served ourselves more food and are just enjoying each other's company. I'm feeling slightly calmer as we finish eating, our plates piled on the table, and I'm achingly aware of how domestic this feels.

"Want to know something funny?" Holt asks, shifting closer on the couch.

"Always."

"My buddy from the MC, Diesel, his ex was getting married. Proper society wedding, the kind where they have assigned seating and seventeen forks. She invited him just to rub his face in it."

"That's cruel."

"That's Diesel's ex. So he decided to show up with a wife."

"He got married out of spite?"

"Fake married. Three-day weekend pretending to be madly in love with this Omega he hired. Matching rings, coordinated stories, even practiced their first dance."

"That's insane."

"It gets better. The Omega he hired? Turned out to be a professional Dom in her spare time. Spent the entire wedding bossing Diesel around, making him fetch drinks, carry her purse. Diesel's ex was so confused that she cried."

I'm laughing so hard I can't breathe. "That's horrible! And amazing!"

"The best part? They're actually married now. For real. Turns out they were perfect for each other."

"You're making that up."

"Scout's honor. Went to their real wedding last year. The Dom made Diesel cry during the vows."

We're both laughing, and somehow we've gotten closer on the couch. His thigh presses against mine, warm even through our clothes. The living room feels smaller, more intimate. Like the air has thickened with something electric.

"You're beautiful when you laugh," he says quietly.

"You don't have to practice compliments. We're alone."

"I'm not." He reaches out, traces a finger along my jaw. "Van was a fucking idiot."

"You don't know the whole story."

"I know enough. I know he tried to own you instead of treasure you. That makes him an idiot."

His hand is still on my face, thumb brushing my cheekbone, and I'm leaning into the touch without meaning to. My skin tingles everywhere he's touching and everywhere he's not. My heart thuds like it's caught between running and surrendering.

"We should kiss," he says.

My brain shorts out. "What?"

His thumb pauses just below my lip. "We're supposed to be dating, remember? Might come in handy if you don't look shocked every time I get close to your mouth."

"That's not why you said it."

"No," he admits, voice low and rough. "It's not."

I should pull back. I really should. But I don't. I'm too caught up in the warmth of his hand, the steady look in his eyes, the tension thrumming in my chest that feels suspiciously like longing.

"Just a practice kiss?" I ask, and my voice betrays me by sounding breathy.

"If that's what you need to call it."

He's so close now that the heat of his breath flares over my cheek. Everything in me wants to lean in, to find out what he tastes like, to see if kissing him is as good as it looks in my head.

I don't know who moves first. Maybe it's both of us. But the moment our lips brush, the fake label we've been clinging to snaps like an overstretched thread.

I press closer, hands finding his firm chest, feeling his heartbeat racing to match mine. His body is solid heat under my palms, and I swear I can feel his pulse beneath my fingertips, a deep, thrumming rhythm that calls to something buried inside me.

He makes a sound low in his throat, almost a growl, and angles his head, deepening the kiss. His mouth claims mine with a slow, aching hunger, tongue tracing my lower lip before slipping inside.

The hand on my waist pulls me flush against him until I'm practically in his lap, my dress sliding high over my thighs. I don't care. All I can feel is the press of his body, the hard line of him beneath me, the way his other hand fists in my hair and pulls, not roughly, but firmly enough that my breath catches and heat floods through me.

He loosens my bun until my hair spills around us, tangling in his fingers. The sound he makes then—like he's lost control of his restraint—has something in me unraveling.

He kisses me like he's been starving. Like he's afraid that if he stops, I'll disappear. His tongue slides against mine, coaxing a soft sound from my throat. I've never been kissed like this, like he wants to worship and ruin me all at once.

When we finally break apart, I'm gasping and my lips feel swollen. His eyes are dark, jaw tight, like he's holding back from taking things further.

"That's... that's definitely not the kind of kiss we can do in front of my mother," I manage.

"Probably not," he agrees, voice low and rough, but he doesn't let go.

"Cindy?"

"Yeah?"

"You can scent me if you want. Properly."

I blink at him, confused, until he undoes two more buttons of his shirt, revealing the taut line of his chest and the edge of a skull tattoo inked into tanned skin. He tilts his head back, exposing his throat.

That kind of openness. That kind of trust. It makes me shudder and curl forward.

"That's... that's really intimate," I whisper.

"We're supposed to be together. You should know my scent."

My hands move on instinct, sliding over the hard plane of his chest. His skin is hot beneath my fingers. I lean in, breath catching as his scent wraps around me. It's stronger here. Spiced caramel, darker and more potent up close. The marshmallow sweetness has a creamy depth, thick and soft, with a hint of vanilla.

I press my nose to his throat and breathe him in deep.

Something inside me breaks and re-forms. Like this was always meant to be.

"Scent match," I whisper against his skin.

His arms come around me, pulling me in so tight I can barely breathe. "I know."

"This can't be real."

"Feels pretty fucking real to me."

I pull back slightly, just enough to see his face. I need space. I need to think. But he doesn't release me. His hand is on my back, warm and steady. His breath fans my cheek.

"We should focus on tomorrow," I murmur. "The plan. That's what matters."

"If you say so." But his eyes are locked on mine, and

they're full of heat. Of questions. Of promises we're no longer pretending to ignore.

He stands, goes to grab his duffel bag, and I try to calm my racing heart. *Try* being the operative word.

Because the second his back is to me, something in my body shifts as if a match has been struck, and now everything inside me is burning. My thighs clench without permission. My breathing goes shallow. There's a heat rolling through me, slow and mean, licking at the edges of my self-control, wanting to see what I'll do when it's gone.

This can't be happening. Not now. Not again.

I press my palms to my knees, grounding myself. But it doesn't help.

The scent of him is everywhere. It lingers in the air, seeps into my skin, and the raw, primal part of me, the heat I've been trying to ignore, is clawing her way to the surface, desperate and feral. And every inch of me wants to roll in that scent. She wants to be *claimed*.

And worse?

Bitten... What I wouldn't give to feel that ache between my thighs.

God, who have I become?

The ache hits low and deep, sharp and undeniable. The kind that demands attention doesn't just want—it *needs*. Pressure. Teeth. Tongue. Cock. Something to ease the pulsing throb between my thighs that's now making me squirm on the damn couch like I'm in heat.

Which I'm not.

I'm not.

I grip the cushion beneath me and focus on breathing, on logic, on anything but the slick heat building between my legs and the way my body is already responding to just the sound of his zipper opening as he unpacks.

"Let's make this place look lived in," he says, all business now.

I manage a nod, even though I'm not sure my brain is functioning. But right now, every single thing he does feels loaded. Erotic.

I watch him unpack. Toothbrush and razor for the bathroom. Normal enough. Then he starts sorting everything on the other end of the couch like he's building little piles for each room, grouping them like some unspoken plan is playing out in his head.

"That's a lot of clothes," I observe, forcing casualness into my voice while my thighs squeeze tighter together.

"Need to make it believable."

He adds folded shirts to one pile, a belt to another. Like he's moving in. Like this is real. Like I'm his and he's just settling into what was always inevitable.

Then he sets down a phone charger, places his watch carefully beside it, and adds a pair of reading glasses to the mix.

"You wear glasses?" I ask, trying to latch on to anything to distract from the inferno in my bloodstream.

"Sometimes. Want to see?"

He puts them on, and thank God I'm sitting down

because scholarly Holt is a version I was not prepared for. He looks like a dangerous professor, the kind that would make you stay after class. The kind who'd bend you over the desk for giving the wrong answer—and I'd suddenly forget how to get anything right.

"That's not fair," I inform him, my voice a little hoarse. "You can't just add accessories and level up in hotness."

He continues unpacking without comment, like this isn't killing me slowly. He pulls out workout bands and places them on the far end of the couch. A tub of protein powder follows.

"Your mother might check the kitchen," he explains.

Then comes a worn cookbook with stained corners.

"No one would believe I live somewhere without recipe books."

Even a pair of scuffed boots land neatly by the side table like they've always belonged there.

"This is very thorough," I say.

"That's me." He takes out a framed photo next. "Harper sent this."

It's us, sort of. Harper's Photoshop skills have combined what looks like a brewery event photo of me with one of Holt at the restaurant. We're not quite together but close enough to look like a couple. I'm laughing at something, and he's looking at me with an expression that will give me fantasies.

"When did Harper do this?"

"This afternoon, apparently. She and Luke have been plotting."

"Of course they have."

By the time he's done, my space looks transformed. Male presence everywhere. The bathroom smells like his soap, and his jacket on the hook carries his scent, his belongings mixed with mine like we've been together for months.

"Perfect," he says, surveying his work.

"Yeah," I agree, looking around my invaded space. "Perfect."

We return to the couch, closer now, the air charged between us.

"We should go over more details," he says. "Just in case."

"Like what?"

"Your favorite things. Morning routine. How you take your coffee."

"Why would my mother ask about my coffee preferences?"

"I should know them. Boyfriends know these things."

So we talk. I tell him about my coffee addiction with cream, no sugar, unless it's Monday—then all the sugar. He tells me he drinks it black like God intended. I learn that he runs every morning at dawn when the world is quiet. He learns that I haven't seen dawn voluntarily in years.

"Biggest fear?" he asks.

"That's getting deep for fake dating."

"Your mother might test me."

"Fine. Ending up like my sister. Married to someone who sees her as decoration. Two kids she never wanted, living a life someone else chose." I pause. "Yours?"

"Failing to protect the people I care about."

The weight of that statement sits between us. Not heavy. Not awkward. Just real. Like the rest of this night.

"Holt?"

"Yeah?"

"What happens after tomorrow? When my mother leaves?"

He looks at me for a long moment. "What do you want to happen?"

"I don't know," I admit. "This is complicated."

"Doesn't have to be."

We're close again, that magnetic pull between us that I don't understand but can't resist.

"I should probably get ready for bed," I say. "Big day tomorrow."

"Right," he says, standing with a stretch that somehow makes him look even broader. "I'd better head off, then."

I follow him to the door, pulse tripping. "Are you really going home, or are you going to sit in your car and watch my place all night?"

He pauses with his hand on the doorknob, eyes narrowing just slightly.

"Harper told me she spotted you guys out there the other night."

The corner of his mouth lifts, slow and wicked. It's the kind of smile that has women questioning their moral compass.

I nearly fan myself.

"Then I insist you stay over," I say, pushing the words out before I lose my nerve. "The couch is super comfy. Long enough to fit you. Please don't stay in the car."

"I've got a good view from the street," he says, like it's the most normal thing in the world. "I'll be more comfortable keeping an eye out. And being a gentleman."

"I won't sleep knowing you're out there in the dark and cold," I argue, crossing my arms. "You'll be ten feet away either way. What's the difference?"

He considers me for a second too long. "This way, I'll spot danger before it reaches you."

I hate that logic. Hate how it makes sense. Hate that it feels like he's drawing some kind of boundary I don't want.

"Wait," I say, before he can pull the door open. "At least let me make you a coffee. And maybe some snacks? You like snacks, right?"

He grins again, like he knows exactly what he's doing. "Only if you're on the menu."

I sputter. "Absolutely not."

"Then I'll take cookies if you have them."

I turn and stalk toward the kitchen because blushing in front of him feels like surrender.

Behind me, I hear him settle into the doorway again. Guard dog mode. Protector mode. The kind of man who watches your front step like it's a war zone and your safety is a mission.

I fill the kettle, breathing in his scent still clinging to the air, wondering how a fake boyfriend can make a house feel more like home when it never really has before.

I think I'm in trouble.

But for once, I don't feel like running.

The cookies are gone. Every last crumb. And yeah, maybe I licked the chocolate off the foil because fuck if I was wasting anything that came from her hands. The coffee is long gone too, the travel mug sitting empty in the console like it served its purpose and died a hero. I've got the heater on low, windows just fogged enough to blur the world without fully blocking it. My phone is face down on the dash after I let the guys know I'm on scope tonight. They'll handle the evening prep while I keep watch, then I'll head back after dawn to help with the marquee and return to Cindy's.

Cindy. Fuck.

She kissed me.

No, that's not right. I kissed her, and she let me, and she kissed me back with that soft, needy sound in her throat I'm still hearing like it's etched into the damn lining of my skull. My fingers tighten around the steering wheel, thumb pressing into the leather where it's already worn smooth. I've been kissed a thousand times, had women beg for more with their mouths and their moans and their heats. But Cindy?

That was different.

That was everything.

And the second I got close, I knew it. She's my scent match. No room for doubt anymore, not after the way her skin warmed under mine, her pulse kicked up, her slick perfuming the air so thick I could taste it without even parting her thighs.

She knows it. Omegas always do. It blooms like something ancient, something primal, something deep in the marrow.

I rub a hand down my face, slowly, then reach to adjust my cock through my jeans because it's still half hard and aching like a motherfucker. It's been hours, and I'm still strung tight from just a kiss and a whiff of her slick. I didn't even get to touch her properly, didn't get to taste her. She was wearing that summer dress, the one that clings in the right places and makes it impossible to think straight, and all I wanted was to tear it in half. Rip it from her shoulders, bare her soft curves, and press my mouth to the heat between her thighs.

She's magic. The kind that ruins a man. And I'm going to let her.

I stare at the side of her house from across the road. Her porch light is still on, like she promised. One dim light upstairs, just enough to tell me she's there and settled. The house is quiet, the neighborhood dead. Trees lining the street sway gently in the breeze, rustling like whispers. A few cats have wandered past. Someone three doors down just got home a little while ago and slammed their car door loudly.

But here? At this location on her street? Still. Silent.

I've got eyes on the front door, on the window that shows a sliver of the living room, and that upstairs light I've memorized. It's the best angle. No dead spots. Nothing she can't scream through if something goes wrong.

Not that anything is going to.

Because I'm here.

I crack the window half an inch and breathe in the cool night air. Still smells like her. I want to drown in it. I adjust my cock again, biting off a curse, jaw tight. I'm not going to make it the week at this rate.

Two hours pass. I'm yawning into my sleeve, trying not to blink too long because I might slip into sleep. I never fall asleep on watch. Ever. But my body is fighting me tonight, and I hate how fucking soft it feels.

Then the lights go out.

Just... off.

No flicker. No fade. Just gone.

Porch and upstairs, both at once.

My entire spine locks.

I lean forward in the driver's seat, eyes narrowed, blood already thundering in my ears. What the fuck?

Maybe the bedroom light, sure. But the porch? She

told me she was leaving it on. Insisted, even. Said she liked knowing I was out here. I watched her switch on the lights earlier, saw the way she went around the house. These aren't set on timers, and they don't trip together like that.

This is wrong.

Every instinct in my body is screaming.

I pop the glove box, grab the blade stashed in a leather sheath, and tuck it into the back of my jeans. I reach under the seat next, where I keep the compartment latched to the rail. Pull out the Glock, smooth and fast, and slide it into my waistband at the front.

My belt is custom. Reinforced. Slim steel hooks beneath the leather designed to hold weapons flat against my body without the bulk of a holster. The guys both have the same rig. We had them made a few years back when shit got hairy with the rival club near Portside. You learn to move fast and smart when there's always a threat on the horizon.

Gun secure. Blade in place.

I open the car door without a sound and step into the night.

The air is colder now, breeze sharper. My boots barely whisper against the pavement as I cross the street, eyes sweeping the surrounding area. No lights on in the neighbor's townhouse. No sign of movement in any window. Nothing but the low hiss of wind through the trees and the pounding of blood in my ears.

Something is off. I feel it in my gut, in the way my

skin prickles like a warning. Like the universe clearing its throat and saying *Pay attention.*

I move faster.

The porch is dark, but I know where the weak step is and avoid it. I don't knock. I don't call out. If something is wrong, announcing myself could make it worse.

Instead, I press my back to the brick wall beside the door and listen. I try the door, and it's locked.

Nothing else.

No footsteps. No voices. Not even the creak of the floorboards upstairs. The quiet isn't peaceful anymore. It's loaded. Tense. Something is fucking wrong.

I move to the edge of the porch and scan the side of the house, looking for shadows, movement, anything that might explain the blackout. Electrical issue? Sure. Could be. But the power lines aren't down. Her neighbor doesn't have lights, but it's been dark since I started my surveillance. The rest of the block is lit up.

No. This isn't random.

I step down onto the path, boots crunching over gravel, and follow it toward the backyard gate. My hand wraps around the latch. Still locked.

I flick it open, slowly and silently, and ease the gate inward.

Darkness presses in around me, the kind that feels like it's breathing, watching. Every step down the side of the house sets off alarm bells in my spine. My palm goes to the blade tucked into my waistband.

I don't want to break in. Don't want to scare her. But if something has happened?

I'll tear the fucking door off its hinges.

Please not her. Not tonight. Not under my watch.

If someone is inside? I'll gut them.

No hesitation.

I knock. Hard. Once. Twice.

No answer.

The silence has weight. Too heavy. Too still.

I step back, tense, assessing the structure. Could be someone inside. Could be nothing. But my instincts are flaring red-hot. That itching, clawing sensation deep in my chest that says something is off.

I shift my weight, muscles coiling. Ready to—

Meow.

The sound rips through the tension like a knife. I whirl around, blade halfway drawn—

A shadow detaches from the darkness.

No. Not a shadow.

A goddamn tank of a cat.

Black. Huge. Tail like a feather duster, fur thick as hell, and glowing green eyes fixed right on me like I'm the intruder here.

Maine Coon. Has to be.

The bastard doesn't flinch. Doesn't blink. Just pads up the path like he owns the place. Like he summoned me.

He strolls right up and plants his fat ass in the middle of the path.

I stare down at him. "The fuck are you supposed to be? King Kong Kitty, or Lucifer perhaps?"

The cat blinks. Slow. Judgy.

"Well, all right, then, Fluffzilla," I mutter, sidestepping the beast. "You'd better get your furry ass home before someone mistakes you for a small bear."

I turn back to the rear door. "Cindy!"

Still nothing.

Then I hear something.

A voice. Soft. Strained.

I freeze, breath locking in my throat.

There's a sound.

Barely audible through the thick walls, but it cuts through the quiet like a blade. Muffled. Distant. I can't even be sure I heard it right. It wasn't a normal noise. It had the shape of a scream, the way it rose too fast and ended too sharply. It doesn't matter that I can't make out the words or that I might be imagining it.

My body reacts before my brain can catch up.

Everything in me goes tight and hot.

Fear crackles up my spine, morphing into rage so fast I see red.

She's in there.

And something is wrong.

I fucking knew Van was going to try something. Knew he was the type of scum who'd wait until I blinked, until I let my guard down. He must've snuck in. Back window? Basement? He's quiet. Cowardly. The kind of bastard who doesn't break down doors... just slithers through cracks and waits to strike when no one is looking.

My hand goes to the back door before I realize I've even moved.

And this time, I don't knock.

I crouch low, fingers brushing the handle.

I reach into the pocket of my shirt and pull the thin roll of tools I always carry with me. One glance over my shoulder to scan the yard again, and then I'm working.

The pick slides in, teeth feeling for the mechanism. Years of experience take over. I don't need to see. Just feel. A soft click, then another. The last tumbler gives way with a whisper of metal.

Then I ease the door open.

I slip inside.

A draft hits me. The air is heavy, warm, but something is off. A little too quiet. My boot nudges something soft, fur brushing my leg, and I jerk, gun raised before I realize it's the damn cat again. It must've followed me, and it's now darting into the house.

"Jesus," I hiss. "Creepy little bastard."

It vanishes into the dark hallway, tail flicking.

I don't care.

I shut the door behind me. Lock it again.

Every muscle in my body is strung tight. I listen, eyes scanning. No sound from the kitchen. No creak from the living room. But then I hear it.

A thump.

Upstairs.

Fuck.

I'm moving before I think. Past the laundry, into the open-plan living room. Moonlight slices through the front windows. I barely register the furniture or the scattered books. All I see is the stairs. Straight ahead.

I take them two at a time, nearly silent, my hand skimming the wall as I go. My pulse hammers. My teeth grind. My mouth is dry, and all I think is if that motherfucker laid a hand on her, he's dead.

No second chances.

No warnings.

I reach the top. The hallway is darker than the rest of the house, the power still out. But I hear her.

"Holt?"

My name. Shaky. High. I lunge for the door.

"Cindy!"

I shove it open. Hard. The wood slams against the wall with a crack that echoes through the house.

And then I freeze.

Time warps. Everything slows. I don't even know how to breathe.

She's in the middle of the bed, moonlight lighting her up. Sheets barely covering her. Her legs are parted under the thin cotton. Her dress is rucked up over her hips. She's panting, eyes wide and dazed, cheeks flushed like she's just—

Then she gasps. Her head jerks toward me. Her mouth falls open in a little moan that turns to shock. The panic hits her late. She fumbles, yanking the sheet, hands flailing, and for a split second, she seems to forget everything else.

Including what she's holding.

Something small. Slick. Pink.

A vibrator.

It flies from her hand as she jerks the covers up to her chin. Pure instinct, probably meant to protect herself, but instead she launches it like a missile.

It hits me right between the eyes.

"Fuck!" I stagger half a step, wiping my brow with the back of my arm as the damn thing bounces off my forehead and lands with a thud at the edge of the bed.

We both stare at it.

Long. Silent. Sheer disbelief.

It's curved. Coated in her slick.

And the scent hits me.

My knees nearly buckle.

Fucking addictive. My cock was already half hard, but now it pulses, thick and aching, straining against my jeans with nowhere to go. I wipe my forehead again, slower this time, as if I can delay the inevitable.

Her gaze flicks between me and the vibrator.

Her eyes go huge.

"Oh my God!" she shrieks, diving under the covers so fast it's like she's trying to disappear into the mattress. "Holt! Shit—I'm so sorry—oh my God, what are you doing?! I want to die!"

The sheet scrunches higher. Her hands go over her head.

She's mortified.

I'm hard enough to tear through denim.

And trying not to fucking laugh.

She still has that damn sheet yanked over her head like it's going to save her dignity. Pillow clutched in one hand, voice muffled beneath the covers as she hisses, "I can't believe this is happening. I can't believe you saw—oh my God—"

I laugh. Deep and raw, because fuck, what else am I supposed to do after nearly shitting myself thinking someone broke in, only to get bitch-slapped in the face by her pretty little pink vibrator?

"My good girl," I say, biting back another grin as I nudge the vibrator off the bed with the back of my knuckle. "If you wanted me to come upstairs, all you had to do was ask."

She groans, high and horrified. "Don't talk to me. I'm dying. I'm already dead."

"Don't think that's how death works." I grab the edge of the sheet and tug it slightly, not pulling it away, just enough to piss her off.

She squeals and yanks it tighter. "Holt!"

"Jesus, woman. It's not like I walked in on you sacrificing a goat. It's just your heat." I fold my arms. "Natural. Beautiful. A little fucking dangerous, if I'm being honest, but God, baby girl, you smell like sin and sugar and everything I've ever wanted."

"You are not helping," she mutters.

"I'm not trying to help. I'm trying not to rip that sheet off and bury my face between your thighs, so frankly, I think I deserve a goddamn medal for standing here talking to you instead."

Another horrified noise. The pillow comes flying toward me, hitting me in the chest. "Out!"

I catch it before it hits the floor, toss it right back onto the bed like I own the place. "Fine. You win." I take a step back, but I don't leave yet. "Though if you need anything, and I do mean anything, I'll be right downstairs. On the couch. Ready. Willing. Very, very able."

She groans louder, and I can't tell if she's laughing or crying. "You're the worst."

"No, sweetheart. I'm the best mistake you're ever gonna make." I grin, letting the cockiness sit heavily between us. "Also, next time you decide to set the mood, maybe skip the whole lights-out-like-a-horror-movie setup. I thought someone broke in."

Her voice goes small. "The lights went out?"

"Yeah. Porch, too. Whole damn house blacked out. Why do you think I came running in here like some crazed lunatic ready to take down an intruder? Thought Van managed to slither in somehow."

"Oh God," she whispers. "I didn't even notice. I was... I wasn't exactly paying attention."

"No shit." I smirk. "You were paying attention to that little pink devil you threw at my face."

"I didn't mean to!" Her voice cracks with half laughter, half mortification. "I panicked."

"Not gonna lie, most creative thing I've had chucked at my head in a while."

She makes a strangled sound, still buried under the sheets. "You'd better not tell anyone."

"Oh, I'm definitely telling the guys—"

"Holt!"

"—after your mom hears the story first."

She whips the sheets down just enough to peek out, wide-eyed and red-faced. "You wouldn't."

I hold up two fingers. "Swear to God. First chance I get, I'm calling her."

"Don't you dare!"

I start backing toward the door, grinning like a bastard.

She groans and disappears under the sheets again. "You're evil. Pure evil."

I pause with my hand on the doorknob. "Maybe. But you like it." And then, before she can launch the whole mattress at me, I slip out and shut the door behind me.

My laughter follows me down the stairs. The house is quiet again, but not in that eerie, something-is-wrong way it was earlier. Now it's warm. Real. Hers.

I pass the laundry room, where the back door is still shut. Locked now. I made sure when I came in. That damn cat is nowhere to be seen, probably hiding in the shadows and plotting my death.

The couch is old, the kind that appears to sink in the middle like it's been through some shit. I kick off my boots, take off the blade and Glock, then drop onto the sofa and let out a long breath.

Fuck me.

I run a hand down to the hard length in my jeans. Still there. Still rock solid.

That scent... her scent. Sweet heat, slick arousal clinging to the air like a drug. It's in my lungs, on my skin, seared into my fucking soul. I adjust myself with a grunt, thumb pressing along the thick ridge. Yeah, no way I'm sleeping tonight.

And that view? Her, sprawled in bed, dress shoved up, moaning my name like a prayer before she even knew I was there?

I'm ruined. Fucked. Completely fucking claimed and she doesn't even know it yet.

That's mine.

All of her.

I rest my head back against the cushion and stare at the ceiling, trying to will my body to calm down. It's a lost cause. The only thing that would take the edge off right now is going back upstairs, pulling that sheet down, and giving her everything she just tried to give herself.

But I won't.

Because she's not just an Omega in heat. She's Cindy. She's fire and "fuck you" and strawberry lip gloss, and damn it, she deserves more than me using her like a fix for an addiction.

Still, I stay. Right here. Guard dog on the couch.

If she needs me, I'll come running. If she wants me, I'll tear the world down to make it happen.

Until then, I close my eyes, cock aching like hell, and whisper to the dark ceiling above, "God help me... I'm going to destroy her."

I wake up to sunlight streaming through my curtains and the immediate, crushing memory of last night. Not the kiss that scrambled my brain cells. Not the scent-matching that rewired my DNA. Not even the way Holt looked at me like I was something worth protecting.

No, I wake up remembering the part where he walked in on me during an extremely private moment with my battery-operated boyfriend, Mr. Bunbury.

Yes, I named my vibrator Mr. Bunbury. After Oscar Wilde's imaginary invalid. Because if you can't have literary references for your sex toys, what's the point of even living?

The memory floods back in technicolor horror. Me, in bed, thinking he was outside in his car, being all noble and protective. Him, coming in, thinking I was being attacked by Van and required Alpha intervention.

Instead, he found me in a very different kind of emergency. The kind where I was arched off the bed, Mr. Bunbury doing the Lord's work, me crying out his name.

Hell!

I pull my pillow over my face and scream into it until my throat hurts.

"This is how I die," I inform the pillow. "Not from Van's psycho stalking or my mother's disapproval. But from pure, undiluted embarrassment. They'll find my body, and the coroner will write 'mortification' as the cause of death."

I can hear him moving around in the kitchen, pans clanking, and the smell of bacon drifts into my room like a peace offering from the universe. My stomach growls, the traitor. Apparently, my digestive system doesn't care about my emotional crisis. But on the bright side, the power seems to be back on based on my flashing clock on the bedside table.

"Okay, Cindy," I whisper to myself, sitting up and catching my reflection in the mirror. My hair looks like I've been electrocuted. "You're going to get up, have a shower, and go downstairs and act like a normal human who definitely doesn't own a vibrator. He probably already forgot about it. Men have a selective memory about these things. It's fine. You're fine. Everything is spectacularly fine."

I stumble to the shower, turning the water as hot as it'll go, hoping to either wash away the shame or boil myself.

"Listen up, self," I tell my reflection in the steamy mirror. "Today your mother arrives, and you need to convince her that you have your life together. You cannot hide in your shower, crying about the fact that the hottest man you've ever met saw you masturbating. You're going to channel Harper. What would Harper do?"

She would probably make a joke about orgasms being good for the skin and offer to lend him her vibrator collection for comparison. Harper has no shame. I need to borrow some of that energy.

"Besides," I say, continuing my pep talk in the shower, lathering shampoo with perhaps more violence than necessary, "he's seen worse. He was in a biker gang. They probably had... I don't know, orgies? Is that what bikers do? Group activities? Oh God, don't think about Holt in an orgy. Don't think about... damn it, now I'm thinking about it."

The water is going cold by the time I finally emerge, wrapped in my fluffiest towel and determination to pretend last night never happened.

"Not today, Satan," I mutter at my reflection, thinking about all the feelings trying to claw their way out of the box I've stuffed them in. The scent-matching that my body recognized even if my brain is in denial. The kiss that made me reconsider my entire understanding of human lips. The way he makes me feel safe and terrified in equal measure. "Today is about surviving Mother. Everything else goes in the mental vault labeled 'Process Never.'"

I dress in my Saturday shopping armor of black leggings with orange spiderweb designs, an oversized cream sweater that falls off one shoulder, and my lucky socks with tiny pumpkins that have googly eyes. We all have our coping mechanisms.

I blow-dry my hair into submission, apply just enough makeup to look alive but not like I'm trying, and stare at myself in the mirror.

"You are Cindy Young. You survived running from your own wedding. You survived Van finding you. You can survive looking at the man who saw you with Mr. Bunbury. You are a warrior. A goddess. A—oh, who am I kidding? I'm going to die."

I open my bedroom door, and the smell of break-fast foods assaults me in the best way. Real bacon. Real eggs. Real toast. Not my usual Saturday breakfast of coffee and whatever is left in the candy drawer.

Each step down the stairs feels like walking to my execution. The embarrassment plank, if you will.

"Morning!" I chirp as I enter the kitchen, aiming for breezy and landing somewhere around constipated cheerfulness.

Holt turns from the stove, and sweet mother of pearl, he looks good. His hair is slightly mussed from sleep, he's wearing a gray Henley that clings to his chest, and his feet are bare, which somehow makes this domestic scene even more intimate.

"Morning," he replies, his voice that croaky rumble. "Figured you'd need fortification before facing your mother."

He's set my table with actual place settings. There's orange juice in a pitcher I honestly forgot I owned, toast arranged in a basket like we're fancy people, and enough food to feed the neighborhood.

"This is... wow. You didn't have to do all this."

"You need to eat. Properly. Can't face a dragon on an empty stomach."

He plates eggs, adding bacon and toast. When he sets it in front of me, steam rising, I might actually tear up a little.

"You okay?" he asks, settling across from me with his own plate. "You know, after last night?"

I laugh, and it sounds like a chipmunk being strangled. "Ha! Last night? What about last night? Nothing happened last night. New day, new opportunities."

He studies me over his coffee mug, and there's something in his eyes, not mockery, not disgust, but maybe understanding? "Cindy—"

"Nope!" I cut him off, shoving eggs into my mouth. "We don't talk about it. It never happened. I was sleepwalking. You were hallucinating. We both had very different, completely unrelated evenings that definitely didn't intersect in any mortifying way."

The corner of his mouth twitches. "Sleepwalking?"

"Vigorous sleepwalking. It's a medical condition. Very serious. No cure."

"Right." He takes a sip of coffee, and I can tell he's fighting not to smile. "Well, for what it's worth, everyone has needs. Nothing to be embarrassed about."

"Anyway, hope you slept okay on the couch," I say, changing the topic, my face burning hot enough to cook the eggs myself.

"Sure did," he answers quickly.

We eat in silence for a moment, and the food is genuinely incredible. The eggs are fluffy, the bacon perfectly crispy, the toast somehow exactly the right golden brown that I can never achieve without setting off the smoke alarm.

"I love watching you enjoy food," he says suddenly. "Your whole face changes. You look... happy."

"Food is one of life's few uncomplicated pleasures," I tell him, then immediately think about Mr. Bunbury and want to crawl under the table.

He reaches across the table, his fingers brushing mine, and I don't pull away even though my skin feels electric.

"We should practice being comfortable with casual touches," he says, his thumb tracing circles on my wrist that should not be as affecting as they are. "Your mother will notice if we're stiff around each other."

"Right. Casual. We're super casual. The most casual couple that ever casualed."

"Ready for today?" he asks, his hand still on mine, grounding me. "Whatever happens, we'll figure it out. I'm good at improvising. If you get stuck or over-whelmed, just squeeze my hand. I'll take over."

"Like a tactical girlfriend extraction?"

"Exactly like that."

I turn my hand over, lacing our fingers together,

practicing. His hand dwarfs mine, warm and calloused and surprisingly gentle.

"Thank you," I say, meaning it. "I know this is a huge ask. Lying to my mother, pretending we're together, giving up your Saturday. I just need her to see that I'm settled, happy, so she'll back off. Maybe if she leaves me alone, Van will too. I love this town. I don't want to run again."

"You're not going anywhere." His grip tightens slightly. "Not from him, not from her, not from this town. I won't let that happen."

The certainty in his voice makes me believe him, which is dangerous for my heart but comforting for my anxiety.

We finish eating, and I start clearing plates, needing something to do with my hands that isn't touching his.

"Can I ask you something?" I say, rinsing dishes because apparently we're having a serious conversation now.

"Go for it."

"How bad were you guys? As bikers? Like, should I be checking for bodies in my basement?"

His laugh is dark chocolate mixed with whiskey. "No bodies. Well, no bodies you need to worry about."

"That's not as reassuring as you think it is."

He's quiet for a moment, and when I turn, he's leaning against my counter, looking like every bad-boy fantasy I've ever had.

"I ran the Savage Reapers," he says finally. "Not just a member. I was the president. The guy making the hard calls, giving the orders others followed."

"You ran an entire motorcycle gang?"

"MC. Motorcycle Club. But yeah, basically a gang." He runs a hand through his hair, messing it up more. "We did things I'm not proud of. Protection rackets, enforcement, moving products that shouldn't be moved. Violence that wasn't always justified, just profitable."

"So why leave if it was profitable?"

His expression darkens, and for a moment, I see the dangerous man he used to be. "We lost someone. Young kid, Danny, barely twenty-two. Prospect who wanted in so bad he'd do anything to prove himself. Took a job he wasn't ready for, walked into an ambush meant for me."

"Oh God."

"Yeah. Kid bled out in my arms while Luke tried to keep pressure on wounds that were never going to close. And then..." He pauses, jaw working. "Then we almost lost Arrow."

"What happened to him?"

"His brother happened. Mack, his younger brother, showed up at the clubhouse, high off his ass on something that made him brave and stupid. Started screaming about how Arrow abandoned the family, left him to deal with their parents' religious insanity alone."

I dry my hands and move closer, drawn by the pain in his voice.

"His parents tried to pray the Alpha out of him. Literally. Starvation, isolation. Arrow got out at sixteen. Mack stayed, and it broke something in him. So when Mack showed up that night, waving a gun around, making threats, one of our rivals saw an opportunity."

"They attacked during a family crisis?"

"The Bones MC didn't give a fuck about family drama. They saw vulnerability and struck. Arrow took three bullets protecting Mack. Three bullets for a brother who went there to hurt him."

My hand finds his arm. "But he survived."

"Barely. Touch and go for weeks. And while he was fighting to live, I realized that next time it could be Luke. Could be me. Could be someone who didn't get lucky. We'd been doing it long enough, made enough money. It was time to get out before the life took everything."

"That must have been hard. Disbanding everything you built."

"I made sure everyone was taken care of. If they wanted to keep working, I found them places with other MCs. If they wanted out, they got enough to start over. And the three of us came here. This is our place now. Where we're settling down, building something that doesn't end with bullets and blood."

"And the Savage Reapers?"

"Gone. Dissolved. Some of the guys joined other

clubs, and some went straight. But the Savage Reapers died the night Arrow almost did."

"That's why you're so protective. Why you all are. You've already lost too much."

"We've lost enough," he agrees, his hand finding mine. "Not losing anything else. Not losing *anyone* else."

The weight of that promise sits between us, and I squeeze his fingers.

"Thank you for sharing."

Silence.

"We should go," I say, breaking the moment. "Farmers' market gets picked over if you don't get there early, and I need ingredients to impress my mother with my domestic goddess capabilities."

"You need a ride?"

"Unless you want me walking five miles to get groceries, yes, please. Plus, you said you need to get back to help Luke and Arrow?"

"Right. Big event tonight at Savor. Arrow is losing his mind about table arrangements."

We clean up the last of the breakfast dishes, and I grab my reusable shopping bags while he grabs his keys.

In his truck, I'm hyperaware of everything. How his hands look on the steering wheel. How he takes up so much space but makes it feel safe rather than claustrophobic. How his thigh flexes when he works the pedals. I really need to stop staring at his thighs.

"So," he says as we drive through town, Halloween

decorations everywhere, "any other maternal land mines I should know about?"

"Oh, just the usual impossibilities. She hates public displays of affection but will judge us if we don't seem intimate. She basically wants us to be both Victorian and passionate, which makes total sense if you've had a lobotomy."

"We'll make it work."

"You sound very confident for someone who's never met Hurricane Victoria."

"I'm good at reading people. I'll know what she needs to see." His hand rests on the gearshift between us, casual but somehow making the space feel charged.

The farmers' market comes into view, rows of white tents bustling with early morning shoppers, produce arranged in Instagram-worthy displays. The parking lot is already half full because apparently everyone in Whispering Grove needs organic kale at eight in the morning.

He pulls into a spot near the entrance and turns to me. "Aren't you forgetting something?"

I blink at him, mentally running through my checklist. "My bags? Check. My wallet? Got it. My sanity? Questionable but technically present."

"A kiss, my sweet girlfriend."

I roll my eyes so hard I probably see my own brain. "We don't have an audience. The farmers' market vegetables aren't going to report back to my mother."

"Practice makes perfect." His hand lands on my

thigh, warm even through my leggings, and my entire leg suddenly forgets how to function. "Besides, I'm not letting you out until you kiss me goodbye. It's what couples do."

"That's extortion."

"That's commitment to the role."

"You're pushy."

"And you're stalling."

I try to lean over for a quick peck, just a brief, clinical pressing of lips that means nothing, but his hand slides to the back of my neck, fingers tangling in my hair, holding me there. His tongue traces my lower lip, and I open for him without thinking, my hands fisting in his shirt to pull him closer. The kiss is hungry, searching, like we're both trying to find answers to questions we haven't asked. He tastes like coffee, and I make a sound that would embarrass me if I had any brain cells left.

When we finally break apart, I'm gasping and my lips feel swollen and sensitive.

"Jesus," I breathe.

He leans close, his lips brushing my ear, and his voice drops to that register that should require a permit. "You know," he whispers, "if you need help with your tension, I'm much better than any toy. I could make you forget everything except my name, then make you scream it so loud the neighbors learn it too."

My entire body goes liquid. Every nerve ending

lights up like a Christmas display. "That's... I... You can't say things like that!"

"I just did." He pulls back, grinning like he knows exactly what he's done to my ability to function. "Text me when your mom arrives. I put my number on a note on your fridge. I'll be ready."

I practically fall out of the truck, my legs apparently made of Jell-O now. "Right. Yes. Texting. I can do that. I remember how phones work. Phones are the things with the buttons."

He laughs, watching me for a moment longer as though he's memorizing this flustered version of me. Then he drives off, leaving me standing in the parking lot trying to remember basic motor functions.

"Get it together, Cindy," I mutter to myself, adjusting my sweater and trying to look like someone who wasn't just thoroughly kissed in a truck. "You cannot melt into a puddle of hormones in the farmers' market parking lot. You have vegetables to buy and a mother to deceive. Priorities."

But as I walk toward the market entrance, I still feel his lips on mine, still hear that promise in my ear, and I know that whatever happens with my mother today, Holt has already completely destroyed my ability to think about anything except what he could do with that mouth.

Good thing the farmers' market sells ice. I'm going to need to bathe in it.

The scent of peaches and fresh basil fills the air, mingling with the sweetness of strawberries piled high in crates. I pop a slice of white nectarine into my mouth from a free-sample tray, the juice slipping down my chin, and grab a napkin as I reach for another. I'm just about to move on to the cherries when a shadow falls over me.

"Careful, sweetheart. Keep sucking on fruit like that and someone's gonna think it's an invitation."

I flinch, nearly drop the sample, and spin on my heel only to come face-to-face with Arrow. Of course it's him. Long blond hair loose and tousled like he just rolled out of bed, mirrored sunglasses pushed up on his head, smirking like he owns the damn sun.

"What are you doing here?" I ask, my voice catching halfway between breathless and annoyed.

"Shopping for a few spices and food. Like you." He lifts a small canvas bag like it's evidence. "We've got a few extra orders, and there were some things we were short on. Sometimes it's easier to come grab them in person."

"Right," I murmur, heart still racing.

Arrow falls into step beside me like we'd planned this and we do it every Saturday. He gestures toward the overflowing crates of produce. "These tomatoes? Death by nightshade's seductive cousin. Used to be called 'love apples.' Back in the 1700s, people thought eating them would drive you mad with lust."

I blink. "What?"

"True story. Everything here has a secret history. This market? It's basically a pornographic museum if you look hard enough."

A laugh bubbles up out of me. I don't even notice we've stopped in front of a stall with bundles of fresh herbs until he plucks a sprig of mint and hands it to me.

"Try it."

"It's mint."

"But it's also a symbol of hospitality, ancient Greek style. You serve mint to guests when you're trying not to stab them."

I stare at him. "Why do you know all this?"

He shrugs. "I read up on every ingredient I serve people. If I'm going to put it on their plate, I should understand it."

"You're like a sexy food historian."

"Exactly the look I was going for," he says dryly, purchasing a packet of six figs. "Try the fig next. No pressure, but Cleopatra swore by them."

I sample things I'd never look at twice on my own. Arrow keeps ordering strange fruit and weirdly shaped root vegetables and chats with the vendors like they're old friends. And with each one, he tosses something into his bag, then reaches out and takes whatever I'm holding so I don't have to carry a thing.

When I try to stop him, he just smirks. "Let me carry your burden, oh maiden of the market."

"You're so weird."

"You like it."

God help me, I do.

He pauses at a shaved-ice stall, slaps a ten on the counter, and says, "One Devil's Punch, extra syrup."

"What's that?"

"Local favorite. Spicy tamarind, sour cherry, and blackcurrant. It's insanity in a cup. You'll love it."

He hands it to me, and the first bite has my eyes widening. "Holy crap. That's—"

"I know." He leans in. "Addictive. Like me."

I roll my eyes, but I'm giggling when I scoop some onto the wooden spoon and offer it to him. He accepts without hesitation, lips brushing the spoon. My stomach does a ridiculous little flip.

"So," he says, casually. "How did practice go with Holt?"

The spoon freezes halfway to my mouth. "Oh, great. All ready."

Arrow arches a brow. "You're a terrible liar. That bad?"

"No!" I say quickly. "It actually went well. Just... me being awkward."

"Hmm." He tilts his head. "So, what'd you do last night?"

I glance sideways at him. "Why?"

"Just wondering if you were thinking about me."

I scoff, blushing. "What were you doing last night?"

"Tearing out old floorboards."

"What?"

"The dining room in our house had this horrible fake oak vinyl. We're putting in reclaimed pine from a century-old schoolhouse."

"Wow. That's... intense."

"You'll see it soon."

I blink. "I will?"

He shrugs. "You know. Maybe. Dinner. Something like that."

I glance down to hide my smile, then look back up only to find him closer. Not touching me, but in my space. His nose dips slightly, his eyes on my neck.

"Did you just… did you just scent me?"

Arrow pulls back with a slow grin. "You caught me. Sneaky, huh?"

"What's your deal?"

He takes a beat too long to answer, then says, "I think you're my scent match."

I stare. "You too, huh?"

"It's not just me being a romantic. I know what I smell."

"Well, like I told Holt, that discussion is on the back burner. I need to survive today before I can take on anything else."

He lifts both hands in mock surrender. "Of course. I'm not going to push you. But I'm not going to let you get away either."

And damn him, he says it with a smile that melts me straight through.

"Holt mentioned your brother," I say, trying to change the subject. "Is he living in town?"

Arrow's expression doesn't flicker, but his answer is short. "He is temporarily."

"You two close?"

"Used to be."

I study him. "You don't want to talk about him."

He shrugs, noncommittal. "Some stories aren't ready to be told."

"I get that." I hesitate. "I have a sister. Juliette. We don't get along. She married some Alpha and moved to Northern Europe. She was happy to go, and I was happy to let her."

He glances at me, then nods slowly. "Yeah. I get that."

"If you're finished, I'll give you a lift home."

That would be perfect.

I follow him to the lot heading for a lone motorbike. Sleek. Matte black. Parked at the far edge, near the bushland. Away from other cars.

"Wait. You want me to get on that?"

He grins. "You can."

"I've never—"

"You'll be fine. I've got compartments for the groceries."

He loads the food, then pulls a second helmet from a side pack.

"Trust me." Something inside me shifts. Maybe I'm still high on the market buzz. Or it's the way he looks at me. Perhaps it's just me, tired of always playing it safe.

"You know what? I can. I've always wanted to try."

His eyes darken slightly. "Love that."

He holds out the helmet. I slide it on, adjusting the strap, then shrug my backpack through both arms. He climbs on and pats the back seat.

My heart hammers as I step closer, grab his shoulders, and swing my leg over. The seat is narrow, close. My thighs hug his. My chest presses into his back.

"That's it," he murmurs, one hand dropping to my thigh and squeezing. "Hold on."

I do. I wrap my arms around his waist and feel the rumble of the engine as he starts the bike. And then we're moving, the world blurring into wind and heat and thrill.

I laugh, loud, wild, free. "Oh my God, this is amazing!"

He pats my hands, steadying me. "I knew you'd love it."

I lean with him into the corners, try not to melt into him entirely. But there's no space. My breasts are flush against his back, and I feel every movement of his muscles as we ride.

And I never want it to stop.

"Hold on, sweetheart," he says over his shoulder, voice muffled but unmistakably cocky. "I take corners like I mean it."

We lean into a turn, and I can't help but laugh, riding the wave of pure adrenaline. The world tilts with us, and I swear I feel the curve in my stomach, in my toes, in places I shouldn't be feeling anything right now.

"You good back there?" he calls, and I swear he's grinning. I can hear it.

"I'm amazing," I shout. "This is insane!"

We weave through the last stretch toward my

townhouse, the world blurring by in a rush of green trees, cracked pavement, and late-summer haze. His hand slides down, fingers brushing my thigh again for a moment. It's so casual. So intimate. So maddeningly hot.

I have no idea what's happening to me.

When we finally pull into the driveway, the bike jerks to a smooth stop. The engine cuts out, and suddenly everything is too quiet. Too still. The only thing louder than the silence is the rush in my head and the tingle between my legs.

I climb off the bike, wobbly, my legs barely functioning. My thighs are trembling. My knees weak.

Oh God.

Did I just orgasm from a motorcycle?

No. No, of course not.

Probably.

Definitcly maybc. I take my helmet off.

Arrow swings off like he's done this a thousand times, and let's be honest, he probably has, but then he turns and takes my helmet from me. His blond hair is tangled at the nape of his neck.

He's watching me, his helmet now in his other hand, his eyes hooded and hungry and way too knowing. I try not to stare at his mouth as he smirks.

"You all right?" he asks as he stashes the spare helmet in one of the compartments.

I clear my throat. "Yeah, for sure. I mean, except for the part where I now need cold water and a rest."

He chuckles. "That bad, huh?"

"That good."

And now I've said too much. I snap my mouth shut.

Arrow steps closer. Just a fraction. But it's enough that I feel it.

"I'll take you for a ride anytime," he says, his tone low. "Even if you ever wanna ride *me* instead."

My soul leaves my body.

I blink at him. "Did you just—"

"Oh, yeah."

I squeak out a laugh. My face is on fire. Literal flames.

"You're unbelievable."

"I've been called worse."

He winks, then reaches into the side compartment of the bike and starts pulling out the bag of fresh produce I bought at the market. He doesn't even comment on how I'm standing there, completely frozen, heart doing an Olympic sprint in my chest while my thighs are plotting to betray me again.

He hands me a bag, his fingers graze mine, and I practically drop it.

"Butterfingers," he teases.

"Bike fingers," I mutter.

He grins widely. "You just say the sexiest things."

"I doubt that."

He's leaning in close so his breath brushes my ear. "You smell like peaches."

My knees buckle a little.

He pulls back slowly, like he knows exactly what he's doing.

"Well," I say, voice too breathy, "I'd better get inside before I melt."

"Want help with the door?"

"Nope," I squeak. "I got it. Definitely got it."

He watches me fumble for the keys like it's the most entertaining thing he's seen all week.

"I'll see you soon, pretty girl," he says as he straddles his bike again, voice smooth and heavy with implication. "Anytime you need a ride—"

"Arrow!"

He revs the engine, helmet on. "Just call."

And with that, he peels down the street, his long hair whipping in the wind, the roar of his bike echoing in my bones like a goddamn mating call.

I watch him go, biting my lip. Still breathless.

Who is this man?

Since when do I fall for bikers?

I stare after him until he vanishes around the bend. Only then do I tear my gaze away and hurry inside with my arms full, cheeks flushed, thighs still humming from the vibrations, and my heart completely out of sync with reality.

Dark past or no, I am so screwed.

I barely get the door closed before I hear the slosh.

Water?

I frown, bag still in my arms, and turn toward the kitchen.

There he is.

Perched like a furry king on my dining table, his massive black tail curled elegantly around his enormous paws, the big fluffy beast is casually sipping from my glass of water.

"Oh, for crying out loud, General Flufferton!"

He pauses mid-sip, blinks at me with those piercing green eyes, then chirps like an offended pigeon.

"Don't you give me attitude," I say, setting the grocery bags down and marching over. "How the hell did you get in here?"

He chirps again, clearly unbothered, then stretches, his full, lion-sized body arching with dramatic flair, and jumps down. It's not graceful. It's a flop. But an elegant flop, as only a Maine Coon can manage. He saunters over and immediately rubs himself against my leg like he hasn't just been trespassing and stealing my beverages.

I sigh, crouch, and scoop him up. He's so heavy that I grunt under the effort, but his fur is like warm silk, his purring thunderous against my chest.

"You are not a small creature," I murmur, pressing my nose into the thick fluff around his neck. "You're a sofa in cat form."

He *mrrrows* in response, rubbing his cheek against mine like we're lovers reunited after war.

"You charming little burglar."

General Flufferton technically belongs to Mrs. Meadow next door. But he's made my place his second home ever since I moved in, sometimes staying three, even four nights at a time. Especially when I break out the rotisserie chicken.

I glance toward the back door.

Still locked.

"Seriously, when did you sneak in?"

He yawns in my face.

I cradle him with one arm and head toward the place next door. Mrs. Meadow has lived here forever, always tending her garden in a wide-brimmed hat and bright lipstick. But she mentioned moving in with her son's family.

I step outside and cross the short walkway to her door, still holding the purring beast like he's my emotional support animal.

I knock.

No answer.

"Mrs. Meadow?" I call.

Nothing.

I step back and glance up at the windows.

No curtains.

My stomach dips. "Wait," I whisper, glancing down at General Flufferton. "Did she... leave you?"

The cat meows, sharp and insistent.

"Oh my God. You were supposed to move too, weren't you?"

He chirps and bumps his head against my chin, like he knows exactly what I'm saying. I look back at the window. Bare. Empty.

She's gone.

"You poor thing." I kiss the top of his giant, fuzzy head. "Okay, okay. Let's find out what's going on."

Back inside, I grab my phone and scroll to the

message Mrs. Meadow's son sent me weeks ago, the one with his number. I'd helped watch General Flufferton when she last visited them for the weekend. Hopefully, he still has the same number.

I tap it and pace, heart fluttering with nerves.

He picks up on the second ring.

"Hello?"

"Hi, this is Cindy from next door to your mom. Sorry to call out of the blue but, uh, General Flufferton's in my kitchen."

A pause. "He's alive?"

I blink. "Yes? Wait, you were looking for him?"

Another pause, then rustling. "Hang on. I'll get her."

There's a muffled call for "Ma! Cindy's got the cat!" and then a click.

"Oh, sweet heavens above, thank God." Her voice trembles. "Cindy? Is he all right?"

"He's purring like a lawn mower and already drank from my water glass."

She laughs. "That boy. I couldn't find him before we left. I thought he'd come back in, but... he didn't. I was devastated. I meant to leave him with my sister."

My heart twists.

"I'm so glad you found him," she says. "I miss him terribly, but... my daughter-in-law is allergic, and, well, we are already moved, and he never did like car rides."

General Flufferton meows again from his perch on my counter, grooming one giant paw like none of this drama concerns him.

"He's been staying with me a lot lately," I say softly. "More than with you, honestly."

Mrs. Meadow laughs. "I always suspected he liked your place better. All those toys and that silly feather thing you bought."

"He lives for the feather thing."

There's a long, quiet moment. I hear her sigh.

"He loves you, dear. I can tell. I'm just so glad he's safe."

Another pause.

"Will you..." Her voice cracks. "Will you love him as much as I did? He may be better at your place than with my sister, who has two dogs."

I look at him. Big, black, fluffy menace of a cat with a chirpy meow and a purr that sounds like a truck engine. He blinks slowly at me, then jumps down and butts his head against my leg again, curling his tail around my calf.

"Of course," I whisper. "You can come visit him anytime."

"Oh, thank you, sweetheart. That means everything to me." There's a pause. "Oh dear, I almost forgot to mention! Since I moved out, the power company is scheduled to shut off my service sometime this week. But you know how these old townhouses are... Wouldn't be surprised if that causes you to have a blackout because of me. Like the time I plugged in my bread maker and took out both our fuses."

I blink. Wait. Was that why the lights went out the other night?

We say our goodbyes and hang up, and just like that... I have a cat.

I stare down at General Flufferton. He meows like it's about time I figured it out.

I scratch behind his ear. "That's one more thing my mother is going to disapprove of."

11

CINDY

The opening beats of a boppy song blast through my kitchen speakers while I pipe yellow filling into the twentieth deviled egg. General Flufferton sits on the chair I dragged in specifically so he could supervise, his massive black Maine Coon body taking up the entire seat. His green eyes track my every movement like I'm performing surgery instead of making appetizers.

"I know, I know," I tell him, adjusting the piping bag. "They're not perfect. But Mother always loved these at Easter, so maybe—" I squeeze too hard, and filling spurts across the counter. "Shit."

General Flufferton chirps at me, that weird little trill Maine Coons do that sounds nothing like a normal cat.

"You're right. I'm overthinking." I wipe up the mess with a paper towel. "But you have no idea how excited

I am to have you as mine now. In a bittersweet way, Mrs. Meadow's moving was the best thing that happened to me this month. Well, there are those three hot bikers... Nope, I can't think about them." I reach over and scratch behind his ears. "Seventy-three years old and moving in with her son's family. Can you believe her daughter-in-law is allergic to cats? Their loss, my gain."

He makes this low groaning sound, like an old man protesting having to get up from his recliner.

"Yeah, well, tough. You're too fluffy for your own good. Wait until I tell Harper about you officially living here. She's gonna go ballistic and camp out on my couch just to cuddle you twenty-four seven."

Another groan, deeper this time.

"Drama queen." I arrange the eggs on an old crystal platter.

My hands shake slightly as I cover the platter with plastic wrap. The kitchen is spotless. I've cleaned it three times today. Fridge stocked with wine, that expensive cheese, fresh fruit arranged in a bowl like some Pinterest board threw up in here.

"Mother is going to accept me as I am," I tell General Flufferton, but it comes out more like a question. "I'm not going to care what she says about my place being small or my job being beneath me or—" I stop, take a breath. "And you're gonna be on your best behavior, okay? No jumping on her lap. She hates cats. Says they're for spinsters and witches."

He slow-blinks at me, completely unbothered.

"Well, maybe I am a witch. A brewery witch. Making potions out of hops and barley instead of eye of newt."

I check my phone. 6:47 p.m. The sun is already setting, October darkness creeping in early. No messages. No missed calls. My stomach churns with each passing minute. Of course she's making me wonder if she's even coming.

"Fuck." I start pacing, General Flufferton's eyes following me back and forth. "She's gonna stand me up, isn't she? She'll message me at dawn when I'm in my ratty pajamas with a face mask on and my hair looking like I stuck my finger in a socket."

Through the window, headlights sweep across my living room wall. A familiar black truck pulls up to the curb. It's Holt's monster of a vehicle.

"Thank God," I breathe, already heading for the door. "I could do with him talking me down from panicking."

But it's not Holt who climbs out of the driver's seat. It's Luke.

Something in my gut twists hard, like when you miss a step going downstairs. Wrong Alpha. Wrong biker. Wrong everything. My phone buzzes and I actually flinch, nearly dropping it.

Mom: *I've made us a reservation at Savor. See you at 8 p.m.*

There's a link to the restaurant website.

I stare at the screen. Read it again. Then once more because surely I'm hallucinating.

"What the fuck?" The words come out strangled. My mind spins like a blender on high speed. She's not coming here? After I cleaned everything, after I bought all this food, after I mentally prepared myself for her to judge every square inch of my space, she books Savor? Arrow's restaurant?

Does she know it's his? Is this some cosmic joke? Or did she pick the fanciest place in town to make this about her, about showing me how a proper dinner should be?

General Flufferton is suddenly at my feet, meowing urgently, pressing against my legs. He always knows when I'm about to spiral. His fur is soft against my ankles, grounding me.

The doorbell rings.

"Right. Luke." I force my legs to move, yanking open the door maybe a bit too aggressively.

He's standing there looking absolutely perfect, because of course he is. Like some fallen angel who decided heaven was too boring. Except—

"Luke! You cut your hair?"

His auburn hair that used to fall past his shoulders in waves is gone. Cut short like Holt's, styled but still somehow disheveled. The copper highlights catch the porch light, making them look like actual flames.

"Hey," he says.

General Flufferton makes a break for freedom, but Luke is already moving, scooping up all twenty pounds of Maine Coon like he weighs nothing. He steps inside, cat secured, and I manage to get the door closed while trying not to stare.

Black jeans that fit him like they were tailored by someone who really, really likes him. Motorcycle boots. A white button-down shirt with tiny black dots, sleeves rolled up to his elbows, showing those thick leather bands around his wrists that he always wears. Below them, the tattoos covering his forearms. Real biker ink. A skull wrapped in chains on his left arm, what looks like a blade or dagger on the right, dark and sharp and dangerous.

And his scent, God, his scent. Leather from his jacket mingles with candied apples and spiced cider, plus that crisp, cold air smell that clings to bikers. My head spins, and I want to lean in closer and just breathe.

"You like the hair?" He's watching me stare, one eyebrow raised, that knowing smirk playing at his lips.

I fan myself with my hand, not even trying to play it cool. "Somehow you're even sexier than before."

"Oh, you thought I was sexy?" That smile spreads across his face, the one that probably gets him out of speeding tickets and into trouble in equal measure.

Heat floods my cheeks, spreads down my neck, pools low in my belly. "I—that's not—shut up."

He sets General Flufferton down, who immediately starts winding around Luke's legs like a traitor. "Didn't know you had a cat."

"He's new. Well, not *new* new. He belonged to my

neighbor, Mrs. Meadow, but she's seventy-three and moving in with her son's family. The daughter-in-law is allergic, so she asked if I wanted him, and obviously I said yes, because look at him." I'm rambling, my mouth running to avoid thinking about how Luke smells like temptation. "Where's Holt?"

Luke walks farther in, casual as anything, and leans against the back of my couch. "Well, funny story."

"Oh my God, what happened to him? Is he okay?" The words tumble out in a rush. My mind immediately goes to the worst places—a bar fight, a bike accident, something violent and dangerous that comes with their territory.

"Yeah, yeah, he's fine. Just knocked his head, mild concussion. They're keeping him overnight at the hospital for observation."

"Hospital? Holt's in the hospital?" My voice rises. "But we practiced together. We had the whole routine down, the story about how we met, what he does for work—"

"That's why I'm here. We'll practice now." He pulls out his phone, checks the time. "It'll be fresh in our minds."

"Okay, but wait—" I narrow my eyes at him. "What *actually* happened to Holt?"

Something flickers across his face. Guilt? Amusement? "You really want to know?"

"Is it like... a biker gang thing?" The words slip out before I can stop them. Images flash through my mind of rival gangs, territory disputes, the kind of violence you see in movies.

Luke barks out a laugh. "No, nothing like that. Though that would be less embarrassing."

"Go on," I ask.

"See, Holt was up on this ladder, fixing the marquee at the restaurant. Real focused, you know how he gets, making sure everything was perfect for tonight." He shifts against the couch. "And earlier, he might have mentioned to Arrow about your little vibrator incident."

The floor drops out from under me. "Wait, fuck, wait—what?" My voice goes supersonic. "Please don't tell me he told everyone about—"

"He only told Arrow." Luke holds up a hand. "But Arrow told me, and, well, it's a hot story." He scratches the back of his neck, looking almost sheepish. "Anyway, I had this squishy dildo at work from some bachelorette party gag gift someone left behind—"

"Wh— Actually, never mind."

"—and I thought it would be hilarious to chuck it at him while he was on the ladder."

"You didn't."

"Hit him right in the face." He demonstrates the trajectory with his hands. "Perfect aim, really. Should've seen his expression—complete shock. Then he wobbled, arms windmilling, and down he went."

"Oh my God." I cover my face with both hands. "I'm going to die. I'm literally going to die of embarrassment right here in my kitchen, and General Flufferton is going to eat my face and—"

"He's fine, though," Luke continues. "Just a bump on the head, couple bruises, and a sore eye. Arrow stayed to handle the restaurant while I took him to the hospital."

I blink at him, lowering my hands. "I don't even know what to say to that."

"You're very red," he observes, that smirk playing at his lips again.

I grab a throw pillow from the couch and launch it at his head. It hits him square in the face with a satisfying *thwump*.

"That's for hurting him!" I grab another pillow. "And embarrassing me!" This one he catches, laughing.

"Which brings me to my next point." He sets the pillow down, and something in his expression shifts, becomes more serious. "My apology. And how I'm gonna make it up to you."

"By not telling anyone else about my mortifying incident?"

"Holt told us all about your mom." He runs a hand through his shortened hair, and I have to clench my fists to keep from reaching out to touch it. "How she'd expect your boyfriend to look like him after Van saw him with you at the Harvest Dance."

My stomach flips, and I stare at his hair. "Oh God, you didn't—"

"Cut it all off to play the boyfriend for you? Yeah."

"For me?" The words come out as barely more than

a squeak. My throat feels tight. "Luke, how long did it take you to grow your hair?"

He shrugs. "Couple years. It's nothing."

I'm shaking now, overwhelmed by the gesture, the sacrifice, the absolute insanity of it all. "I'm so sorry, but also thank you, but also you're a complete jerk for the dildo thing and—"

He crosses the space between us in two strides and pulls me into a hug. I'm enveloped in that hunky scent, his arms solid and warm around me. My body goes haywire, heart racing, skin tingling, heat pooling everywhere it shouldn't. This is fake. This is pretend. This is—

"It'll be okay," he murmurs into my hair, and I can feel the rumble of his voice through his chest. "I promise."

"I doubt it." My voice is muffled against his shirt. "Today is turning out to be completely horrendous, and you want to hear something that'll make it worse?"

He pulls back slightly to look at me, hands still on my shoulders. "Hit me with it. Can't be worse than giving Holt a concussion with a sex toy."

"I just got a message from my mom."

"Yeah?"

"She's not coming here."

His brow furrows. "She's not?"

"She booked us a table at Savor. For eight o'clock. In an hour."

His mouth actually drops open. Like, full, jaw-unhinging surprise. "Arrow's restaurant?"

"Yep." I laugh, but it has a hysterical edge to it.

"Fuck."

"Yeah."

"Does she know it's his place?"

"I have no idea! Maybe? Most likely not. It's the fanciest place in town, so probably she just picked it to make me feel inferior." I gesture wildly at my kitchen. "I cleaned everything three times, Luke."

"Hey." His hands remain on my shoulders, thumbs rubbing small circles that should be comforting but just make me more aware of him. "Look at me."

I do. His gray-green eyes are steady, focused entirely on me.

"We're gonna figure this out. But first, you need to breathe."

"I am breathing."

"No, you're hyperventilating. There's a difference." His hands slide down to my arms. "In through your nose. Come on."

I inhale shakily.

"Good. Now out through your mouth."

I exhale.

"Again."

We breathe together for a minute, and gradually my heart rate slows from hummingbird to skittish squirrel.

"Better?"

"Marginally." I step back, needing distance from his touch. "Maybe let's practice our backstory."

He smiles gently, but I can't afford to read into it.

"Let's just get our story straight," I say, putting space between us.

"Right," he says after a beat. "Strictly facts."

But the way he's looking at me? There's nothing fake about it, and that's the problem.

12

I follow her up the stairs, watching the way her hips sway in that dress, the way her hand grips mine like she needs the connection. My fingers tighten around hers automatically. This woman has no fucking idea what she does to me.

Her bedroom is exactly what I expected and nothing like it at the same time. Sage green walls, string lights creating shadows and warmth, books stacked on every surface like she's building a fort out of words. The air is thick with her scent, that clove-studded orange mixed with sugar brittle that makes me want to bury my face in her neck and just breathe.

She rushes to her closet, yanking out dresses as if the place is on fire. One catches on a hanger, and she tugs harder, nearly taking the whole rod down.

"Shit, shit—" She stumbles backward, three dresses clutched to her chest.

I catch her elbow, steady her. "Easy there, tornado."

"I'm fine. I'm totally fine." She's not fine. Her pupils are wide, chest rising and falling too fast. "Which one?"

She throws them on the bed, and I study the options. The first is emerald green. Modern cut, thin straps, the fabric feels soft. The second is some pink monstrosity with ruffles that must have escaped from 1987 and needs to be put out of its misery. The third is a navy blue, sleek, contemporary dress.

"Not the pink," I say immediately. "Burn that one."

"What's wrong with—" She looks at it, really looks. "Oh God, why do I even own this? I think my sister gave it to me."

"Okay, so green or blue first?"

"Green."

She gathers it up and heads for the walk-in closet, and Christ, watching her move is torture. She shuts the door behind her.

"So," her voice streams out, "we should nail down our story. Like, we'll say we met at the Harvest Dance. Last October. We've been together for a year."

I sit on the edge of her bed, trying not to think about her stripping in there, fabric sliding down skin.

"And you were wearing that burgundy sweater. You kept playing with your necklace," I add to our story.

The door opens and I'm fully alert.

The green dress molds to her body like water,

flowing from her chest down to just above her knees. The straps are delicate, as if I could snap them with one finger. The color brings out the glow in her skin, all cream and gold, and when she turns to show me the back, I notice how it dips low, exposing the line of her spine, the delicate wings of her shoulder blades.

"Thoughts?" she asks, doing another turn that makes the skirt flare.

I have thoughts. Lots of thoughts. None of them appropriate. "I'm lost for words."

"That bad?"

"That good." I clear my throat, shifting on the bed because my jeans are suddenly too tight. "But maybe too sexy for Savor with family." Not to mention, trying to keep my hands off her.

"Right. Of course." She disappears back into the closet, and I hear the rustle of fabric. "First kiss? We need a first-kiss story."

"After our third date. We went to see that movie… what's it called? The one with the guy who inherits his grandmother's bookstore?"

"*The Words Between Us*? You love rom-coms."

"I really do. I usually watch them after a long and stressful day. It helps calm my racing thoughts."

The closet door opens again, and fuck me sideways.

She's in a new, black dress now, must have had it in there already. It's modern, sophisticated, with a halter neck that leaves her shoulders bare and a skirt that hits mid-thigh. The fabric clings to her curves, shows off legs that go on for miles. But it's the way she's standing that gets me, uncertain, one foot turned in slightly, hands smoothing down her sides nervously.

"This one's probably too much," she says quickly. "I bought it on sale and never wore it because—"

"Because you'd cause car accidents."

Her hands stop moving. "What?"

"You walk into Savor wearing that, every man in that place is going to forget how to use a fork. Including me."

"You're being ridiculous."

"I'm being honest. Your mom will hate it because you'll outshine her without even trying."

She looks down at herself, and I notice the exact moment she actually realizes that what I see is true, the way the dress has her looking powerful, sexy, untouchable. "Maybe that's what I want."

"Yeah?"

"No. Maybe. I don't know." She presses her palms to her cheeks. "God, why is this so hard? It's just dinner. It's just my mother. It's just—"

"Hey." I stand, cross to her. "Breathe."

"I am." She takes a shaky breath, another. I don't touch her even though every instinct screams at me to pull her close. She needs to choose that.

"Okay, so not this dress," she says finally. "The navy one."

Back into the walk-in closet she goes. I return to the bed, but this time I lie back, staring at her ceiling where she's stuck glow-in-the-dark stars in actual constellations. Of course she has.

"Our first fight," she calls out. "We need a good fight story."

"Why?"

"Mother always says relationships without fights are fake. Like you're both pretending to be perfect instead of being real."

"Fine. We fought about... my ex."

"You have an ex?"

"Everyone has exes, Cindy."

"I mean, one that would cause a fight?"

"She showed up at the brewery. You were working. She made some comment about how I was slumming it, dating a bartender."

"I'm not a bartender. I'm a brewer."

"That's exactly what you said to her. Right before you poured a half-finished beer over her head."

"I did not!"

"In the story you did. Then you stormed out, I followed you, and we had a massive fight in the parking lot about trust and jealousy and whether I was defending you enough."

"Were you?"

"No. That's why you were right to be pissed. I was trying to avoid drama instead of standing up for you."

"And how did we make up?"

"I showed up at your place with coffee, a huge box of chocolates, and an apology. Told you that you were worth a thousand of her, that I was an idiot, that I'd never let anyone disrespect you again."

"Did I forgive you?"

"After you made me grovel for an hour."

She laughs, real this time. "Good. I have standards."

The closet door opens, and my mouth goes dry.

The navy dress is perfect. It's modern but classic, wrapping around her body in a way that suggests rather than reveals. The V-neck is deep enough to be interesting but not scandalous. The fabric nips in at her waist, showing off her curves, then falls to just below her knees in a way that nudges at me to push it up.

"This one?" she asks, but she already knows. It's obvious in the way she stands taller and her hands rest confidently at her sides instead of fidgeting.

"That's the one."

"You're sure? Because I have others—"

"Cindy." I sit up, meet her eyes. "You could wear a garbage bag and still be the most beautiful woman in that restaurant. But this dress is armor. It says 'I'm successful, I'm confident, and I don't need your approval.'"

"I do, though. Need her approval. I hate that I do, but—"

"No, you don't." I stand, walk to her slowly, giving her time to back away if she wants. She doesn't. "You want it. There's a difference between wanting something and needing it."

"Semantics."

"Truth." I stop just close enough that I can sense the heat radiating off her skin. "You've built a whole life without her approval. You've got a job you love, friends who'd kill for you, a place of your own, a demon cat, and now you have us—me, Holt, and Arrow."

We're standing too close. Her pulse flutters at her throat, and her pupils dilate when she stares at me. Her scent is stronger now, sweeter, and it's taking everything I have not to lean down and taste it at the source.

"Luke?"

"Yeah?"

"What if she sees right through this? What if she knows we're faking?"

"Then we sell it better."

"How?"

"Like this." I reach up, tuck a strand of hair behind her ear, let my fingers trail down her neck. She shivers. "Every couple has tells. Little things they do without thinking. The way they lean into each other. The way they touch casually. The way they look at each other when they think no one's watching."

"And how do we look at each other?" Her voice is barely a whisper.

"Like we can't believe our luck. Like we're both waiting for the other shoe to drop. Like we want to devour each other but we're trying to be civilized about it."

"Is that how you're staring at me now?"

"You tell me."

She studies me for a long moment, and something shifts in her expression. "I need to… I should put on makeup. And shoes. And—"

She turns too fast, snags her foot on the edge of the rug, starts to fall. I catch her around the waist, pull her back against my chest. We freeze like that, her back to my front, my arms around her, both of us breathing too hard.

"You okay?" My voice comes out rough.

"I'm—" She turns in my arms, looks up at me, and suddenly we're inches apart. "I'm terrified."

"Of your mom?"

"Of this. Of you. Of how real this feels when it's supposed to be fake."

My hands tighten on her waist. "Cindy—"

"I know we just met recently and this is simply a favor. I know you're only here because Holt got hurt. But when you stare at me like that, when you touch me, I forget it's pretend."

"What if it's not?"

The words hang between us, too heavy, too real.

"What if it's not pretend?" I continue, because I'm already in too deep. "And what if this is the most real thing I've felt in years?"

"You could have anyone."

"I don't want anyone. I want—"

She kisses me.

It's soft at first, tentative. Then I groan against her mouth, her hands fist in my shirt, and suddenly we're drowning in each other. My hands slide into her hair, angling her head so I can deepen the kiss, and she makes this sound—half whimper, half moan—that shoots straight to my cock.

"Fuck," I growl against her mouth. "You're gonna kill me."

"Good way to go, though."

"The best."

I walk her backward until her legs hit the bed. She falls back, pulling me with her, and then I'm covering her body with mine, careful to keep my weight on my forearms. She arches up against me, and I nearly lose it right there.

"We should—" She gasps as I kiss down her throat. "We should maybe stop."

"Do you want to?"

"No. God, no. But my mom—dinner—"

"We have time." I pull back to look at her, sprawled on the bed, dress riding up her thighs, lips swollen from kissing. "Let me help you relax. Let me take care of you."

"I don't know if—"

"Trust me." I kiss her again, slower this time, coaxing rather than demanding. "All that tension, all that anxiety, let me take it away. You'll walk into that restaurant feeling powerful. Confident. Like you own the fucking world."

She studies me for a long moment, then nods.

I start at her ankles, pressing kisses to the inside of each one. She giggles, and it's the best sound I've heard all day.

"Ticklish?"

"Perhaps."

I file that information away for later, then continue my path up her legs. By the time I reach her thighs, she's not giggling anymore. She's breathing in short gasps, hands fisted in the comforter, hips lifting slightly off the bed.

"Please," she whispers.

"Please what?"

"I need... I don't know what I need."

"I do."

I push her dress up slowly, inch by inch, the fabric catching against my knuckles as I remain kneeling on the floor between her legs. She's watching me, barely. Her breath catches, eyes fluttering shut like she can't bear the weight of how I'm staring at her.

My gaze drags lower. Then I spot a flash of color, soft lavender lace stretched over warm skin.

Fuck.

Heat rolls through me. I press my palm against her thigh, needing the grounding pressure, needing something to keep me from tearing those panties in half.

"Christ," I whisper.

Her cheeks go pink, and still she doesn't open her eyes. I nudge her dress higher, past her hips, bunching it around her waist. It's not just the sight of her; it's the way she responds, soft and silent, trusting me with her whole body.

"Look at you," I breathe, voice thick.

She barely opens her eyes, like she doesn't realize she's undoing me one heartbeat at a time.

"No," I murmur. "Don't hide from me. Open your eyes fully. I want you to watch what I'm going to do to you."

I lean in closer to her inner thigh and kiss it, slow and reverent. "You're fucking perfect."

Then I breathe her in.

My dick throbs, painfully caged behind my zipper. She smells like heaven and sin mixed together, sweet, musky, absolutely fucking addictive. The kind of scent that sears itself into memory and makes a man lose his goddamn mind.

I slide my hands beneath the waistband of her panties, the lace clinging for a second like it doesn't want to let go. She lifts her hips in silent permission, and I drag the lacy material down her thighs, my knuckles grazing over soft skin, over heat, over places I ache to taste.

I take my time. Watching.

Her thighs tremble just slightly as I slide the panties past her knees, down her calves, and finally off her ankles. I toss them aside without looking, my eyes locked on the spot she tried to hide from me. The small strip of blonde hair. The blushing pink lips.

She's already glistening.

Wet. Swollen. Her folds delicate and flushed, so

fucking pretty that I can't move for a second. I just admire everything she's offering me.

I press my hands to her inner thighs and part her legs.

And there it is.

The most intimate, vulnerable pussy laid bare for me.

Pink and wet and aching. My name is written all over her.

My throat goes dry.

I look up and find her watching now, lips parted, breath stuttering out of her.

"Fuck," I whisper, voice wrecked. "You're dripping for me."

I bend forward, breath ghosting over her slit, and smile as she shivers beneath it.

"You're going to let me break you, aren't you, baby?"

I lean in closer, unable to resist. The first taste ruins me. Warm, wet, addictive like nothing and no one else. I groan into her, dragging my hands up the insides of her thighs, spreading her wider as I settle between them. She's flat on her back, breathing hard, eyes wide as if she can't believe this is happening.

She tries to close her legs, just slightly, not enough to stop me, but enough to make me lift my head.

"I've never… No one's ever done this to me before."

Her cheeks flush, hands fisted in the sheets. Shy. Vulnerable. So goddamn beautiful I can hardly take it.

I press my mouth to the inside of her thigh.

"Then I'm going to make it unforgettable," I murmur against her skin, fucking excited to think I'll be the first man to ever eat her sweet pussy. "You'll never doubt how good it can feel again."

I kiss higher, feel her tense beneath me, then let my breath spill hot over her hole where she's wet and aching. My thumbs glide along the softest parts of her inner lips, coaxing them open for me with my touch. Her body gives way slowly, trembling, glistening, flushed and exposed.

She gasps when my tongue drags the length of her, the sound torn from her as if she wasn't expecting it. I work her slowly, savoring every twitch of her thighs, every shaky breath. My fingers follow, sliding through the slick heat, and I ease two inside her, inch by inch. Tight. Hot. She takes me so sweetly it nearly breaks me.

She's quiet, but her body says everything. The way her hips shift just barely toward my mouth. The way her hands twist in the sheets like she's holding herself together. And she keeps staring, holding my gaze as I flick her pink pussy.

I curl my fingers deeper, pressing into her tight heat until I feel her squeeze around me. My tongue doesn't let up. Instead, I drag it over her clit again, then flick harder, faster, more ravenous. I want her overwhelmed. I want her gasping for air and crying out my name with that sweet, broken voice.

Her thighs tremble around my head, hips jerking, trying to ride the rhythm I've set. She's so wet, dripping down to my knuckles, coating my mouth like she was made for this. Made for me.

I growl low into her, the sound vibrating through my tongue, and her whole body jolts like I hit a live wire.

"That's it," I mutter against her. "Just like that. So fucking responsive. You gonna come for me, little Omega?"

Her back arches. My fingers curl again, rougher this time, stroking deep with every thrust. She clenches so tightly it knocks the breath out of me.

I'm rock hard and leaking, cock straining for any kind of contact, but I can't stop. Not when she's falling apart like this.

I unfasten my fly one-handed, pull myself free, and hiss through my teeth at the relief. My hand wraps around my cock, slow strokes matching the rhythm of my tongue.

"You feel what you're doing to me?" I rasp against her clit. "I'm fucking leaking for you, baby. Making a mess all over myself, and I haven't even been inside you yet."

She whimpers, thighs trembling, breath coming fast and shallow. My jaw aches from the way I'm devouring her, but I don't stop.

"You don't even know," I groan, "how perfect you taste. How good you squeeze around my fingers. You were made to be wrecked like this."

I fuck her with my hand, slick and deep and filthy, dragging my tongue over her in quick, relentless licks until she's writhing. Her hips roll, chasing every stroke like she's desperate for more, but it's mine to give. I'm the one unraveling her. I'm the one who gets to watch her come undone.

I groan against her, grinding into my fist harder now. It's not enough, never enough, but it keeps the edge off. Just barely.

Her body starts to tighten, muscles clenching, her hands fisting the sheets. She's so close. So goddamn close.

"Let go," I growl into her, voice rough and low. "Give it to me. Come on my fingers. Come all over my fucking tongue."

Her whole body shudders as she comes, jaw clenched, a scream on her lips, eyes squeezed shut. She pulses around my fingers, soft and frantic, flooding my mouth with a sweetness I never want to forget.

I don't stop until her legs start to shake, until her hips twitch like it's too much. Only then do I ease up, slowing my fingers, gentling my tongue. I press kisses into the trembling skin of her thighs like I'm grateful. Like I'm worshipping her. Because I fucking am.

I lift my head, breathless, and look at her. She's staring at the ceiling, eyes glassy, lips parted, chest rising and falling like she's just survived something holy.

And I lose it.

I reach blindly for the scrap of lace I tossed aside earlier. Her panties. Still damp with her heat, still carrying her scent. I grip them in one hand, brace the other against the bed, and stroke myself hard and fast. It only takes seconds. I've been teetering on the edge since the first sound she made.

Her name breaks from my lips as I come, hips jerking, cock throbbing in my fist. I spill into the delicate fabric, breathing her name like a prayer, like a curse.

I wipe the head against the soft lace, her scent and mine tangled together. I close my fist around it and breathe in deep, dizzy with it.

When I look back up, she's still watching me.

I smile, wiping my mouth with the back of my hand.

Her taste still clings to my lips. Her scent is thick in my lungs.

And I know without a doubt that she's mine now.

"How do you feel?" I ask softly.

She doesn't answer right away, just breathes, lips parted. "That was incredible," she whispers. "I could definitely do that more often."

I chuckle, loving seeing her this way.

After tucking my cock back into my pants and zipping up, I get to my feet and help her sit up, smoothing her dress back down. She looks at me, eyes still glazed, and reaches for my belt.

"Let me—"

I catch her hands. "This was for you."

She grabs me by the shirt and tugs me down to her, then kisses me, deep and dirty, tasting herself on my tongue. When she pulls back, we're both breathing hard.

"I'm going to shower," she says, standing on shaky legs. "Try not to miss me."

"Already do."

She pauses at the bathroom door, glances back at me. She bites her lip, doesn't say a word, and then disappears into the bathroom.

My cock throbs. Fuck, I don't think I know what I've got myself into.

The shower starts, and I fall back on her bed, licking my lips, tasting her there. I probably reek of her now, her scent all over my face, my hands, my clothes. I should probably care about that, should wash up before we go, but fuck it. Let everyone know. Let her mother smell it and know that her daughter is desired, wanted, cherished.

She's mine. She doesn't know it yet, probably isn't ready to hear it, but she's absolutely fucking mine. My scent match, my perfect fit, my beautiful disaster of a woman who's captured my attention.

Soon, the shower shuts off, and I sit up, trying to look less like I've been rolling around in her bed thinking about her. She emerges wrapped in a towel, steam billowing around her like she's some kind of water nymph, and I have to clench my fists to keep from reaching for her.

"Don't look!" She darts for the closet, and I catch a glimpse of pale shoulder, the curve of her calf, before she disappears.

"Wouldn't dream of it," I lie, absolutely dreaming of it.

"Almost ready," she calls. "Just need to put the dress back on and do my face."

"Your face is perfect already," I call back.

I push off the edge of the bed and stroll toward the bathroom, the door half cracked, steam still curling out into the bedroom from her shower. The air inside is warm and wet, thick with her scent clinging to every surface.

I glance down as I reach the sink, watching my hands in the soft light, fingers still slightly tacky, smeared with the evidence of her. Some of it has dried at the edges of my knuckles, glinting faintly like a secret I don't plan on giving up. I give them a scrub.

Then I bring them to my nose and breathe her in.

Fuck.

Still sweet. Still warm. Still *hers*.

I swipe a wet hand across my chin, wiping at my mouth even though I already know the taste is still there, stubborn and addictive. A smear of her on my lower lip, caught in the stubble on my jaw. I fucking love that.

Her scent is all over me, soaked into my skin like I marked her just by touching her.

I grip the edge of the sink and stare into the mirror, still half hard, jaw tight, heart pounding with the kind of hunger that doesn't just fade.

She has no idea what she's done to me.

She emerges five minutes later, dressed, lips painted deep red, some kind of shimmer on her eyelids.

She looks expensive, untouchable, like the kind of woman who'd never give a guy like me a second look.

Except she is giving me a second look. A third. A fourth.

"What?" she asks.

"You're going to surprise her."

"My mom?"

"Everyone. Every person in that restaurant is going to wonder who you are, why they don't know you, how they can get to know you."

"You're being ridiculous."

"I'm being honest. Come here."

She walks over slowly, careful in her heels. I stand, towering over her even with the added height, and she has to tilt her head back to look at me.

"You're going to walk in there on my arm," I tell her. "And your mother is going to see that you're happy. Successful. Desired. Everything she thinks you couldn't be without her approval."

"What if I fall apart?"

"Then I'll put you back together." I cup her face in my hands. "That's what boyfriends do."

"Fake boyfriends."

"Right. Fake." But there's nothing fake about the way I kiss her forehead, her cheeks, the corner of her mouth. "Ready?"

"No."

"Perfect. Let's go shock some suburban sensibilities."

She laughs. "Is that your plan?"

"Part of it."

"What's the other part?"

"Making sure you know your worth and ensuring she knows it too. Also, maybe, if I'm really lucky, convincing you that this doesn't have to be fake."

She stares at me. "Luke—"

"For now, just let me be your boyfriend and worship you the way you deserve."

She kisses me then, soft and sweet. "Thank you. For being here. For... everything."

"You don't have to thank me for doing something I want to do."

"You want to have dinner with my mother?"

"I prefer it was just you. Your mother is simply an unfortunate side effect."

She laughs as we head downstairs. General Flufferton watches us with judgment from his perch on the couch.

"Be good," Cindy tells him. "No parties."

"He's definitely throwing a party," I say.

"Probably. He's very social for a cat who pretends to not like strangers."

"Sounds like someone else I know."

"You wish." She bumps me with her shoulder, and I catch her hand, lace our fingers together. It feels natural, right, like our hands were designed to fit together.

"Luke?"

"Yeah?"

"I'm really glad you're here."

"Me too."

And I am. Because as we walk toward the door and get into the car to reach dinner with her nightmare of a mother, toward whatever comes after, I know one thing for certain: I'm going to make this woman mine. Not just for tonight, not just for her mother, but for real. For keeps. Forever.

I'm very good at getting what I want.

And what I want is Cindy.

13

CINDY

Luke pulls Holt's massive truck up to Savor's side entrance, and my stomach drops at the sight of the packed parking lot. Every space filled, people milling around the entrance, waiting for tables. Saturday night at the hottest restaurant in town, of course Mother would pick this.

"It's like the whole town's here," Luke mutters, maneuvering the beast of a vehicle into the loading zone.

He throws it in park with the confidence of someone who's never gotten a ticket in his life.

My hands won't stop shaking. I clasp them together, but that just makes the shaking more obvious.

"Hey." Luke's hand covers both of mine. "You're gonna be fine."

"You don't know my mother."

"No, but I know you. And you're tougher than you think."

Arrow appears at the entrance just as we climb out, and my stomach flutters at the sight of him.

He's dressed in black jeans and a fitted slate-gray button-up with the sleeves rolled to his elbows, showing off forearms dusted with tattoos and corded muscle. The top two buttons are undone, revealing just a hint of ink at his collarbone and enough skin to make my mouth go dry.

There's a towel slung over one shoulder, a pen tucked behind his ear, and a worn leather apron tied low around his waist. He looks every bit the owner and every bit the problem, as if he stepped out of a gritty-chef calendar shoot and into real life.

His blond hair is pulled back into a messy knot, a few strands falling loose around his temples and his eyes. He scans the parking lot until he finds me heading his way.

That crooked smile tugs at his mouth, lazy and knowing, like he's already got my number and he's just waiting for me to admit it.

"Your mom's here," he says without preamble. "After you texted us on your drive over that she booked here, I found her easily. And you're in for a surprise."

"God, don't say that." My voice cracks. "Today has already had too many surprises."

"Well, she's the one who booked the big group table for twelve, and everyone's here but you two."

The ground tilts beneath my feet. She brought nine

other people with her? That's not dinner with my mother. That's a fucking ambush.

"Oh, fuck me, no she didn't!"

My breathing dips, too fast, and my head spins slightly. I'm about to have a full panic attack in the parking lot of Savor. The edges of my vision blur. My heartbeat sounds too loud in my ears.

"I can't do this. I can't—"

"Hey, hey." Luke is in front of me suddenly, hands on my shoulders. "It's going to be okay."

"It doesn't feel like it."

Arrow moves to my other side, and between them I feel less like I'm going to float away. "You're not alone here," Arrow adds, his deep voice steady. "We've got your back."

"She brought nine more people to meet my fake boyfriend."

"Then we give them a show," Luke says simply, not appearing alarmed in the slightest.

"Let's take you both in through the front so it doesn't look sus," Arrow continues, and his dark eyes sweep over me with genuine appreciation. "And by the way, you look absolutely gorgeous."

He winks, and despite the terror clawing at my chest, my traitorous body responds with a flutter of my heart. Even in the middle of a panic attack, I'm apparently not immune to his charm.

"Oh, fuck, I almost forgot." Heat floods my cheeks. "Don't call me Cindy. My real name is Cynthia."

Luke grins. "I know. Heard Van call you that at the Harvest Dance, remember?"

Arrow clears his throat. "Shall we? Your audience awaits."

God, that terrifies me.

Luke takes my hand, fingers interlacing with mine, and I let myself lean into his strength. As we enter the restaurant, heads turn. A table of college girls actually stops mid-conversation to stare at Luke, mouths parted, eyes wide, like they've just seen a celebrity walk in.

And honestly? I get it.

In his crisp button-down and dark jeans, with that fresh haircut sharpening every brutal line of his face, he looks like a man you dream about and never survive. Effortlessly hot. Lethal in the prettiest way. The kind of man who could break your heart just by smiling, and they want him to.

Arrow leads us through the main dining room, past tables of curious diners trying not to stare, through the back door and outside where—

"Holy shit," I breathe.

The marquee is stunning. Like something from a magazine or a movie about rich people's garden parties. White fabric drapes from the beams of a peaked pergola towering at least fifteen feet high, with tiny lights strung throughout, swaying gently in the open night air. Crystal chandeliers hang at intervals, casting rainbow patterns when they catch the light.

Heating lamps disguised as elegant bronze sculptures keep the October chill at bay.

The table is even worse. Or better, depending on how you look at it. It's oval, stretched to accommodate twelve place settings, and covered in white linen. Silver chargers under bone china plates, more forks and spoons than anyone needs for one meal, and crystal glasses. The centerpieces are elaborate arrangements of burgundy and cream roses mixed with eucalyptus and something that might be actual gold-dusted branches.

And around that table, ten faces turn to look at us.

My throat closes up. They're all here. Family members who've made me feel small, insufficient, not quite enough.

At the far end of the oval sits my mother, positioned like a queen holding court. Victoria Williams. She looks exactly as I remember. Cream silk blouse, pearls that belonged to my father's grandmother, steel-gray hair styled in that way that looks effortless but takes two hours and a professional. Her eyes, the same hazel as mine but colder, lock on to me with laser focus.

To her right, two empty chairs wait like threats.

"You got this," Luke whispers in my ear, his breath warm against my skin. "You don't owe them anything."

There's Mother's Aunt Beatrice, seventy-five and mean as a snake, dripping with diamonds. My cousins

Sarah and Emma with their matching husbands, both named James, which would be funny if they weren't such assholes. Father's nephew Trevor and his fiancée, Monica, who looks like she'd rather be anywhere else. My Omega cousins, the twins Lisa and Laura, already whispering behind their hands like we're still in high school.

I lift my chin, summoning every ounce of fake confidence I've learned from watching Harper bulldoze through life.

"Look who finally arrived!" Mother's voice carries across the space, pitched to sound delighted but with that undertone that says *You're late and everyone knows it.*

Luke's hand tightens on mine, and then he's moving forward, dragging me with him.

"Amazing to meet you all!" His voice booms with the kind of confidence I'll never have. "I'm Luke, Cynthia's main squeeze."

Sarah actually snorts wine through her nose. Emma's husband, James One, snickers. Mother's smile freezes like someone hit pause on her face.

"Hi, everyone," I manage, surprised that my voice works at all. "What a surprise to see you all here."

"Surprise?" Mother stands, arms open like she wants a hug. "Sweetheart, I told you we were having dinner."

"You said *we*. You and me and my boyfriend. Not the entire extended family tree."

"Don't be dramatic." She air-kisses my cheeks, European style, which she started doing after one trip to Paris. "Everyone's been dying to meet your young man."

We make our way to our seats, Luke's hand on my lower back warm through the fabric of my dress. I sink into the chair next to Mother, and Luke settles beside me with Aunt Beatrice on his other side. We're trapped, bookended by judgment.

"So this is him," Mother says, examining Luke as though he's a horse she's considering buying. "You're quite… large."

"Mother!"

"What? It's an observation." She turns to Luke. "Cynthia, introduce us properly."

"Mother, this is Luke Brennan. Luke, my mother, Victoria Williams."

Luke leans over me to give her a hug, and I watch Mother's eyes widen as she's engulfed by his arms. She's not a small woman, but he makes her look delicate.

"My, you are a very big boy, aren't you?" She pulls back, eyes immediately zeroing in on the tattoos visible on his forearms where his sleeves are rolled up. Her fingers reach out, actually tracing the skull wrapped in chains. "And such interesting artwork. Is this real?"

"All real," Luke confirms, not pulling away even though I can feel the tension radiating from him. "Got this one when I was nineteen. Buddy of mine had just opened his shop, needed practice. Hurt like a bitch—sorry, hurt quite a lot, but worth it."

"Luke, she doesn't need to know—"

"No, no, I'm fascinated." Mother's fingers are still on his skin, and I want to slap them away. "Each one must have a story. This blade here, is that significant?"

"Got that one after a particularly rough period in my life," Luke explains. "See, I was working security for this company that dealt with—well, let's just say they weren't entirely above board, and there was this incident with a shipment—"

"Luke." I put my hand over his. "She doesn't need your whole life story."

"But I want to hear it," Mother insists, finally releasing his arm. "After all, you've kept him such a secret. We have so much catching up to do."

The interrogation begins immediately.

"So how exactly did you two meet?" Aunt Beatrice leans forward, her numerous necklaces clanking.

"The Harvest Dance last year," Luke answers. "Halloween night. She was dressed as... what was it, baby? A witch?"

"Brewery witch," I mutter.

"Right, brewery witch. Creative. Anyway, I saw her across the room and just..." He makes a gesture like his head exploded. "Had to meet her."

"Really?" Sarah's voice drips with disbelief. "Our little Cynthia caught your eye in a room full of people?"

"Couldn't miss her if I tried. She was arguing with some guy about IPA versus stout, just going off about hop varieties and malt profiles. Sexiest thing I'd ever seen."

Emma chokes on her wine. "Sexy? Beer knowledge?"

"Intelligence is sexy," Luke says simply. "Passion is sexy. Your cousin has both in spades."

"And what do you do for work?" Trevor asks, raising an eyebrow.

"Security," Luke replies. "Private protection, asset management, that sort of thing."

"Like a bodyguard?" Lisa or Laura, I can never tell them apart, asks, staring at him like candy.

"Sometimes. Other times it's more about securing locations, making sure valuable items get from point A to point B safely. It's varied work, keeps me on my toes."

"Sounds dangerous," Mother observes, that fake concern creeping into her voice.

"Can be. But I'm very good at what I do." Luke grins. "Plus the danger pays well. Very well. Just bought a place up near the mountains, actually. Six bedrooms, pool, huge land, the works."

"Six bedrooms?" Aunt Beatrice's eyes narrow. "That's quite large for a single man."

"Well, I'm not planning on staying single." His arm slides around my shoulders, pulling me against his side. "Am I, baby?"

My face burns. "Luke—"

"And what exactly made her so special?" Mother is watching him closely now. "What drew you to our Cynthia specifically, not just her talking about beer?"

I swallow hard.

"You mean besides the fact that she's gorgeous?" Luke squeezes my shoulder. "She's brilliant. Funny. Independent. Doesn't take shit from anyone… sorry, doesn't take nonsense from anyone. Called me on my bullshit within five minutes of meeting me."

"Language, please," Mother says coolly.

"Right, sorry. I work with a rough crowd sometimes, forget my manners."

"Are you from around here?" Monica speaks up.

"Born and raised. Never saw much reason to leave. Everything I want is right here." He glances over at me when he says it, and my stomach does that swooping thing again.

There's a beat of silence, like they're all recalibrating, unsure of what to do with the man who's clearly staking a claim.

"And your parents?" Aunt Beatrice asks. "What do they do?"

I stiffen. They aren't even pausing with their grilling.

"They died when I was eight. Car accident."

My heart hurts, as I had no idea either, so I lean in closer to him, whispering, "So sorry."

"Oh." Even Aunt Beatrice looks momentarily human. "I'm sorry."

"Long time ago. Made me who I am, you know? Had to grow up fast, learn to take care of myself."

I glance at him, something tight and hot blooming behind my ribs to hear his pain. And they're still not asking *me* anything.

"So you have no family?" Emma asks, and it sounds like she's pointing out a deficiency. A lack. Something she's relieved not to see in her dating pool.

"I've got chosen family. Brothers who'd take a bullet for me. And now I've got Cynthia." He presses a kiss to my temple, soft but claiming. "That's more than enough."

It should make me melt, and part of me does, but the rest of me is just... aware. Aware that I'm sitting here at a table of people who haven't asked me a single thing. Not about my job. Not about my life. Not about why I didn't call.

"How romantic," Sarah says in a tone that suggests it's anything but.

I smile tightly, sip my water, and resist the urge to ask if they even remember why I left in the first place. Or if they just needed someone new to judge now that I've stopped making it easy for them.

A shadow falls across the table, and I glance up, expecting Arrow. But the figure placing a drink in front of Luke is wearing server attire—black pants, white button-up, and—

Wait...

A black eye patch. Like a pirate. Like a fucking pirate.

It's Holt.

My brain stutters. He's supposed to be in the hospital. Concussion. Rest. That's what Luke said.

But here he is, very much upright, and apparently working.

"Your usual, sir," he almost growls, setting down what might be the most ridiculous cocktail I've ever seen. It's bright blue with an umbrella, a sparkler, what looks like dry ice making it smoke, and at least three different fruits garnishing the rim.

Luke doesn't miss a beat. "Ah, my favorite! Thanks, man. You know me so well."

Before I can say a word, he kicks the back of Luke's chair hard enough that Luke jerks forward, catching himself on the table with a grunt.

I blink, still stuck on the damn eye patch. What the hell kind of hospital discharge includes accessorizing like a villain in a Halloween play?

"Oops, sorry, sir. These new shoes are slippery."

"No problem," Luke says cheerfully, taking a sip of the monstrosity. "Happens to the best of us."

Everyone is watching Luke drink this ridiculous cocktail that's still smoking and sparkling, and he's playing it completely straight, like this is actually something he orders.

"Interesting choice," Mother observes.

"I like to live dangerously," Luke says, pulling out a piece of pineapple and eating it. "Plus, look at this presentation. It's art."

I catch Holt's eye as he's backing away, and he smirks before disappearing toward the kitchen. My brain is spinning. Holt is here, not the hospital. This is insane.

"Cynthia, you're being very quiet," Mother observes. "Don't you want to tell everyone about your life? Your little job? What have you been doing instead of being with your family?"

I cringe on the inside. "Work as an assistant brewer at a local brewery. I'm learning the trade."

"Of course you are," she says in that tone that means *How amusing that you think this matters.* "But how is that sustainable long-term? Surely you don't expect Luke to wait around while you chase your little business ventures."

"I'm not chasing anything," I say, voice tight. "I've built something. It matters."

"Don't get defensive, sweetheart. I'm only thinking practically. Luke here seems like a man who knows what he wants. Doesn't that include family? A more... settled future?"

I open my mouth, ready to fire something back, but Luke gets there first.

"I adore that she's a career woman," he says smoothly. "It's one of the first things that drew me to her. She's ambitious. Passionate. The kind of person who *doesn't* wait around for life to happen. She builds it herself. And I support that completely."

He looks directly at my mother as he says it, his thumb brushing the back of my hand under the table.

"She's not playing at anything," he adds. "She's doing it. And doing it damn well."

Mother's smile tightens, but she doesn't respond.

Aunt Beatrice sips her wine, clearly disappointed that no one is spiraling yet.

"I think what Cynthia does is incredible," Luke

continues, drawing the spotlight firmly back to me. "Do you know how complex brewing is? It's chemistry and art combined. She's been developing this seasonal ale that's going to put the entire brewery on the map."

He says it like it's a fact, like it's already happening. Like he's proud of me in a way no one at this table ever has been.

And for once, I let myself breathe in that pride. Let it settle deep.

Mother tilts her head. "That's quite a sales pitch, Luke. You should consider politics."

"No need," he replies easily. "I already got what I wanted."

"Beer," Aunt Beatrice says dismissively. "Such a masculine pursuit."

"Some of the best brewers in the world are women." I snap the words out before I can soften them.

"Of course they are, dear," she replies with a tight smile that makes it clear she believes the exact opposite.

Arrow appears then, saving me from saying something I'll absolutely regret.

"Good evening, everyone. I'm Arrow, owner here at Savor. I wanted to personally welcome you and take any additional drink orders."

He starts at the far end of the table, but when he gets to Luke, he just says, "Your usual, sir, again?" with a perfectly straight face.

"Already got it, thanks." Luke raises his ridiculous blue cocktail.

Arrow continues around, and I order wine with a desperate edge that makes him pause.

"Make it a large," I mutter.

"You bet," he assures me quietly.

Once he has all the orders, he clears his throat, drawing everyone's attention. "We've prepared a special banquet menu for your group tonight. Seven courses, beginning with an amuse-bouche of butternut squash soup with brown butter and sage, followed by a mixed green salad with pomegranate vinaigrette and candied pecans..."

He goes through each course with the kind of detail that has even Aunt Beatrice looking impressed. When he finally leaves, Mother immediately reaches for Luke again.

"So tell me, Luke," she begins. "Working in security must mean odd hours?"

"Sometimes. But I make my own schedule, mostly. Perks of being the boss."

"You own the company?"

"Co-own with my friend. We started it together."

Luke slips his hand into mine beneath the table and squeezes.

"And this business of yours," Mother continues, "it's successful?"

"Very," he says without hesitation. "We've got contracts all over the state. Just landed a deal with—" He pauses. "Actually, I probably shouldn't say. Client confidentiality and all that."

"Of course," she replies, clearly irritated that she can't measure him by name-dropping alone.

Luke shifts in his chair slightly, his thumb brushing over the back of my hand now. I don't realize how tight my shoulders have been until they start to ease.

"Cynthia thinks I look hot in a suit too," he adds casually, flashing me a grin that's half devilish, half sweet.

I nearly choke on my breath.

"Luke!"

"What?" He shrugs, eyes twinkling with mischief. "You said so. I just like being accurate."

"Moving on," I say, louder than necessary, cheeks burning.

Sarah leans forward, all fake innocence. "When was this? While you were getting ready together?"

"She was helping me pick out a shirt," Luke says smoothly, letting go of my hand just long enough to rest it on my thigh. Warm. Grounding. Possessive in a way that has my heart fluttering.

Emma's eyes narrow, gleaming with interest. "So... you got ready at her place?"

"No," Luke says easily. "My place. She lives with me."

Silence falls like a dropped glass.

My breath catches. My heart kicks hard against my ribs.

He said it so casually. So matter-of-factly. Like it's not a bomb in the middle of a table full of people who didn't even know we were serious. We had agreed to say we lived together to show that we were serious.

Mother's expression freezes. "She... *what?*"

Luke doesn't flinch. "She moved in a while ago. I've got the space. And I like having her there."

Aunt Beatrice makes a noise into her wineglass that could be a cough or a judgmental scoff. Probably both.

"She's not a guest," Luke adds, thumb brushing softly over my thigh again. "She's home."

His words land in my chest like an anchor and a match all at once.

And this time, I don't look away. I let them all see me steady myself under his touch, let them see me choose not to shrink.

Mother sets down her wineglass with a delicate clink. "So she moved in before I even had the chance to meet you?" Her voice isn't raised, yet it slices through the table like a blade. Laced with judgment. I shift uncomfortably in my seat. However, Luke and I practiced our background. "And she's an Omega," Mother adds, glancing at me but speaking to the table. "Living with an unmated male without so much as a conversation with her parents? It's... concerning."

My stomach twists. There it is. The thing she's been dancing around since I walked in the door: her belief that I've embarrassed myself. That I've stepped outside the boundaries of what's acceptable for someone like me.

"I wasn't aware she needed permission to decide

where she sleeps," Luke says, voice low and even. "She's an adult. She makes her own choices."

Mother's smile is brittle. "She's still an Omega. And Omegas—"

"Are not property," Luke cuts in, sharper now.

There's a pause, and then he adds, quieter but heavier, "She lives with me. She's mine to protect now. Not yours to manage."

The weight of the words drops hard between us. Not loud, but final.

Aunt Beatrice glances at her plate. Emma reaches for her wineglass like it's a life raft. The air has changed—charged, humming with the kind of tension that makes people forget how to breathe.

But I don't hide.

I lift my chin and meet my mother's stare head-on. "You don't get to decide what kind of Omega I am," I say, my voice steadier than I feel. "Not anymore."

"You don't understand what this looks like," she says, her composure slipping. "You moved in with a man I've never met. An Alpha. Before there was any formal arrangement. Before a mating mark. What was I supposed to think?"

Luke shifts beside me. "There is a mark," he says. Quiet. Certain.

Mother's lips part. Her gaze flicks to my neck, but I know she won't see it. Not unless I show her. Not unless I want her to.

"She didn't tell you," Luke continues, threading his fingers through mine. "Because she knew how you'd react. But you should know, she's already mine. Fully. Claimed." He pauses, his gaze steady as he adds, "Marked, too."

Everyone stills.

Aunt Beatrice blinks. "Marked?"

Luke doesn't flinch. "With my bite. High on her inner thigh."

I cringe hard. Why did he have to add that part?

Aunt Beatrice gasps outright, hand flying to her chest.

Someone makes a strangled noise that might be a cough or a laugh she's trying to swallow.

And my mother, her cheeks flush a deep, blotchy red. Whether it's from fury or humiliation, I'm not sure.

"You—" she starts, but Luke doesn't give her space to spiral.

"She asked me to," he says simply, like it's the most natural thing in the world. "Because she trusts me. Because it was her choice. Not yours."

My pulse thunders, but I don't look away. I squeeze his hand tighter.

"I didn't hide it because I was ashamed," I say. "I didn't tell you because I didn't want this"—I gesture to the table, the tension, the judgment hanging heavy in the air—"to ruin something that belongs to me."

"He doesn't belong to you alone," Mother snaps, regaining some of her steel. "You're an Omega. Your choices reflect on your family, as does your choice of Alpha."

"No," I say, breath catching. "My choices reflect *me*. And I don't need to be managed. I need to be respected."

Luke's hand slides up to rest on the small of my back, steadying, claiming. His voice drops low, intimate but firm.

"She's not under your roof anymore. She's under mine. And I won't apologize for taking care of what's mine."

Silence stretches, coiling tighter.

Mother stares at me like she's seeing a stranger.

"I'm not ashamed of what we are," I go on. "And I'm not looking for your approval unless you mean it."

Luke doesn't let go of my hand. Not once.

"She's safe," he says. "Happy. And not alone anymore."

For a moment, my mother says nothing. Just lifts her glass again, like it's all suddenly too heavy to face head-on.

But I see the fracture in her composure, the tiny line where the mask slips. Her Omega daughter, marked without her blessing. Not waiting for a white dress or a contract. Just... loved. Fully. Fiercely.

And I realize something else too.

I didn't come here to win her over.

I came to show her I'm already whole.

The drinks arrive, saving us from more commentary. I grab my wine and take a probably unladylike gulp.

"Pace yourself, sweetheart," Mother says. "You

know how you get. All emotional. Weepy. Remember at Cousin May's wedding?"

"I was seventeen!"

"Still."

I take another gulp out of spite.

The first course arrives, and for a blessed few minutes, everyone is occupied with soup with dumplings. But the reprieve doesn't last.

"So where do you see this relationship going?" Aunt Beatrice asks Luke between spoonfuls.

"Wherever Cynthia wants it to go," Luke says easily.

"That's not very decisive," Mother replies.

"It's realistic. Relationships are partnerships," he adds.

"But surely the man should lead?" That's from Laura. Or Lisa. One of the interchangeable cousins.

Luke glances her way, unfazed. "Why?"

"Because that's how it's done," Mother replies, as if it's law. "The man pursues, the woman accepts or declines."

"Sounds boring," Luke says with a low chuckle. "I like that Cynthia goes after what she wants."

Mother's gaze slides to me. "And what does she want?"

My fingers tighten around my wineglass. "To build something real."

"And hiding from your family is part of that?"

I blink. "Excuse me?"

"You disappear for almost two years," she says

softly. "No call. No visits. And now you show up with this…" She waves vaguely toward Luke. "This person we've never heard of."

"This person has a name," I say carefully. Calmly. "Luke."

"Of course. Luke." Her lips twist like she's tasting vinegar. "Such an informal name. Is it short for Lucas?"

"It is," Luke says smoothly. "But only people I don't like call me Lucas."

The silence that follows is sharp enough to cut. Mother's mouth tightens, but she doesn't reply.

The area is warm. Too warm. My dress sticks to the back of my knees.

"I think I need some air," I say, rising from my seat.

"Cynthia." Mother's voice is clipped. "Sit down."

"I just need a minute." I keep my tone even, calm.

"You just got here."

"I know," I say, smoothing the fabric of my dress. "But I'd rather step away than say something I'll regret."

Her eyes narrow. "You're being dramatic."

"Maybe," I admit quietly, offering a thin smile. "But that's better than being rude."

The silence that follows isn't approval. It's control being tested.

Luke doesn't move. He stays seated, calm and unreadable, but I feel the weight of his attention tracking every step as I ease my chair back.

His hand rests on his thigh. "She'll come back when she's ready," he says, voice even, gaze steady.

Mother doesn't respond, but her mouth tightens.

I don't wait for permission. I walk out from under the marquee and cross part of the courtyard to head into the restaurant building, hands loose at my sides. But the moment I pass the doorway into the bathroom, my breath shudders out of me.

Not because I regret leaving.

But because for the first time, I didn't ask.

"Oh my God, I might die tonight," I whisper to myself.

The bathroom is a sanctuary of marble and soft lighting, the only quiet place I've found since we arrived. I run cold water and wet a paper towel, pressing it to the nape of my neck. My reflection stares back, eyes too bright, cheeks flushed, lipstick too perfect like a lie I'm trying to keep together.

"You're fine," I murmur. "You've got this. Smile. Nod. Pretend." I suck in a breath. "Show off Luke. Make them see that you're happy."

It's such a lie that my stomach churns. But it gets me moving.

After using the toilet and washing up, I smooth my dress, square my shoulders, and open the bathroom door—

Right into a solid wall of muscle.

"Shit!"

Hands catch my arms, strong and grounding. I look up, startled, and meet Holt's gaze. His scent smothers me instantly.

Spiced caramel, toasted marshmallow, and vanilla.

It rolls over me like heat, and my body reacts before my mind does. Knees wobbling. Skin flushing. Heat pooling low.

And then I see the bruising beneath the edge of his eye patch, and the adrenaline spikes for another reason.

"Oh my God. Luke told me you got hurt!" The words tumble out, breathless. "Are you okay? He said *concussion,* but, your eye, what are you doing here?"

Holt steps in close, fingers curling around my wrist, and walks me backward a few paces, guiding me into a shadowed corner of the hallway. It's quiet here. Dim. The buzz of voices from the dining room fades to static.

His scent follows, thick and dominant. I breathe it in too fast, too deep, and it clouds everything.

"I'm so sorry I couldn't be the one," he adds, voice low and rough like gravel dragged across velvet. "I saw you at the table with Luke and knew I could have done better."

"Holt..." My fingers twitch toward the bandage under his patch. "You should be resting. Not here—"

"I couldn't stay away," he insists, and there's a tremble under the steel of his tone. His good eye burns into me, sharp and raw. "I need to know you're okay. I need to smell you for myself."

Before I can answer, he steps closer.

Too close.

His chest brushes mine, and the air thickens, heavy with unspoken need. I sway forward just an inch, maybe two, but it's enough.

His nose dips to the curve of my neck, breath brushing skin. He doesn't touch, not really. Just inhales.

And I break.

My legs weaken, thighs pressing together involuntarily. A whimper slips out, barely a sound, but it's real, and I hate how much I want to lean into him. Let him scent me deeper. Let him *claim*.

"Holt," I whisper. "Please don't…"

"Tell me to stop," he says, voice tight with restraint, even as his fingers skim my wrist, tracing the skin like he's branding it. "Tell me right now, and I'll walk away. I swear it."

But I don't.

Because the truth is, I don't want him to stop. Not really. Not when my insides are screaming, scent rising in soft betrayal of everything I'm trying to hold back.

"You smell like you're mine, even if I can scent Luke on you," he breathes, voice cracking on the last word. "I hope you know we are all prepared to share you."

It aches how much I want it to be true, but part of me refuses to believe such men would be interested in me beyond helping me out.

"Luke is doing an amazing job," I whisper, but the words don't carry conviction. Not when my body is betraying every syllable, trembling under Holt's scent when I should focus on the dinner.

"He's doing okay," he breathes, then smirks. His hand presses to the wall beside my head, caging me with heat and shadow. "Doesn't change how much I wish it were me out there with you."

I should step away. Say something to shut this down. But I can't move. Can't breathe.

His forehead touches mine, and it's too much and not enough all at once. His breath ghosts over my lips, thick with restraint.

"I should stay away right now," he mutters. "You've got the dinner to deal with."

Yet he doesn't move.

Neither do I.

Not when my skin is buzzing and my body is already leaning into him, scent curling in a traitorous wave that recognizes him. Wants him. Just as it did with Luke earlier. I keep trying to shove these cravings down, lock them up tight, but they're rising now, molten and insistent, like a volcano threatening to blow.

"I don't know what I'm doing," I whisper, throat tight. "I'm trying to do the right thing."

His good eye darkens. "Then don't say it."

"Say what?"

"That you don't want me."

Because I do.

And we both know it.

His mouth crashes into mine with a desperation that steals my breath. His hands frame my face, holding me like I might disappear if he lets go, and I melt into him instantly. This kiss is consuming, demanding, like he's trying to prove something or maybe claim something. My hands fist in his shirt, pulling him closer, and he unleashes a low growl that sends heat straight through me.

His tongue traces the seam of my lips, and I open for him, tasting whiskey. One hand slides into my hair, tilting my head for a better angle, while the other grips my waist hard enough that I'll probably have bruises. I don't care. I want bruises. I want evidence that this happened, that this gorgeous, dangerous man wanted me this badly.

He kisses me like the world is ending and we'll never get another chance, and I'm the only thing that can satisfy him. When he nips at my bottom lip, I gasp, and he swallows the sound, pressing closer until there's no space between us. I can feel every hard line of his body, the heat of him through our clothes, and it's still not enough. My hands slide up his chest, feeling the muscles tense under my touch, and he makes a sound that's almost pained before kissing me even deeper.

"Oh. My. God." Sarah's voice cuts through the haze.

We freeze, still pressed together, and whip our heads around to see my cousin standing at the end of the hallway, mouth hanging open, eyes bright with the glee of someone who just won the gossip lottery.

"Oh, fuck," I breathe against Holt's mouth.

Sarah turns and practically runs back toward the door that leads out to the marquee.

Great job, Cindy…

14

LUKE

I'm drinking this ridiculous blue monstrosity of a cocktail, trying not to laugh at whatever the fuck Arrow and Holt think they're doing. The drink tastes like someone melted a candy store and added rum, but I'll be damned if I let them see me flinch. The sparkler has finally died out, leaving little black specks floating in the blue liquid that probably aren't meant to be there.

Holt is clearly jealous as fuck that I'm here with Cindy instead of him. The way he keeps *accidentally* hitting my chair every time he passes? Amateur hour. A bruised shin isn't going to throw me off my game.

I smirk into my drink, feeling Cindy tense beside me every time her mother opens her mouth. Which is constantly. The woman is like a shark that'll die if it stops moving, or in her case, stops talking. But I've got this. I've talked my way out of police stations, into locked buildings, and through three state lines with contraband. One bougie mother isn't going to—

The cousin, Sarah, I think, the one with the pinched face like she's constantly smelling something bad, practically runs to the table. She's actually gasping as though she's just witnessed a murder. Or won the lottery. With this family, probably the same thing.

Everyone stares at her. Even the mother stops mid-sentence, which might be a fucking miracle.

"Oh my God," Sarah pants. "I just spotted Cynthia kissing the eye-patched waiter in the hallway!"

The silence that follows is beautiful. Absolute. The kind where you can hear someone's wineglass settling against their plate three seats away.

Then everyone turns to stare at me.

Well played, Holt. Well fucking played. Goddammit.

My brain kicks into overdrive. Option one: act shocked and betrayed, storm off dramatically. Problem: leaves Cindy alone with these vultures. Option two: laugh it off, make it nothing. Problem: Sarah is practically vibrating with the scandal of it all, and these people are looking for blood. Option three: own it completely, make it weird for them instead of us.

I go with option two with a twist of three.

"Ha!" I bark out a laugh that's probably too loud. "Classic Cynthia. She's always been a prankster." I take another sip of my blue nightmare, casual as fuck. "The waiter is a friend of ours. In fact, Arrow, the owner, is also a close friend. She's just being friendly."

"That didn't look friendly to me," Sarah insists, eyes glittering with malice. "He was practically humping her against the wall."

"Sarah!" Victoria's voice is sharp, but she doesn't follow up with anything. They're all watching me now, waiting for the explosion. The betrayed boyfriend. The scene.

Fuck that.

I need to play this right. Can't look weak, can't look cuckolded, but also can't throw Cindy under the bus when she walks back. These people are looking for any crack in the armor, any sign that their precious Cynthia is the fuckup they want her to be.

Time to be the boyfriend who's so confident, so secure, that kissing friends is just normal Tuesday shit.

Before I can get another word out, Cindy appears at the entrance of the marquee. She's pale except for her lips, which are definitely pinker than before, slightly swollen. Fuck me, Holt really went for it. Her hair is a tiny bit mussed, and there's panic, defiance, and maybe a touch of well-kissed satisfaction in her expression.

I give her my biggest, tightest smile. The one that says "We need to talk" while looking like "I love you so much."

"Baby, so good to have you back!"

I stare at her, trying to communicate "Play along or we're fucked" with just my eyes. She sits, and I immediately wrap my arm around her back, pulling her against me hard enough that she lets out a little *oof*.

"Funny thing," I say, laughing like this is the best joke I've heard all year. "Sarah here insists you were making out with the pirate waiter, but I was just explaining that Holt is a friend and you two are close."

I lean in to kiss her temple, whispering against her skin, "The wolves are ready to attack."

She stiffens for a second, then lifts her chin in that way that means she's about to get defiant. Good. Defiant Cindy is better than panicked Cindy.

"It's true. He's a friend," she insists, voice steadier than I expected. "We're all close, actually. Nothing to worry about." Then she grins, and I know she's about to say something that'll either save us or damn us. "I mean, he's a very good friend of ours, and he's super European with all the kisses. You should see him and Luke go at it."

She chuckles, and I raise an eyebrow at her. The fuck is she doing?

But then I see the way the family is leaning in, confused but intrigued. She's making it weird for them. Brilliant.

"Oh, yeah." I grin, deciding to run with it. "I get in there. Tongue and all."

I'm chuckling now, and Cindy cuts me a side glare that promises retribution later. Worth it for the way Aunt Beatrice looks like she's swallowed a lemon whole.

"It's nothing," Cindy says firmly. "Absolutely nothing to worry about."

"Right," I add, looking around the table with my

best shit-eating grin. "But it's nice to see the family so concerned about Cynthia. Really heartwarming."

The sarcasm is thick enough to cut, but I keep smiling. Let them figure out if I'm serious or not.

Arrow appears then like some kind of restaurant ninja, all smooth and in control. "The next course is ready to be served. Pan-seared scallops with cauliflower puree and pancetta."

He looks at me with a question in his eyes, and I just shrug. Best thing we can do now is act like it's nothing and move forward. These people are watching us like we're their personal reality show.

The waiters emerge with plates, and of course Holt is among them. Every eye in the place tracks his movement as he approaches our table. He's grinning, practically bouncing on his feet.

As he sets a plate in front of me, he clips my chair again. Harder this time.

"Oops," he states, not even trying to sound sorry. "These new shoes."

Two can play this game, asshole.

I pull Cindy closer. "Come here, my gorgeous Omega." Then I kiss her. Not a peck, not a friendly smooch, but a real kiss. The kind that stakes a claim. The kind that says *mine* in a language everyone understands.

She makes a surprised sound against my mouth, but then she's kissing me back, and for a second, I forget we're performing. Her lips are soft, and she tastes like wine and something sweet, maybe lip gloss. When I pull back, her eyes are a little glazed.

Holt has stopped moving. Just standing there holding an empty tray, watching us.

Yeah, that's right, fucker. We share Omegas no problem, but you trying to sabotage me? That's a different game entirely.

Cindy nudges me slightly, coming back to herself, then grins at her mother. "Try the food, Mother. You'll be blown away."

Victoria picks up her fork as if it might be poisoned, eyes never leaving us.

Holt comes back with the next round, and this fucking time, he actually spills salad into my lap. Mixed greens with what feels like an entire bottle of vinaigrette.

"Oh, shit," he says, not sounding sorry at all. "Let me—"

"It's fine!" I laugh, probably too loud, grabbing my napkin. The dressing is already soaking through my jeans. "Happens all the time. Slippery hands, right?"

Victoria's eyes narrow to slits. "Are you sure you two aren't fighting over my daughter?"

The table goes quiet again. These people love their dramatic silences.

Cindy laughs, but it's got an edge of hysteria. "If that were true, then I'd just take them both as my Alphas."

I swear to God you could hear a pin drop. Hell, you could hear a feather drop. In space.

"Cynthia!" Victoria's voice could freeze hell. "Wash your mouth out this instant."

"Mother, I was joking—"

"In our family, Omegas only take one Alpha." She's using that tone that probably traumatized Cindy as a kid. "I know many don't care about propriety anymore, and it's trendy to be... progressive. But no Williams succumbs to that kind of behavior."

"It's not about succumbing—" Cindy starts.

"Men shouldn't grovel after Omegas," Victoria continues like Cindy hasn't spoken. "It should be the other way around. An Omega should be grateful for an Alpha's attention, not collecting them like... like trading cards."

"Trading cards?" Cindy's voice is incredulous.

"You know what I mean."

"I really don't."

I decide to jump in before this escalates. "I'd support Cynthia if she wanted another Alpha."

Every head swivels toward me.

"Nothing wrong with adapting to modern traditions," I continue, casual as fuck while wiping salad dressing off my lap. "World's changing. People are finding what works for them instead of what worked for their grandparents."

"That's very... progressive of you," Aunt Beatrice says.

"Very realistic of me," I correct. "Cynthia is incredible. Of course other Alphas would want her. I'd be more worried if they didn't."

"You wouldn't be jealous?" One of the twins asks.

"Of what? I'm the one here with her, aren't I?" I squeeze Cindy's hand. "Besides, jealousy is just insecurity with a fancy name."

"How modern," Victoria says coldly.

"How honest," I shoot back.

We all turn to our food, which is admittedly fucking amazing. Arrow might be a pain in my ass, but the man and his team can cook. The scallops are perfect, buttery and sweet, and the cauliflower puree is so smooth it's basically silk.

I keep Cindy's hand in mine while we eat, rubbing my thumb over her knuckles. She's still tense, but every touch seems to relax her a fraction. I can't stop thinking about earlier, going down on her in her bedroom, how she tasted, how she sounded when she came.

My cock throbs, and I shift in my seat. *Hell, not now.* But my brain is already painting pictures: Cindy spread out on this fancy table, dress pushed up, me between her thighs, making her forget every single person here exists. Making her scream my name loud enough that her mother would have an actual heart attack.

"Luke?" Cindy's voice breaks through my fantasy.

"Hmm?"

"Mother asked you a question."

Shit. "Sorry, I was distracted by how beautiful you look tonight."

Smooth save, if I do say so myself.

Arrow returns to check on everyone, moving

around the table with the kind of grace that comes from years of dealing with difficult customers. When he reaches Victoria, she practically lights up.

"The food is absolutely divine," she gushes, and it's the first genuine thing I've heard from her all night. "Actually, I wanted to ask. Do you ever host weddings?"

Arrow pauses, scratching his chin.

She gestures to the far end of the table where a nervous-looking couple sits. The guy, Trevor, I think, next to a tiny blonde Omega who has barely said a word all night, appears to be trying to become invisible.

"Trevor and Monica are getting married," Victoria continues. "They wanted a Halloween wedding, very last minute, I'm afraid."

"We don't usually—" Arrow starts.

"But surely for family?" Victoria's voice has that edge that means she's not really asking. "It would be small, intimate. Nothing you couldn't handle."

Arrow looks at me, and I can read the "What the fuck?" in his eyes perfectly.

"As long as it's small," he says finally, probably because he knows Cindy needs this to go well. "I don't see why not."

Victoria claps her hands. Actually fucking claps like she's five years old.

"Wonderful!" Then she turns to me, and every instinct I have starts screaming *Danger!* "Luke, dear."

Nothing good ever starts with that.

"You wouldn't mind hosting a small wedding at your huge mansion, would you? Arrow can serve the food at your place too."

I blink. "What?"

"Well, it's such short notice with Halloween about two weeks away, and you just finished telling us how spacious your home is."

The table is watching us again. This is a test. A trap. She wants me to admit I don't have a mansion, or refuse and look like an asshole.

"That's really short notice, Mother," Cindy says quickly. "I don't think—"

"Oh, sweetheart, anything's possible if you put your mind to it." Victoria's smile is as sharp as glass. "Right, Luke? Such a good way to be welcomed into the family, by helping us."

She's got me boxed in neat as you please. Say no, and I'm the asshole who won't help family. Say yes, and I've got two weeks to open the home I live in with Arrow and Holt to them.

"But you don't have time to arrange a wedding," I say. "Living so far away—"

"Well, then it just means I'll have to stay in town until the wedding." Her smile widens. "Get everything arranged with a few of our family members. It's the least I can do."

Cindy goes rigid beside me. Her mother, staying in town until Halloween. Planning a wedding. Being around constantly.

I glance at Arrow, who shrugs and gives me a tiny nod.

For Cindy, I think and squeeze her hand.

"I don't think it'll be a big ask," I say finally. "We can help them out."

Cindy's head whips toward me, eyes wide.

"Didn't we have something that weekend?" she asks, jaw clenched so tight I'm worried she'll crack a tooth.

"Oh, sweetheart," Victoria coos. "Surely nothing is more important than family."

Cindy stares at me, and there's something desperate in her eyes. But also... trust? Maybe? She gives the tiniest nod.

"Yes," I say, sealing our fate. "We're happy to host a small wedding."

Cindy's eyes widen even more, and she exhales so loudly that everyone hears it. Her whole body is tense against mine, vibrating with the need to run or fight, or both.

"How wonderful!" Victoria claps again. "Trevor, Monica, isn't that generous?"

Trevor looks like he wants to die. Monica hasn't moved. Might actually be frozen in place.

"Super generous," Trevor manages.

"We'll start planning tomorrow," Victoria announces. "I'll need to see the house soon, of course."

"Of course," I echo, already mentally exhausted from these games.

"And, Cynthia, you'll help. It'll be such good practice for your own wedding."

"My own—" Cindy starts.

"When the time comes, naturally." Victoria's smile could cut diamond. "Though, at your age, one shouldn't wait too long. You need to act while your heat is active. And eggs don't last forever."

"Mother!"

"What? It's biology, sweetheart."

Cindy is shifting in her seat, looking ready to explode. Her hand in mine is shaking, and there's a flush creeping up her neck that means she's about to say something that'll make this worse.

"More wine?" I ask the table at large. "I think we need more wine."

"Excellent idea," Arrow adds after standing there in silence. "I'll have someone bring more bottles."

Holt appears with wine, because of course he does. As he pours, he manages to spill just a tiny bit on my shoulder.

"Oops," he says again.

"You're having a rough night," I observe. "Maybe you should take a break."

"I'm fine," he declares, staring at me with his one good eye. "Just getting warmed up."

"Boys," Cindy says, warning in her voice.

We both look at her and then at each other. There's a moment where I genuinely consider punching him right here at this fancy table in front of her whole family. It would almost be worth it.

"Another excellent course," Victoria announces, pulling attention back to herself. "Though I do wonder about the portion sizes. In my day, we didn't need seven courses to feel satisfied."

"Different times," I say. "Now people want the experience, not just the food."

"Hmm." She makes it sound like I've said something stupid.

The next course arrives. It's some kind of fish with a sauce that probably has a French name I can't pronounce.

The rest of dinner is more of the same. Subtle insults disguised as questions. Judgments wrapped in concern. Holt bumping into me every time he passes. At one point, he actually drops a fork on my foot. The tines first, because of course.

But I handle it all with a smile. Because that's what you do for the people you care about.

"Dessert!" Arrow announces, and I've never been happier to hear that word in my life. "Chocolate lava cake with vanilla bean ice cream and raspberry coulis."

"How decadent," Victoria observes.

"How delicious," I counter, already digging in.

It is divine. Rich and warm and exactly what I need to get through the rest of this nightmare.

"So, about the wedding," Victoria starts, because apparently we're not done with that particular torture.

"What about it?" Cindy asks, voice flat.

"We'll need to coordinate. Colors, flowers, food."

"It's Trevor and Monica's wedding," Cindy points out.

"Yes, but they're young. They need guidance."

Monica looks like she wants to say something but doesn't. Trevor just stares at his dessert.

"I'm sure they have their own ideas, especially if they want it Halloween themed," I say.

"Do you?" Victoria asks them directly.

"We... we thought black and orange," Monica whispers. "Halloween decorations."

"How... festive." Victoria's tone suggests she'd rather die. "We'll work on that."

"But—" Monica starts.

"Trust me, dear. You'll thank me later."

Monica shrinks back into her chair. Cindy's hand tightens on mine.

"Let them have what they want," Cindy says. "It's their wedding."

"And they want my help," Victoria says smoothly. "Don't you?"

Monica nods, but it looks forced. Trevor doesn't even respond.

"See? Everyone's happy."

No one looks happy. Except maybe Sarah, who's probably already planning how to gossip about tonight to everyone she knows.

"Well," I say, standing and pulling Cindy up with me. "This has been lovely, but we should get going."

"Already?" Victoria frowns. "But we've barely caught up."

"Work tomorrow," I lie. "Early morning."

"On Sunday?"

"Security never sleeps."

"How inconvenient."

"How profitable."

She stands too, and suddenly everyone's getting up, that awkward dance of goodbye hugs nobody wants.

Victoria air-kisses Cindy again, then turns to me.

"It was... interesting meeting you, Luke."

"Likewise."

"Take care of my daughter."

"Always."

"We'll see."

The threat is subtle but clear. She's not done with us. Not even close.

We make our rounds, saying goodbye, which takes forever because rich people apparently need to air-kiss and make false promises about getting together soon with every single person individually. Aunt Beatrice actually pats my cheek like I'm five, telling me *I'm rough around the edges but moldable.* I resist the urge to bite her fingers.

Finally, fucking finally, we're turning to leave. I can see the exit, freedom just twenty feet away. My hand finds Cindy's lower back, guiding her toward salvation.

"Cynthia, sweetheart," her mother calls.

We both freeze.

"Do you have a moment, please?" She's already walking out of the marquee and into the restaurant toward a hallway that's away from the main dining room.

Cindy turns to follow, and I move inside the restaurant with her, but Victoria stops at the hallway entrance, one perfectly manicured hand raised.

"Just my daughter and me, if you don't mind."

She says it like it's a request, but her eyes make it clear that it's not. This is a dismissal. A power play. A reminder that no matter what happened at dinner, Cindy is still her daughter first, my girlfriend second.

Cindy stares at me, and there's something desperate in her eyes. But also resignation. She knows this dance.

"I'll be right back," she says quietly.

I want to say no. Want to tell Victoria to fuck off, that Cindy doesn't have to go anywhere she doesn't want to. But this isn't my fight. Not yet.

"I'll be right here," I tell Cindy, making sure Victoria hears the promise in it.

Her smile is all ice. "This won't take long."

She turns and walks down the hallway, clearly expecting Cindy to follow. And after a moment, Cindy does, shooting me one last look over her shoulder before disappearing around the corner.

Sometimes the hardest thing to do is nothing at all.

15

CINDY

The hallway stretches longer than it should, or maybe that's just my anxiety making everything feel distorted. Mother's heels click against the hardwood while I follow, each step feeling as though I'm walking toward my own execution.

She stops near a small alcove with two chairs and a ridiculously expensive-looking orchid on a side table. Of course she'd pick the most private spot possible. No witnesses for whatever psychological warfare she's about to unleash.

"Sit," she commands, and I hate that my body obeys automatically, twenty years of conditioning overriding my adult autonomy.

She doesn't sit. Instead, she stands over me, hands clasped in front of her like she's about to deliver a sermon. After that dinner, the interrogation, the judgment, and the wedding ambush, I'm as stressed as I've ever been. My nerves are shot, my head is pounding, and I can still taste the wine I gulped down while trying to survive. Might as well hear whatever insanity she's cooked up now. Get it all over with in one horrible night.

"You may think I'm a fool," she begins, voice eerily calm. "And it hurts me to think you do. But I bring the family here, create this opportunity for reconciliation, and you turn up with that man, thinking I wouldn't see right through your charade."

My blood turns to ice. Every cell in my body goes cold.

Fuck. Were we that obvious? That bad?

"I don't know what you're—"

"A man like that would never be interested in you, Cynthia." She says it so matter-of-factly. "You're making a mockery of our name with this pathetic display."

Something hot and sharp rises in my chest, cutting through the ice. I pull my shoulders back, trying to find some spine in the wreckage of my confidence.

"That's just cruel, Mother. To not even accept that I could attract a man like Luke." My voice quivers but I push through. "Or even Holt, for that matter."

She shakes her head slowly, that pitying look that used to reduce me to tears as a teenager. "What was that about? Kissing someone else? Did you pay him too so you could show us all how these men want you? How desirable you are?"

My hands clench in my lap, nails digging into my

palms. "I'm really getting angry now—" I start, but she cuts me off with a sharp gesture. However, I ignore her. "Look, you invited me to dinner. I didn't want to catch up, and then you brought everyone to bombard me. I had no clue you were bringing so many people!"

"If you're not going to be honest with me, Cynthia, I will find out the truth." She leans forward slightly, and I smell her perfume, the same Chanel she's worn my whole life, now forever associated with criticism and disappointment. "That's the reason I'm staying in town. To find out what you're hiding from me."

"There's nothing—"

"And when I find out that you aren't really with Luke…" She pauses for effect, letting the threat build. "I will drag you back home by any means necessary. You can either stop embarrassing the family name voluntarily, or I'll stop it for you."

I'm stunned. Angry. Sick with how small she makes me feel even now, after two years of freedom. But more than that, I'm terrified because I know she means it. This isn't an idle threat. Mother has connections, money, and a vindictive streak wider than the Mississippi.

"For your information," I hear myself saying, voice stronger than I feel. "Luke and I love each other. We've even talked about marriage."

Fuck. Digging myself deeper. But at this stage, I'll say anything to get her out of my life. Because she's the kind of person who would actually stay in town for a year just to prove me wrong. I shouldn't care. I'm an adult. I have my own life. But I also know she wouldn't be above having someone literally kidnap me if she thought it would save the family reputation.

And I'm exhausted. So fucking exhausted. I just want to be left alone.

"Then it's easy," Mother says, and her smile is the one that used to precede the worst punishments. "You have until Halloween at the wedding to show me this is real."

"What?"

"About two weeks. Prove to me that this relationship is genuine, and I give you my word that I'll leave you alone for good." She tilts her head. "I know that's what you want, nothing to do with your own mother."

"Maybe—"

"We will disown you, just so you know." She says it conversationally, as though she's mentioning the weather. "Your father is furious. But that's what you want, isn't it? To be free of us?"

I can't speak. Can't breathe. After everything, it comes down to this—two weeks to prove that a fake relationship is real or lose my freedom forever.

"The choice is yours, sweetheart." She pats my arm, the touch burning through my dress. "Halloween. The wedding. Show me that what you have with Luke is real, or come home where you belong."

"I-I don't need to show you any of that," I stammer, and she glares at me.

"Then expect to see a whole lot more of us in your life here in town or wherever you run, as we will find you," she snaps, her threat clear. She's not going to leave me alone, is she? Proving to her I'm in a relationship is my way out, though part of me worries she won't give up even then.

She turns and marches out, leaving me alone in the hallway with an expensive orchid and the ruins of my life.

I'm trembling. My whole body shakes with rage and fear and this bone-deep tiredness that makes me want to curl up on the floor and just give up.

I hate her. God, I loathe her so much it feels like poison in my veins. The idea of leaving town plays through my mind—pack up General Flufferton and disappear, start over somewhere she'll never find me. Vancouver maybe, or Portland, or, hell, Alaska.

But I'm tired of running. So fucking sick of looking over my shoulder, jumping at shadows, wondering when she'll show up to drag me back to *that* life. This is my chance to settle it once and for all. Two weeks of convincing performance, and I'm free forever.

My nerves pull tight at the thought of making this believable. Luke has already done so much. Cut his hair, faced down my family, and offered his house for a wedding. Can I ask him to keep pretending, to sell this lie even harder?

But I don't just have Luke.

I have three men who live in that mansion. Who've each shown me more kindness in a few days than my family has in years. Three dangerous, complicated, beautiful men who might just be crazy enough to help me pull this off. Men who insist I'm their scent match —I don't know about that yet because my emotions are so out of control that I don't know what I'm feeling. But maybe that will work in our favor…

So, the question is, how far am I willing to go to sell this lie?

I straighten my back, stand, and walk out of that hallway. I just take Luke's hand when I reach him and let him guide me toward the exit. His fingers interlace with mine immediately, no questions asked, and we escape into the October night.

The cold air is freedom after the suffocating atmosphere. Luke helps me into Holt's massive truck, and we pull away from Savor without a word. He drives for a few minutes, then parks under a huge oak tree a few roads down, its branches creating shadows in the streetlight.

We sit in silence for a moment before he reaches over, his hand warm on my knee. "What did she say? Are you okay?"

I turn to face him, and the words pour out. How she saw through our fake relationship, said he'd never be interested in someone like me. The threat to drag me home. The ultimatum—prove it's real by Halloween or lose my freedom forever.

"That fucking bitch." His hand tightens on the steering wheel until his knuckles go white. "You could have any man you wanted. She's just belittling you so you'll run back to her." He turns to me, eyes fierce. "Fuck if I'll allow that."

I'm shaking now, the adrenaline crash hitting hard. Luke reaches over and pulls me against him, awkward with the center console between us but somehow still comforting.

"So we need a plan," he says into my hair. "You know I'm in. You don't even need to ask. Fuck, if we need to, we'll get married tonight. I'll get you a big fat diamond ring and prove her wrong."

A giggle escapes me, surprising us both. Part of me thinks it's actually romantic, this crazy offer from a man I barely know.

"She won't believe it if it happens that fast. It has to seem real. She has to see the reality of our romance play out."

"Well then, I know what we're going to do." He pulls back to look at me. "You're coming to our place tonight, and we're talking it out. Then stuffing our faces with ice cream."

I laugh, a real one this time. "I actually would like that. But oh, I need to get General Flufferton, my cat. He's alone at home."

"Done." He starts the car immediately. "Let's go get your demon cat."

As we drive, he glances at me. "I've met people like your mother. Super manipulative, always moving the goalposts. No matter what you do to prove yourself, she won't believe it because it's not about the truth. It's about control."

"So why bother?"

"Because we do this for you, not her. We get

through the wedding, and if Arrow and Holt buy into it too, which they will, what's she going to do if we keep you at our side constantly? Can't prove it's fake if we never break character."

"I guess." I stare out the window, watching Whispering Grove blur past. Mixed emotions churn in my stomach—gratitude, fear, and this horrible guilt about dragging these men into my family's insanity.

We reach my townhouse, and Luke follows me inside and picks up General Flufferton, who immediately starts purring at the sight of him.

"Pack some clothes," Luke says. "We're not letting you stay here alone tonight with your family in town. You need company."

I grin despite everything and grab a bag, throwing in clothes and essentials. On impulse, I also take the box of cookies I made yesterday and some of the food from the fridge, all the stuff I'd prepared thinking Mother would come to my place.

"Can't let it go to waste," I explain.

Soon we're back in the truck, bags in the back, General Flufferton in my lap trying his best to migrate to Luke's lap despite the fact that he's driving.

"I could calm you down again," Luke says with a wicked grin. "Like before."

But I'm laughing. "You wish."

"What? I was having fantasies about it during dinner. Devouring you right there on that fancy table."

I gasp, heat flooding through me. "You were not!"

"Was too. You in that dress, looking all elegant and untouchable? Made me want to touch everything."

General Flufferton chooses that moment to balance on the center console with his front paws on Luke's shoulder, sniffing his hair.

"I think someone approves of you," I say.

"Goddamn, this cat is huge. It's like a panther. Is it going to maul me?"

"Only if you stop petting him."

Luke manages to drive one-handed while scratching behind General Flufferton's ears, and my traitorous cat purrs loud enough to rival the engine.

Then we turn into a driveway, and my mouth drops open.

There's a security gate with a keypad and cameras. Luke punches in a code, and the gates swing open to reveal a driveway that seems to go on forever, winding up toward the mountains.

"What the—"

And then I see it.

The house, no, the mansion, which sits at the base of the mountains like something out of a magazine. It's enormous, all stone and wood and huge windows that probably have million-dollar views. The grounds are manicured but not fussy, with huge old trees and a pool house off to one side. There's a six-car garage, outdoor lighting that gives everything a warm glow, and is that a fucking fountain?

"You live here?" My voice comes out squeaky.

"All three of us, yeah."

The house itself is a mix of modern and rustic, with dark wood beams and stone accents.

"Are you three secret billionaires?" I breathe. "My mom might faint at seeing this. She'd probably try to marry you herself."

Luke fake gags and we both laugh, the sound slightly hysterical. General Flufferton nudges his head against Luke's arm until he gets more pets.

"Told you he likes you," I say.

We climb out, me holding the cat while Luke manages all my bags, and head to the huge front double doors. When he opens one and switches on the lights, my eyes bulge out.

The entryway is two stories high with a grand staircase that curves up. The hardwood floors gleam, dark and rich, leading to rooms that branch off in multiple directions. There's art on the walls and a chandelier that's modern but elegant, all crystal and clean lines. To the left, I glimpse what must be a living room with leather furniture and a fireplace big enough to roast a whole pig. To the right, a dining room with a table for twelve.

"You definitely did well in your previous jobs," I say with a wink.

He chuckles. "Come on, let me show you around."

I set General Flufferton down, and he immediately starts exploring, tail high with confidence. We follow at a more sedate pace, Luke's hand on my lower back guiding me. Every room is gorgeous and masculine but warm, expensive but lived-in. There's a large, modern kitchen with everything you need, a media room with a screen that takes up an entire wall, and even a library that smells of leather and old books. Because of course the broody Beasts have a fairy-tale library. What's next, enchanted furniture?

His hand keeps finding reasons to touch me, guiding me through doorways, steadying me on the stairs, brushing hair from my face. Each touch sends electricity through me, and I'm hyperaware of how alone we are in this huge house.

"And this," he says, opening a door on the second floor, "is something that came with the house, but we enhanced it."

I step inside and freeze. "Is this... is this an Omega heat room?"

"Yeah. We kept it, thinking someday we'd settle down, find someone who'd need it."

The room is incredible. Soft lighting, temperature controls on the wall, soundproofing evident in the thick door. The bed, or more like nest area, really is massive and sunken slightly into the floor, surrounded by built-in shelving filled with blankets, pillows, and throws in every texture imaginable. There's a walk-in bathroom with a shower big enough for six people and a tub that's basically a small pool.

"We stocked it with supplies," Luke explains, opening some drawers. "Still need to add food, snacks, hydration stations, our clothes..."

I peek into one drawer and immediately slam it shut, face burning. The assortment of... items... in there is extensive. Lubricants in every variety, toys I've only seen in online stores that I'd never admit to browsing, massage oils, things I don't even recognize.

"Wow, you were thorough," I manage.

"Only the best for Omega needs."

I walk around the room, trailing my fingers over the soft fabrics, the little details that show thought and care. It's so comfortable, so perfectly designed, that part of me wants to curl up in that nest right now and never leave.

"This is dangerous," I say without thinking.

"What?"

"This room. It's too perfect. Makes me want things I shouldn't want."

Luke strolls closer, and suddenly the room feels much smaller. "Like what?"

I swallow hard. "Like staying."

The word hangs between us, heavy with implication.

"I'd love that. Let me make you hot chocolate," he says. "We can relax because meeting your family was damn tense and exhausting."

"Tell me about it."

We head back downstairs, General Flufferton racing ahead of us like he already owns the place.

"I need to put some of the food in the fridge," I say, grateful for something normal to focus on.

In the kitchen, we work side by side, me finding space in their large, double-door refrigerator, him making hot chocolate from actual chocolate, not powder. General Flufferton supervises from his perch on the counter, occasionally batting at Luke's hand for attention.

Part of me can't help imagining what it would be like living in a place like this. Waking up to mountain views, cooking in this dream kitchen, curling up in that library with a book. Having these men around, their laughter filling the empty spaces, their presence making it feel like home.

But guilt crashes through the fantasy. These men have been nothing but kind to me, and I'm dragging them into my family's insanity. What if there's only so much of that they can take? What if Mother's manipulation drives them away? What if—

"Stop overthinking," Luke says, handing me a mug of the richest hot chocolate I've ever seen. "You get this concentrated expression on your face. Like you're arguing with yourself." He touches my cheek gently. "We're in this because we want to be."

"You barely know me."

"I know enough."

"My family is insane."

"So are ours, just differently."

"My mother will make your life hell."

"She can try." He grins. "I've faced down worse than one controlling mother."

"Have you?"

"How hard can it be?"

I laugh despite myself. "Famous last words."

"Worth it, though." He's looking at me with that

hypnotic stare again, the one that leaves me forgetting why this is supposed to be fake. "You're worth it."

And for a moment, in this too-perfect kitchen with the best hot chocolate I've ever had and a man who makes me feel things I shouldn't, I almost believe him.

Luke shows me to the guest room with warm lighting, soft bedding, and lots of space. I take my time getting changed, letting the quiet settle around me for a minute, giving myself a moment to breathe.

Now I'm back in the living room, wearing comfortable clothes, the ones I grabbed during my hasty packing. Worn jeans that feel like pajamas, and an oversized burgundy sweater. My feet are bare, toes digging into the plush rug.

The living room is huge, with the stone fireplace taking up most of one wall. The TV is mounted above the mantel, one of those ridiculous sizes that make you feel like you're in a movie theater. The L-shaped couch faces both the fire and the screen, dark leather that's butter-soft and deep enough to get lost in.

I'm curled into one corner with General Flufferton sprawled across my lap, purring like he's having a conversation with himself. Luke made me a grilled cheese because he insisted that I'd barely touched my dinner with all that chaos, and it's perfect. Golden brown, cheese oozing, cut diagonally because apparently that's the only proper way.

Luke is sitting on the adjacent section of the couch, and I keep stealing glances at him. He's changed into worn jeans and a black T-shirt that stretches across his chest when he moves. His bare feet are propped on the coffee table, and he keeps running his hand through his short hair as though he's still not used to the length. Or maybe he's restless. His fingers drum against his thigh, then still, then start again.

The space between us feels electric. I want to move closer, to curl into his side as if I belong there. My body keeps betraying me, leaning toward him, tracking every movement of his hands, noticing how his throat moves when he takes a drink. The heat from the fire has nothing on the heat building under my skin every time our eyes meet.

On the TV, *Bon Appétit, Your Majesty* is playing. It's about a modern pastry chef who's mysteriously transported to the Joseon era in Korea and has to convince the palace she's not a lunatic.

"She's arguing with the prince right now," Luke says. "She doesn't believe he's actually royalty but thinks it's cosplay or a prank."

"She just called him a pampered aristocrat with delusions," I mutter, smirking over my mug.

He laughs. "Latest episode I watched, she tried to make a French dessert with no modern tools and nearly got chased out of the kitchen."

"You really love this show."

"I'm invested." He grins. "Been waiting for new episodes every Thursday. We're only on episode nine overall."

General Flufferton stretches up and snags the

corner of my sandwich, coming away with a string of cheese.

"General! That's not yours!"

He ignores me completely, purring louder as he chews his prize.

Luke laughs. "I literally just gave him fresh salmon. The expensive stuff from the fish market."

"Clearly, stolen cheese tastes better." I guard the rest of my sandwich. "It's the thievery that adds flavor."

"Criminal cat. He'll fit right in here."

I take another bite, careful to keep it away from grabbing paws. "Speaking of which... if you could time-travel anywhere, where would you go?"

He rubs his chin, thinking, and I get distracted by his hands. Those fingers that were inside me earlier today. The scrape of stubble under his palm. His bottom lip caught between his teeth as he considers.

"Prohibition Chicago," he says finally. "1920s."

"Seriously? With Al Capone and tommy guns?"

"Think about it. Everything was illegal, but everyone was doing it anyway. Speakeasies hidden behind barbershops. Jazz music. Everyone dressed sharp even though they were all criminals." He shifts, and his knee brushes mine, sending electricity up my thigh. "Plus, I'd have been perfect for it. Protection for bootleggers, security for illegal clubs. Same shit I do now but with better music."

"And significantly more murder."

"Details." His grin is wicked. "Besides, I've survived

worse than—" He catches himself. "I mean, I'm tough. I'd manage."

"Sure you would, tough guy." I roll my eyes but I'm smiling. "Let me guess—you'd romance some flapper and die in a shoot-out."

"Nah. I'd find my dame and convince her to run away with me to Paris or something. Live the expatriate life. Write terrible poetry. Drink absinthe."

"You write poetry?"

"Terribly. There's a difference."

"Show me sometime."

"Never." But he's staring at me with heat in his eyes. "Your turn. Where would you go?"

"Ancient Egypt. Specifically, Cleopatra's court."

"Of course you'd pick the cat civilization."

"They were gods there! Worshipped! Mummified when they died!" I gesture at General Flufferton. "He would have been treated like royalty."

"He already is."

"Plus those clothes, the gold, the makeup, the headdresses. And I'd finally solve the mystery of the pyramids."

"There's no mystery. It was thousands of workers and clever engineering."

"But what if it wasn't?" I finish my sandwich, licking cheese off my finger and definitely not noticing how Luke's eyes track the movement. "What if there was something else? Lost technology or—"

"Aliens. You think it was aliens."

Before I can defend my position on ancient aliens,

General Flufferton notices my empty plate. The betrayal in his green eyes is Oscar-worthy. He stands, stretches dramatically, and saunters over to Luke, climbing directly onto his chest with zero regard for organs or breathing.

"Jesus, fuck—" Luke wheezes as the huge cat settles on his sternum, nose to nose with him. "This is how I die. Suffocated by a judgmental cat."

General Flufferton chirps, pressing his forehead against Luke's chin in a headbutt that's somehow both aggressive and affectionate.

"He's testing you," I inform him. "Seeing if you're worthy of his affection."

"By crushing my lungs?"

"It's a rigorous screening process." I giggle at the sight.

The cat starts purring so loudly that it sounds like a motor, kneading his paws into Luke's chest.

"Okay, but aliens," I continue, trying not to laugh at Luke's face. "We can't be alone in the universe. The math doesn't work. Billions of galaxies, trillions of stars—"

"Oh, I agree completely." He manages to shift the cat slightly so he can breathe. "We're probably some alien kid's science project that got a C minus."

"Gave them consciousness but they still destroyed their own planet. Mediocre effort."

We're laughing when the front door opens, cold air sweeping in along with Arrow and Holt. They stop in the entryway, taking in the scene, me curled up,

Luke trapped under my cat, both of us grinning like idiots.

"Looks cozy," Arrow observes, shrugging out of his leather jacket.

"What happened after we left?" Luke asks.

"Waited for them to clear out. Your cousin Sarah was holding court by her car for twenty minutes in the parking lot, probably still talking about the hallway incident," Holt says.

My stomach drops. "Oh God."

"Hey." Arrow's voice gentles. "How are you doing? That was intense."

"I'm..." I pull my sleeves over my hands, a nervous habit. "I'm better now. Away from them. That was more than I expected."

"Ambush," Holt says simply. "Your mother planned that."

"Yeah." I sink deeper into the couch. "That's her specialty."

Arrow stretches, cracking his neck. "All right, I need to get out of these jeans before they become a second skin."

Holt gives a short laugh. "Yeah, I should change too."

They head upstairs, and Luke immediately tries to extract himself from under General Flufferton.

"Come on, buddy. Let me up."

The cat digs his claws in just enough to make a point.

"I need to get snacks for your mom."

General Flufferton instantly hops down and follows Luke to the kitchen, tail high, supervising as he raids the pantry.

"Luke, I just ate—"

"Not enough. Never enough. You picked at that fancy dinner like a bird."

He comes back with his arms full of three kinds of chips, chocolate bars, what resembles homemade cookies, cans of soda, bottles of water, and even a bowl of grapes.

"Did you rob a convenience store?"

"I didn't know what you'd want." He arranges everything on the coffee table like offerings. "I just want you happy. Fed. Comfortable."

The sincerity in his voice makes my chest tight. General Flufferton weaves between his legs, purring his approval.

"You're going to spoil me."

"That's the plan."

Before I can respond to that loaded statement, Holt comes back downstairs, and my brain empties completely.

Gray sweatpants that sit low on his hips, showing the V of muscle that disappears beneath the waistband. A white tank top that does nothing to hide the strength of his chest, the intricate tattoos covering his arms. His dark hair is mussed, and the medical eye patch somehow makes him more attractive, like danger personified.

He grabs a beer from the kitchen and drops onto

the couch on my other side, close enough that his thigh presses against mine. The heat of him seeps through my jeans immediately. My body responds to his closeness without permission, skin flushing, pulse jumping.

"Better not be watching ahead without me," he says, nodding at the TV, where the pastry chef is now teaching palace maids about a certain dish.

"Starting from episode one for Cindy," Luke assures him.

"Good." Holt takes a long pull of his beer, and I watch his throat work, the way his lips wrap around the bottle.

"After sending me that nuclear cocktail, you deserve punishment," Luke adds.

"That was payback for the concussion," Holt protests.

"And then you made it worse by kissing her in front of the family spy!" Luke replies.

My face heats. "Sorry about that. Terrible timing."

Holt's hand lands on my thigh, heavy and warm. "Not sorry. If Luke wanted the fake boyfriend role so bad, he gets to deal with the complications."

"You're just pissed I got there first," Luke shoots back.

"You got there because you gave me a head injury."

"Okay!" I interrupt, burning with embarrassment. "Can we not discuss the... incident? How's your eye?" I ask Holt. "Really?"

Holt's mouth opens to speak, but—

"Arr, matey, it be healin' right fine!" Arrow's voice

carries from the stairs in the worst pirate accent I've ever heard. "Though me depth perception be shot to hell, yarr!"

"Stop," Holt groans, but his lips twitch.

"What's that? Can't hear ye over the sound of me peg leg!" Arrow joins us, and my mouth goes dry for entirely different reasons.

His dark hair is wet from a shower, slicked back from his face, emphasizing those sharp cheekbones and dangerous eyes. He's wearing black slacks and a thin white T-shirt that clings to his chest, bare feet silent on the hardwood. He appears relaxed but ready to spring into action at any moment.

"Ye scurvy dogs best be treatin' me wench right!" He's really committing to this terrible accent.

"Arrow, I swear to God—" Holt starts.

"Or I'll make ye walk the plank into… uh… the pool!"

We're all laughing now, even Holt, though he tries to hide it behind his beer.

"You're all idiots," Holt mutters. "But you—" He squeezes my thigh, and I nearly combust. "You, I don't regret. That kiss was worth the chaos it caused Luke."

Arrow grabs another pack of chips and drops onto the couch between me and Luke, bouncing us all. I'm now pressed in with him and Holt, hyperaware of every point of contact. Arrow's arm goes across the back of the couch behind me, not quite touching but close enough that I sense the heat.

"So," Arrow says, voice back to normal. "We're really hosting a wedding here?"

Guilt crashes through me. "I'm so sorry. She just sprung it on us and—"

"Not your fault," Luke says firmly.

"Still. You can say no. Tell her the house isn't available or—"

"We're doing it." Luke's voice brooks no argument. "Besides, that woman needs to see exactly what she's messing with."

"What do you mean?"

Luke looks at the others, some silent communication passing between them, then tells them everything. The ultimatum. The threat to drag me home. The demand to prove that our relationship is real by Halloween.

"She said what?" Arrow's voice goes deadly quiet.

"She can't—" Holt starts.

"She can. She will." I twist my sleeves anxiously. "You don't know her. She has connections, money, this vindictive streak that—" I stop, swallow hard. "I'm so sorry for dragging you all into this disaster. Now you see why I ran. Why I changed my name. They destroy everything."

"Cindy." Luke moves closer. "Look at me."

I do, reluctantly.

"We're not going anywhere."

"This isn't pretend," Holt says quietly. "Not for us."

My heart stops. "What?"

"You're our scent match." Arrow's voice is matter of

fact. "All three of us react to you. You react to us. That's not fake."

"But—"

"Give us a chance to court you," Holt interrupts. "Properly. The way you deserve."

"We'll take you on real dates," Arrow adds. "Show your mother what actual romance looks like. Not that arranged bullshit she tried to force on you."

"Anything you need," Luke says. "We've got about two weeks to prove this is real because it is real."

I stare at them, these three dangerous, beautiful men who are offering... everything. "You're serious."

"Dead serious," Luke confirms.

"All three of you want to... date me?"

"We want more than that," Holt says quietly. "But we'll start with dates if that's what you're comfortable with."

My eyes burn with unshed tears. The hope in their faces, the sincerity, the way they're all leaning toward me, is overwhelming.

"I don't—I can't—" I take a shaky breath. "What if she wins? What if she proves it's fake somehow?"

"How can she prove something false?" Arrow asks.

"She's smart. Manipulative. She'll find a way to twist things—"

"Then we don't give her anything to twist." Luke's hand finds mine. "We show her the truth. That you're ours."

"That we're yours," Holt corrects.

"That this is real," Arrow finishes.

I stare at them, these men who barely know me but are ready to fight my mother for me.

"Halloween wedding," Luke muses. "Your mom is gonna hate every second of what we create."

"Hell yeah. We'll make it the gothest fucking wedding ever." Arrow grins. "Really lean into the Halloween theme."

"Skeleton centerpieces," Luke suggests.

"Black roses," Holt adds.

"Costume requirement," Arrow finishes.

I laugh despite everything. "Monica would actually love that."

"Then that's what she gets." Luke squeezes my hand. "Your mom has to smile through it all since she asked for our help."

The conversation continues, plans getting more ridiculous, and I find myself relaxing incrementally. But underneath the laughter and planning, dread curls in my stomach.

My family is poison. They seep into everything good and taint it, twist it, break it down until nothing is left but resentment and pain. These men who smell like they belong to me, who leave me desiring them, who study me like I'm precious, they don't understand what they're signing up for.

My mother will dig. She'll manipulate. She'll find every weakness and exploit it. And when she does, when she proves this is all fake—even though it's becoming terrifyingly real—she'll destroy them just for the sport of it.

"Your mom is about to learn not to fuck with what's ours," Holt says, the other two nodding.

The possessive growl in his voice warms me up. General Flufferton chooses that moment to walk across all our laps, demanding our attention, and the tension breaks into laughter.

But as I sit here, surrounded by these men who've decided I'm worth fighting for, I can't shake the feeling that I'm leading them into a war they can't win.

My mother always wins.

Always.

16

ARROW

The morning sun cuts through the October cold as I roll my Ducati out of the garage. Matte black paint shines in the light like a loaded weapon, every line sharp and coiled with intent. The engine purrs with that quiet, deadly hum that turns heads and makes SUV drivers double-check their mirrors. It's modified for speed and control with upgraded exhaust, track-tuned suspension, and clip-ons positioned exactly where I need them for riding that toes the line between thrill and felony. Then I'm off around the front door of the house.

Cindy is waiting on her front steps, bundled in that burgundy sweater that makes her skin look like cream, worn jeans that hug her gorgeous ass. Her soft curls glint in the morning light, all honey and gold, and when she sees me, her whole face transforms. That nervous smile, the way she tucks hair behind her ear, the little bounce on her toes... fuck me, this Omega is going to be my undoing.

"Your chariot awaits," I call out, pulling up to the curb.

She eyes the bike with a mix of excitement and terror. "I'm ready to ride with you again."

I grin, handing her the spare helmet, matte black with a tinted visor. "Safety first. Can't have *my* Omega getting damaged."

Her cheeks pink up, but she doesn't correct me. Progress.

She swings her leg over, settling behind me, and the first contact of her thighs against mine sends electricity straight to my cock. Then her arms wrap around my waist, tentative at first, like she's afraid to hold too tight.

"Closer," I growl. "Unless you want to fly off when I hit third gear."

She scoots forward, pressing her entire front against my back, and Christ. Her tits crushed against me, her thighs bracketing mine, her hands splayed across my stomach, I can feel her heartbeat through my leather jacket, quick and nervous. Her scent wraps around me despite the wind, that sweetness that makes me want to shout *Mine, claim, protect.*

"Hold tight," I warn, then gun it.

She squeaks, arms tightening to the point of pain, and I can't help but grin inside my helmet. The industrial district flies by, old warehouses being converted to trendy bullshit, graffiti giving way to commissioned murals, brew pubs and artisan whatever-the-fucks sprouting like mushrooms after rain. Whispering Grove Brewing Company sits in the middle of it all, a restored brick building with huge windows and a sign that tries too hard to look vintage.

I pull into the employee lot, killing the engine. The sudden silence feels loud.

"You can let go now," I say, amused.

"Give me a minute." Her voice is muffled against my back. "My legs forgot how to work."

I help her off, steadying her when she wobbles. Her face is flushed, eyes bright, and she's grinning like she just got off a roller coaster.

"That was terrifying," she says. "When can we do it again?"

"Anytime you want, gorgeous. I'm your personal taxi service now."

"I really should get a car—"

"Why? So you can sit in traffic like every other sucker while I'm out here living free?" I pull off my helmet, shaking out my hair. "Besides, I like having you plastered against me. Best part of my morning."

She ducks her head, but not before I catch her smile. "Thanks, Arrow. Really."

"Go brew your beer, woman. I'll pick you up at five."

She heads toward the employee entrance, and I watch every step because I'm a weak man and that ass in those jeans is a religious experience. She turns at the door, waves, and disappears inside.

I turn around, and that's when I spot him.

Across the street, maybe ten yards down, leaning against a busted streetlight like he owns the fucking sidewalk. Even without the helmet, even with the distance, I'd know that cocky stance anywhere.

Mack.

My baby brother, the walking disaster. He's watching the brewery entrance where Cindy just disappeared, and every protective instinct in my body goes nuclear.

I fire up the Ducati, not bothering with the helmet, which I keep in front of me. The engine roar echoes off the buildings as I tear across the street, sliding to a stop inches from his feet. Gravel sprays, and he doesn't even flinch.

"Nice entrance," Mack says, that shit-eating grin I remember from when he was twelve and setting fires in the backyard. "Very dramatic."

He looks rough. But not as bad as last time. Still has our mother's sharp cheekbones, our father's dark eyes, but there's a hardness there that wasn't present when he was a kid. His hair is longer, tied back off his face, new tattoos creeping up his neck. He's wearing ripped jeans, combat boots, and a leather vest over a black Henley.

"What the hell are you doing here?" I demand, not getting off the bike. "How did you know I'd be here?"

"Nice to see you too, brother." He spreads his arms like he wants a hug. "It's been years."

"Yeah, since you called from county lockup needing

bail money. I remember real well. Assault with a deadly weapon, wasn't it?"

He rolls his eyes, the gesture so familiar it hurts. "Fuck, man. I fucked up. Let it go."

"Not just once."

"I know, I know." Something is different. The manic energy that usually radiates off him like heat waves, it's muted. Controlled. "Look, I'm trying to—"

"What do you want this time?" I cut him off because Mack's apologies are like his promises—worth less than the air used to speak them.

He stretches his shoulders. "Nothing. I'm here for a job, figured it might be good to see my older brother. Maybe patch up some things."

I scoff before I can stop myself. It's automatic, like breathing. This usually means he needs money, a place to crash, or someone to take the fall for whatever stupid shit he's gotten into.

The last time I saw him, he'd shown up at Savor during the dinner rush, high as fuck, screaming the same thing about how I abandoned him, how I left him in that house with those monsters. Made a scene, broke dishes, scared customers. I had to physically throw him out while he cried and cursed me in equal measure. The time before that, he'd stolen my bike and wrapped it around a telephone pole. Cost me fifteen grand to rebuild.

But before all that, before the drugs and the crime and the endless fucking disappointments, he was just my little brother. The kid who'd sneak into my room during Dad's prayer sessions, when the screaming got too loud. Who'd share his dinner when they put me on restricted rations for defiance. Who cried for three days straight after the beatings when he got caught helping me.

I was sixteen. He was thirteen. And I left him there. Fuck, it still guts me because then things might have turned out differently.

"What job?" I ask, already knowing I won't like the answer.

His eyes flick to the brewery. "That chick on your bike. Your girl?"

Every muscle in my body goes rigid. "You'd better fucking believe it. But she's not for your eyes."

"Hey, I get it." He holds up his hands, and there's something in his expression... like resignation? "But that's the thing, Arrow. I'm here because of her, and we need to talk. There's something you need to know."

The words hit like ice water. Van. It has to be fucking Van. That piece of shit has reach, connections, the kind of money that buys muscle. And Mack, my desperate, always broke brother, would be exactly the kind of muscle he'd buy.

"For fuck's sake," I spit. "Fine. Follow me to the restaurant. We'll talk there."

I don't wait for a response, just tear out of the industrial district like hell itself is chasing me. In my mirrors, I find Mack scrambling to keep up, though he always could ride like the devil taught him personally. We weave through morning traffic, splitting lanes, running yellows that are definitely reds by the time we clear them.

Savor is empty when we arrive, won't open until lunch. I use the side entrance, flipping on lights as I go. The kitchen crew is already prepping—I can hear them chopping, can smell onions and garlic hitting hot oil—but the dining room is all mine.

I grab two beers from behind the bar, pop the caps with the edge of the counter, and slide into a corner booth. Mack follows.

"Place looks good," he admits. "Successful."

"It is." I push a beer across to him. "Now speak."

He takes a long pull, either gathering courage or buying time. With Mack, it's always hard to tell.

"A few days ago, I took a job through an MC." He's peeling the label off his beer, a nervous habit. "For some guy called Van. Wanted someone to do surveillance, maybe apply some pressure. On a girl."

My hand tightens on my bottle until I'm surprised it doesn't shatter. "Go on."

"It was for a pretty Omega, blonde, working at some brewery." He meets my eyes. "I had no fucking clue she was yours, Arrow. I swear on Mom's grave—"

"Don't think Mom's dead."

"Whatever. You know what I mean." He leans forward. "The job was simple. Watch her. Make her nervous. Maybe stage a few accidents, nothing serious. Make her want to leave town."

"And you took it."

"I needed the money." His voice cracks, just a

little. "I've been trying to get in with the Savage Sons MC. Some of the old crew from the club you were in, Savage Reapers. This was supposed to be my trial run, so they offered me the job and were liaising directly with Van. And I had to prove I could follow orders, be useful before they considered taking me."

"That's your career aspiration? A biker gang?"

"It's protection. It's belonging somewhere." The words hang between us, heavy with accusation: *You left me with nowhere to belong.*

"So, what, you came to scare my Omega and earn your patch?"

"I came to do a job. Then I saw you with her this morning, and—" He shrugs. "Blood's blood, Arrow. Even after everything."

I want to believe him. Want to believe there's something of my little brother left in this damaged man. But Mack has burned me too many times, each betrayal cutting deeper than the last.

"You approach her?" I ask.

"Never. Saw you with her for the first time today, called it off immediately."

"And the Sons?"

"I'll tell them you're involved. They know your reputation, know what the Reapers did. They won't touch anything connected to you."

We sit in silence, drinking our beers. The kitchen noise fills the space, the familiar rhythm of prep work, my crew getting ready for another day. Normal sounds from my normal life, while my past sits across from me with tired eyes and shaking hands.

"You look tired," I tell him.

"Thanks. You look like a sellout." He grins. "Fancy restaurant, clean clothes. Playing citizen."

"It's called growing up."

"Or forgetting where you came from."

"I know exactly where I'm from." The words come out harder than intended. "A house where Dad tried to beat the Alpha out of me and Mom prayed over my unconscious body. Where they locked me in the cellar for presenting, like it was my fucking choice. Where they made you watch—"

"Stop." His voice is small. "I know. I was there."

"Were you? Because I remember begging you to come with me. To get out before they broke you too for fighting against them."

"I was thirteen!"

"And I had nowhere to go. No money or contacts." I lean back, suddenly exhausted. "But I still wanted you with me."

"Then why didn't you come back?"

The question that's haunted me for years. Why didn't I go back for him? Pride? Fear? The knowledge that I was barely surviving myself, working shit jobs for cash under the table, sleeping in the bike shop's back room, fighting for money when honest work dried up?

"Because I was a coward," I admit. "Because I

convinced myself you were better off with them than homeless with me."

"I wasn't." His voice is flat. "They got worse after you left. After he couldn't fix one son, he went crazy and took it out on me for no reason."

I know what that means. The prayer sessions that left bruises. The restriction diets that bordered on starvation. The isolation, the manipulation, the careful destruction of anything that might make you feel strong or worthy or whole. My insides go cold.

"I'm so fucking sorry," I say, and mean it. "I should have—"

"Don't." He waves me off. "We both made choices. Mine were just shittier than yours."

"Clearly." I gesture at the restaurant around us. "Look how far my shitty choices got me."

That gets a small smile. "You always did land on your feet. Like a fucking cat."

"Mack." I wait until he meets my eyes. "Stay in town for a bit. Don't join the club. We'll work something out."

His whole face changes, years dropping away until I can see the kid he used to be. "Yeah?"

"Yeah. But listen closely. If you dick me around again, if you lie to me, if you go near Cindy or do anything to hurt her, I will personally kick you out of town. And you can consider yourself no longer having a brother. We clear?"

"Crystal." He nods quickly. "I'm trying to change, Arrow. Really trying. Getting money honestly where I can, staying clean. Well, mostly clean. Weed doesn't count."

"Weed never counts."

"See? You get it." He finishes his beer. "I should call Jon at the Sons. Tell him I'm out for good."

Jon. That name punches through the haze in my mind like a fist.

I remember him from our Savage Reaper days. He's sharp-eyed, a slick talker, always two moves ahead, and never afraid to get his hands dirty.

Smart as hell. Too smart.

The kind of guy who smiles while working angles no one else can even see.

I wouldn't call him a friend, but I'd never underestimate him.

And I damn sure wouldn't lie to him unless I was ready to burn everything down after.

"Yeah, you should." I stand, heading toward the front of the restaurant. "I'll be up here doing manager shit."

I busy myself with the previous night's receipts, but I'm listening. Mack's voice carries even when he's trying to be quiet, and I'm catching some of the words.

"Yeah, it's Mack... No, I'm out... The Omega's connected... Arrow... Yeah, that Arrow... My brother..."

There's shouting from the other end, tinny through the phone's speaker.

"I don't give a fuck what Van offered to pay... No, you don't understand. Arrow will... Don't threaten me, you piece of..."

More shouting. Mack's responses get shorter, sharper.

"Fine. Whatever... For your own sake, you'd better turn this job down."

He hangs up, and I count to ten before walking back.

"How'd that go?" I arch a brow.

"About as expected. They're pissed. Van's going to be furious." He shrugs, then hesitates. "But Jon says they'll pass on the job."

I tilt my head to the side. "You sure that's what he said?"

"What do you mean?"

"I mean I want to ensure that you're being truthful with me."

Mack gives me a flat look. "Believe me or not, Arrow. I said what needed saying. If Jon is smart, he'll listen."

I don't respond right away. There's a knot in my gut that hasn't loosened, but then again, I get that feeling with anything Mack does.

Still, I force a smile and glance at the time. "Come to the festival tonight. We're running a food truck in Miller's Field. You can help out, catch up with Luke and Holt."

He nods. "Yeah? Be good to see them again."

"We're partners. In everything."

"Even the Omega?"

"Especially the Omega."

He lets out a low whistle. "Didn't think you'd be the type to share."

I grin. "That's none of your business. Just show up around seven. And, Mack? Don't make me regret this."

"I won't." He heads for the door, pauses. "Arrow? Thanks. For not throwing me out on my ass."

"Haven't decided I won't yet. Day's still young."

He laughs, and for a second, it's like we're kids again. Before the violence, before the breaks, before Dad joined a fucking cult and everything went to shit. Then he's gone, his bike roaring to life outside, and I'm left alone with the ghost of every choice that led us here.

My phone buzzes. Text from Luke: *How's our girl?*

Delivered safe. Got a situation though. Mack was watching Cindy for a job.

The fuck? Van?

The fucker hired him to scare Cindy.

The three dots appear and disappear several times before Luke's response: *I'll kill him.*

Which one?

Both. Start with Van, make Mack watch, then him.

He's coming tonight. He called it off in front of me.

You believe him?

I think about Mack's face, the exhaustion there, the resignation. The way he said *Blood's blood* like it still meant something after everything.

Maybe. I'll keep an eye on him.

Good. How's Cindy?

I imagine her pressed against me on the bike, the

way she held on like I was the only solid thing in her world. The little sounds she made when we took corners too fast. How she smelled like home and sex and mine all at once.

Perfect. Absolutely fucking perfect.

You're so gone on her.

Says the man who cut off all his hair for one date.

Worth it.

Yeah, I type, looking around my restaurant, thinking about my brother, my Omega, my complicated fucking life. *It always is.*

17

CINDY

The festival grounds pulse with October energy. Strings of orange lights crisscross overhead like fire against the darkening sky, the smell of fried everything mixing with woodsmoke from the bonfire that's already drawing moths and teenagers in equal measure. Kids shriek on carnival rides that look one bolt away from disaster while their parents clutch beer in plastic cups. Our brewery's booth sits between a taco truck pumping out mariachi music and a delicious-smelling churro stand.

Harper is wrestling with our banner while I arrange sample cups, but her purple-tipped black hair keeps whipping into her face with the evening breeze.

"Son of a—" She spits out hair for the third time. "Should've brought hair ties."

"Here." I dig one out of my pocket, always prepared because anxiety means always having backup everything.

"You're a goddess." She yanks her hair into a ponytail. "Okay, now explain again, and slowly, what the actual fuck happened to Hot Holt's eye."

I glance over at the food truck where he's helping Luke and Arrow set up. The medical eye patch is stark black against his skin, making him look like a dangerous pirate who might rob you blind and then cook you the best meal of your life. He catches us staring, and his good eye narrows in a way that leaves me grinning. God, even injured he radiates that sinful power I love.

"Did someone finally punch him for being too hot?" Harper continues, not bothering to lower her voice. "Because I've considered it. It's honestly unfair to the rest of us mortals."

"Arr, me hearty!" Arrow's voice carries from the truck in that horrible pirate accent he used back at their mansion. "The scallywag be recoverin' from a fearsome battle with a ladder that won, may it rest in pieces!"

"Very funny," Holt growls, but I spot his lips twitching. "Fuck you, Luke, very much for this."

Luke doubles over laughing, nearly dropping the box of supplies he's carrying. The movement makes his shirt ride up, exposing a strip of skin and those V-lines that disappear into his jeans. I'm gawking. "Worth the concussion!"

Harper grabs my arm hard enough to leave marks. "Excuse me, what? Concussion? Ladder? Luke? I need details immediately. Like, Emergency Broadcast System immediately."

I lean in close, keeping my voice low even though the guys are too far to hear over the festival chaos. "So remember my accidental vibrator incident I told you about?"

"How could I forget? That was the highlight of my whole month."

"Well, Holt told Arrow about it. Then Arrow told Luke."

"Okay, following so far."

"Luke happened to have a squishy dildo from some bachelorette party, and he threw it. At Holt. While Holt was on a ladder."

Harper's mouth drops open. Then closes. Then opens again. She looks like a fish having an existential crisis. "A dildo? And it caused him a concussion?"

"Holt fell off the ladder. Hit his head. Hospital. The whole thing."

"This all started with your accidental throwing of a vibrator?" Harper's voice rises to a pitch that makes nearby dogs concerned. "This is better than any Netflix show. This is premium cable!"

"Can we please not—"

"No! We cannot move on from this!" She's practically vibrating with glee, bouncing on her toes. "There's a whole soap opera here, and you're going to tell me everything while we set up. Every. Single. Detail."

She drags me behind the table at our booth, positioning us far enough from the guys that they can't hear but close enough that I can still see them. And God help me, I can't stop watching. Luke's arms flex as he lifts equipment, muscles moving under ink. Arrow's shirt rides up when he reaches for something high, showing abs that could grate cheese. Holt moves with the grace of a god despite the injury, every motion deliberate and somehow sexual even when he's just carrying boxes.

My body feels too warm, oversensitive. Every breeze has me shivering. Every accidental brush of Harper's arm has me flinching. It's like my skin is two sizes too small, and the only thing that would help is letting those three men put their hands—

"Stop eye-fucking them and start talking," Harper demands. "Start from the beginning. And include the dinner from hell. Your Satan's spawn of a mother. Everything."

So I tell her everything while we work.

"And she gave you two weeks to prove that your relationship is real, or she'll drag you home?" Harper stops in the middle of adjusting our banner. "Like, physically drag you? Is she the mafia?"

"She might as well be," I say, half smiling at how stupid it sounds, yet I know she will do anything in her power.

"Fuck!" Harper shakes her head. "And then what?"

"Well, the guys asked me to move in."

Harper drops the stack of coasters she's holding.

They scatter across the grass like confetti at the world's saddest party. "You didn't?"

"Yep, Saturday night. Well, only for a night at first. Then I agreed to stay there at least until Halloween. I spent all of yesterday moving some of my stuff to their place and setting up the guest room as mine. They also insist on taking me to and picking me up from work, so I came here with them straight after work."

"That's why—" Her eyes go wide. "I offered to pick you up, and you said you had a ride and—holy fucking shit, Cindy. You're living with three Alphas? What happens when your heat comes?"

"Hell, I don't know, but maybe it will stay away. And it's just until after the wedding. To make it believable."

"Uh-huh. Sure. Temporarily." She air-quotes so hard she might dislocate something. "And how's that working out? Platonically sharing space with three men who look at you like you're a seven-course meal and they haven't eaten in a year?"

I busy myself with arranging sample cups in obsessively perfect lines, my hands shaking slightly. "It's fine."

"Cindy."

"It's complicated."

"Cindy."

"Okay, fine! It's torture!" The words explode out of me. "They're everywhere, being gorgeous and helpful and sweet, and they smell so good it makes my brain melt into my underwear. Luke made me breakfast—

pancakes shaped like hearts, Harper. Hearts! Holt fixed my bedroom door that was squeaking without me asking. Arrow brought me coffee exactly how I like it, and I never told him how I liked it!"

"And?"

"And they want this to be real. All three of them."

Harper fans herself with a coaster. "And you don't?"

"I do. God, I do. So much it hurts." I risk another glance at them. They're all watching me now, three sets of eyes that set my skin on fire. Luke winks. Arrow smirks. Holt just stares with an intensity that makes me clench my thighs. "But what if it gets ruined? Everything my family touches turns to shit. What if my mom finds some way to destroy this? I don't think I could survive having them torn away from me."

"Okay, but what if—" Harper groans, cutting herself off, checking under the table. "Damn it, I have to grab the kegs before the boss man shows up and gives me that look like I've failed at life." She lifts a brow at me as she turns toward the cooler. "But we're not done talking. If I were in your shoes? I'd be paying those Alphas a visit in their bedrooms. Every night."

I blink. "Wow."

"I mean, come on." She pauses mid-step, grinning over her shoulder. "You know Alphas are beasts in bed. Can you imagine what they could do to you? Like, *tied-up, can't-walk-straight, rearranged-your-soul* levels of good."

"Harper."

"What? You're thinking it."

She tosses me a grin and stares out toward the parking area, where the kegs are still sitting in the back of the van.

"I'm just saying," she says. "If I had three Alphas in one house? I'd be rotating rooms like a damn tasting menu. One each night—hell, maybe double up."

I shake my head, trying not to laugh. "Harper."

"What? You *know* they're probably insane in bed. Alphas don't play. You'd be lucky if you could walk after."

I open my mouth to fire back something equally inappropriate, but Harper is already halfway to the van, tossing a smug look over her shoulder.

A minute later, she's trudging back toward the table, hauling the first keg against her hip with both arms, wobbling a little under the weight but determined not to ask for help.

She nearly reaches our booth when a male's voice calls out, "Need help with that?"

Harper half turns toward the sound.

I catch the way her grip loosens, her head tilting slightly as she takes him in.

Tall. Lean. Striking, with dark hair pulled back in a messy knot that somehow still looks deliberate. Sharp features, confident posture. There's a faint resemblance to Arrow, not enough to draw attention, but something in the movement, the sharp-eyed stillness, the quiet edge under the charm. Brown eyes flick over

Harper like he's reading a situation and enjoying every second of it. Is that his brother?

Harper is gawking now, still holding the keg like she's forgotten what it's for. "Absolutely. They're in my van and it's unlocked. I'm Harper, by the way." She sets the keg down and extends her hand, batting her eyelashes hard enough to cause weather patterns.

"Mack." He takes her hand and holds it a beat too long. "Beautiful name for a beautiful woman."

Harper giggles. "You're sweet. Come on, big boy, let's see those muscles work."

She dumps the keg near me, smiles crazily, and heads toward the parking area with Mack. I watch Harper deploy every weapon in her flirtation arsenal— the hair flip, the accidentally-on-purpose brush of fingers, the laugh that's pitched just right to stroke a man's ego. Mack is eating it up, flexing unnecessarily when he lifts the first keg, making sure his shirt rides up to show abs.

"So you met Mack."

I jump, nearly knocking over my carefully arranged cups. Arrow has appeared beside me, silent as smoke despite being six feet, four inches of solid muscle.

"Crap! Bells! Wear bells or something!"

"Where's the fun in that?" He's watching his brother with an expression I can't read. "That's my brother, by the way."

"I can see the resemblance." Now that I know, it's obvious. Same bone structure, same dangerous beauty. "He seems... nice. Helpful."

Arrow groans, running both hands through his hair, and his biceps flex. My mouth waters. Literally waters. What is wrong with me?

"Yeah, that's what everyone thinks at first. That's what the judge thought too, right before Mack stole his gavel."

"He stole a judge's gavel?"

"During his own hearing. For stealing garden gnomes."

"Oh, wow."

"Forty-seven of them. From all over the county. He was building what he called an army of judgment in someone's ex-girlfriend's yard." Arrow is still watching Mack, who's now carrying a keg on his shoulder while Harper makes appreciative noises that border on pornography. "That was actually one of his tamer phases. The year before, he convinced half of Tucson he was a traveling priest and performed thirteen weddings."

"Were they legal?"

"Fuck no. He was high on mushrooms for most of them."

I can't help but laugh. "You're making this up."

"I wish." But he's smiling now, that rare genuine grin that transforms his face from dangerous to devastating. "Look, Mack's... complicated. Good heart, terrible execution. Like, historically terrible. Biblical-plague levels of terrible. He's trying to get his shit together, but he's got a pattern. Shows up, charms everyone, means well, then somehow you're explaining to the cops why your car is in a pool and all the lawn flamingos in the neighborhood are arranged in a pentagram."

"That's oddly specific."

His expression darkens. "I left home when he was thirteen. Left him there with our parents, who thought beating the fear of God into kids was literally in the Bible. Every bad decision he's made since then is partly on me."

The pain in his voice hits harder than I expect. Before I can stop myself, I reach out and touch his arm. His skin is warm beneath my fingers, solid. The contact sparks something sharp and electric that shoots up my arm, but I don't pull away.

"Arrow—" I start, but the name catches on something in my throat.

Because for the first time, I see not just the attitude and swagger he wears like armor, but also the damage underneath. Not so different from my own. We both come from houses where love was a weapon, not a shelter. Parents who knew how to tear us down better than anyone else ever could.

The realization steals my breath a little.

We're more alike than I ever wanted to admit.

"Just tell Harper to be careful. Mack's got a way of making you believe he's changed right up until he proves he hasn't. Usually explosively."

Mack and Harper return, Mack carrying another keg like it weighs nothing. His shirt is fully untucked now, and Harper is touching his arm every three seconds as though she's checking whether he's real.

"Let's go, Mack," Arrow says, his tone suggesting this isn't a request. "We've got prep work."

"Already? But I just met this angel." Mack grins at Harper, all dangerous charm.

"Now."

The brothers stare at each other, some silent battle happening. Tension rolls off Arrow, Mack's jaw working. Finally, Mack breaks.

"Nice meeting you, Harper." He takes her hand and kisses it like some discount-romance-novel hero. "Maybe I'll see you around."

"Count on it," Harper purrs.

They leave, Arrow's hand on Mack's shoulder either guiding or restraining him. Harper fans herself with both hands.

"Did you see those abs? Those arms? That whole 'I make terrible decisions and you can be one of them' energy? And he's a Beta like me. It's perfect."

"He's Arrow's brother. And Arrow says to be careful. Apparently, Mack has a complicated history involving theft, fraud, and lawn flamingos."

She stares at me for a long moment. "Says the girl shacking up with three bikers who probably have actual body counts." Harper grins wickedly.

"Touché." I laugh despite myself. "You win. Go forth and make your own terrible decisions."

"Planning on it. Mama needs a bad boy to ruin her credit score."

"Harper!"

"What? I'm being honest about my goals."

"Ladies!" a familiar male voice booms across the grass.

Garrett approaches with Ruby at his side, and they're such a perfectly matched set that it aches in my chest. He's all broad shoulders and brewery owner confidence, flannel and worn jeans. Ruby is gorgeous in that effortless way that takes three hours, with reddish-blonde waves around her face, amber eyes bright with warmth, and curves that her sweater dress can't hide.

They met at a beer festival, both showcasing their own brews, and somewhere between shared taps and friendly rivalry, things turned personal. Though neither likes to talk about how Ruby nearly lost the bar that her aunt left her to an asshole cousin.

"Boss man!" Harper salutes with a sample cup she pulls from nowhere. "And boss lady! Here to check that we're not giving away all your beer to minors?"

"Here to enjoy the festival," Garrett corrects, his arm around Ruby's waist with casual possession. "Plus, Ruby wanted to check out the competition."

"There's a new brewery setting up?" I ask.

Ruby nods. "Saw two, actually." Then she leans in, smiling. "So, Harper tells me you've got yourself three hot Alphas?"

Garrett chuckles under his breath.

I shoot a glare at Harper, who looks entirely

unbothered. Of course she told people. She *thrives* on being the town's unofficial PR machine.

"It's nothing yet," I say quickly, trying to wave it off.

Harper pretends to choke on air. "Sure," she wheezes. "Absolutely nothing."

Ruby laughs. "When I met Garrett, Knox, and Dominic, I tried to keep my distance too. But sometimes the universe doesn't care how ready you are. When it's your pack, it finds a way."

I glance at the three men at the food truck, and my heart flutters. "How do you handle it?" I ask, glancing back her way. "The fear that it could all fall apart... or that you won't be enough for all of them?"

Ruby considers that, her fingers absently twisting a lock of her hair.

"You don't *handle* it like a problem," she says gently. "You trust the bond you're building and take it one day at a time. Communicate. Let them show up for you, and let yourself be seen, even when it's messy. Especially when it's messy."

Her words settle deeper than I expect, quiet and sharp, like the truth always is.

Ruby bumps her hip lightly against mine. "You'll get there. And hey, tomorrow night is 'adults only' at the festival. No kids, no rules, just costumes, drinks, and all the fun."

Garrett sighs like he's already resigned to it. "Mandatory costumes. The committee was very clear."

"I'm definitely going," Harper announces. "I

already have my costume. Sexy witch, but like, actually sexy, not Spirit Halloween sexy."

"I don't have anything prepared—"

"The guys will help," Ruby suggests with a knowing smile. "Trust me, Alphas love dressing up their Omega."

"We're not—I'm not their—"

"Yet," Ruby interrupts. "You're not their Omega yet. But, honey, the way they're looking at you?"

I turn to glance at the food truck. All three of them have stopped working to stare at me. Luke is holding a spatula like he's forgotten what it's for.

My body responds instantly with heat flooding my system, skin hypersensitive, that telltale ache between my thighs that's been getting worse all day. My heat is coming quicker than it should. And being surrounded by three Alphas who smell like everything I've ever wanted isn't helping.

"You're already gone on them, aren't you?" Ruby asks me.

"Completely fucked," Harper answers. "In the best way. Look at her. She's practically vibrating."

"I'm not—"

"Your pupils are dilated, you keep rubbing your thighs together, and you're producing enough pheromones to start a riot," Harper lists clinically. "When's your heat due?"

"Harper!"

"Okay, this is my exit time," Garrett says and wanders to another booth.

"What? It's a valid medical question."

"Soon," I admit quietly. "Maybe a week."

Ruby's lips pinch. "And you're living with three unmated Alphas?"

"It's fine," I say quickly, maybe too quickly. "They have a heat room. It's fully equipped. I'll be fine."

"A heat room," Ruby repeats slowly. "That they built. For an Omega. That they're now living with."

"It came with the house," I mumble, even though I'm not sure that makes it any better.

Ruby gives me a look that's equal parts sympathy and *girl, please*. She pats my arm gently. "Cindy, just so you know, you're playing with fire."

I let out a breathy laugh, but my stomach twists. Because she's not wrong. I'm practically curled up in the fire, pretending not to notice the burn.

"More like bathing in gasoline while juggling torches," Harper adds cheerfully. "But in a fun way!"

I force a smile, but my thoughts are already spiraling. I don't even know who I am when I'm in heat—what if I say something I can't take back? What if I *want* things I shouldn't?

What if they see the real me and don't want me?

Ruby squeezes my hand like she can hear the thought as clearly as if I'd said it out loud. "It'll be all right," she says softly. "Just... don't deny what's inevitable. Sometimes fate doesn't wait for permission."

She offers a small smile, then glances over her

shoulder. "I should go find Garrett before he accidentally adopts another lost tourist."

I watch her disappear into the crowd, her presence lingering like comfort and warning all in one.

The evening crowd has started to thicken, laughter and music rising with the cool fall air. We get busy pouring samples, but I'm hyperaware of the mingling scents of Alphas all around me, the weight of three specific gazes that never seem to leave me.

A customer accidentally brushes my hand when I give him his sample, and I nearly moan. Just from a finger brush.

This is bad. This is very, very bad.

"You okay?" Harper asks during a brief lull.

"I'm…" I press the back of my hand to my forehead. I'm not feverish yet, but I'm warm. Too warm in a way that feels like a warning. "I think it might be sooner than a week."

"How soon?"

"Days? Maybe less?"

"Holy shit," Harper gasps.

"It wasn't supposed to happen this fast," I mutter. "It's probably their scents triggering it early—"

"You think?" Harper laughs, but it's tinged with real concern now. "Babe, you need to talk to them. Like, actually talk to them. Before this turns into a meltdown with naked consequences."

I look back at the food truck. Luke is juggling sauce bottles to entertain a couple of kids, his movements easy and playful. Arrow is focused, plating something that looks way too good for a food truck. And Holt... Holt is watching me like he already knows something is wrong.

As if sensing my stare, he sets down what he's doing and starts walking over, completely unreadable.

But before he reaches me, Harper gently grabs my arm and leans in close.

"Hey," she says, voice soft but steady. "It's going to be okay. You'll see."

I swallow hard.

"I'm serious," she goes on. "I'm here for you, no matter what. But you've got to stop overthinking and start feeling. Focus on what they make you feel. That's real. That's what matters. And your mom?" She shrugs. "She'll see it eventually. I feel it in my bones."

I glance toward the truck again. Holt is still walking, his gaze never leaving mine. Luke is grinning at something Arrow said. And suddenly, the weight on my chest doesn't feel so heavy.

Maybe she's right.

Maybe it's time to stop fighting every instinct and see where they take me.

Maybe for once it's safe to let myself want something.

Maybe it's not about surviving this time. Maybe it's about choosing something that finally feels right.

18

CINDY

My bedroom in their mansion is bigger than my entire living room, kitchen, and bathroom combined. The king-sized bed swallows me whole, expensive sheets that feel cool against my overheated skin. General Flufferton is sprawled across the foot of the bed, purring in his sleep, completely unbothered by my restlessness.

It's past eleven, and I've been lying here for an hour, staring at the ceiling, trying not to think about the three Alphas somewhere in this house. Luke's room is down the hall to the left. Holt's is across from his. Arrow's is at the far end, the master suite he insisted I should take instead, but I refused because that felt too much like accepting something I shouldn't.

The lamp casts soft shadows on the walls, and I've kicked off the covers twice already. I'm slowly cooking from the inside out. This isn't normal pre-heat warming. I've been through two heats to know the difference. This is something else. This is being surrounded by Alpha pheromones, by their scents that have seeped into every corner of this house despite them trying to be respectful and give me space.

I press my palms to my cheeks, touching the heat there. My tank top clings to my skin with a light sheen of sweat, and my sleep shorts are restrictive even though they're my loosest pair. Everything is too much and not enough at the same time.

I can't focus on anything except the knowledge that they're so close.

My body thrums with awareness, every nerve ending hypersensitive. I'm burning up. And my scent must be broadcasting my arousal through the entire house. Unmated Omega in pre-heat, surrounded by unmated Alphas. This is how those tales start, the ones mothers tell their Omega daughters to keep them safe. Except I don't want to be safe. I want—

No. I can't think about what I want. Because what I want is to walk down the hall and knock on one of their doors. Or all of their doors. What I want is to give in to this need that's eating me alive from the inside out.

I sit up, startling General Flufferton, who gives me a disgruntled look before resettling.

"I'm going to get a drink," I tell him. "Cold water. Arctic water. Icy enough to shock some sense into me."

He chirps sleepily and gets up, arching into a stretch, then hops off the bed with a plonk.

The house is quiet when I open my door. No lights visible under any of the other doors. Good. They're asleep. I can sneak down to the kitchen, get water, maybe stick my head in the freezer for a minute, then come back up without anyone knowing.

The stairs don't creak—of course they don't—because everything in this house is perfectly maintained, but General Flufferton rockets past me, nearly sending me tumbling.

"Traitor," I whisper after him as he disappears into the darkness below, losing sight of him.

The kitchen is all shadows and moonlight streaming through the enormous windows. I don't turn on the lights, not wanting to announce my presence. The refrigerator hums quietly, and I open it, letting the cold air wash over me. It helps, a little. I grab the water pitcher, condensation cold against my palms, and pour a glass.

The first sip is heaven, icy enough to make my teeth ache. I drink half the glass in one go, then press the cold surface against my forehead, my neck, trying to cool the fire under my skin.

"Can't sleep?"

I shriek, jumping and sending water everywhere, down my front, across the counter, onto the floor. The glass slips from my hand but doesn't break, just rolls across the granite with a sound like thunder in the quiet kitchen.

"Shit! Sorry, I didn't mean—" Arrow steps out of

the shadows by the pantry, and my brain stops functioning entirely.

He's wearing low-slung pajama pants and nothing else. His chest is art, all angled muscles and ink I want to trace with my tongue. The V of muscle at his hips points down like an arrow—pun fully intended—to what those pajama pants are barely concealing. His hair is messy, as though he's been running his hands through it, and his eyes are locked on—

Oh God.

My white tank top is soaked, completely see-through, clinging to every curve. My nipples are clearly visible, hard from the cold water and, if I'm honest, from him being half naked in front of me. I snatch a kitchen towel, dabbing uselessly at myself, which only makes it worse because now the fabric is rubbing against sensitive skin, and he's still staring.

"That really isn't helping," he says, voice rougher than usual.

His eyes have gone dark, pupils wide, and his chest rises and falls faster. He's almost feral, predatory, as if he's two seconds from pouncing. Every instinct I have screams at me to run, to get back to the safety of my room before—

But my body betrays me. Instead of running, I stay frozen, clutching the useless towel. Instead of fear, heat pools low in my belly, that ache becoming a throb. Instead of backing away when he takes a step closer, I lean in.

"I should—" I start.

"Should what?" He's close enough that the inferno radiating off his skin engulfs me. "Go back to bed? Where you'll lie awake thinking about this? About us?"

"I don't—"

"Don't lie to me, Cindy." Another step. He's got me backed against the counter now, not touching but close enough that I notice the pulse jumping in his throat under the moonlight pouring into the kitchen. "I smell it on you. How turned on you are. How much you want this."

"That's just—it's pre-heat. It doesn't mean—"

"Bullshit." His hands come up to rest on the counter on either side of me, caging me in. "This started before your heat. This started the moment we first met."

"Arrow—"

"Tell me you don't want this." His face is so close now that his breath flutters across my lips. "Tell me to back off and I will. I'll go upstairs right now, and we'll pretend this never happened. But if you don't tell me to stop—"

My hand moves without permission, pressing against his chest. His skin is hot, smooth over hard muscle, and his heart is racing under my palm. "We shouldn't."

"We absolutely should." His hand covers mine. "We should have done this days ago."

He leans in, lips barely brushing my ear. "You are

fierce and beautiful, and I want to squeeze you against that wall and kiss you until you can't remember why you want to return to your room."

A whimper escapes me, and his responding growl turns my knees to putty.

"I know I shouldn't," I whisper, my other hand coming up to rest on his chest because apparently I have no self-control at all.

His nose trails along my jaw, not quite touching but close enough that I shiver. "Don't fight it."

"How do you—how do you want me?" The question slips out before I can stop it.

He pulls back to look at me, and the intensity in his eyes makes me grateful for the counter holding me up. "Every way. Any way. Soft and sweet. Hard and rough. On this counter. Against that wall. In my bed until you forget any other man exists."

"Oh God." My fingers curl against his chest, nails scraping lightly, and he hisses.

"But right now?" His hand comes up to cup my face, thumb tracing my bottom lip. "Right now, I just want to kiss you until you stop overthinking everything."

"I'm not—"

His mouth crashes into mine.

It's nothing like I expected. I thought Arrow would be controlled, the way he is in his kitchen. Instead, he kisses like he's starving and I'm sustenance. He closes the space between us, one hand tangling in my hair while the other grips my hip, pulling me against him. I gasp at the contact, and he takes advantage, his tongue sliding against mine in a way that leaves my whole body lighting up.

My hands glide up his chest to his shoulders, holding on as he devours me. When he nips at my bottom lip, I make a needy and desperate and completely shameless sound.

"Fuck," he groans against my mouth. "The sounds you make."

He lifts me onto the counter like I weigh nothing, stepping between my spread thighs, and the position puts us at the perfect height. He's so damn hard against me through the thin fabric of our pajamas, and I roll my hips without thinking, seeking friction.

"Careful," he warns, but he's moving too, grinding against me, and I'm suddenly seeing stars. "Keep that up and I won't be able to stop."

I laugh and swoon at the same time.

He draws back to look at me, and we're both breathing hard. My lips are swollen, my skin oversensitive, and I've never wanted anything as much as I want him to keep touching me.

"Cindy—"

I kiss him this time, pouring all my frustration and need and want into it. My legs wrap around his waist, pulling him closer, and he groans into my mouth. His hands are everywhere—my hair, my waist, sliding up my ribs but stopping just short of where I want them most.

We're moving, though I'm not sure how... him

walking into the living room while carrying me, still kissing like we'll die if we stop. My back hits a wall, and I gasp, the cool surface a shock against my heated skin.

He's kissing down my neck now, finding that spot that melts me. "Tell me how you want it." His voice is pure gravel now, Alpha command bleeding through. "Let me hear what you need."

I'm blushing so hard I must be glowing. "Rough. I want it—God, I *need* it—rough and hard. This ache is destroying me. I can't think about anything except—"

"Except what?" He purrs the words, which undoes me.

"You inside me," I whisper, and his whole body shudders.

"You're going to be the death of me." He's kissing me again, harder this time, more desperate. "The way you smell and taste, these fucking noises you make—"

His hands slide higher under my tank top, palms hot against my skin, and I arch into the touch. He moves slowly, torturously, pushing the fabric up inch by inch while his mouth continues its assault on mine.

"So beautiful," he murmurs against my lips. "So fucking perfect."

When he finally pulls the tank top over my head, the cool air makes me shiver. Or maybe it's the way he's devouring me with his stare like I'm a feast and he's been starving for years.

"Please," I breathe, and he groans.

"Say my name."

"Arrow."

"Again."

"Arrow, please—"

He kisses me slowly, then starts moving down. His lips trail fire down my throat, across my collarbone, and when he reaches my breasts, I have to bite my lip to keep from crying out. We can't wake the others. "Let me hear how good this feels."

"What if someone hears us?"

"Let them hear," he murmurs, his gaze on my breasts. "So they know what they're missing."

"We can't—they'll—"

"They'll what? Come down here? Join us?" He glances up at me, eyes dark with desire. "Is that what you're afraid of? Or what you want?"

I can't answer because he's using his mouth again, teeth scraping lightly before he sucks hard, wrapping those lips around a nipple with just enough pressure to make me arch against him. He's not gentle. He doesn't ease me into it. He *devours*, like he's been waiting and I'm the only thing that'll satisfy him.

My hands tangle in his hair, fisting it to hold him there, or maybe to anchor myself because my body is unraveling. I'm gasping, panting, these helpless little sounds spilling out of me without permission. My thighs are shaking, heat pulsing between them in waves that have nothing to do with my cycle and everything to do with *him*.

He switches sides without warning, biting just enough to make me flinch, then soothing the sting with his tongue. Every nerve in my chest is raw and lit up, as if he's rewired me with nothing but his mouth.

"I'm going to ruin you," he whispers against my skin, his voice dark and reverent. "Going to take you apart piece by piece until you can't remember why you were fighting this."

"Don't stop," I gasp. "God, yes, please—"

The living room is all shadows and moonlight, and I should be embarrassed about being half naked in such an open space, but all I can focus on is Arrow's hands, his mouth, the way he's making me feel like I'm flying apart.

I slide down his body until I'm on my knees in front of him, looking up at his shocked expression.

"Cindy, you don't have to—"

"I want to." My hands go to his waistband, and I stare at how hard he is, the outline clear through the thin fabric. "I need to taste you."

"Fuck." His head falls back, hands clenching at his sides. "You can't just say things like that."

"Why not?" I tug down his pajama pants slowly, revealing him inch by inch, and— "Oh my God."

He's massive. Thick and hard and perfect, and for a second, I have doubts, because how is that going to fit? But then I remember this isn't my first time doing this. There was that Beta waiter back home who I practiced on, much to my parents' horror when they found out, so I know what I'm doing. Sort of.

I wrap my hand around him, and he groans like I've punched him.

"Baby…"

I lick from base to tip, tasting salt and skin and Arrow. His hands tangle in my hair, not forcing, just holding, and when I slide my lips over his tip, he moans. So I slip him into my mouth.

"Jesus fucking—your mouth—"

I hum around him, which makes him grunt louder, and then I'm finding my rhythm. I remember what that Beta taught me, about using my hand and mouth together, about paying attention to reactions, about enthusiasm being more important than technique.

And I'm enthusiastic. The way his thighs tremble, the taste of him, it's all going straight to the fire between my thighs. I'm so turned on that I can't stand it, my shorts drenched, and without thinking, my free hand slips into my sleep shorts.

"Are you—fuck, Cindy, are you touching yourself?"

I moan around him in response, my mouth moving up and down his shaft, my fingers finding that bundle of nerves that's been aching all day. I push them between my swollen, silky lips and groan at the touch. The dual sensation of him in my mouth and my own fingers is overwhelming in the best way.

"Fuck yes, just like that. But I want, I need to touch you—"

But I don't let go, don't stop, just increase my pace on both fronts. I'm close, so close, and when Arrow's hips start to stutter, when his grip in my hair tightens—

"Cindy, I'm going to—you should—"

I don't pull away.

Instead, I stare up at him as I take him deeper. My lips stretch wide, my jaw aching, and still I keep going, slowly, until the thick head hits the back of my throat. He's so big that it burns a little, and I *love* it. My eyes water as I push further, swallowing around him, my tongue pressed tight to the underside.

His hand finds the back of my head. Not forcing, not yet, but holding. Applying just enough pressure that my pulse stutters. It's possessive. Guiding. Exactly what I crave.

"Fuck, baby," he groans, his voice wrecked. "Look at you. Taking it so well."

I hum around him, the sound deep in my throat, and it makes him shudder. My hips rock, desperate for friction, my fingers working, rubbing my clit in frantic circles. I'm soaked, hot, every nerve on fire just from having him in my mouth, tasting his skin, hearing the noises he makes.

He starts to move, shallow thrusts into my mouth that grow a little rougher with each pass. I let him. Want him like this, unleashed, undone. His grip tightens in my hair, his breaths ragged, his groans tumbling out with every wet slide of my lips over his cock.

"You were made for this," he pants. "Fuck, your mouth, your throat, they feel better than anything I've ever had."

He throbs against my tongue. He's close, evident in the way his legs tense and his rhythm falters.

"You gonna swallow all of it for me?" he growls, low and primal. "Gonna be my good girl and drink it down?"

I moan around him in answer, pressing my thighs together as my own orgasm tightens, crashes, heat flooding me as I rub harder, lost to the intensity of it all.

He jerks in my mouth with a harsh, broken sound, the kind of growl that feels like it should be dangerous. And then he comes. Hard. A thick, hot flood that fills my mouth, and I don't hesitate. I swallow it down fast, greedy, even as more follows, and still, I don't stop. His grip holds me in place, trembling fingers buried in my hair as he hisses.

"Good fucking girl," he rasps. "So good, so perfect, fuck, you drank it all. Jesus."

I finally release him, breathing heavily, my lips swollen and slick. His cock remains hard, glistening with spit, a drop of cum lingering at the tip. He stares down at me, ready to ruin me all over again.

And maybe I want that too.

He sinks to his knees in front of me, his thumb brushing the corner of my mouth, catching the shine there and dragging it slowly across my lips. His eyes are dark, pure Alpha, and his voice drops to a dangerous purr.

"You have no idea what that did to me. Seeing my cock in your mouth? Watching you *need* it that bad that you came on your own fingers?" He leans closer. "That was the hottest fucking thing I've ever seen. You on your knees, dripping and desperate with my cum still on your tongue? Baby, I'm never gonna stop wanting that."

"You're going to kill me," I murmur, my voice still hoarse from everything we just did. My knees feel like jelly, and my heart won't stop thudding against my ribs.

Arrow smiles, slow and devastating, then draws me to my feet like I weigh nothing at all. "Nah, baby. Not kill you." His fingers dig into the elastic of my sleep shorts. "I'm gonna fuckin' make you scream. That mouth"—he groans, eyes dipping to my lips like he's still seeing himself there—"was just the beginning."

I can't breathe. My blood is rushing south again, my body already aching for more. And I love how he says it. How rough he gets. How his voice goes thick and low when he wants me.

I reach for him. "Then do it. Fuck me like I belong to you."

His mouth crashes into mine, messy and hot, while his thumbs hook beneath the waistband of my shorts, dragging them down slowly.

But then—

Movement catches my eye.

A flicker in the dark, just over Arrow's shoulder.

My breath stutters, body stilling mid-kiss as my gaze snaps toward the dining table at the far end of the open-plan space.

And that's when I see them.

Holt and Luke.

Sitting like twin shadows in the dim glow from the kitchen, both with a glass of something. Clearly breathing heavily. Staring at us like they're barely holding on.

My stomach drops. My face floods with heat.

Arrow turns slightly, following my frozen line of sight, and groans, dragging a hand down his face. "Fuck."

I squeal, high-pitched and horrified, pulling my shorts up. Then I snatch my tank top off the floor and clutch it to my chest.

"Oh my God," I whisper. "Ohmygodohmygod—"

"Cindy—wait—" Arrow tries to catch me, his tone somewhere between apologetic and still aroused.

Too late.

I bolt for the stairs, half naked, heart pounding like I've just sprinted out of a nightmare. Or a fantasy. Or maybe both.

"Seriously? You had to ruin the perfect moment?" Arrow groans.

"Hey!" Luke fires back. "We were here first."

"And you just sat there?" Arrow sounds like he wants to throttle him.

"Well, we weren't gonna interrupt," Luke says, and I *hear* the smirk in his voice. "Would've been rude. And honestly? That was better than any damn movie."

"I was gonna fuck her right there," Arrow growls.

I don't hear the rest. I'm already in my room, door slammed shut behind me, my back pressed against the wood as I try to breathe.

My body is flushed and electric, my thighs sticky, my skin still tingling from where Arrow's mouth had been. I let out a shaky laugh, half hysterical, half turned on, and slide to the floor.

What the *hell* did I just do?

And worse—

Why do I want to do it again?

Why do I want *them* to see?

Still clutching my tank top to my chest, my whole body throbbing with aftershocks and mortification.

What the hell was I thinking?

My lips are swollen, my thighs still trembling. My mouth tastes like him. My skin feels branded by his hands. And now they've *all* seen me. Not just Arrow, but Holt and Luke too. Watched. Hard. Unmoving. Like they were *waiting* for something.

A knock rattles the door behind me, and I jump like I've been electrocuted.

"I'm fine," I call too quickly. My voice is high and cracked. "Totally fine. All good. Everything's fine!"

Silence.

"Cindy. Can I come in?" Arrow says in that gravel-smooth voice.

I hesitate. My hand hovers over the doorknob.

"I don't want you thinking that was a one-time thing. Or that it changes anything about how attracted I am to you."

My breath catches.

"I'm just... tired," I say weakly. "And a little—embarrassed."

More silence. "You don't need to be embarrassed. Trust me. Holt and Luke are gonna be awake all night, *dying* to get those images of you out of their heads."

I let out a strangled sound. "That's really not helping."

A low chuckle from the other side of the door. "Sorry. Just... trying to make you feel better."

"You're making me feel *something*, all right."

He goes quiet again, like he's letting me choose what happens next and waiting to see if I'll open the door.

I don't.

But I press my palm against the wood between us. Needing to feel something grounded.

"You really don't think it was just for fun so you can gloat in front of your friends?" I ask quietly.

"Not even a little," he says. "You're gorgeous, you're smart, you're filthy in the best fucking way... and when you dropped to your knees for me, I nearly lost my mind. I count myself lucky for having met someone as incredible as you."

My face burns. But I can't help the tiny smile.

"You're trouble, Cindy," he murmurs. "But the good kind."

I lean my forehead against the door, heart still racing, trying to slow the spiral of embarrassment and afterglow and want.

Silence stretches, just long enough that I think he's gone.

"Well... sweet dreams, my good girl."

My knees threaten to give out again.

I melt. Actually melt into the wood like it could catch me.

And when I'm sure he's really gone, I whisper to the closed door, "Yeah. I think I'm in big trouble moving in here."

The dining table needs an exorcism. Maybe some sage burning. Hell, throw in whatever ritual removes the memory of last night permanently branded into the wood grain. Because sitting here eating pancakes for breakfast while pretending I didn't watch Cindy on her knees, taking Arrow's cock into her mouth like she was starving for it —fuck. My dick has been semi-hard since last night, and no amount of cold showers or jerking off is fixing this problem.

I tear into another chocolate chip pancake with my hands, ignoring the fork completely. Arrow has gone overboard as usual, five different kinds spread across the table. Chocolate chip, blueberry, banana walnut that smell like a bakery, plain ones for the boring people, and something with bacon pieces that shouldn't work but absolutely does.

The sun streams through the kitchen windows, highlighting the banquet Arrow created.

My eye feels strange without the patch. Good strange, but strange. Like when you wear boots every day and then suddenly go barefoot. Everything feels too exposed, too bright. The hospital doc said two to three days max when they discharged me, and it feels ready. No permanent damage except to my dignity and my ability to look at dildos without laughing.

"Weird seeing you with both eyes again," Luke mutters, but he's not really present in the conversation. He's on his fourth cup of coffee, and his leg won't stop bouncing under the table. Man looks like he went ten rounds with his demons and lost. His hair is sticking up in twelve directions, dark circles under his eyes, and he keeps adjusting himself under the table when he thinks no one is looking.

"The eye patch was working for you," Arrow adds from where he's still flipping pancakes at the stove because apparently five types weren't enough. "Had that whole dangerous pirate thing. Women love that mysterious injured-Alpha shit."

"Fuck off," I grunt, but I watch Cindy's reaction from the corner of my eye.

She's sitting across from me, systematically destroying her third stack of pancakes. Actually eating, not picking at her food like she's afraid of carbs or whatever bullshit the Omega magazines tell them to worry about. There's maple syrup on her bottom lip, and she licks it off slowly, probably not even aware she's doing it. My cock jumps, and I have to shift in my seat.

Arrow finally sits down with his own plate, taking the head of the table like the control freak he is. Luke is to Cindy's right, close enough that their elbows keep bumping when they reach for things. She's wearing a white button-up shirt, and every time she laughs, which is often because Luke keeps stealing bacon from Arrow's plate, her shirt pulls across her bust, giving me a tiny sneak peek at her lace bra. The sight goes straight to my balls.

"So the Halloween festival tonight," Arrow starts, pouring himself orange juice. "The part where they kick all the kids out and let adults actually have fun. We should go as a group."

I grab the bacon plate before Luke can raid it again. "Last year, some eight-year-old threw up on my boots after too much cotton candy."

"That's what you get for being scary," Cindy teases, and, hell, when did she get comfortable enough to tease me? "Poor kid probably took one look at your resting murder face and lost it."

Luke snorts coffee through his nose, which starts him coughing and laughing at the same time. "Resting murder face! Fuck, that's perfect."

"I don't have—"

"You absolutely do," Arrow confirms, grinning. "It's why we keep you around. Natural security system."

"Speaking of tonight," Cindy continues, wiping syrup from her fingers in a way that shouldn't be erotic but absolutely is. "Harper is going, and I need a costume. We all do, right?"

"Leave it to me," Luke announces, suddenly looking more animated than he has all morning. His eyes get that gleam that usually means he's up to something. "I'll handle costumes for everyone. We need coordination. Unity. Visual impact."

I set my coffee mug down hard enough to rattle the saltshaker. "Absolutely not. I don't do matching anything. We're not a boy band. I'm not showing up like we raided the same Pinterest board."

"Not matching," Luke insists, gesturing wildly like that helps. "Coordinated. Themed. Totally different vibe."

Arrow is already laughing, that slow, dangerous kind of laugh that suggests he's about to make this worse. "You mean like last year? When you tried to get us to be the Teenage Mutant Ninja Turtles?"

"That was genius," Luke says, deeply offended. "And you're a coward for bailing."

"We're in our thirties," I remind him, unimpressed.

"Technically, Holt, you're the only one in your thirties," Luke says smugly, like that somehow justifies anything.

"Still not dressing as a turtle."

Cindy glances between us with this half-amused, half-bewildered expression, as if she's still not convinced we're actual adults. "Okay, so what are you planning this year?" she asks Luke, her voice suspicious enough to count as a warning.

"I'm with her," I say, jabbing my thumb in Cindy's direction. "I want a full briefing before I agree to anything. You've got a track record of... creative disasters. Like the Elvis year," I say, ticking them off. "The sexy-elf charity debacle. The time you ordered full-body spandex morphsuits in neon."

"Those were festive!" Luke demands.

"They were a cry for help," Arrow adds.

Cindy chokes on her coffee. "Wait. Sexy elves?"

"Nope." I shake my head. "Absolutely not. That story is sealed in the vault."

"I need to know," she says between laughing fits. "I feel like this is critical information."

"You don't," I say flatly. "No one does."

"But I'll tell you what I'm not doing," she continues, pointing her syrup-covered fork at Luke like it's a dagger. "I am not showing up in some revealing Halloween costume. You know the kind. Lingerie with animal ears. Or a nurse outfit that's basically a bra and optimism. That's a hard no."

The entire table falls into silence.

I'm certain we're all picturing it, because I sure as fuck am.

Arrow has his fork in a death grip, Luke is halfway through a bite and frozen solid, and me? I'm pretty sure I forgot how to chew. Cindy in lingerie. With ears. A little cotton tail. Stockings. Maybe heels. Definitely heels.

"Not... necessarily the worst idea," Arrow says carefully.

"Nope!" Cindy flushes, but she's laughing. "If I'm in lingerie, you three are wearing those novelty animal thongs. Full commitment. Ears. Trunks. No escape."

Luke instantly lights up. "I call the anaconda. Gotta be accurate."

"Right," I say, deadpan. "Because you're known for your massive constrictor energy."

"I'd need the elephant," Arrow continues, not missing a beat. "Trunk capacity. Superior engineering."

"You two are dreaming," I cut in, still trying not to smile. "Clearly, I'd need the blue whale. Largest mammal on earth."

"That's not even an option!" Luke shouts.

"And yet," I say, tearing off another piece of pancake, "I'm still making it work."

Luke squints at me. "Have you been Googling exotic underwear again?"

I raise my brows. "You act like I ever stopped."

Cindy buries her face in her hands, shoulders shaking with laughter. "This is hands down the weirdest breakfast conversation I've ever had."

"There are also giraffe ones," Arrow says as if he's giving a TED talk. "For the height-inclined."

"How the hell would that even work?" I ask, already regretting the question.

"The neck goes up your torso. Real innovative design."

"Damn," Cindy gasps, flinging a strawberry at him like it's a weapon. It hits dead center on his cheek, leaves a little red smear, and Arrow just grins, then eats it.

"No more zoological sex ed at breakfast," she declares, trying to sound stern while laughing.

"You opened the floodgates," Luke says, shrugging.

"I was trying to steer us away from lingerie animal cosplay!"

"Bit late for that after last night," I mutter without thinking.

The second it's out, I know I fucked up. The words hit the table like a shot glass dropped from a rooftop. Cindy's face flames, Arrow raises an eyebrow like he's ready to fan the flames, and Luke? He's full-on choking on his coffee again.

"I meant—"

"We all caught the meaning," Arrow says cheerfully, patting Luke's back as he wheezes.

Cindy downs her orange juice as if it's a shot of tequila. I watch the way her throat works, the flutter of it, and yeah, abort. Not doing this mental reel during pancakes.

I take her glass, refill it just to keep my hands busy, and she gives me this look of apology.

"Fine," she says, voice a little rough. "Costumes are your thing, Luke. But if I end up looking like a Halloween meme come to life—"

"You won't," he cuts in quickly. "You'll look insane. In the best way."

Cindy snorts, shaking her head, but there's color blooming on her cheeks again.

"Swear on my highly curated sense of aesthetic," Luke adds, tracing an overdramatic *X* over his heart.

I catch the way Cindy's gaze follows the motion, the way she bites her lip like she's not even aware of it.

And just like that, breakfast turns into another minefield I'm not sure I'll make it out of intact.

The table falls quiet for a minute, rare for us. The kind of lull that only comes after laughing too hard, too long, and now everyone is digging into their food.

Then I take a bite of pancake, and the taste hits me harder than expected, too sweet, too familiar. Banana walnut. Warm, soft center. Just like the ones my grandmother made the one time she visited us at my parents' place. She had come to fix things between my parents, I think. She cooked breakfast for everyone and tried to make us act like a real family. For one morning, it almost worked. No yelling, no deals being made, no guns on the table. Just pancakes. Even I got to eat as much as I wanted.

Didn't last.

The pancakes remind me of shit I haven't thought about in years. My father, when he was between jobs, which meant between crimes, sometimes tried to play house. Made breakfast like normal families. Except normal families probably didn't have weapons in the cereal boxes or use breakfast conversation to plan drug routes. I started running packages when I was thirteen, small stuff at first. Then guns. Then worse things.

Mom had vanished when I was ten. Tuesday morning she was there; Wednesday she wasn't. Dad said she'd run off with some Beta from her work. The Russians he owed money to said different. Amazing how people can just disappear when someone needs to clear a debt. Never did find out which version was true. Never really wanted to know.

"You okay?" Cindy's voice pulls me back. She's looking at me with those eyes that see too much, catch too many details.

"Fine. Just remembering why I usually don't eat pancakes."

"Bad memories?" she asks, and her foot bumps mine under the table. Not accidentally.

"Something like that."

Her foot stays against mine, just that small point of contact, and it settles something in my chest I didn't know needed settling.

Cindy's phone buzzes. She glances at it, eyes widening. "Shit. I'm going to be late. Work. I need to —" She's already moving, grabbing the last sip of her juice like it might buy her time.

I'm on my feet before I've even made the decision. "I'll drive you. Need to hit the hardware store anyway."

She stops halfway to the stairs, eyes flicking to me. There's hesitation in the wrinkle between her brows, like she wants to accept but isn't sure she should. "You sure?"

"Already getting my keys."

"Let me grab my bag." She heads upstairs.

The second she disappears, Arrow leans back in his chair like he's been waiting for this moment. That smug grin spreads across his face like oil. "Hardware store?"

"Fuck off."

"That was smooth, jumping up to drive her," Luke adds, voice dry. "Worried we might get there first?"

"Worried you two idiots would make her later than she already is." I down the rest of my coffee. It burns, bitter and sharp, and I welcome it. "Someone's got to be responsible."

Arrow's lips twitch "Responsible, huh? Interesting choice of word."

"After last night," Luke mutters, voice dropping like a stone, "game's officially on."

"What game?" Arrow asks, all wide-eyed innocence.

"The one where we all try not to lose our minds and fail spectacularly." Luke snorts, but his jaw is tight. "My money is on Holt. He's been wound tighter than a garrote wire since she walked in."

I don't respond. Can't. Cindy's footsteps echo down the stairs, and then she's there.

And I forget how to fucking breathe.

She's changed into work clothes for a business meeting today. Shouldn't be a big deal. But the sexy, pencil skirt clings to her like sin, and that button-up blouse is doing its best but barely managing containment. The top button is undone. Maybe the second one too. Just enough skin to tease, just enough leg to cause my cock to throb. She's pulling her hair into a loose ponytail, baring the soft column of her neck.

"Ready?" she asks, and I realize I've been staring so long that she's started to shift, uncertain.

"Yeah." My voice is low, rough. I don't clear it.

Two minutes later, we're in my truck. The engine hums, tires crunching gravel as we head toward the mountain road. Her scent hits me before I even shut the door. Clove-studded orange, sugar brittle, and pumpkin spice loaf. But there's more to it today. Deeper. Sweeter. Ripe.

Her heat is getting closer. I feel it in my bones. In the way my hands itch on the steering wheel. In the curl of something primal inside me that wants to turn the truck around, drag her back inside, and make her forget what time is.

She shifts beside me, adjusting her bag, and her thigh presses against the seat in a way that's fucking indecent. She crosses her legs. Uncrosses. The skirt rides up. A sliver of skin flashes, pale and soft, and all I can think about is how warm she'd be if I touched her there. How fast she'd come undone.

The silence stretches. Only the radio hums quietly, playing some moody song neither of us is listening to. I know she's thinking about it too. I sense it in the air, charged and dangerous, like the moment before a storm breaks.

"We should probably talk." Finally, she speaks.

I glance at her.

My grip on the wheel tightens. "About what?"

She doesn't look away. "You saw."

Not a question.

I don't answer.

"I didn't plan it. That wasn't—" She cuts herself off, breath hitching like she's sorting through thoughts that don't want to line up. "It just happened."

I exhale through my nose, keeping my eyes on the road. "You don't owe me an explanation."

"I know I don't," she says quickly. Then, softer: "But I want to give you one anyway, as it's your home too and we had kissed and…"

There's silence between us, but it isn't empty. It's full of everything we're not saying.

"It felt like more," she whispers. "Even with you. Especially with you."

Those words hit harder than I expect. Not because she was with someone else last night—I can live with it being Arrow. We all can. That's the whole damn point of our pack sharing an Omega.

But because *it* meant something.

Because she's saying what I felt too. What I *still* feel every time she glances my way like I'm already hers. As if there's space for *all* of us and a one-off thing.

"I meant what I said," I murmur. "You come first, and we all want to share you. However this plays out. However long I have to wait."

"I guess I was embarrassed, and this is all so new to me," she says.

"I'm not hurt," I say, and this time, it's not a lie. "I just… want more of you. We all do."

Her breath catches. Her thighs press together. She

doesn't respond, but the silence now thrums like a struck wire.

We're both trying to be patient.

We're both failing.

She makes this small sound, not quite a gasp. "I was caught off guard."

"But you enjoyed it. I could smell it. Every second of it."

Her face flames. "God, that's—you could—" She groans and rolls down her window like she needs the cold air to keep from combusting. Wind rushes in, whipping her ponytail around.

"This is torture," she says breathlessly. "My body is completely out of control around you three. Moving in was probably a mistake."

"No," I say, voice low. "No mistake."

My hand moves without permission, finding her bare thigh just above the knee. Her skin is soft, warm, so fucking tempting. She inhales sharply at the contact.

"You're exactly where you're supposed to be."

She turns toward me, eyes wide. "You say that like you believe it."

"I do." I glance at her, jaw clenched. "You're ours, Cindy. Already ours. I'd burn the whole fucking world to prove it, and I'd do it with a smile if it meant getting close enough to breathe you in. Deep. Like I'm starving."

Her scent spikes, and my cock responds instantly,

pressing hard against the seam of my jeans. I shift in my seat, hand tightening on the wheel.

"I need to take it slow," she says, voice unsteady. "My body clearly isn't listening, but my heart—" She swallows. "I need to be sure."

"Sure of what?"

"That this is real. That you want *me*, not just this heat or whatever bond is making everything feel so intense. I have baggage, Holt. My family…" Her voice dips. "They ruin whatever they touch."

"Then they can try and see what happens." My voice is pure gravel now. "Your mother doesn't scare me. I've stared down men twice my size with guns to my head and walked away smiling. I've seen what real monsters look like, gorgeous. And I became one of them just to survive."

She flinches but doesn't look away.

"When I was younger, I believe my father traded my mother to cover his debts. When I was seventeen, I lit a match on a building because that's what loyalty meant back then. No idea if anyone was in there. When I was nineteen, I left someone in a dumpster, bleeding a lot, for touching a girl who'd said no. It didn't matter who he was. He learned not to do it again."

She stares at me.

"I've done things I'll never come back from," I say, parking the truck and cutting the engine. "But I'd do them all over again, every one of them, if it meant keeping you safe. If it meant earning even a piece of whatever you're giving out so freely and still calling a mistake."

She swallows hard, blinking like she's trying to hold back something sharp and real. "You make it sound so simple," she says, voice low. "Like protecting me wouldn't come at a cost. Like you know what you're signing up for."

I reach over, thumb brushing her cheek.

"Let your family come for you," I murmur. "Let the whole goddamn world come. I'll still be here. Standing between you and whatever storm hits. I'm ready."

Her expression softens. Then she leans across the console and kisses me.

It's not desperate.

It's not even hungry.

It's soft, like she's afraid that wanting me too much might shatter something between us.

My forehead drops against hers, breath shaky.

"I think about you," I whisper. "Constantly. In every room. In every silence. When I touch you, it feels like the universe is holding its breath. Like I've been waiting a thousand lifetimes just to taste the stars on your skin."

Her lips part. No words. No breath.

Just that look that says she feels it too.

The one that might just undo me.

"I don't know what I did to earn any of that," she says finally. "But I've never wanted anything more."

She stares at me as if I'm the only steady thing in a world that's always spun too fast.

When she pulls back, we're both breathing hard.

"I should go," she whispers.

"Yeah."

Neither of us moves.

"Tonight," she says. "The festival. It's a date?"

"It's whatever you want it to be."

She smiles, small but real. "It's a date. With all three of you." Then she disappears into the brewery, and I sit there like an idiot, watching her go. Her taste lingers, her scent drowns me, and my cock is so hard it hurts.

I think about what Luke said. The game. Who'll crack first.

Looking at where she disappeared, tasting her on my lips, I know I'm fucked. Completely, thoroughly fucked.

But as I drive away, window down to clear her scent, I realize something: I want her to ruin me. Crave for her to take everything I am and reshape it into something that deserves her. Desperate to mark her skin.

The game isn't who cracks first.

It's whether any of us survive her at all.

20

CINDY

The mansion still doesn't feel real. Even after several days, I keep expecting to wake up in my townhouse with General Flufferton judging me for oversleeping and discover this was all some elaborate fever dream. But here I am, toeing off my work shoes in the entryway of a house that belongs in magazines, listening to Luke talk with excitement.

"Perfect timing!" His hands are clasped together like he's about to reveal Christmas presents in October. "Costumes are in your rooms. No complaining, no negotiating, no returns. Just get dressed and get back down here before I die of anticipation."

"What did you do?" I ask, already nervous but also thrilled.

All day at work, I haven't been able to stop thinking about Holt. His gruff voice in the truck saying my family couldn't break him. But more than that, the way his whole face transformed when he picked me up after work. Pure, uncomplicated joy at seeing me, like I was the highlight of his entire day.

Growing up, no one was ever excited to see me. Maybe my aunt on the rare occasions I could visit her, but those moments were few and far between, precious because of their scarcity. My parents saw me as either a disappointment or a commodity to trade for social standing. Van saw me as property he'd purchased but hadn't taken delivery of yet. To have someone's face light up just because I walked through a door? It's the most wonderful thing I've ever experienced.

"Arrow is already up there getting changed," Luke says, snapping me from my thoughts.

From upstairs, Arrow's voice carries clearly through the house. "What the fuck is this supposed to be? Luke, I swear to God, if this is some kinky bullshit—"

"Just put it on," Luke yells back, cupping his hands around his mouth. "It's classic Americana!"

"Classic, my ass!"

Holt appears behind me from the doorway. He takes one look at Luke's expression and groans.

"Please tell me you didn't do something that's going to get us arrested for public indecency."

"Everything important is covered!" Luke protests. "Just go look, big man. Trust me, you'll love it. Or at least you won't immediately set it on fire, which is really all I can ask for with you three."

"Your confidence is overwhelming," I say, but I'm

already heading for the stairs, curiosity winning over caution.

"LUKE!" Arrow's voice booms again. "Why are these pants made of velvet? Do you know what velvet does to my thighs?"

"Makes them look amazing?" Luke suggests hopefully.

"Makes them look like I'm smuggling hams!"

I rush to my room, pushing open the door to find General Flufferton sprawled across my pillow. He wakes with a chirping meow that sounds accusatory, immediately demanding attention by aggressively headbutting my hand.

"Hello, my precious demon," I coo, scratching behind his ears the way that makes him purr like a broken motor. "Guess what? Luke got us costumes and —oh. My. God."

I actually squeal. Like a teenager-at-a-concert squeal.

Laid out on my bed is a light blue gingham pinafore dress with a white blouse underneath, complete with puffy short sleeves that have tiny pearl buttons. Ruby red shoes that shine like fresh blood in the lamplight. White socks with little lace edges that are somehow both innocent and not. And the pièce de résistance, a small dog-shaped brown handbag.

"He made me Dorothy!" I'm laughing and spinning even though no one can see me except General Flufferton, who appears deeply unimpressed. "That means the guys are—oh, this is going to be hilarious."

I shut my door and lock it for good measure, then rush to change. Through the walls, I hear the guys complaining but can't make out their words.

It's already getting dark outside, past seven, since Holt insisted on stopping for burgers on the way home. We sat in his truck in the local burger joint's parking lot like teenagers hiding from their parents, special sauce dripping onto napkins neither of us had enough of.

He ate with one hand, scrolled through his phone with the other, occasionally showing me videos of cats being assholes. It was weirdly intimate. Sharing messy food in comfortable silence, him handing me extra napkins without being asked, just knowing I'd need them, was perfect.

Back in the bathroom, I take a quick shower. I towel-dry my hair, then blast it just long enough that it won't drip, leaving the waves to fall loose.

When I get back to my room, I pause at my underwear drawer.

No one is going to see what I'm wearing. The dress is modest enough, hitting mid-thigh. But still... my fingers hover over the sensible cotton options before drifting to the red lace thong I bought on a whim months ago after Harper dragged me into a clothing store.

The tag is still on.

Not anymore.

"It matches the shoes," I tell General Flufferton, who's watching me with those judgmental green eyes.

"That's the only reason. Color coordination is important."

He slow-blinks, which, in cat language, means either "I love you" or "You're full of shit." Knowing him, probably both.

The costume fits perfectly. How did Luke know my size so accurately? The dress hugs my waist before flaring out, the gingham design somehow both wholesome and flirty. The blouse buttons properly without gaping at the chest, miracle of miracles. The shoes fit like they were made for me, and when I do an experimental walk, I don't immediately fall over.

I do a twirl in the mirror and laugh at myself. I look like Dorothy if Dorothy had grown up, developed curves, and decided Kansas was overrated.

General Flufferton meows at the door, demanding freedom with increasing volume.

"Okay, okay. You'd think I was holding you prisoner."

I let him out, and he immediately rockets down the hall to Arrow's partially open door, his tail a flag of feline determination.

"Hey there, Sir Floof." I hear Arrow's voice go soft and gooey. "Come to see the disaster Luke created? At least someone appreciates my suffering."

Smoochy sounds follow, the kind that would ruin Arrow's dangerous reputation if anyone heard them. For someone who looks like he eats nails for breakfast and has definitely hidden bodies, Arrow turns into absolute pudding around my cat.

Downstairs, I find Luke waiting on the couch.

He's dressed as the Scarecrow, but makes it fashionable. Patched pants in various shades of brown and tan that sit low on his hips. A raggedy jacket, patches and tears revealing his entire torso, held partially closed by a rope instead of a belt. He's wearing nothing underneath, just his bare chest with its lean muscle and scattered tattoos. There's actual straw sticking out of his sleeves, his collar, even tucked behind his ears. His hair is styled to stick up in twelve directions like he's been electrocuted, and somehow it works.

"Holy shit," I breathe, eloquent as always.

"Right back at you, Dorothy." He stands, circling me slowly like a predator who's spotted dinner. "Sexiest Kansas farm girl I've ever seen. Makes me want to skip down your yellow brick road. Click your heels three times. Find your Emerald City."

Then he's kissing me, backing me against the wall with intent, and coherent thought evacuates the premises. His mouth is demanding, hungry, tongue sliding against mine. My knees forget their job. His hands grip my waist through the thin dress, and I moan into the kiss without meaning to. My fingers tangle in his jacket, pulling him closer, feeling straw scratch against my palms.

Someone clears their throat with the volume and duration of a foghorn.

We break apart to find Arrow and Holt at the bottom of the stairs, and I start laughing so hard I actually snort, which makes me laugh harder.

Arrow is the Cowardly Lion, and he looks simultaneously ridiculous and somehow still intimidating. Brown velvet pants that definitely make his thighs look powerful rather than ham-like, despite his protests. A matching brown velvet jacket that's fighting for its life across his shoulders. But the collar is a masterpiece of faux-fur absurdity, so enormous that it frames his face like a mane made of brown cotton candy. He looks like a lion who got stuck in a craft store explosion. But it matches his dark blond hair.

Holt is the Tin Man, wearing silver-gray pants and a jacket that looks like someone attacked it with metallic spray paint. Multiple coats, by the looks of it, some spots darker where the paint pooled. Silver gloves and painted boots that were definitely black yesterday. And there's an actual funnel attached to his head with what appears to be elastic string.

"We look fucking ridiculous," Holt states flatly, the funnel bobbing when he talks.

"We look amazing!" I counter, still giggling every time the funnel moves. "This is perfect! We're the whole *Wizard of Oz* gang! This is genius!"

Arrow groans. "We're dressed as a children's movie."

"A classic film!" Luke protests, throwing his arms wide, which sends more straw flying.

"I look like I lost a bet with a hardware store," Holt mutters, holding up his silver-gloved hands.

"You look like a sexy robot," I offer, which has Luke snorting behind me.

"Sexy robot. The pinnacle of masculinity," Holt says. "Really gets the gears grinding. 'Oh, baby, upgrade my firmware.'"

"At least you're not covered in crushed velvet," Arrow mutters, dragging a finger under the collar threatening to devour his jawline. "I feel like I'm being slow-roasted inside a limited-edition teddy bear."

"You make a very regal lion," I assure him, reaching up to adjust a piece of his mane that has started to wilt. "Powerful. Ready to conquer."

"I'm supposed to be cowardly," he replies, brow furrowing. "It's kind of the whole bit."

"Then maybe stop giving off the vibe of a guy who'd win a bar fight just by looking bored."

"And I'd still win."

"If I'm going to die inside, I at least want to do it with a caramel apple in my hand," Holt adds.

Before we leave, I duck into the kitchen.

General Flufferton is already glaring at me as he runs alongside me into the kitchen. I pour a bowl of the only food His Royal Highness deems edible after rejecting three other brands like the furry little food critic he is. And a fresh water bowl.

"We won't be long," I whisper, leaning in to scratch him between the ears. "Defend the homeland. Scratch any burglars. You know, standard cat ops."

He meows once. Then he dives into the food.

Once outside, we pile into Holt's truck, where I end up in the front seat. Arrow and Luke are in the back,

Arrow's fluffy mane taking up enough space to qualify for its own zip code.

"I can't see a damn thing," Luke gripes. "I'm getting Simba'd in the face back here."

"Good," Arrow says, not even pretending to sound sorry. "Let it deepen your character."

The costume makes it hard to sit normally, the dress riding up no matter how much I tug it down. Holt's hand rests on the gearshift, knuckles occasionally brushing my knee when he changes gears, and each touch sends little electric shocks up my leg.

"So," Luke says as we cruise down the winding road toward the festival, his chin resting between the front seats. "We should practice our characters. Get into the roles. Method acting."

"Absolutely fucking not," Holt replies, jerking the wheel just enough to send Luke flying backward with a squawk.

Arrow snorts. "You deserved that."

"Come on!" Luke protests from the back seat. "Arrow, you're the Cowardly Lion. Give us a roar. Or maybe a whimper. Dealer's choice."

"I'll give you something, all right," Arrow growls. "A demonstration of natural selection."

"See? That's perfect! Lions are noble but deadly."

"Lions are also known for eating their young," Arrow adds, glancing out the window. "Want a demonstration?"

I laugh, twisting in my seat to glance back at them. Arrow's mane is half in Luke's face. Holt's funnel glints in the streetlights, and I feel… weirdly content. Like I've stumbled into some chaotic fairy tale I didn't audition for but somehow got cast in anyway.

"I don't think any of you actually know the story," I say. "The lion is sweet. Scared of everything. He just wants courage."

Arrow raises a brow. "Have you met me? I don't do scared. I do scary."

"And I respect that," I say, biting back a grin. "But you do kind of growl when people try to hug you."

Luke pokes Holt in the shoulder. "The Tin Man needs oil for his joints. You should walk stiff. Like you've got a stick up your—"

"Finish that sentence and you're walking to the festival," Holt cuts in, not even looking away from the road.

"That's not very Tin Man of you," Luke states. "He's gentle. Emotional. Just wants a heart."

"I'll show you emotional," Holt mutters. "It's called rage."

"Incredible," I deadpan. "We've managed to traumatize the entire cast of *The Wizard of Oz* in under five minutes."

"And I'm the Scarecrow," Luke declares proudly. "Which works because I'm brainless, right? That's what you were all thinking."

"No one said that," I lie, then pause. "Out loud."

"First accurate thing he's said all night," Arrow mutters.

"You two are assholes," Luke says with a chuckle. "Not the fun kind. The judgmental kind."

The truck quiets for a moment, only the hum of the tires and the soft shuffle of Arrow adjusting his overly large mane. The playlist Holt queued up earlier keeps playing softly, some moody, guitar-heavy track I don't recognize, but it fits.

"Have any of you actually seen the movie?" I ask, glancing around suspiciously.

Silence.

Not guilty silence. The kind that comes with a sprinkle of panic and a dash of shame.

"Luke?" I prompt.

He clears his throat. "I may have... Wikipedia'd it yesterday."

"*Luke.*"

"What? I knew there was a yellow road and possibly some flying monkeys. That counts for something."

"There's definitely a witch," Arrow adds. "Green face, riding around on a broom, cackling. Classic witch shit."

"And a house falls on her sister," Luke chimes in. "Right? So really, the story begins with an act of homicide."

"Technically manslaughter," I say. "Unless Dorothy aimed."

"I knew I liked her," Holt mutters.

"Of course you did," I say under my breath, turning back to the windshield.

Holt's hand brushes mine on the console. Not on purpose, but I don't move away. Neither does he. And in this truck, full of velvet, fur, synthetic silver, and emotional chaos disguised as humor, something warm settles in my chest. Like I've already found something worth holding on to, even if I can't name it yet.

The festival grounds are already in sight, and packed when we arrive, the sky painted in those perfect October colors of orange bleeding into purple, last gasps of pink before full darkness takes over. The air smells like everything good about fall, kettle corn and apple cider, that crisp leaf smell that only happens this time of year.

The parking lot is chaos. Teenagers in reflective vests direct traffic with the seriousness of air traffic controllers. We pile out of the truck, and I smooth my dress down.

We follow the slow stream of festivalgoers toward an arched gateway made of black wrought iron wrapped in twinkling orange lights and thick spider-webbing. A giant skeleton grins down from above, animatronic eyes glowing red as it creaks to life with a motion sensor and lets out a hollow, echoing *boo*. Around us there's laughter, the occasional scream from the haunted maze, and the tinny jangle of a nearby merry-go-round.

Inside the festival grounds, the path opens up into a wide clearing filled with vendor booths, flickering jack-o'-lanterns, and oversized decor straight out of a Halloween fever dream. Hay bales double as benches, and a scarecrow DJ spins music beneath a canopy of black and gold flags flapping in the breeze.

"Photo opportunity!" a man calls out cheerfully, waving one arm while balancing a massive camera rig with the other. He's stationed right in front of the main attraction, a genuinely impressive haunted house that looks like it was designed by someone with both a budget and psychological issues. "All festival photos will be available for viewing and purchase at the exit tent!"

Arrow makes a face like he's just been told he has to sing karaoke. "Hard pass."

"Come on," Luke urges, already nodding to the man with the camera setup stationed near the huge haunted house façade. The photographer grins as we approach.

"Right this way, Wizard of Oddballs," the man announces.

"Wizard of shut your face," Holt mutters under his breath, adjusting the silver funnel on his head.

We arrange ourselves. Holt on my left, Luke on my right, Arrow on Luke's far side. The photographer starts snapping immediately.

"Lion, stop looking like you're planning murder!"

"Tin Man, the funnel is crooked!"

"Scarecrow, more straw is falling out!"

"Dorothy, perfect, don't change a thing!"

He takes a photo of us posing. Then he takes another one of all three of the men leaning in to kiss my cheeks at once. I burst out laughing as Arrow's mane tickles my neck and Luke's straw pokes my shoulder. The flash goes off mid-giggle.

"Beautiful!" the photographer exclaims. "That one's definitely going in the festival highlights reel. Check the tent later!"

I step back, cheeks flushed from the attention, the laughter, the unspoken heat of being surrounded like that.

The festival stretches out ahead of us like a storybook come to life. Stalls offer pumpkin spice funnel cakes, maple-bacon kettle corn, caramel apple cider, and a suspiciously gray pumpkin cotton candy that I make a mental note *not* to try.

Overhead, strings of orange and purple lights crisscross like a glowing canopy, woven with fake autumn leaves so convincing I have to resist the urge to catch one. Every surface is lit up, jack-o'-lanterns grin from haystacks, tabletops, and wooden shelves, each one unique. Some are terrifying, others artistic masterpieces.

Somewhere, a band plays a rock cover of "Monster Mash," managing to make it weirdly aggressive and catchy. The bass vibrates through the ground as people in every costume imaginable wander past—Spice Girls with glittering makeup, four different versions of Pennywise, ranging from nightmare fuel to sad clown, and what appears to be an entire bachelor party dressed as breakfast cereals.

"The haunted house already has a long line. We

should go to the hayride first," Arrow says, pulling us forward through the crowd.

Luke takes my hand as we weave through people, his fingers interlacing with mine like it's the most natural thing in the world. His hand is huge, warm. My skin tingles at every point of contact, warmth spreading up my arm and settling somewhere in my chest.

"Cindy?" a female voice calls out. I know that voice, and every muscle in my body tenses.

I turn to find my cousin Sarah, dressed as what can only be described as a sexy witch who lost most of her costume in a terrible accident, looking my way.

"Sarah." My voice comes out steadier than I feel, which is a minor miracle.

Her eyes rake over me, taking in the Dorothy costume, then the men, lingering on my joined hands with Luke with the kind of focus usually reserved for finding Waldo. "Interesting costume choice. Very... wholesome."

Luke pulls me against his side, arm sliding around my waist possessively, hand splaying across my hip in a way that's definitely not wholesome.

"Babe, we're going to miss the hayride," he says, voice carrying that edge of impatience guys get when they want to be anywhere else.

Then he kisses me.

Not a peck. Not a performance. He kisses me like we're alone in his bedroom, as though he's been thinking about this all day. His tongue sweeps into my mouth, tasting like mint. His hand tangles in my hair, messing up whatever style I'd achieved. The other hand pulls me closer until I'm pressed against him completely, feeling every hard line of his body.

When he pulls back, I'm dazed, lips tingling, probably looking thoroughly kissed. Sarah's mouth is hanging open like she's witnessing a miracle or a tragedy, possibly both.

"Nice seeing you," Luke tells her cheerfully, as if he didn't just stake a claim in front of God and everybody. "Enjoy your night!"

He guides me away, hand firm on my lower back.

"Let's go," Luke says, loud enough for Sarah to hear. "Tonight is about having fun. You're ours for the evening. Forget everything else exists."

I glance back once. Sarah is still watching, probably already composing the family group-chat message. Good. Let her report back that I'm happy, that I'm not the family failure hiding in a small town. Let her tell my mother how Luke kissed me like I was precious and necessary.

"Thank you," I whisper to Luke as we walk behind Arrow and Holt.

"Any excuse to kiss you," he replies. "Plus, your cousin looks like she sucks lemons for fun. Figured I'd give her something actually sour to chew on."

I burst out laughing as Holt slows down on my other side, taking my free hand and lifting it to his lips for a kiss that's somehow just as possessive.

We reach the entrance to the hayride, a wooden

arch that appears to have been built by someone with a Gothic sensibility and a love of the dramatic. A sign painted in what's supposed to look like blood reads ABANDON HOPE ALL YE WHO ENTER — MADMAN'S LAST RIDE.

"Subtle," Arrow observes.

The haunted hay wagon is actually an old wooden cart that looks like it was dragged from the set of a horror movie, left to age for a decade, and then dragged back—weathered boards that have definitely seen better days, rusted metal fixtures that probably violate several safety codes, and beams of wood as seating. It's attached to a tractor.

"This is definitely interesting," I say as the guys help me climb in, Luke's hands on my waist lifting me easily.

"Where's your sense of adventure?" Luke asks, though he's also eyeing the rusted bolts suspiciously.

I try not to flash everyone as my dress rides up, quickly smoothing it down once I'm seated. The wagon has bench seating along both sides, our legs dangling out through gaps in the wooden slats that serve as minimal protection from falling out. We are facing the outside of the wagon. Five other people are already aboard—a couple dressed as a zombie bride and groom, complete with fake blood and torn formal wear, two women costumed in what might be vampire flight attendants, and a guy who's either dressed as a serial killer or just has an unfortunate fashion sense.

Holt sits on my left, his thigh pressed against mine

from hip to knee. Luke is on my right, close enough that I can smell the straw mixed with his cologne. Arrow is beside Luke, his mane taking up lots of space.

The tractor roars to life with a belch, and we lurch forward into the woods. The path is barely visible, just two ruts in the dirt that the wheels follow, and the trees close in immediately like they've been waiting. Someone has strung lights sporadically to create ominous shadows, not enough to actually see what's making those rustling sounds.

"Welcome, damned souls," the driver calls back in a raspy voice that's trying too hard, but we appreciate the effort. "To Henley Farm, where the corn grows tall, the nights grow cold, and the screams... well, the screams never stop."

"Starting strong with the melodrama," Arrow mutters, but he's grinning.

The tractor pushes us deeper into the woods, and whoever designed this really committed to the atmosphere. Fog machines hidden in the trees create thick mist that swirls around the wagon. Hidden speakers play ambient sounds of chains rattling, distant screams, and children singing nursery rhymes, which is somehow the worst part.

"Legend says," the driver continues, really leaning into his role, "that Farmer Henley went mad one October night in 1887. Killed his whole family with a rusty scythe, then himself. But on nights like this, when the veil is thin and the moon is high, he returns. Looking for new souls to harvest. New blood to—"

Something rustles in the trees to our left. We all turn—

A figure bursts from the bushes, wielding a chainsaw that's definitely running but hopefully bladeless. He's wearing a bloody apron over overalls, face hidden by what appears to be a leather mask. Everyone screams, including me and the guys.

"That was a warrior's cry," Holt claims, voice slightly higher than normal.

"Practice shouting," Arrow corrects, hand over his heart.

"I was warning you all," Luke adds. "Through screaming."

I'm laughing too hard to call them on their bullshit. The chainsaw figure chases the wagon briefly, really committing to the bit, before disappearing back into the woods.

We round a bend and enter what's supposed to be an abandoned farm but is clearly a section they've set up specifically for scares. Broken fence posts lean at impossible angles, a scarecrow that's definitely going to move because that's how these things work, and... is that a body hanging from a tree?

"Oh, that's just a mannequin," the driver says casually. "Probably. We think. No one's checked recently."

The scarecrow does indeed move, lurching toward the wagon with jerky movements that would be scary if the actor weren't clearly fighting with the costume. One of the vampire flight attendants shrieks. Luke grabs my hand.

"You're safe," he murmurs in my ear, breath warm against my skin. "I'll protect you from the fake and the real monsters."

"My hero," I tease and lean into him because his warmth feels good in the cooling night air.

More figures jump out as we continue, a headless horseman whose head under his arm has an LED light in it for some reason, zombie farmers who shuffle, something in a wedding dress that's actually genuinely creepy with the way it moves.

Then the tractor stops in a clearing.

"What's happening?" the zombie bride asks nervously.

A figure emerges from the cornfield. Tall, wearing overalls and a straw hat, carrying a scythe in one hand and—

"Is that a dildo?" someone asks, not even trying to be quiet about it.

It absolutely is. A large purple anatomically ambitious dildo that the figure is now waving around like a battle flag.

The entire wagon goes silent for three full seconds. Then everyone bursts into hysterical laughter.

"Local legend says"—the driver tries to continue seriously, but he's clearly fighting not to laugh—"that Farmer Henley wasn't just mad. He was also a pirate before he became a farmer. Lost his eye in a battle at sea, which drove him to madness and... unusual appetites."

"A pirate farmer?" Holt asks, glaring at Luke and Arrow. "That's the story we're going with?"

"The high seas of Kansas!" Luke shouts, tears streaming down his face from laughing.

"Captain Henley, they called me," Farmer Henley wails, waving both scythe and sex toy with equal enthusiasm. "Scourge of the seven seas! Master of... navigation!"

"Navigation!" Arrow wheezes, and I'm laughing wildly. "With his purple compass!"

"Legend says he buried his treasure right here," the driver continues, completely committed now. "But what kind of treasure, no one knows."

"I think we can guess," the zombie groom manages between gasps as the wagon starts moving again.

"Revenge for me eye!" Farmer Henley screams. "And me... other things!"

"This is the best and worst thing I've ever experienced," I wheeze, sides aching from laughter.

"You assholes set this up, didn't you?" Holt warns.

The rest of the ride is almost anticlimactic after that. More jump scares, more fog, a pretty convincing werewolf who might have actually been scary if we weren't all still giggling about Captain Farmer Henley. Finally, we're back where we started, everyone climbing out on shaky legs.

Arrow lifts me down from the wagon, hands lingering on my waist longer than necessary. Heat pours from his touch.

"Enjoy that?" he asks, voice low enough that only I can hear.

"That was amazing. Ridiculous, but amazing."

"Our whole night has been ridiculous." His eyes drop to my lips. "Doesn't mean it's not perfect."

"MAZE TIME!" Holt announces, already striding toward a field where enormous hedges have been grown and groomed into walls taller than any of us. "And before anyone argues, Cindy starts with me. It's only fair."

"How is that fair?" Arrow protests, jogging to keep up behind us. "You had her on the hayride. Luke got to kiss her in front of her cousin. My turn."

"This isn't a custody arrangement!" Luke's voice is exasperated, but there's laughter bubbling under it.

"It is now." Holt already has my hand in his, possessive and decisive, tugging me with him through the crowd. His grip is warm and solid, his fingers curling over mine like he has every right to them. "Luke, Arrow, go get snacks or something. Win her a prize. We'll meet you after."

"Fuck, this is your payback for the pirate story, isn't it?" Luke shouts after us, throwing his arms up.

Holt doesn't even glance over his shoulder but chuckles as he drags me toward the towering hedge maze glowing ahead.

The entrance of ivy-covered lattice looms like a mouth ready to swallow us whole, arching overhead, threaded with flickering fairy lights and black paper bats that flutter in the breeze. A fog machine pumps lazy curls of mist around our ankles as we step beneath the archway, and just like that, the sounds of the festival begin to fade, muffled by the thick green walls that rise at least ten feet high on either side.

We plunge into the maze quickly.

The hedges are dense and dark, the kind of living barrier that swallows light and sound. Up close, the leaves are sharp-edged and waxy, and it's clear this isn't some flimsy setup thrown together for decoration. This thing is *real*—designed to trap, confuse, disorient.

Small solar lights dot the gravel pathway, casting just enough glow to keep us from walking headfirst into a wall, but not enough to see more than a few feet ahead. It's like being inside a cathedral that's tall and quiet, with every footstep muffled by crushed leaves and damp earth.

"I know this maze well," Holt says as we take our third left turn without hesitation. He sounds almost smug. "Helped design it, actually. The owner is an old friend who owed me a favor from... never mind what from."

I stop short and yank my hand out of his, giving him a wide-eyed look. "That's cheating!"

His brows lift. "Cheating?"

"Where's the adventure if you already know the way?"

He steps closer, and the narrowness of the path means I have to tilt my head up to meet his eyes. The light hits his face just enough to make his smirk visible, and the way he looks at me then? It's like I'm the only thing that's ever mattered.

"The fun is catching you," he says softly.

The words sink into me like ink into paper, slow and staining. There's something about the way he says it, all calm, certain, as if he's already pictured exactly how this ends. It sends a shiver down my spine that has nothing to do with the crisp October air.

My heart stutters. I try not to let it show.

"Only if you can catch me," I shoot back, trying for playful, but my voice comes out breathless.

Then I bolt away, grinning, laughing, sprinting down the next turn without waiting for his reply. My shoes crunch on gravel as I dodge past a hanging skeleton prop and weave around a corner lit with a jack-o'-lantern whose grin is way too smug.

Behind me, there's a low, amused curse, and then the sound of boots pounding after me.

The game is on.

I dart down a side path, my laugh echoing off the hedge walls. The dress flares as I run, ruby shoes clicking on the packed-dirt path. He's behind me, not running but walking with purpose.

"Cindy," he calls. "You can't escape. This maze is huge, but not infinite. And I know every dead end, every loop, every secret passage."

"Then I'd better run faster!" I state, taking a right turn at random, grinning.

"Run all you want. I like the chase."

God help me, that voice. Deep and certain and

amused, like he's enjoying this game as much as I am. I peek around a corner to an empty path stretching ahead. I dart across to another section, trying to put distance between us, but his footsteps are there, steady and unhurried.

"You know what happens when I catch you?" His voice seems to come from everywhere and nowhere, the acoustics of the maze playing tricks.

"*If* you catch me," I call back, breathless from running and anticipation.

"When," he corrects, and suddenly he's there, stepping out from a path I didn't even see.

I shriek and try to dodge, but he's faster than someone his size should be. He suddenly catches me around the waist, lifting me clean off my feet. I'm laughing and struggling half-heartedly as he throws me over his shoulder in one smooth motion, my protests lost in breathless giggles.

"Got you," he growls, hand on the back of my thighs to keep me steady.

"Now you're mine."

"I can walk!" I exclaim, but I'm not really trying to get down.

"Soon." He's carrying me deeper into the maze, to a section that seems older, where the hedges are thicker and the paths narrower.

He stops at what looks like a solid wall of hedge, then shoulders through what's actually a concealed opening. The branches part around us, and he pushes them back into place behind us. We're in a small clearing, maybe ten feet across, hay strewn on the ground like someone prepared this. The sounds of the festival are muted here, distant. The moon is directly overhead, providing silvery light that makes everything look like a dream.

"You planned this," I accuse as he sets me down, but I'm not really upset. My heart is racing, skin tingling where he touched me.

"Might have made some arrangements for us to be alone... a kind of date that involves chasing you." He doesn't step back, keeping me caged between him and the hedge wall. "Asked the owner to maintain this spot specially. Told him it was for a marriage proposal."

"Holt—"

"Was I lying?" His hands come up to frame my face, thumbs stroking my cheekbones. "Because the way I see it, you're already ours. We're just waiting for you to realize it."

My whole body flushes hot at his words, at the certainty in them. "You can't just decide—"

"I can. I have. We all have." His thumb traces my bottom lip. "You think I was going to let you escape from us? Return to that townhouse alone? Or pretend this isn't real?"

"This is going too fast."

"I know you take your coffee with usually no sugar and lots of cream. I know you sing off-key in the shower when you think no one's listening. I know you check the locks three times before bed because you're still scared someone's going to come for you." His voice drops lower. "And I can tell you've been wet since we left home. I can smell it on you, how much you want this."

"God..."

"I can be your god, if that's what you want?" He grins sinfully. "Tell me you don't want this and to take you back to the others right now, and I will. We'll go eat caramel apples and pretend I don't know what your lips taste like. Pretend I haven't been thinking about you all day, every day, since you walked into our lives."

I stare up at him, his funnel hat long lost somewhere in the maze, eyes dark with want in the moonlight.

"I can't tell you that," I whisper.

"Then tell me what you can say."

"Don't take me back. Don't pretend. Don't stop."

He makes a sound that's pure Alpha satisfaction, and then his mouth is on mine and everything else ceases to matter.

21

The festival noise fades to a distant static. The maze walls become protective rather than confining. Even the October chill disappears, replaced by heat that starts where his lips meet mine and spreads through every cell of my body.

"You'd better keep it down," he whispers against my mouth. "Unless you want everyone to hear us."

I giggle like a teenager, which should be embarrassing but somehow isn't. "Then maybe we shouldn't do anything that would make me loud."

He laughs, low and rumbling, the sound vibrating through his chest where I'm pressed against him. "I never run from danger. Or risks. Especially not when the risk looks like you in this dress."

Then he's kissing me again, and this isn't the desperate hunger from before. This is deliberate, thorough, like he's memorizing the exact way our mouths fit together. His hands frame my face, thumbs stroking my cheekbones as his tongue traces the seam of my lips. I open for him immediately. My hands grip his silver-painted jacket.

He walks me backward until my back hits the hedge wall, the branches giving slightly under my weight. One of his hands slides into my hair, angling my head for better access, while the other grips my waist. The kiss deepens, becomes something more urgent, more necessary. I make a sound I've never made before that's needy and desperate, and he swallows it, pressing closer until there's no space between us.

"You've been driving me crazy," he whispers when we break for air, both of us panting.

"Since last night. You've been struggling, haven't you?" I murmur.

"You have no fucking idea," he growls, then his hand comes down on my ass in a light spank that makes my eyes fly wide.

"Hey!"

"Been wanting to do that since you bent over to feed the cat in this dress."

Before I can respond, he's lifting me like I weigh nothing, carrying me to where the hay is spread thicker. The walls tower around us, creating our own private world. Above, stars scatter across the sky like someone threw diamonds on black velvet. The moon is almost full, providing enough light to see but not enough to feel exposed.

He sets me down gently on the hay, then shrugs

out of his ridiculous silver jacket. He's wearing nothing underneath, and I'm drooling. His chest is all muscle. Tattoos wind across his skin, dark ink that looks silver in the moonlight.

"Thank God," he mutters, tossing the jacket aside. "That thing was suffocating me. Spray paint doesn't breathe."

Then he's lying beside me, kissing me again with an intensity that makes my head spin. My hands explore his bare chest, following ink, feeling muscles contract under my touch. He's so warm, like a furnace, and I press closer, wanting that heat.

"I need you," I whisper against his mouth, surprising myself with my boldness. "I've been thinking about this, about you, constantly."

"Fuck, Cindy," he groans.

His hands glide up my thighs under the dress, making me squirm with anticipation. He lifts up my skirt, and his eyes go dark when he sees what I'm wearing underneath.

"Red lace," he says, his voice turning rough. "Matching your shoes. Beautiful."

"I thought—I wanted—"

"They need to come off," he demands, already hooking his fingers in the sides.

"We shouldn't—not here—"

But he's already tugging them down, and I lift my hips to help because my body has completely disconnected from my brain. Part of me is screaming that this is too public, too dangerous, but the bigger part that's been burning for days doesn't care. The danger makes this moment better somehow, the possibility of being caught adding an edge.

He tucks the red lace into his pocket with a grin that's pure masculine satisfaction. "Mine now."

"Thief," I accuse, but I'm breathless, already anticipating what comes next.

He kisses my neck, finding that spot that makes me melt, while his fingers trace up my inner thighs. I spread my legs wider without thinking, and he makes this sound of approval that goes straight to my core.

"I can barely hold it together," I gasp as his fingers inch higher. "You're teasing me so bad."

"You want me to touch you higher?" His voice is dark, knowing. "Is that what you're asking for?"

"You're pure evil," I whisper, breath catching on the words.

Holt's answering grin is slow and wicked, a promise that coils heat low in my stomach. He leans in close, his breath brushing my ear. "You like it," he murmurs.

Then he touches me, gently at first, just a drag of fingertips closer to my bikini line that causes every nerve to spark awake. The hay rustles beneath me as I arch, trying to chase the warmth he gives and takes away in equal measure.

"Shh," he says, but the sound isn't a warning. It's more like worship disguised as a command.

When his hand slides downward, the first touch of his fingers across my lower lips has me gasping, the air leaving my lungs in a sharp, helpless sound. My whole body responds to him, to the press of his fingertips.

"Look at you," he whispers, watching my face. "So sweet. So ready."

I can't look away. The intensity in his gaze leaves the world tilting, the weight of it a promise and a threat all at once. Each slow stroke pulls me higher as my thighs tremble, and I forget the world beyond his touch.

"Tell me," he breathes, lips grazing my throat. "Does it feel good?"

"Amazing." It's barely a sound, more breath than voice.

He doesn't rush. His touch is maddening in its slowness, like he wants to memorize the way my body reacts, how I breathe, how I break. His fingers drag through the slick between my thighs with such careful precision that it borders on cruelty. Every movement is a tease, never quite enough to push me over, but always circling the edge like he knows exactly what I need and refuses to give it too soon.

My hips lift instinctively, chasing the desire he keeps pulling away. I'm trembling now, muscles drawn tight, every nerve screaming for more. I dig my nails into his shoulders, trying to stabilize myself, but he only groans like the sting excites him. It makes me feel powerful and undone all at once.

"Fuck," he whispers, voice rough against my throat. "You feel like sin."

Then his mouth is on my collarbone. When he drags his teeth lightly over the neckline of my dress, the fabric gives a little. A quiet sound escapes me, half gasp, half invitation. He follows it, tugging until the material slips lower, releasing my breast. His breath fans across my skin before his mouth closes over my hardened nipple, a slow kiss that makes my whole body tighten.

I moan, hungry goose bumps covering me.

His tongue flicks over the hard center before sucking it deeper. I cry out, too far gone to care who hears. The scrape of his stubble burns in the best way. Each pull of his mouth on my nipple tugs at something low in my belly.

It's at this moment that he presses a finger into me, and I shudder, the sensation overwhelming, incredible, leaving me starved for more. Then he pushes a second one in while he sucks down hard on my nipple, not releasing me.

The pressure of his fingers builds and builds, going faster, harder, my hips rocking to meet him, until I feel like I'm going to burst apart in his hands.

When the orgasm breaks, it's all light and pulse and breath, his name caught in my throat as he holds me through it, murmuring something I can't quite catch except for one word: beautiful. But I don't remember a climax ever feeling this intense, this spectacular.

I gasp for air, finally opening my eyes. He's still watching me. There's nothing playful left in him now, only hunger in his gaze. And he pulls his fingers out of me, leaving me gasping, needing them back.

"That was incredible."

He grins mischievously. "Are you ready for more, then?" he asks.

I nod, then find my voice. "I want this. Want you. But... you'll be my first."

His whole face changes. The smile that spreads across his features is brilliant, boyish almost, completely at odds with his usual intensity.

"Cindy," he breathes, kissing me softly. "Thank you for trusting me with this gift. I'll remember this forever."

We kiss for long moments, sweet and deep, before I pull back and he says, "We could wait. Until we're home—"

"No," I interrupt. "I want this here. Now. I want a story for my first time, something wild and fun. I haven't felt this alive in so long."

I'm already reaching for his belt, fingers fumbling with the buckle while he remains lying beside me in the hay. He helps, lifting his hips so I can pull his pants down enough. When I wrap my hand around his huge cock, we both groan. He's big, thick and hard and perfect, and I stroke him, loving how it feels.

"Fuck," he hisses, catching my wrist. "Can't do that or this'll be over before it starts."

"How do you want me?" I ask, feeling brave and reckless.

"On your back," he instructs, shifting and positioning himself between my thighs, where he kneels before me. "I want to see your face. Want to watch you."

He stares down at where I'm spread out for him, my skirt up to my waist, and the expression on his face makes me feel like a goddess. "So fucking perfect," he murmurs. "Absolutely delicious."

He grips his cock and leans in closer, aligning himself at my entrance, the broad head pressing against me. "Ready?"

"Beyond ready," I breathe.

He pushes in slowly, carefully, watching my face for any sign of discomfort. There's resistance at first, my body adjusting to his size, then a sharp pinch that makes me gasp.

"I've got you," he soothes, staying perfectly still. "Take your time."

The pain fades quickly, replaced by a fullness that's overwhelming but incredible. When he's finally all the way inside, we're both breathing hard.

"You okay?" he asks, jaw clenched with the effort of staying still.

"Yes. God, yes. Move, please."

He starts slow, gentle rolls of his hips that already have me seeing stars. Each movement sends sparks through me, pleasure building. He pulls down the other side of my top, revealing both breasts to his hungry gaze.

Just then, we hear voices nearby, familiar ones.

"Where the hell did they go?" Luke's voice fades away.

"They've been gone forever," Arrow adds, sounding annoyed.

I giggle against Holt's shoulder, and he grins, never stopping his movements.

"Should we—" I start.

"Absolutely not," he states, increasing his pace slightly. "They can wait."

His grip shifts suddenly, a rough hand sliding beneath my knee to lift my leg around his waist. I gasp, instinctively clutching at his shoulders, but he doesn't thrust, just holds me there, aching.

"You remember telling Luke you wanted it hard?" Holt's voice is a rasp, every syllable dipped in hunger. "Rough?"

I nod, too breathless to speak, too far gone to pretend otherwise.

He presses in deeper, hips grinding slowly and heavily. "Say it."

"I do," I gasp. "God, I do. I want—" My voice fractures. "I want all of it."

He groans, the sound hot and close. "You have no idea what that does to me."

The ache between my hips burns hotter, sharper, and I meet him as he plunges into me, each motion harder now, deliberate, dragging sounds out of me I didn't know I could make. He shifts his grip again, pulling back onto his knees, lifting my ankles in his hands, and angling me deeper.

"I can go further like this," he mutters, watching me with that wolfish gleam. "But I'm holding back. First time and all."

My eyes flutter. "Don't. I can take it."

His head drops forward, teeth gritted. "Fuck, you're perfect."

Then he slams in, the sharp slap of skin against skin swallowed by my moan, raw, needy. The hay scratches at my back as I arch, my nails grabbing for his arms, trying to hold on as sensation crashes through me.

"Like that?" he growls, hips snapping.

"Yes. Oh my God—yes, Holt—"

"You're so goddamn tight," he hisses. "So wet. Fuck, gripping me like you don't wanna let go."

He doesn't slow. Doesn't give me space to think. Just drives into me like he's trying to burn the need out of both of us. The pressure builds too fast, the stretch and heat blurring into something unbearable. I don't want it to stop.

And then—

The world twirls as I come undone and climax. Every sound fades except the low rumble of his voice against my skin. My thoughts scatter, and there's only heat, pressure, and him, everywhere. I reach for words and find none, only broken sounds that don't belong to a language.

He murmurs something I can't make out, something that resembles praise or maybe prayer, and the sound of it unravels what's left of me. My body answers on instinct, muscles tightening, breath catching, vision flickering white at the edges. I don't even realize I'm shaking until he gathers me closer, one hand at the back of my neck, balancing me.

When the trembling finally eases, I'm still half lost, still catching my breath against his chest. The hay prickles my skin, his heartbeat thunders under my ear, and for a moment, it's as if the entire world has gone still.

"You were so damn beautiful when you came," he whispers.

Then suddenly he's pulling out, still hard, and I make a sound of protest.

"Wait, you didn't—"

"Not here," he says, though his jaw is clenched with the effort of stopping. "When I come with you for the first time and knot you, I want to be able to hold you after. For hours. As much as this is killing me."

"You're really sweet," I say, touched by his restraint.

"Only for you, Cindy." For a moment, Holt doesn't move. He just glances down between my thighs, where I'm spread open for him, and something in his expression goes soft. He licks his lips as the hunger in his eyes doesn't fade; it deepens. "You're a sight I'm never forgetting," he says.

My cheeks burn. I start to get up, but he stops me long enough to steal another kiss, slow, lingering, a promise tucked between breaths.

Then he grins, that crooked, dangerous smile reappearing. "We should get you decent before those two come looking for us."

I laugh, shaky but real, and let him help me to my feet.

I smooth my skirt back down my thighs and cover my breasts, fingers trembling a little, still buzzing from everything we just shared. Holt shifts beside me, tucking himself away with a low breath, doing up his jeans.

My gaze drops to the curve of his back pocket, and there it is. Red lace.

I reach out and pluck it free.

"Hey," he says, lips quirking. "Those are mine now."

I laugh as I step into them and drag them up under my skirt. "You can come get them later," I say.

His stare hits me square in the heart. Hot. Direct. Full of promise.

A shiver dances over my skin, settling low. Heat pools deep in my belly, and I'm already aching again. If we were anywhere else and alone, I might go all night. My body is on a high, and I worry that my heat is making an appearance earlier than expected, just like I'd mentioned to Harper. Something I might have to deal with tomorrow.

We leave the secret section through the shrubby wall, then round a corner and nearly collide with another couple. My stomach drops.

It's Monica and Trevor, who are getting married

soon. Their eyes go wide, taking in our joined hands, my messed hair, Holt's possessive grip.

I try to pull my hand away, but Holt holds firm.

"Hi," Monica squeaks. "We were just—we got lost—"

"Maze is tricky," Holt says calmly. "That way leads to the exit."

They practically run in the direction he pointed, whispers starting before they're even out of sight.

"Holt!" I hiss. "They're going to tell everyone!"

"Good." He draws me closer against his side, completely unbothered. "Let them know you have three boyfriends. Your mother wanted a show, right? Let's give her one."

Despite everything, I laugh. "You're terrible."

"You love it."

I do. I really do.

And if my mother catches wind of this? Well... she already hates everything I do. This'll just be one more sin to stack on the pile.

Three boyfriends? She'll choke on it.

She made it clear that our family doesn't do things like that.

Well. Clearly, I do.

We finally find the exit, where Luke and Arrow are waiting, both looking annoyed. But as we get closer, their expressions change. They inhale deeply, nostrils flaring, and their eyes go dark.

"You fucking didn't," Luke says, staring between us.

"In the maze?" Arrow adds. "Seriously?"

"Please tell me it's not that obvious," I plead.

"Only up close," Luke says, eyes still dark with want. "We're obsessed with your scent. Have been since day one."

"We should grab some food if you two are up for it," Arrow says, voice strained.

"Bathroom first," I say, desperate to clean up a bit.

They walk me to the restrooms like bodyguards, and as I'm exiting, I spot Harper.

"Cindy! Cindy, is that you?"

Harper appears in what might be the best costume I've seen all night. She's Morticia Addams, complete with the long black dress that hugs every curve, dramatic makeup, and a wig that touches the ground. She looks gorgeous and gothic and perfect.

"Harper! You look amazing!"

"I know, right? But, oh my God, you look—" Her eyes narrow. "You look like you just got properly fucked in a—"

She stops because someone appears at her elbow.

Mack. Arrow's brother. In leather pants and a white poet's shirt unbuttoned to his navel, probably supposed to be a vampire or something.

"Oh, are you two…?" I breathe, looking between them.

Harper grins, completely unrepentant. "Oh, yes."

This is going to be interesting.

22

CINDY

"Harper, are you sure about this?" I ask, eyeing Mack, who's standing there looking like trouble decided to dress up as a romantic vampire for Halloween. His leather pants sit low on his hips, the poet shirt unbuttoned to show a chest covered in tattoos that look like they were done in someone's garage at 3:00 a.m. after too much tequila. He's got that same dangerous energy as Arrow, the kind that makes sensible people cross the street, but where Arrow's danger feels controlled, calculated, Mack's feels like a firecracker with a lit fuse.

"Oh, I'm very sure," Harper purrs, running her hand down her Morticia dress. The slit goes up to her thigh, and I catch Mack's eyes tracking the exposed skin like he's memorizing it. "He's been absolutely sweet all night. A perfect gentleman. He even won me a stuffed octopus at the ring toss."

"An octopus?" Luke asks, confused.

"It's Halloween-themed," Mack explains, producing a black-and-orange octopus from his back pocket and handing it to Harper. It's not huge, but it's adorable and wearing a tiny witch hat. "Harper said she likes things with tentacles."

"I meant anime," Harper protests, but she's clutching the octopus like it's precious.

Arrow appears beside his brother, and seeing them side by side is like looking at two versions of the same person, one who chose therapy and one who chose wildness. Same sharp cheekbones, same eyes that see everything, same way of standing like they're ready for a fight. But Arrow has laugh lines, and Mack has worry lines.

"We need to talk," Arrow says to Mack, jerking his head to the side.

"Jesus, here we go," Mack mutters but follows him a few feet away.

They're not far enough. We can all hear every word.

"You hurt her," Arrow says, voice low and dangerous, "and you'll regret coming to town. I'll make sure of it. We clear?"

"Yep, already told you I won't," Mack says, meeting his brother's eyes without flinching.

"I'm serious, Mack. This isn't one of your schemes. Harper's not some mark or a good time. She's family."

I pause, loving the way he referred to Harper as family, like I'm already considered that to the three of them. My heart flutters.

"You think I don't know that?" Mack's voice rises slightly.

"Your track record says—"

"Fuck that." Mack runs his hand through his hair, the same gesture Arrow makes when he's frustrated. "I've never felt this way about any woman. Ever. She makes me want to be better. Makes me think maybe I could be."

"Wanting and doing are different things."

"I know that. But I'm trying, Arrow. For the first time in my life, I'm actually trying."

I sidle up to Harper, who is watching the brothers, holding her octopus.

There's a moment of silence where the brothers just stare at each other.

Holt has been quiet through this whole exchange, but now he steps forward, and somehow that's scarier than Arrow's threats. "Harper can take care of herself," he says quietly. "But she shouldn't have to. You make her take care of herself because of your bullshit, and what Arrow does to you will look like mercy compared to me and Luke."

"Jesus, it's like having seven angry dads," Harper says and laughs, not intimidated in the slightest. "I can handle myself. Been doing it for years. Survived my actual dad, survived my ex, survived that time Cindy convinced me to try CrossFit—"

"Drama queen."

"Muscle failure queen, thank you very much."

"Can we please eat?" Harper continues, adjusting

her grip on the octopus. "I'm starving, and there's this amazing food truck section that'll blow your minds. Plus, watching you all threaten Mack is making me hungry. Violence always does."

"That's concerning," Luke observes.

"That's hot," Mack counters, which has Arrow groaning.

We follow Harper through the festival, and it's like navigating a Halloween obstacle course.

The food truck area is its own ecosystem of amazing smells. String lights crisscross overhead in orange and purple, casting everything in warm Halloween colors. Picnic tables fill the space between trucks, most occupied by others. The competing smells shouldn't work together, with Korean BBQ mixing with gourmet grilled cheese mixing with what appears to be a truck selling nothing but variations of mac and cheese, but somehow it's perfect.

"Now this place"—Harper points to a bright green truck with *Julio's Authentic Tacos* painted in faded red and yellow, next to a cartoon taco in a sombrero that's *borderline* offensive but still weirdly adorable—"makes the best Mexican food you've ever had. I'm talking religious-experience tacos."

"That's a lot of pressure for a taco," Holt adds, brows raised.

"Trust me. I once saw a grown person cry into his torta," Harper says.

"Was that you?" I ask.

Harper doesn't answer. Just smiles at me.

"I'll order for everyone," Arrow declares, already peeling off toward the truck. "I speak fluent taco. Plus, Julio owes me a favor from when I taught him how to properly season his meat."

"Of course you did," Luke mutters.

"I'll come too," Mack adds, trailing after his brother.

We find a picnic table of wood carved with initials, hearts, crude drawings, and one particularly aggressive declaration: *Brad + Janet 4Ever*, which looks like it was done with a butter knife. Orange and black streamers are wrapped haphazardly around the posts, with fake spiders hanging from fishing line overhead. Every time the wind picks up, one of them jerks around like it's coming to life, causing at least one person nearby to flinch and swat at the air.

Luke slides in beside me, instantly throwing his arm across my shoulders. "So, are we officially the scandal of the festival now, seeing as you have family members here, or do we need to light something on fire?"

I laugh even though I haven't told him that we bumped into more family in the maze.

Across the table, Harper snorts. "Oh, you lit something, all right. Half the town saw you guys threatening a man earlier near the animal petting zoo. I'm pretty sure the goat fainted."

"You're welcome," Luke says with a grin. "We aim to traumatize the livestock."

"You're hilarious," I mutter, pressing in closer to him.

"To be fair," Harper adds, "the dramatics were kind of hot. I mean, if someone cornered *my* stalker and gave him the Alpha death glare—"

"I meant every word," Luke states.

Holt drops onto the bench on my other side. His thigh brushes mine, and I sense the tension that's been curled inside me all night uncoil just a little.

"Yeah, you nearly broke his nose with your stare," Harper says, rolling her eyes. "Seriously, it was very sweet of you all to be looking out for me too."

Luke just grins.

Holt leans back slightly, arm draping over the back of the bench, glancing my way and blowing me a kiss. I shudder all over in the best possible way.

Across the table, Harper's stuffed octopus stares blankly at me from where it's sitting.

I stare at Luke, who grins my way, and at Arrow, who's talking animatedly to the food truck guy.

I'm falling for them.

Harder than I planned. Faster than I should.

And I should be worried, but I'm not. I want a family of my own who adores me as I am. What scares me is that I might lose it all.

"So," I say, leaning forward, eyeing Harper, "is Mack treating you well? Like, *really* well?"

Harper's expression shifts instantly, mouth tipping into a dreamy little smile I've never seen on her.

"You have *no* idea how well," she says, practically glowing. "We've been talking all night. Like, *actually* talking. He asked about my job, my family, and so much more. I think he's interested in my *brain,* not just my"—she gestures dramatically at her corseted cleavage, which honestly deserves its own moment of appreciation—"assets. Though, make no mistake, he's very interested in those too. Like, laser-focused interested."

"And that's different from other guys, how?" Holt asks, genuinely curious.

"Most guys? They see the boobs and lose all higher brain function. The rest of me might as well be background noise. Mack, though..." She shakes her head in disbelief. "He's literally been stopping *me* from climbing him like a tree. Says he wants to 'do this right.'" She even makes little air quotes. "Who says that? What kind of tattooed bad-boy criminal says that with a straight face?"

I glance at her, something warm blooming under my ribs. "The kind that's trying to be better."

Her eyes meet mine, softer now. "Exactly. He feels... good. Solid. Like maybe he's made mistakes—"

"He has," Luke interjects, not even pretending to hide it. "Like, *a lot* of mistakes."

"—but he's trying to be better," Harper finishes, ignoring him completely. "That's hot. Redemption is hot."

There's a beat. Holt and Luke exchange a look across the table like they're silently playing some game of unspoken male telepathy.

Harper narrows her eyes. "Okay. What? What was that look? Don't make me throw the octopus."

"Mack's got... history. The kind that usually doesn't end with happy backyard barbecues."

"So do you three," she fires back immediately. "You think Cindy doesn't know that? Doesn't *see* it?"

I blink at the sudden spotlight. But she's not wrong.

"Whatever you've done," she says, sweeping her hand across the table like she's dealing cards, "you're here now. Trying. That counts. She gets that."

They all go quiet.

"We're reformed. Or... y'know. *Reforming.* Like an old boy band, but with more brooding and fewer haircuts," Luke adds.

"Very few haircuts," I mutter under my breath, side-eyeing Holt's always messy hair.

He catches it and smirks.

Harper shakes her head, grinning now. "You're all adorable together."

Holt doesn't speak, but under the table, I feel the brush of his pinky against mine.

A quiet reminder.

He's listening.

Watching.

Arrow and Mack return soon after, carrying two trays loaded with enough food to feed a small village. The smell hits immediately of grilled meat, fresh cilantro, lime, onions, and that perfect char that only comes from a well-loved grill. Tacos wrapped in white paper already showing grease spots, tortas the size of my head stuffed with everything imaginable, chips still warm from the fryer, guacamole, elote covered in white cheese and chili powder that's going to get everywhere.

"Oh my," Harper breathes. "It's beautiful."

"I got you the pescado especial," Mack tells Harper, setting down a container in front of her with the care usually reserved for religious artifacts. "You mentioned earlier that you loved fish tacos with mango salsa. Extra lime, light on the cilantro because you said it sometimes tastes like soap."

Harper actually swoons. Like, full hand to her forehead, eyelashes fluttering, might need smelling salts swoons.

"You listened," she says, voice soft and filled with wonder. "You actually listened to my food preferences."

"Course I did," Mack says, sliding in beside her, his leg immediately pressed against hers. "Everything you say is fascinating. Even the twenty-minute rant about how the *Twilight* movies ruined the books."

"They did!"

"I know, gorgeous. You explained it. In detail."

Arrow makes a gagging noise that turns into a very fake cough when Harper glares at him with the force of a thousand suns.

"Sorry," he says, not sorry at all. "Allergic to feelings."

"You're allergic to your brother being happy," Harper shoots back.

Arrow laughs, and I notice his shoulders relax slightly.

"They look good together," I whisper to Holt and Arrow beside him.

"Yeah," Arrow concedes quietly. "She makes him smile real smiles. Haven't seen those in years."

"That's good," I say.

"Speaking of which, you look fucking edible tonight, Dorothy," Arrow adds. "Good enough to eat. Makes me want to click your heels three times and take you home right now."

Harper is giggling at us while leaning in closer to Mack.

I blush. "Arrow, we're in public."

"So? Didn't stop Holt earlier."

"That was different," Luke adds, his hand on my thigh, traveling up.

"We're eating!" I squeak, grabbing his wrist to stop his hand's journey.

"So!" Harper says loudly, clearly trying to distract from whatever she's seeing on my face. "Tell me about this mansion you've all moved into. Cindy says it's incredible, but she tends to understate things."

I laugh, as she isn't wrong.

"You should come see it sometime," Luke offers through a mouthful of taco, somehow still managing to look attractive despite having salsa on his chin.

"Well, my guest bedroom has its own bathroom

with a tub that's basically a small pool. Plus heated floors! My feet have never been so happy."

"Your home now," Holt reminds me, his voice gentle but firm. "Not just your bedroom. The whole thing. Every room, every inch of it."

"Still getting used to that," I say softly.

It strikes me suddenly, sitting here surrounded by laughter, that this is what normal feels like. This is what I missed all those years growing up.

Friends who actually like me. Men who look at me like I'm something precious instead of a burden or a commodity. Harper smiling. Arrow and Mack debating whether a hot dog is a sandwich. Luke's hand warm on my thigh. Holt's presence solid beside me. The comfortable company of people who choose each other.

Is this what life could have been like if I hadn't had my family suppressing me? All those years of being told I wasn't enough, was too much, needed to be smaller, quieter, less. And here I am being exactly myself, laughing too loudly, eating my fourth taco without apology, covered in hay from rolling around with Holt, dress probably ruined, and these people want more of me, not less.

"You okay?" Arrow asks quietly.

"Just thinking."

"About?"

"How different everything is now. Good different. A few weeks ago, I was living in a townhouse, keeping low, and jumping at every knock on the door. Now I'm with three Alphas, my best friend is dating a potentially reformed criminal but hasn't been this happy in years, and I just... I keep wanting to pinch myself. Make sure it's real."

"It's real," Holt assures me, the other two smiling my way. "We're real. This is real."

I go back to eating and embrace the peace settling over me.

When we're gathering our trash, my phone buzzes. I pull it out and notice that it's from Mother.

My blood turns to ice... anything from her sets me off.

I will come over in the morning to see this mansion. For wedding purposes, of course. Please send me the address.

My whole body goes rigid. The warmth of the evening, the comfort of being surrounded by people who actually like me, and the safety I felt evaporate instantly.

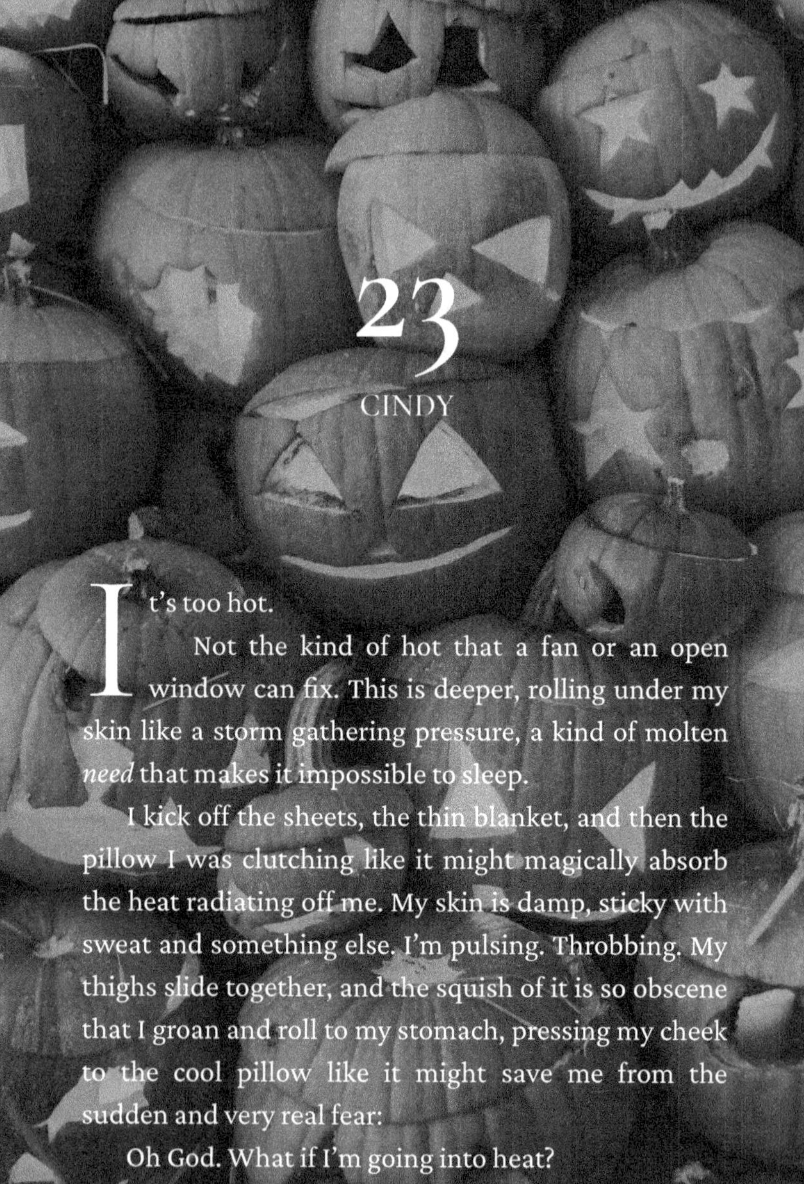

23

CINDY

It's too hot.

Not the kind of hot that a fan or an open window can fix. This is deeper, rolling under my skin like a storm gathering pressure, a kind of molten *need* that makes it impossible to sleep.

I kick off the sheets, the thin blanket, and then the pillow I was clutching like it might magically absorb the heat radiating off me. My skin is damp, sticky with sweat and something else. I'm pulsing. Throbbing. My thighs slide together, and the squish of it is so obscene that I groan and roll to my stomach, pressing my cheek to the cool pillow like it might save me from the sudden and very real fear:

Oh God. What if I'm going into heat?

A *real* heat. The kind that throws your body into losing control, rewrites your brain, makes you feral.

And of course it's showing signs of arriving now. Because tomorrow my mother is coming over. Here I am, slick like someone cracked an egg down the inside of my thigh, panting into my pillow like I've just run a marathon and wishing, *aching*, for the Alphas.

It's not fair. I've tried everything to cool down. A cold compress. Ice water. But nothing works. It's what he did to me in that maze. The feel of him inside me. The way I came apart for him, like I'd been waiting my whole life for that moment.

And then he stopped, still hard and thick and heavy in his pants.

"Goddammit," I mutter, slapping my forehead with the back of my hand. "Why am I like this?"

I try rolling onto my side. Then my back. Then the fetal position.

Nope. Still horny. Still overheating. Still one sharp memory away from marching across the house and climbing into Holt's bed like a crazy person.

I swing my legs over the edge of the bed. Bad idea. As soon as I shift, I feel the wet slide of slick on my thighs, like proof that, yep, my hormones have declared war on reason. I try to stand, but my legs wobble, and I have to brace a hand against the night-stand to keep from face-planting.

So much for dignity.

I shuffle toward the bathroom, feet slightly sticking to the wood floor with each step. "Sexy," I whisper to myself. "So sexy. If there were a pageant for disaster Omegas, I'd win by a landslide."

I fumble with the bathroom light, blinking against the glow. In the mirror, I look like a woman on the verge of spontaneous combustion. Flushed cheeks. Dilated eyes. Hair a mess. There's even a mark on my neck where I must've clawed at myself in frustration.

Jesus.

I peel my sleep shorts down and grimace at the stringy trail of slick that clings to my thighs. I'm soaked. And not in a cute, romance-novel kind of way. No, I'm *viscous*.

I grab a washcloth, run it under cold water, and do a quick cleanup.

I sit on the toilet lid and drop my head into my hands.

"I should go to bed," I whisper. "I should definitely *not* go to Holt's room."

Except I'm burning.

And I remember the way he looked at me earlier, like he couldn't believe I was real. But he didn't finish.

He *stopped* so I could come, and then he held me, and helped me clean up, and smiled when I stole my underwear back like a little gremlin.

He was sweet. And dirty. And *perfect*.

Would it really be so wrong to show up in his room right now and return the favor? Just to say thank you? Just to sit on his lap and...

Okay, this is spiraling.

I splash cold water on my face and glance at the mirror again.

"You owe him," I tell my reflection. "And you're a giver."

God, even my reflection is blushing.

Still, the image sticks. Me. Him. My thighs straddling his. That big hand splayed across my back as I ease down over him, finally taking him inside me the way I've needed since the maze.

I groan into my hands.

"Okay," I whisper, standing. "Just going to see if he's awake. That's all. Maybe he's having trouble sleeping too. Maybe he's lying there thinking about me and how rude it was to leave him like that."

I pause. "And if not... maybe I can just lie there and be held. Right? That's fine. That's normal."

Except I'm already walking down the hallway.

I tiptoe, heart pounding harder with every step. I'm not even sure why I'm trying to be quiet. It's not like I'm sneaking out of my parents' house. This is my house. Sort of. Temporarily. With three dangerously hot men I've apparently decided to thirst after all at once like a hormonal raccoon.

I pass Arrow's door and freeze.

It's cracked open, just enough to catch a sliver of warm light spilling across the floor from his bedside lamp. I peer in without meaning to, and my lips curve in spite of myself.

He's passed out diagonally across the bed, one leg hanging off the edge, hair tousled like he lost a wrestling match with his pillow. And sprawled across his stomach, purring like an idling engine, is the General. The fat Maine Coon has claimed him like a furry overlord, one paw resting over Arrow's bare chest like he's keeping him hostage.

I smother a laugh behind my hand.

Arrow snuffles in his sleep and mutters something about "Don't touch my fries," and I quickly move on before I wake him. The smile sticks as I continue down the hall, my body still aching but my mood lifting slightly.

Am I really doing this?

By the time I reach Holt's door, the doubt sets in. My feet slow. My fingers hover near the wood but don't touch it.

What am I doing?

I should turn around. Go back to bed. Do literally anything other than throw myself at the one man who makes me come undone with a single look. Especially when my hormones are rioting and I'm one step from throwing myself into a bathtub full of ice cubes.

But then I remember his mouth on mine. His hand between my legs. The way he looked at me when I shattered against him.

I close my eyes and press my forehead to the door.

"This is a terrible idea," I whisper. "It's a mistake."

And maybe it is. But my skin burns and buzzes, and I know that if I go back to bed, I won't sleep. I'll just lie there thinking about us in the maze. Wanting him. Spiraling.

So maybe, just maybe, being with him will ease the ache. Just enough to get through the night. Just enough to survive my mother's judgmental stare tomorrow without climbing the walls or dry-humping the furniture.

I take a breath, straightening my spine.

Just a quick visit. Just a little relief. Then I'll deal with everything else tomorrow.

The door creaks slightly as I push it open, heart hammering in my throat like I'm about to do something dangerous.

Probably because I am.

The room is bathed in silver moonlight. The curtain by the open window flutters lazily in the breeze, casting shadows across the floor. The air smells like him. And there, sprawled on the massive bed, is Holt.

He's on his stomach, the sheet barely clinging to his hips. His broad back is all hard planes and muscles that shift subtly with every breath. One leg is bent, the other stretched out, and the sheet dips low enough to give me a perfect view of the curve of his ass. Moonlight drapes over him like he's been carved out of shadow and sin.

Hell.

He resembles a predator resting between hunts. Like something out of the kind of books I used to hide under my mattress. The ones where the heroine knows better but climbs into bed with the beast anyway, because some aches don't go away with reason.

This is a mistake. I know it is.

My mom is going to be here tomorrow. I'm slick and restless, and one wrong word could spiral this whole truce into disaster. And yet here I am, sneaking into Holt's room like some kind of horny cartoon burglar.

I should walk away.

I don't.

"I was wondering how long it would take before you came to me, little Omega." His voice slices through the dark. He doesn't even turn his head to face me.

I freeze. "You were awake?"

"Close the door."

My fingers fumble behind me, finding the knob and nudging the door shut with a quiet click. The room feels even darker now, more intimate. My skin prickles.

I walk toward the bed, heart racing. He rolls over slowly, the sheet slipping down his body like it knows better than to stay in the way. And then he's on his back, naked, hard, and completely unbothered by any sense of modesty.

I actually gasp. His cock is erect and standing upright.

Is it the lighting? The moon? Because he looks bigger than he did in the maze. More intimidating. His chest rises and falls slowly, arms folding behind his head like he's some kind of god waiting to be worshipped. Every muscle is cut and powerful, shadows playing across his abs and down the V of his hips.

I should say something witty. Clever. Anything. But my brain has been reduced to static.

His gaze rakes over me. "Clothes off, beautiful

Omega," he growls, eyes gleaming in the dark. "Unless you came here just to stare."

That voice. It goes straight to my core. Deep. Commanding. Raw hunger laced with dark amusement.

"This is a terrible idea," I whisper.

"Then make your decision quickly. I'm dying over here."

My lips part. My breath stutters. Heat flashes across my skin. My hands fumble at the hem of my shirt, tugging it off, trying to pretend that I'm not trembling. His gaze follows every inch of skin I expose, and when my shorts drop, he exhales like he's been punched.

God, he's watching me like he's starving.

When I'm naked, I stand there for a beat too long. Vulnerable. On display.

His jaw clenches, and I can see just behind his eyes how close he is to pouncing.

"Come here," he says. "Slowly."

So I do. Crawling onto the bed, trying to look seductive but probably looking like a baby giraffe learning to walk. My knees sink into the mattress, and I move toward him, his gaze locked on my every movement.

Every inch I close feels like an electric wire tightening between us. I don't know what's going to happen once I reach him. Only that I won't be leaving this room the same.

And maybe that's exactly what I want.

His grin is sharp. Dangerous. "We're going to fix that ache, aren't we?"

He sits up, all that muscle flexing like a threat. I'm on my knees, and suddenly he's right there, towering in front of me. He reaches over to his nightstand, pulls open the drawer, and brings out something dark and soft.

Fabric cuffs.

I swallow hard.

He dangles them from two fingers.

My breath hitches. "Oh."

He leans in. "These stay on until you say otherwise. Is that okay?"

I nod, but he waits.

"Yes," I say, voice small.

"And if you want to stop at any point—"

"I'll tell you."

He nods once, then reaches behind me. His big hands are surprisingly gentle as he gathers my wrists together and fastens the cuffs. The soft fabric hugs my skin. I shiver.

"You're shaking."

"Not because I want to stop."

His eyes flare at that. "Good."

Then, to my complete surprise, he flops onto his back and throws his arms behind his head again like he's presenting himself.

"All right, sweetheart. You get first go. Climb on, cowgirl, and show me what you want."

My throat dries up. He's stretched out like a damn

fantasy, golden skin and all that carved muscle, and that cock, God. So hard. So huge. Waiting for me.

I straddle his hips, my knees on either side of him. His cock presses against me, and I moan under my breath, unable to help it.

"You're soaked already," he murmurs.

"You're the reason."

I rock my hips slightly, teasing him, and his eyes darken. "Is this what you pictured in the maze?" I whisper. "Me riding you, making you beg?"

His jaw flexes. "You're playing with fire."

"Maybe," I tease.

His hands twitch behind his head, but he doesn't move.

"I've been thinking about how you felt inside me. How thick you were. How good it was."

His groan is guttural.

I shift my hips, the tip of him brushing my slick entrance.

"You okay?" he asks, voice tight.

"Yes."

"Then take what you need."

I do.

Slowly. Inch by inch. The stretch burns in the best way. My eyes flutter closed, mouth falling open as I sink onto him.

He's thick. Deeper than I remember. Or maybe it's just that I'm finally seeing all of him, claiming him without any maze walls or rushed moments.

When I settle down, fully seated, he curses, "Fuck, Cindy."

"Still in charge?"

"For now."

"Then don't move."

His smirk is pure sin. "Yes, ma'am."

I start to ride him. Slowly at first, letting myself adjust, feeling every inch of him. He watches me closely.

My slick is everywhere. It drips, and the wet sounds as I move are obvious, but I don't care. I've never felt more powerful, more wanted.

"You look so fucking incredible," he rasps. "Your tits bouncing, your lips all parted like that. You were made for this."

"For you?" I tease, breathless.

He growls. "No doubt in my mind."

I lean back slightly, changing the angle. Stars explode behind my eyes.

"Fuck, Holt—"

"I've got you," he says, voice trembling with restraint. "Ride me as long as you need. I'll be here. I'll always be here."

And with that, I know I'm not just losing control; I'm giving it to him. Willingly. Desperately.

And it's never felt so good.

My thighs quake as an orgasm slams into me unexpectedly. I shudder, moaning, trying not to wake up the whole damn house.

"Fuck," he hisses.

His hands suddenly fly to my waist, his breath coming fast as I grind against the thick length beneath me. He groans low and deep, his voice ragged. "That's it. Soak me. Drip all over me, pretty girl."

And I do.

I keep coming undone, my body trembling as wave after wave overtakes me. My wrists pull against the restraints as I fall apart. I'm panting, dazed, as the rush fades.

As I float down from the heavens, his hands grip my waist tighter. "Not done yet."

He sits up suddenly, so fast it makes me squeak, and lifts me off his cock as if I'm nothing more than a doll. He sets me back onto my knees gently and smirks. "Fair's fair. My turn."

I giggle breathlessly. "You make me nervous when you say it like that."

His expression softens. "I'd never do anything you don't enjoy, sweetheart. You say the word, I stop. Always."

I nod, breath hitching. "I know. I trust you."

He kisses my cheek and slides out of bed, only to kneel behind me on the mattress, that hulking body moving like a predator. The brush of his cock between my thighs is teasing, promising.

"Lean forward for me," he murmurs.

I do, chest to the bed, cheek against the sheets. He places a big palm on my spine, running it slowly and warmly down to my lower back, coaxing me into position. I gasp as he eases my knees wider, baring me.

"Perfect," he breathes. "The view from here... fuck, Cindy. I'll never stop cherishing it."

My moan is raw and hungry because I feel that desperation in his voice, the way he worships every inch of me.

Then he's there. His cock at my entrance.

And he slides into me with a long, deep thrust that knocks the breath from my lungs. I cry out. The stretch, the pressure, it's everything. It's him.

"Tell me if I'm too much. Too hard," he says, voice a rough whisper.

I groan, my hips pushing back against his. "It's how I want it."

He growls a feral, possessive sound and claims me like he's starving. His hands grip my hips tightly as he thrusts, slowly at first, dragging it out until I'm squirming, begging for more. Each movement is dominant, letting me feel every inch of his cock driving into me.

He leans over me, his chest brushing my bound arms, his mouth hot at my ear. "You feel that? That's me owning you. Filling you so deep there's no space left for anyone else."

"Holt..." I pant his name, desperate.

He grips my hair, not hard, just enough to tilt my head. "You're mine, Cindy. My perfect fit. My addiction."

I can't form words. All I can do is take it. The rhythm builds, relentless, controlled. He watches the way I take him, the way I fall apart. I can also feel him in my spine, my toes curling, sweat slicking our bodies.

"You're taking me so well, fuck," he groans. "So greedy for it, aren't you?"

I whimper, the tension in my core spiraling. "Please. Please, Holt."

His hand dips between my legs, fingers finding my clit, and that's it.

I shatter.

It's white-hot, a climax that steals the air from my lungs and the strength from my limbs. My cry is muffled by the sheets, my hips jerking as he rides me through it.

He's panting, losing control. His fingers dig into my hips as he thrusts harder. "Gonna fill you up, Omega. You want that? Want to be full of me?"

"Yes," I sob. "God, yes."

And that's all it takes.

He growls, hips jerking. "Fuck, that's it. Gonna knot you, baby. Brace yourself."

His knot swells inside me, locking us together. I feel every thick inch of him pulsing, stretching me to the edge of pain again, but it's laced with mind-numbing pleasure. I whimper, helpless and full.

He doesn't stop moving, slow thrusts meant to milk every last drop of his release.

"So tight," he groans. "You're holding me so well."

He's flooding me, thick warmth spreading, the pressure intense. I can't move, can only moan and writhe beneath him, completely undone.

As the wave finally ebbs, he lets out a deep, satisfied sigh and reaches for my wrists.

The cuffs click open, falling away as he scoops his big hands under me, sliding around to cup my breasts.

"Come here," he murmurs.

Still joined, he lifts me gently until I'm upright, my back against his broad chest, both of us on our knees.

He holds me like I'm precious, his knot still inside me, and the way it pulses with every little twitch has me moaning.

"How are you feeling, my little Omega?"

I'm gasping, boneless in his arms. "I had no idea what to expect being with an Alpha and being knotted. It's... it's there. So much. A tiny hurt... but also so good."

He chuckles, warm against my neck. "You feel incredible. Embracing me so tightly." He leans in and presses a kiss to my ear, then down to my neck, and lower yet. "Beautiful," he whispers. "You're mine. Ours."

Then he bites me.

Right in the curve of my neck.

I cry out, the sharp sting turning into a rush of euphoria that leaves me trembling.

I've just been marked.

And I never want this moment to end.

His knot is still swollen inside me, locking us

together, his arms wrapped tightly around my middle. His chest rises and falls against my back, slowing now, but steady. Warm. Real.

I've never felt this wrecked and this whole all at once. My body aches in the best way, stretched and sated and safe. The storm of need that had me crawling to his room now feels like a distant memory, soothed under the weight of his possessive hold.

He brushes his nose along the shell of my ear, then presses a kiss to the back of my neck. "Still breathing, sweetheart?"

I let out a soft laugh, too content to open my eyes. "Barely."

His chuckle rumbles against me, deep and pleased. "You did good."

"Mmm." My head tips back slightly, resting against his shoulder. "You did better."

A comfortable silence settles between us, broken only by our breathing and his occasional soft stroke across my skin. I sense every inch of him inside me. But it's no longer overwhelming. It's grounding.

My eyelids are heavy now. Sleep pulls at me, warm and drugging. Then the words fall out. "I'm falling for you," I murmur, almost too soft to hear. "For all of you. And it scares the shit out of me."

His arms tighten around me just a little. No teasing, no slick response. Just the quiet exhale of a man who hears what I didn't mean to say out loud.

"You're safe here," he says, his voice a low promise

against my skin. "No one's going anywhere. We fucking adore you."

I want to believe him.

I think part of me already does.

The last things I feel before sleep pulls me under are his lips brushing my temple and the steady beat of his heart against my back.

24

LUKE

The doorbell chimes through the house, and I'm already moving toward the front door. Mid-morning, right on scheduled torture. Victoria Williams. Fuck me.

I catch sight of Cindy in the hallway, and something stops me cold. She's leaning against the wall like she needs it for support, one hand pressed to her stomach. Her face is flushed, a thin sheen of sweat on her forehead.

"You good?" I ask, keeping my voice low.

She straightens too quickly, pasting on a smile that doesn't reach her eyes. "Fine. Totally fine."

Bullshit. Cindy is throwing off every red flag in the book. Her scent, Christ, her scent is different. Still that sweetness she carries, but underneath it, there's something deeper now. Richer. It makes my teeth ache and my dick twitch, and I have to force myself not to do something stupid like pin her against the wall and taste her neck.

She's doused herself in perfume. Floral, cloying stuff that would make most people gag. To an Alpha's nose, though? Might as well be waving a neon sign that says *Omega in Pre-Heat*.

Speaking of which, she keeps trying to place her hair over the bite mark on her neck, but I spotted it first thing this morning. Faint, fresh, and unmistakably Holt's. As if I hadn't already heard him last night, fucking our Omega like a man possessed. Like she was his to claim first.

But my time is coming.

And fuck, the wait is driving me insane.

The doorbell rings again. Insistent.

"I'll get it," I say. "You should sit down or something."

"I'm fine." She pushes off the wall, swaying slightly. "I can greet my mother."

"Yeah, you look real steady there, sweetheart." The endearment slips out, and I watch color flood her cheeks. Not from the heat. From me.

Her eyes flash. "I got this."

I hold up my hands, but I can't stop looking at her mouth. "Just saying you look like you're about to keel over and you got me worried."

"I called in sick to work this morning," she says, like that explains everything. "I still have to finish some stuff on my laptop later. Just... stressed."

Another lie. She's terrible at lying. Her pulse jumps

in her throat every time, and I want to put my mouth right there, feel it flutter against my tongue.

Fuck. Get it together.

The doorbell rings a third time, followed by sharp knocking.

"Jesus Christ," I mutter. "That woman's got no patience."

I pull open the door before Victoria can start beating it down. She's standing there in a cream-colored suit, a designer handbag on one arm, and heels. Her hair is styled in some complicated twist that screams expensive salon. Everything about her is polished, pressed, perfect.

And she's alone.

I expected her to bring a team of followers... someone at least. But no, Victoria Williams makes her entrance solo, like she doesn't need backup to intimidate the hell out of people.

Her eyes, same hazel as Cindy's but cold where Cindy's are warm, sweep over me.

"Mrs. Williams," I say, flashing my best charming smile. "Good to see you again."

"Luke." She steps inside without waiting for an invitation, her heels clicking on the hardwood. Her gaze travels over the entryway, the chandelier, the curved staircase. I can practically see her calculating square footage and property value. "Where's Cynthia?"

"Right here, Mother." Cindy appears in the hall-way, and I don't miss the way she keeps her distance.

At least ten feet between them. No greeting beyond those few words.

Victoria notices too. One perfectly shaped eyebrow arches. "Are you feeling all right? You look flushed."

"I'm fine." Cindy waves a hand dismissively. "Just warm. You know how it is."

"It's quite cool in here, actually." Victoria's tone is light, pleasant even, but there's an edge underneath. "And you're perspiring. Are you coming down with something?"

"I called in sick this morning," Cindy says quickly. "Don't want to get you sick too, so I'm keeping my distance."

I jump in before Victoria can press. "How about that tour? You wanted to see the place, right?"

Victoria's attention shifts to me. "Yes. I'm very curious to see where we will hold the wedding and where my daughter is living." She pauses, letting the implication hang. *Living with a man she barely knows.*

"It's my mansion," I say smoothly, falling back on the agreed lie. Simpler than explaining she's dating all three of us. For now. "And Cynthia calls this her home too."

Behind her mother's back, Cindy shoots me a grateful look. Then she grimaces, one hand going to her stomach again.

Fuck. We need to get Victoria out of here. Fast. Because Cindy's scent is getting stronger by the second, and it's taking every ounce of control I have not to react. My pulse is hammering, and there's a low ache building in my balls.

"Right this way." I gesture toward the living room, keeping my voice light and easy. Tour Guide Luke, at your service. "We'll start with the main floor, work our way up."

Victoria steps into the living room, and I watch her take it all in. The floor-to-ceiling windows overlooking the mountains. The custom furniture, leather and dark wood that Arrow picked out because he has opinions about shit like that. The art on the walls that Holt insisted we needed.

Her expression doesn't change, but I catch the way her fingers trail over the back of the couch. Testing the quality of the leather. The way her gaze lingers on the view.

"Very nice," she exclaims in a tone that manages to sound both impressed and like she's found it barely adequate. "Quite spacious."

Cindy hovers in the doorway, not quite coming in. Her face is even more flushed now, and she's breathing a little too fast.

I keep talking, drawing Victoria's attention away. "Kitchen's through here. We made sure it was top of the line. Lots of counter space, professional appliances."

The kitchen makes Victoria's eyebrows rise just slightly, but I catch it. The massive marble island, the Wolf range, the Sub-Zero fridge. Arrow would have my balls if I admitted I barely know how to use half this shit.

"Impressive," Victoria says, running a manicured hand over the counter. "This must have cost quite a bit. How could you afford it?"

"Mother," Cindy calls from the doorway, her voice strained. "You can't just ask people—"

I laugh, waving her off. "It's fine. Yeah, it wasn't cheap. But worth it." I lean against the island, giving Victoria my most disarming grin. "All inheritance from my parents. They had good taste and better investments."

It's complete bullshit. My parents left me jack shit except a juvie record by proxy, but Victoria doesn't need to know that. She just needs to think I'm legitimate money, not club money.

Her eyes narrow slightly, like she's trying to decide if she believes me. "I see. And what did they do?"

"Real estate development." I'm pulling this straight out of my ass now. "West Coast, mostly. Sold the company after they passed."

"How tragic," Victoria says in a tone that suggests she doesn't find it tragic at all. "You must have been quite young."

"Young enough." I push off the island. "Want to see the backyard? That's the real showpiece."

Cindy makes a choked sound from the doorway. When I glance over, she's gripping the doorframe like it's the only thing keeping her upright.

Victoria turns toward her daughter. "Cynthia, are you certain you're all right?"

"Fine." Her voice is barely steady. "Just… gonna grab my laptop. Work stuff."

She disappears before Victoria can protest, and I have to physically stop myself from going after her.

Victoria watches her go, lips pressed into a thin line. "She's acting very peculiar."

"Probably just tired from being sick." I steer her toward the back door, desperate to keep this moving. "Come on, wait till you see this yard."

I lead her outside onto the patio, and even I have to admit it's a hell of a view. The yard stretches out in front of us, a perfectly maintained lawn that some landscaping company charges us a fortune to keep green, flower beds that Arrow insisted on, and beyond that the natural forest leading up into the mountains.

"We've got about five acres total," I explain. "Had the previous owner's garden redone, brought in some designer from Seattle who charged us an arm and a leg to plant a bunch of native species. Said something about eco-sustainability and watershed management."

Victoria is looking at me like she's trying to figure out if I'm serious.

I keep going. "Yeah, apparently we've got some rare moss situation happening by the lake. Guy said we might be able to get a tax write-off for it." I wave my hand vaguely toward the tree line.

"Really," Victoria says flatly.

"Scout's honor." I'm grinning now, this last part all

true. "Though, between you and me, I think he was just running up the bill."

Her mouth twitches. Almost a smile. "That does seem more likely."

I gesture toward the small lake glinting through the trees. "That's where we're thinking for the wedding. By the water. Figured it'd make for nice photos."

Victoria moves to the edge of the patio, her sharp gaze assessing the distance. "That's quite far from the house."

"Nah, five-minute walk, tops. We'll set up a path with lights, maybe some of those luminarias?"

"And for inclement weather?" Victoria asks.

"We'll have a backup plan. Tent, maybe. Or move it to the covered patio." I nod toward the large pergola structure off to the side. "That can hold about a hundred people if we set it up right."

The back door opens. Cindy steps out, still no laptop in sight, and the wave of scent that rolls off her nearly drops me where I stand. Her perfume cloud has gotten stronger. She must have sprayed on more, but underneath it, her heat is unmistakable.

My mouth waters. My hands clench into fists. Every instinct I have is screaming to get rid of Victoria, throw Cindy over my shoulder, and take care of her the way she needs.

"What do you think, Mother?" Cindy's voice is too bright, too forced.

Victoria turns, and her nose wrinkles slightly. "Cynthia, your perfume is rather strong."

"Is it?" Cindy touches her neck. "Sorry. Might have overdone it."

"And your scent seems... off." Victoria frowns. "You should have that checked. Could be a hormonal imbalance."

I nearly choke. Yeah, it's a hormonal imbalance, all right. Called heat combined with perfume throwing her mom off. Good.

"I'm fine, Mother. Really."

Victoria doesn't look convinced, but she turns back to survey the yard. "The property is quite impressive. Though I do wonder about the practicality of such a large space for just two people."

Ah, shit.

"Oh, I've got roommates," I say, keeping my tone casual, knowing it needs to come out eventually. "Arrow and Holt. We all live here."

Victoria's head snaps around. "Roommates."

"Yeah. Big house, seemed stupid to have it sit empty."

"I see." Her voice has gone very cool. "And where are these roommates now?"

"Out running errands," I say. "They'll be back later."

Victoria glances over at Cindy, who's desperately trying to look anywhere but at her mother. "You're living in a house with three men."

"I have my own room," Cindy states quickly. "My

own space. For privacy. Until Luke and I properly marry."

"How very… modern." Victoria's tone could freeze hell. For a long moment, she stares at me. I can see her trying to find something to criticize, some angle to attack, but I'm not giving her an opening.

Finally, she turns away. "I'd like to see Cynthia's room."

Fuck. Of course she would.

"Sure thing, Mother."

I lead them back inside, trying not to notice that Cindy is stumbling slightly. "Right upstairs."

The stairs are torture. Cindy makes it up three steps before she has to stop, one hand pressed to the wall, breathing hard. Sweat beads at her hairline, and I can smell the heat rolling off her in waves.

It's affecting me too. My skin feels like it's on fire, my jeans are too tight, and there's a low growl building in my chest that I have to physically swallow down.

Victoria notices. Of course she does. "Cynthia, perhaps you should lie down."

"I'm fine." Cindy forces herself up another step. "Just out of shape."

"You're twenty-two," Victoria says dryly. "Not ninety."

I take the stairs two at a time, partly to speed this along and partly because if I stay close to Cindy much longer, I'm going to do something supremely stupid. "The guest room is down this hall."

I push open the door, and Victoria steps inside. It's

a nice room. We made damn sure of that. Queen bed with a quality mattress, dresser, chair by the window, attached bathroom. Cindy's stuff is scattered around like she actually lives here. Clothes on the chair, shoes by the closet, her work bag on the desk.

Victoria takes it all in, and I brace for criticism.

"It's adequate," she says finally. Which, coming from her, might as well be a glowing review.

Cindy appears in the doorway, leaning heavily on the frame. Her pupils are wide, and she's trembling.

I need to get Victoria out. Now.

"So," I say brightly, "what do you think? Will this place work for the wedding?"

Something flickers in her expression. Not quite approval. But close. "Yes," she says slowly. "I suppose this will... do."

"Excellent." I'm already moving toward the staircase, practically herding her out. "Let me walk you to your car."

"I should say goodbye to Cynthia—"

"She's not feeling well," I interrupt, flashing an apologetic smile. "Better not risk getting too close, right? Don't want you catching whatever she's got."

Cindy makes a strangled sound behind me. "I'll call you later, Mother. Promise."

Victoria doesn't look happy about it, but she lets me guide her back downstairs. Every second ticks by like a countdown, my control fraying at the edges. My hands are shaking. There's a fine tremor running through my whole body, and it's taking everything I have to keep walking normally instead of sprinting back to Cindy.

We reach the front door, and I pull it open maybe a little too fast.

"Thank you for the tour, Luke." Victoria pauses on the threshold, fixing me with that sharp gaze. "Take care of my daughter."

"Always," I manage. My voice sounds wrecked even to my own ears.

She gives me one more assessing look as if she knows something is wrong but can't quite figure out what, then nods and heads to her car. A black Mercedes, because of course it is.

I watch until she's pulling out of the driveway, then shut the door and lock it.

"Cindy!" I call, already heading for the stairs. My voice comes out as almost a growl.

No answer.

I take the stairs three at a time, my heart pounding. Every breath is full of her scent, stronger now, calling to every instinct I have. The guest room is empty. The master suite. Nothing.

"Cindy, where are you?"

Still nothing, and fuck, I'm starting to panic.

The front door opens, and I glance downstairs. Arrow and Holt strut inside, and I nearly tackle them in my rush to get downstairs.

"What the fuck?" Arrow drops the grocery bags he's carrying. "Who died?"

"Cindy's mother just left," I say quickly. I hear how

close to the edge my voice is riding. "And Cindy—fuck, something's wrong. She's going into heat."

Holt goes very still. "You're sure it's not pre-heat?"

"Her scent is different. She's flushed, sweating, can barely stand up straight. She's been trying to hide it all morning." I run a hand through my hair, pulling hard. "And it's killing me. I can barely think straight."

I'm already moving, following the pull of her scent, but it's everywhere. "We need to find her, as she's not answering. Now."

We spread out, searching the house. Living room, kitchen, both offices, the gym. Nothing. Then Holt stops in the hallway, head tilted.

"Smell that?"

I do. Her scent, stronger now, thick enough to choke on. Coming from the east wing, where we set up the Omega heat room. A space we built just for such a moment.

We follow the trail down the hall. The door to the heat room is closed, and when I push on the handle, it's locked. From beyond it, I can hear water running. The shower.

I knock, trying to keep my voice steady. "Cindy? I know you're in there."

The water cuts off. Silence at first.

"I'm okay." Her voice is hoarse, strained, and it sends a bolt of pure need straight through me.

"Then why are you in this room?" I ask.

Footsteps. Getting closer to the door. "Just needed some Omega time to myself."

"Open the door, Cindy." Holt's voice is low, gentle. "It's okay."

More silence. Then a sharp cry, cut off like she's trying to muffle it. The sound of something hitting the floor.

"Fuck this." Arrow is already pulling out the skeleton key we have for the house that he keeps on his key ring.

He unlocks it, pushes it open, and we all pause.

Cindy is on the floor beside the bed, wrapped in a towel. Her hair is soaking wet, dripping onto the hardwood. She's shaking, breathing hard, and the scent of her heat slams into us like a physical force.

Oh, fuck!

My control shatters. My hands are shaking, vision is narrowed to just her, and there's a roaring in my ears that drowns out everything else. Want. Need. *Mine.*

She lifts her gaze up to us, eyes wide and dark. "I-I'm fine."

"You're not fine," I say, and my voice comes out as almost a snarl. "Are you going into heat?"

"Don't say that." She tries to stand, fails, and slumps back against the bed. "I'm just stressed. My mother, and the house, and—"

She cries out, doubling over. Her hands clench the towel, and I can see slick dampening her inner thighs.

We're across the room in seconds. I drop to my knees beside her, and the strength of her scent up close makes my vision blur. Sweet, rich, *ours.* Every instinct I have explodes to life, demanding that I take care of her, claim her, make her ours in every possible way.

"Your scent is so strong," I manage, my voice barely human. "Beautiful one, you don't need to suffer alone. Fuck, we won't let you."

Holt crouches on her other side. Arrow hovers behind us, his usual smart-ass expression gone. He looks as wrecked as I feel.

"Please." Cindy's voice breaks, and there are tears streaming down her face now. "I don't... I don't know how to deal with this intensity. This hurts so much more than my previous heats."

Something in my chest cracks wide open. I reach for her, cup her face in my hands, feel her burning skin against my palms.

"That's why we're here," I say quietly. Holt brushes wet hair back from her face. "That's what we're made for. To take care of you through this."

"We won't let you hurt," Arrow adds. His voice is softer than I've ever heard it. "That's not happening."

I can see the moment she breaks. Her shoulders sag, and she leans toward us like she can't help it. Like our presence alone eases the ache building in her body.

"Come on," I say, barely holding it together. "Let's get you into the nest."

The heat room has a massive bed—California Omega King made for at least six adults, piled with blankets and pillows that we scented for her. Nest material.

We help her up, and she climbs onto the bed with

shaking limbs. The moment she's surrounded by our scents, she lets out a shuddering breath.

"Better?" Holt asks.

She nods, curling into the pillows. We settle around her, Holt on her right, Arrow to her left, me in front, where I can see her beautiful face.

My hands are still shaking. I'm barely holding back, every muscle locked tight with the effort of not just taking her right now.

"This is what it's supposed to be like," Holt murmurs. He's running his hand up and down her arm in slow, soothing strokes. "You, surrounded by your pack. Safe. Protected."

"We're here for everything," Arrow says. "Every need, every ache."

Cindy's breathing is still ragged, but the panic in her eyes is fading. She looks at each of us in turn. We're not scared, not running. We want this. Want *her*.

"It hurts," she whispers.

"I know, baby." I reach out, cup her face in my hand, and my thumb strokes her cheek. "But we're going to make it better. I promise."

She leans into my touch, and fuck, the trust in that simple gesture destroys me. My control is hanging by a thread.

"You don't have to be afraid," Holt says. "Your body knows what it needs. We're right here." I move my hand from her arm to her hip.

For several minutes, we just hold her. Touch her.

Let her feel us surrounding her, grounding her. She's still trembling, but it's different now. Less pain.

When she leans in and presses her lips to mine, I taste desperation and need and everything I've been craving.

I kiss her back, trying to keep it gentle even though everything in me wants to devour her. Her mouth is so soft, so sweet, and when she whimpers against my lips, I nearly lose it. Her hand finds Arrow's thigh, gripping tightly. Her leg hooks over Holt's, pulling him closer.

She needs to feel all of us at once. Needs the pack connection as much as she needs the physical relief.

When she pulls back, she's panting. "I can't... I need..."

"We know," I say. My voice is wrecked, barely recognizable. My whole body is vibrating with need. "Are you ready for us, then?"

"All of you." She's looking between us, wild-eyed and desperate. "It's going to take all of you. No matter how long this lasts."

Holt's hand tightens on her hip. Arrow makes a rough sound in his throat. And me? I'm trying like hell to keep control when all I want to do is rip that towel off and bury myself in her until we both forget our own names.

But she deserves better than that. Deserves us at our best, not just our base instincts.

Cindy reaches for the towel. Her hands are shaking as she pulls it loose, letting it fall away.

Fuck me!

She's perfect. Curves and soft skin, full breasts with tight nipples, and yes, there's a scar on her arm, burn damage, from what I can see, but it doesn't matter. A small strip of blonde hair between her thighs. Nothing matters except the fact that she's ours, she's here, and she's offering herself to us.

She should be shy. Should be nervous. But the heat has burned through all that. She's watching our faces, the way we stare at her, and she fucking *loves* it. I can tell by the way her breath catches, the way her thighs press together seeking friction.

"You're beautiful," Arrow breathes.

Her thighs are slick, glistening. Arousal dripping down her inner legs, her body preparing itself. I have to swallow hard.

"Look at you," I rasp. "So fucking ready for us."

She whimpers, spreading her legs slightly. An invitation. A plea.

Arrow is breathing hard. "Cindy—"

"I need you all." She's crying now, overwhelmed by sensation, by need. "Inside me. I can't stand the pain anymore."

Holt kisses her shoulder, his teeth grazing her skin. Arrow trails his fingers up her side, leaning in closer, making her arch. And I move in, pressing my forehead to hers, breathing in her scent until it's all I know.

"We've got you," I whisper. "You're safe. You're ours. And we're going to take such good care of you."

Her heat crashes over her in waves, and we're there to catch every single one.

25

CINDY

One moment, I'm flushed and needy, basking in the warmth of being surrounded by my Alphas. The next, it's a wildfire under my skin. My breath hitches, and the ache is somehow worse.

My heat is too early. Too strong. I can barely think through it.

The scent of my Alphas fills the room, thick and potent. It spins my head. My heart pounds.

I'm in the center of an enormous bed, naked and beyond fucking needing. I'm desperate.

Their hands roam with maddening attention, gliding over my hips, brushing the insides of my thighs, tracing every dip and curve like they've been dreaming of this moment. I arch involuntarily as Holt's palm spreads across my belly, the warmth of his skin sinking into mine, grounding me while everything inside threatens to unravel. Arrow's fingers trail up my ribs, making me shiver, while Luke's mouth finds the soft spot below my ear, his breath hot and teasing.

My thighs remain open, the sheets cool against the backs of my knees, but I can't stay still. The tension coils in my belly like a storm gathering. A whimper escapes before I can stop it, raw and desperate.

I twist against the pillows, back arching, muscles trembling with need that borders on agony. I'm soaked, aching, completely undone, and they haven't even truly started yet.

"I know heat is painful," I whisper, breathless. "But this is the first time I've actually been looking forward to putting out the flames. Because with you three? It's going to be unforgettable. I just know it."

Arrow chuckles darkly, his lips brushing my ear. "You're damn right it is."

I yelp when Holt kisses the spot just under my ribs. Ticklish. I giggle despite the ache, and Holt grins like he's discovered treasure. "Sensitive here?"

I nod, biting my lip. "Apparently."

Luke shifts to kneel between my legs, that slow, wicked smile tugging at his mouth. His fingers trace down my stomach, and the touch burns hotter than it should. Every inch he covers leaves a trail of awareness behind, like sparks catching on dry grass. I suck in a breath that doesn't quite fill my lungs.

The space between my thighs throbs with desperation, a pulse I can't ignore. When his fingertips dip lower, I twitch, my hips tipping forward in a plea I'm too far gone to hide. He just watches me, that smug glint in his expression saying he knows exactly what he's doing.

Then Arrow's hand wraps around my left thigh, while Holt's palm mirrors the touch on the right. Their strength brackets me, coaxing me open wider. The mattress shifts beneath us, the sound of breath and fabric and heartbeats blurring together until I'm not sure which pulse belongs to whom.

Cool air hits me, and I shiver from the way they stare at me. Not a single word passes between them, but it feels like being studied, memorized, worshipped. Heat curls through me so sharply it almost hurts. I should cover myself, hide from the intensity of it, but instead I tilt my chin up, defiant and trembling, silently daring them to keep looking.

Holt's breath brushes my ear. "You're perfect like this," he murmurs.

The words slide through me, soft and possessive, and something deep inside me yields to it. I melt, pulse skipping, the ache between my legs deepening until it's almost unbearable.

Luke grins.

And then he moves.

His tongue finds my pussy. Heat sparks, and I jerk with a startled gasp, my back arching off the bed.

My hips buck, needy, frantic, but Arrow and Holt don't let me go anywhere.

Luke drags his tongue through my folds again. Deeper. Slower. Like he's tasting something forbidden. A low sound slips from me, half moan, half beg.

"Holy fuck, the way she reacts," Arrow growls, leaning over me. "Keep her like that. Let me—"

His mouth finds my nipple, sucking it into heat and pressure that steal what's left of my breath. Holt's hand replaces his mouth on the other breast, teasing it with his thumb before his lips close around it too, rougher.

I sob.

I'm unraveling. Writhing.

"Too much?" Holt murmurs, voice dark and gentle at the same time.

I shake my head violently, hips grinding up into Luke's mouth.

"Not enough," I whisper. "More. Please—fuck—I can't—"

Luke groans like I just said the filthiest thing. He dives back in, relentless now, tongue moving faster, more forceful, as if he wants to break me open and drink down whatever is left. He sucks on my clit while he pushes two fingers into me, and I cry out. He's pumping fast, hard, destroying me.

My head thrashes against the pillow. My thighs tremble against their grips. My body is burning, shaking, chasing something just out of reach.

Holt's lips move to my neck. "Good girl. So fucking beautiful. Look at you, can't even keep still."

"She loves it," Arrow adds, fingers stroking around my breast, watching me quake. "She's going to come so hard she'll scream herself hoarse."

I do.

It rips out of me, loud, raw, unstoppable. My entire body locks up and shatters in their hands, wave after wave dragging me under until I can't tell where they end and I begin.

Luke pulls back, lips wet, panting against my thigh. But his fingers keep moving, and I jolt, twitching, over-stimulated. Then he adds another. A third.

I choke on my breath. "N-no—fuck—I don't think it'll—"

"It will," Luke growls, grinning up at me, hair falling into his eyes. "Look at you, baby. You're taking all three."

My protest melts into a cry, high and wrecked. My body tightens, straining against them, hips lifting off the bed as my slick folds stretch around his fingers.

Arrow groans like he's in pain. "Fuck, I love watching her get like this."

Holt strokes a thumb across my nipple. "Look how she clenches your fingers, sucking them back in."

"You're pulsing around my fingers, gorgeous," Luke grits out. "God, you're perfect."

I writhe, pushing closer into Holt's hand, then to Arrow's mouth as he latches on to my breast, sucking hard again. I cry out, completely undone. Their mouths, their fingers, their voices, it's all too much.

And not enough.

The pressure builds, unbearable and electric. Every nerve in my body is alight, skin burning, mouth open in silent, desperate gasps. Now they're all watching Luke finger me. All groaning. All obsessed.

Luke twists his fingers just right, and everything snaps.

I scream, bucking against him as the orgasm hits like a tidal wave. It's too much. It's not enough. I fall apart again, harder than before, pleasure ripping through me like I'll never come down.

Arrow curses. Holt curses. Luke doesn't stop until I'm shaking, begging, tears on my cheeks from the force of it.

"I've got you," Arrow says, catching one of my flailing arms and drawing it to his chest. "Breathe, baby."

Luke finally pulls back, mouth and chin slick, fingers dripping, expression smug and ravenous all at once. "Still not done with you, baby."

"Please," I pant, blinking tears from my lashes. "Need all of you. It's like that climax barely tamed the ache."

They groan in unison like I've just gifted them a fantasy.

Holt presses his forehead to mine. "You want us to wreck you, baby girl?"

"Yes." I bite my lip, body arching into his touch. "Ruin me."

Luke's hand slides between my thighs again, teasing. "This pussy's not satisfied until we're all inside her."

"And even then," Arrow adds, licking up my neck, "she'll beg for more."

I nod frantically.

Because they're right.

Because I can't stop craving them.

Because I want to be destroyed, in the best, most beautiful way.

I push up and grab Luke by the front of his shirt, pulling him into a kiss. "God, I love how I taste on you," I pant into his mouth, dizzy with need, writhing under his touch. "Please... I need you inside me."

Luke growls, that deep, feral sound vibrating against my lips. "You want to be mine, baby?"

I nod, already trembling. "I want all of you."

That's all it takes.

Around me, there's fabric rustling, the heavy sound of shirts being pulled over heads, belts unbuckling, zippers sliding down. My vision blurs at the Alphas stripping for me. Broad chests, rippling abs, heavy cocks standing hard and proud. I can't breathe. They're all muscle, all heat and hunger, and it makes me ache in ways I didn't know I could. This is raw and primal, and I'm all for it.

Luke tosses his clothes aside, his thick cock bobbing free. My gaze locks on it, on all of them, really, and I lick my lips as I watch Luke wrap his hand around the base, stroking slowly, savoring it like he knows how much I want to squirm.

Arrow grins down at me, not even pretending to hide how he watches my thighs tremble. "She's shaking already."

Then Luke lays himself over me, the other two watching.

My legs spread and wrap around his waist on instinct. My body knows this. It's crying out for him.

"You sure, baby?" Luke's voice is rough, cracking with restraint. "Once I start, I'm not stopping until you're marked."

"Yes," I whisper, so hoarse I barely hear it. "Please."

He lines himself up, his thick cock already pressing at my entry. I feel his size instantly as he pushes in slowly at first. I suck in a breath, one hand gripping his shoulder, the other fisting the sheets. Every thick inch stretches me wide, my walls fluttering around him, my breath caught in my throat.

"Oh, fuck," he groans, burying himself deep. "You're so fucking tight."

I cry out, pleasure spearing through me so sharp it almost hurts. "Luke..."

"You take me so good, sweet girl," he growls, hips rolling as he starts to move. "You were made for this. For us."

The stretch is brutal, but my body loves it. My hips lift to meet his every thrust, slick and heat making everything impossibly perfect. Around me, the other two draw close, their hands on my thighs, my breasts, their mouths grazing my shoulders.

"You're everything," Arrow murmurs near my ear, kissing just below it. "Look at how you cling to Luke. I fucking love it."

"You're ours," Holt adds, voice a gravelly low hum against my collarbone. "And you know it."

Luke leans in and growls in my ear, "You want to wear my mark like you wear Holt's?"

"Yes," I gasp. "Please... please..."

His teeth graze over my skin, and my entire body tenses with anticipation, slick pulsing between my legs as he builds up momentum, thrusting into me over and over. I'm breathless.

"Beg for it," he demands.

"Fuck me. Mark me," I whimper. "Make me yours. Claim me."

He sinks his teeth into the softness of my upper breast and thrusts deeper, groaning against my skin as I scream, legs tightening around him, nails clawing into his back. It's too much. Too good. Everything burns in the best way. And he fucks me like a machine, the whole damn bed shuddering.

"You see that?" Holt's voice is low, possessive. "That's ours."

Arrow murmurs, "So fucking perfect."

Luke keeps going, pounding into me faster, sweat dripping down his brow, hips snapping hard. He's too far gone. His body slams into mine with brutal force, and I moan like I've lost my mind. I want it. I want all of it. My body demands more.

But just when I feel the pressure building again, right on the edge, he growls and pulls out, dragging my whimper from deep inside my chest.

"You want us?" Luke pants, his cock twitching against my stomach, still hard, and not coming yet. "Then you'll have all of us."

He shifts aside, and before I can catch my breath, Arrow slides between my legs, gripping my thighs. His cock is thick and veined, flushed and ready.

"I've been waiting to feel you," he mutters, pressing his head against my soaked entrance. "Bet you're still twitching from Luke."

He pushes that heavy cock into me slowly, watching my face, and I arch again, sobbing at the pressure, the fullness. He's wider, stretching me again in new ways, and I cry out as he bottoms out with a groan.

"Fuck me, you're perfect," he hisses. "Hot and soaked. That pretty cunt already swallowed me whole."

My hips jerk, body rolling up into him. I can't stop the moan that rips out of me.

Holt leans over me, one hand on my breast, kneading, while he watches Arrow fuck me slow and deep. "You like it when we take turns on you, baby? You want to know how different we all feel?"

"Yes," I choke out, tears in my eyes from how intense everything is. "God, yes."

Luke leans in, pressing his forehead to mine. "You're ours now." And he runs this thumb across the bite mark where he drew blood over my breast.

Then Arrow starts to move faster. Every thrust punches the breath out of me. The room tilts. I sense every ridge of him, every vein, dragging inside me. My toes curl, and I clutch at his back, keening when Holt reaches an arm between Arrow and me, and his thumb rubs my clit.

"Let her feel it," Holt mutters, teeth at my ear. "Let her come on your cock, Arrow."

"I'm close," I sob. "I'm—please—I'm gonna—"

Arrow growls. His hand curls around the back of my neck as he leans down, breath hot against my skin.

"Time to make it official," he rasps.

And then his teeth, sharp and unrelenting, sink into the opposite side of my neck to where Holt bit me. Pain flares white-hot for a split second, stealing the air from my lungs, but then it crashes into a wave of pure, overwhelming heat. My body jerks beneath him, caught in that line between agony and euphoria. I half scream, half sob, my fingers clawing at him, my pussy clenching around him like I'm trying to hold on to something solid in the flood swallowing me whole.

The moment his teeth break the skin, something in me snaps.

It's not just a bite. It's a *claim* completed by three Alphas, and my body knows it, feels it, accepts it in a way that goes beyond flesh. The marks sear into me, into the bond that ties us together, and I *feel* Arrow, Luke, and Holt now, feel that their presence is another heartbeat pounding inside me. It's raw, primal, unshakable.

He licks the wound slowly, tongue soothing over the sting until it pulses with warmth and settles into a deep, aching throb.

"You're perfect like this," he murmurs against my skin. "Wearing our marks, naked, and dripping."

My scent shifts, thick and saturated with bond-slick heat, the instinctual, biological reaction to being fully owned by my pack. I'm no longer unclaimed. I'm theirs. The marks burn with a living heat that glows through my skin and settles into my bones.

Emotion wells up alongside the pleasure, a tidal wave I can't outrun. Tears sting my eyes, not from pain or fear, but from the intensity of it all. The way my body recognizes them, *wants* them, *belongs* to them. The bond settles over me like a second skin, alive and electric.

Arrow lifts his head and looks down at me, his eyes wild with hunger, lips smeared with my blood and sweat, and in that moment, I've never felt more desired... more *theirs*.

Then he groans and slams into me, and my climax shreds me from the inside out. I scream again, louder this time, mouth open in a silent cry before sound rips from my throat. My whole body shakes as he fights through it, fucking me hard until I can't take another second.

And then, with a curse, he pulls out, panting, cock glistening.

"Fuck," he snarls. "She's too sweet. I nearly—"

"My turn," Holt growls, already sliding into place.

He doesn't wait.

With one hard thrust, he fills me, taking me with force. I cry out again, but this time I'm ready. My hips roll up, greedy, already chasing more. He's just as powerful and dominating as he was last night.

He's rough. Brutal in the way I crave. His grip bruises. His body pounds into mine like he has something to prove. Holt has always been the one who marks with force and keeps others away.

But now, I'm open to all of them. And he's staking his claim all over again.

He growls, teeth scraping my neck where he's already marked me. "We're gonna knot you, beautiful."

I call out, not just from the promise but also from the pleasure. He's hitting something deep, something primal, and my legs shake violently.

"Do it," I sob. "Take me. Make me yours."

He hisses a curse and buries himself to the hilt, then slows just enough to draw it out, his voice guttural. "You want to be filled by all three of us, baby? You want to be dripping for days?"

I nod frantically, beyond words, every inch of me quivering under him. "Give it to me—"

Holt draws out of me with a groan, and my whole body jolts, still trembling from the high Arrow just gave me. My lips part, but no sound comes out as I try to breathe, try to remember how to exist in a body that no longer belongs to just me.

"Come here, beautiful," Holt murmurs, and I blink up to find him crouched at the edge of the bed, his arms out.

He lifts me effortlessly, like I weigh nothing, cradling me against his chest. I melt into him, my skin still flushed and damp. He carries me across the room, and that's when I notice a fireplace tucked into the corner. But Holt flicks a switch, and suddenly the room is bathed in a golden, flickering glow.

He kneels and lowers me onto a thick, furry blanket spread in front of the fire. The plush softness kisses my knees, and I gasp at the contrast of warmth on one side, the fire's heat on the other.

Then they join me. All of them. Holt moves aside to let his friends come closer.

Arrow kneels in front of me, completely naked, eyes burning. Luke settles behind me, his warmth seeping into my spine as his arms cage me gently. I'm caught between them, their scents surrounding me, their hands brushing along my ribs, my thighs, my hips.

My head falls back against Luke's shoulder. I'm trembling again, but it's not from nerves this time. It's from want. Craving. My body hums, alive and greedy. I turn my face and steal a kiss from Arrow, and he groans into my mouth like I've just saved him.

Luke kisses my neck from behind, while Arrow's mouth on mine is devastatingly addictive. I'm drowning in attention. Then Arrow shifts, drawing me closer, lifting one of my thighs with his strong hand and guiding it around his waist, then the next leg until I'm in his embrace, legs hugging his hips.

He grips my hips and lowers me onto his waiting cock, and I gasp as he finds me again, sliding in deep. There's no hesitation. No pause. Just perfect, overwhelming thickness.

A sound escapes me. Not a moan. Not a gasp.

A purr.

It rises from my chest without warning, vibrating against Arrow's mouth as he kisses me again. He grins against my lips. "There she is."

Behind me, Luke's hand slides down, firm against my spine, then lower. His fingers trace between my ass cheeks, and I stiffen from the anticipation. My breath catches.

"I'll be slow," he whispers, his lips brushing my ear.

"I want it," I whisper back, shocked by how much I mean it.

At first, his finger teases my ass, and I squirm on Arrow's cock, gasping, the dual sensation already wrecking me. Then he presses his big cock into me slowly, opening me with care. My mouth falls open.

"Yes," I breathe.

Arrow rocks up into me gradually, the sensation different but just as exciting, and I shudder.

Luke pushes deeper, and I moan.

It's so much. So full. I don't know where one sensation ends and the next begins. They move in a rhythm, Luke behind me, Arrow in front of me, finding a pace that has me purring.

My head falls back on Luke's shoulder again, my arms draped around Arrow's neck. I can barely hold myself up, but they do. They hold me like they were made to. Arrow's hands grip my hips, grounding me as Luke gropes my breasts.

Then Holt steps forward.

I blink, tears already burning the corners of my eyes from the overload. Holt is hard. Bare. Towering over us with the firelight showing every carved edge of him. His eyes are locked on mine as he fists the base of his cock, dragging the tip along my lips.

He doesn't need to say a word. I open willingly.

He guides himself into my mouth, and I take him deeper, letting my jaw stretch to accommodate him. My mouth is slick, eager, and I suck him down, working him the way I know he needs.

The moment is obscene. Beautiful. All three of them inside me in some way, their bodies claiming every part of mine. I'm gasping for air, drooling around Holt as I bounce between Arrow and Luke, our breaths loud and desperate.

They fall into a pattern.

Arrow groans. Luke growls. Holt curses, his hand tangling in my hair.

I'm losing myself, unraveling, every nerve on fire.

"You're gonna take our knots, baby," Luke grits out.

Arrow licks at my neck over the mark he left earlier. "Then we'll rest, and when you're ready, we'll do it again. And again."

I cry out, or try to. My mouth is full, but a whimper escapes around Holt as he pushes deeper.

They keep moving, slow and relentless, filling me, stretching me, loving me in every way they know how. I'm climbing again.

And then I detonate.

It hits like lightning. My entire body locks, my

vision whites out, and I scream around Holt's cock, the sound muffled but desperate. They don't stop. Not until they're following me over the edge.

Arrow groans and stills in front of me, his knot swelling as he locks deep. Luke curses, thrusting once more and then pressing in tight, his knot stretching me.

Holt spills into my mouth with a growl, and I swallow greedily, dazed and whimpering.

It's too much.

I can't take it.

I'm crying, gasping, trembling.

But I love it.

"So full," Luke says, voice shaking. "You're taking everything."

"Gonna knock you up, baby," Arrow whispers against my cheek. "You'll be so beautiful, swollen with our babies."

"Pregnant and barefoot, glowing in our bed," Holt murmurs. "You were made for this. Made for us."

I sob.

Not from pain.

From love.

Holt pulls out of my mouth gently, wiping the corner of my lips with his thumb. I lick it. My chest heaves as I gasp for air.

The ache is gone.

For the first time in what feels like forever, I feel sated. Not just in my body, but in my soul.

I feel loved.

Cared for.

Wanted.

Tears spill freely down my cheeks, and I don't try to hide them.

Holt cups my jaw, brushing them away with his fingers.

"You deserve all of this," he whispers. "Everything."

"Even when I didn't think I did?" I rasp.

"Especially then," Luke adds, pressing a kiss to my shoulder.

"You're ours," Arrow adds, his voice cracking. "And we take care of what's ours."

I let them hold me.

Let them rock me.

Let myself believe that maybe, just maybe, I was never too broken to be loved this completely.

26

I'm standing at the kitchen island, supposedly reviewing the final guest list for the wedding, but I don't really care or want to know who is attending. It's like my mother thinks if she runs it all past me, I'll somehow care. I don't. Plus, I can't focus on a damn thing right now.

My hand trembles as I try to write a note in the margin. The pen skips across the paper, leaving an illegible scrawl because I can't keep still. Can't think straight.

It's been days since my heat ended. Days of slowly coming back to myself, of the fog lifting, of being able to string together coherent thoughts that don't revolve around need and aching and *more*.

But apparently my body didn't get the memo.

The remote-control vibrator Luke convinced me to wear this morning hums to life, and I gasp, gripping the edge of the counter as my knees nearly buckle. The low, steady pulse presses right against my clit, sending a ripple of pleasure through my core. It's not overwhelming, but it's the kind of sensation that coils deep inside, insistent and slow, like a fuse lit beneath my skin. My breath catches as my body clenches around nothing, aching for more, my thighs squeezing together in a futile attempt to dull the delicious pressure building with every passing second.

"Luke," I call out, trying to sound annoyed instead of desperate. "This isn't fair."

His laugh comes from somewhere behind me. "You said you'd wear it. I'm just making sure it's working properly."

"It's damn working." My voice comes out breathless.

The vibration stops, and I sag against the counter, trying to catch my breath. The guest list blurs in front of me. Thirty people. Cousins and Mother's friends, mostly. A few distant relatives who probably think this whole thing is scandalous.

I don't care anymore. Three days until the wedding, and all I can think about is the fact that Arrow is at the restaurant and Holt went into town for supplies, and they left me alone with Luke, who hasn't stopped having a hard-on.

Who apparently woke up today and decided delicious torture was on the agenda. I can't complain, because I jumped at the chance, so really, am I any better than him?

I touch my neck absently, fingers finding a bite

mark there. They're all healing but still raised, still sensitive. Every time I touch them, they tingle. Like they're alive. Like the men who put them there are reaching through the marks to remind me I'm theirs.

Claimed.

The thought sends a shiver through me that has nothing to do with the toy currently nestled inside me.

I can't imagine my life without them now. It's only been a month, less than that, really, but the idea of going back to my townhouse, to eating dinner alone, to waking up in an empty bed? It feels impossible. Wrong.

The vibrator kicks on again, stronger this time, and I cry out before I can stop myself.

"Luke!" I spin around, and he's right there. Leaning against the doorway with that lazy grin, phone in his hand. Remote access.

"What?" He's the picture of innocence. "Just testing the settings."

"I'm trying to work."

"Work." He says it like it's a foreign concept. "On what, exactly?"

I wave at the papers scattered across the counter. "The seating chart. Making sure we have enough chairs."

"Arrow's got all that handled." Luke pushes off the doorway, and I watch him cross to me with predatory grace. "You know he made three spreadsheets, right? Color coded. We're good."

"Still. I should—" The vibrator pulses in a pattern

that makes my knees weak, and I grab the counter again. "Stop that."

"Make me." He's close now.

I'm leaning toward him. "Arrow and Holt will be back soon."

"That's okay." His hand settles on my hip. "And you're already so worked up. Can see it on your face."

He's not wrong. Ever since the heat ended, it's like my body doesn't know how to settle. Every touch arouses me. Every glance from one of them leaves me fantasizing about them devouring me. It should be fading by now, shouldn't it? The lingering effects of the heat?

But if anything, it's getting worse around my men.

"This is your fault," I tell him. "You're the one who suggested I wear this thing."

"Suggested." His smile widens. "Pretty sure I dared you and you jumped at the idea."

I grin evilly.

He adjusts something on his phone, and the vibration changes. Slower. Deeper. "How's it feel?"

"Like I'm about to melt."

His free hand comes up to cup my face, and I'm caught between the gentleness of his touch and the relentless sensation between my legs. "You love it."

"The wedding is in three days," I say, trying to focus on literally anything else. "We still have so much to do."

He leans in, nose brushing my temple. "And we

also need to ensure all your needs are met. That's my priority."

The marks on my neck tingle, and I gasp.

Luke notices. Of course he does. "They're still sensitive?"

"Yeah." I touch Holt's mark, and it's like I can feel him even though he's not here. "It's weird. They keep… reacting."

"That's our bond." Luke's voice is soft now. Serious. "Part of being marked. You'll always feel us, even when we're not around."

The idea makes me feel safe.

"I can't imagine not having them anymore," I admit quietly. "Not having you three."

His hand moves from my face to my hip, tightening his grip. "Good. Because you're stuck with us now."

"What a way to phrase it."

"You know what I mean." He pulls back enough to look at me, and his expression is so open it has me swooning. "Contract or no contract, wedding or no wedding—you're ours now. We're not letting go." Something flashes in his eyes. Heat. Possession.

The vibrator kicks into high gear, and my response dissolves into a moan.

I'm grasping his arms now, my fingers digging in. "You're a tease."

"Never said I'd play fair." But he turns it down, just enough that I can breathe again. "Been thinking about you all morning. Can't focus on anything else."

He presses closer, and his cock is there. Hard. Straining against his jeans. The bulge is obvious, heavy and thick, and I shudder all over at the promise.

I ignore everything else.

He growls, low and rough, and then his mouth crashes against mine. The kiss steals my breath, his tongue sliding against mine with a hunger that borders on ferity. I cling to his shirt like it's the only thing keeping me upright.

The vibrator is still going, and it feels like it's synced to my pulse. It drives heat through me, winding tighter, spreading low in my stomach until my whole body trembles. Luke's chest is solid against mine, his breath harsh.

"Stop teasing me," I gasp when he breaks the kiss, my lips swollen, my voice wrecked. "I need—"

His hand drags down my spine, the touch rough enough to make me shiver. "I've been watching you all morning," he murmurs, his voice dark and low against my ear. "Watching you try to focus on that damn guest list while your thighs pressed together, while this little toy hummed between your legs. Watching you squirm."

My breath stutters. "You're terrible."

He grins, wicked and sure. "You love it." He turns me around to face the counter before I can answer, his body crowding mine until my hips press into the counter. His breath ghosts against my neck. "Admit it."

I don't have to, as my body betrays me. I arch back

against him, the inferno between us unbearable, every nerve ending screaming for him to touch me. My chest heaves at the solid press of him against my ass, thick and hard through his jeans.

His hands find the hem of my skirt, pushing it up, bunching the fabric around my waist. Cool air hits my thighs, and I shiver. Then his fingers hook under the thin elastic of my thong, tugging it down slowly, almost tauntingly. The friction of it sliding over my skin leaves me breathless.

"I need these off," he growls.

I kick them aside, breath hitching, pulse hammering like it's trying to escape my chest.

Then Luke's hand slides between my legs, and the first sweep of touch has me moaning. I'm soaked and aching.

His fingers slip between my folds, touching the toy partly inside me, partly against my clit, his breath shuddering out against my neck.

"Fuck," he murmurs. "Still buzzing."

He tugs it out gradually, dragging it across every oversensitive nerve. I tremble, whimpering as the slick toy slides free with a wet sound, leaving me hollow and desperate.

Luke lifts it, lets me hear the soft hum before switching it off, and then tosses it onto the counter with a quiet clatter.

"You wore it all morning for me," he whispers, mouth brushing the shell of my ear. "Dripping for hours. And now look at you..."

He spreads my legs open with one hand, then runs his touch between my thighs again. "So fucking ready."

I can't even form words. Just a strangled groan as I purr for him.

He curses softly, like he's fighting for control. Then I hear the sharp rasp of his zipper, the sound electric in the charged air. My pulse jumps.

The next moment, the thick, hot head of his cock presses against my ass, then slides down between my crack. I tilt my hips out, ready.

"Easy," he murmurs, one hand gripping my waist, the other steadying me against the counter. His voice is rough with restraint. "Let me in slowly, sweetheart. Let me feel you take me."

But patience isn't in me anymore. I push back against him, desperate, and his quiet groan tells me I've shattered whatever control he had left.

He presses the tip to my entrance and shoves himself in, and the ache is perfect. I'm still tender from the heat, from days of being thoroughly used, but it's the good kind of ache. The kind that reminds me I'm alive, desired, marked.

"Fuck." Luke's voice is wrecked. "I swear your pussy is made of gold. Can't get over how good you feel."

I laugh, breathless. "That's the worst dirty talk."

"Don't care." He pulls back and thrusts again, harder this time. "It's true. Every time I'm inside you, I think I'm gonna lose my mind."

He sets a steady rhythm, and I'm gripping the

counter so hard my knuckles are white. The papers scatter, the pen rolls off onto the floor, and I don't care. Can't care about anything except the feeling of him inside me, filling me, claiming me.

His hands are on my hips, holding me in place. "Gods, I can't get enough. Just spent days devouring you and I still want more."

"Then take it," I gasp.

He does. His pace increases, rougher now, and he's hitting deep. The angle is perfect because I'm seeing stars with every thrust.

My phone rings.

We both freeze.

"Don't answer it," Luke growls, but he doesn't stop moving. Slow, shallow thrusts that keep me on edge.

I glance at where my phone is buzzing on the counter. Harper's name lights up the screen.

"I have to." I reach for it with a shaking hand. "It's Harper."

"Fine. Make it quick." Luke pulls back, then slams forward, and I barely manage to swallow a scream. "But I'm not stopping."

"Luke—"

"Answer. The. Phone." His voice is dark, commanding, and it sends a thrill through me.

I swipe to answer, bringing the phone to my ear. "Hey, Harper."

"Hey!" Her voice is bright, cheerful. "Just wanted to confirm that we're still on for pizza night tonight?"

"Yeah." Luke thrusts again, and I have to press my free hand over my mouth. "Yeah, we're still on."

"Seven o'clock at your place, right? Mack is super excited."

"That works." I'm trying so hard to sound normal, but Luke is keeping up a steady pace now. Not stopping. His hands tight on my hips, angling me just right. "That's—that's perfect."

"You sure you don't want us to bring anything?" Harper asks. "I know Arrow said he's handling the food, but—"

"No, don't—" Luke hits a spot that makes my toes curl, and I have to turn a moan into a cough. "Sorry. Don't bring anything. Arrow has gone kind of crazy with the food."

Luke leans forward, his chest against my back, his mouth at my ear. "Good girl," he whispers, voice low enough that Harper can't hear.

I'm going to die. I'm actually going to die right here in this kitchen.

"You okay?" Harper's voice sharpens with concern. "You sound weird. Out of breath."

"I'm fine." I press my forehead against the cool marble counter. "Just getting a few things done. Running around, you know."

Luke shifts the angle slightly, and oh God—

A moan slips out before I can stop it.

"Cindy?"

"Yeah, sorry." I'm giggling now, can't help it. The absurdity of this situation. Trying to have a normal conversation while Luke is inside me, while I can feel every inch of him stretching me. "Yes. See you later for pizza. Don't need to bring anything. I mean it."

She's laughing. "Okay, but I'm bringing wine anyway." Harper pauses. "Are you sure you're okay? You sound really—"

"I'm great." Another thrust, and I bite my lip hard. "Perfect. Totally normal. See you at seven."

I hang up before Harper can ask any more questions, dropping the phone onto the counter.

Luke immediately speeds up, pounding into me hard enough that I have to brace myself. "That was so fucking hot," he growls. "Watching you try to stay quiet. Knowing I'm inside you and she has no idea."

"You're terrible," I gasp, but I'm pushing back against him, meeting every thrust.

"Yeah, but you love it."

The phone rings again.

I blink, dazed, clinging to the counter while Luke is still deep inside me. "Are you kidding me?" I gasp, twisting to see the screen.

Holt.

Oh God.

Before I can slap a hand toward the red button to make it stop, Luke grabs the phone.

"Hey, babe," Holt's voice crackles through the speaker.

And then Luke slams into me hard.

I nearly drop to my knees, a moan tearing out of me before I can stop it. "Oh—"

There's a pause on the other end. "Cindy? What the hell was that?"

"I'm fine," I choke out, breathless. "Totally fine. What's up?"

Luke's eyes gleam with mischief. He grins and goes faster.

Slap. Slap. Slap.

"Jesus Christ," Holt growls. "Are you getting fucked right now?"

"We're just a little busy. You know how it is," Luke answers for me.

He thrusts again, hard enough to make the slap echo through the kitchen, and I swear I see stars.

"You fucking bastard," Holt snarls. "You're fucking her. You answered the damn phone while you were inside her?"

"Sorry," I whisper, not sure if I'm apologizing to Holt or the gods or my trembling knees.

"Don't apologize," Holt snaps. "You've got nothing to be sorry for. He's just rubbing it in because I'm not there."

Luke chuckles darkly, cocky as hell. "Not rubbing it in. Yet."

"You smug piece of shit—"

I grab the phone, barely able to speak between breaths. "Holt. I love you. But I swear to God if you don't hang up, I'm going to combust."

"I hope you do," he mutters. "Explode all over his cock. Then save some of that heat for me."

Then the line goes dead.

Luke tosses the phone aside with a satisfied grin. "He started it."

I shove back against him, voice cracking. "Then finish it."

His hand slides around to where we're joined, fingers finding my clit. "Come on. Let me feel you come."

It doesn't take much. I'm already so close, wound so tight from the vibrator and the risk of being caught and just him. The orgasm hits me hard, and I'm shaking, crying out his name, barely able to stay upright.

His hips jerk against mine and stop. "Fuck, Cindy. Fuck. I want you upstairs so I can knot you."

We stay like that for a long moment, both of us breathing hard.

"Wow. You two done christening the kitchen, or should I come back later?"

I *squeak* and twist my head toward the doorway.

Arrow is there. Leaning against the frame like he's got all the time in the world. Grocery bags at his feet. Grinning like the devil just gave him a private show.

"Oh my God," I gasp, pushing off the counter in a panic, cheeks blazing.

Luke pulls out of me, unapologetic and still fully hard.

"Jesus," Arrow groans, shielding his eyes with one hand. "Could you *not* point that thing at me? This isn't a duel."

"You're the one who walked in." Luke shrugs,

reaching for a kitchen towel way too slowly. "Maybe knock next time before entering *my orgasm zone.*"

Arrow barks out a laugh, eyes glued to me instead of Luke. "Sorry. Wasn't expecting live-action porn between the bananas and the eggs. Hi, babe."

I scramble to grab my panties, the vibrator, and my phone, trying to smooth my dress and failing miserably.

Arrow's gaze drags over me as if I'm the damn buffet.

"You're glowing, you know that?" he says, still grinning. "All flushed. It's adorable."

"Stop looking at her like that," Luke mutters.

"Then stop fucking her in communal spaces," Arrow fires back, though he's not even trying to look away. His grin just *grows.*

Luke rolls his eyes, tossing the towel over his shoulder. "We were gonna head upstairs."

"Oh?" Arrow quirks a brow at me. "The heat room is free, last I checked. Want some company?"

"No," I say too fast, backing away. "Nope. I'm good from you both. I just need, uh, hydration. And space. To breathe."

They both take a step toward me.

"Sounds good," Luke says, voice low.

"Let's go," Arrow echoes, already moving to scoop up the grocery bags with a wink. "I brought popsicles."

"Oh my God," I squeak, bolting out of the kitchen through the side door that brings me out into the hall-way, with my face on fire. "You two are insane!"

Heavy footsteps follow me. Not fast. Just enough to make it clear I'm being hunted.

"Hey, babe?" Arrow calls up the stairs. "You dropped your panties!"

"Shut up!" I shout, laughing and running, completely overwhelmed, and deliriously happy.

I can't believe this is my life.

And I'm not sure I want to change a damn thing.

27

Three Days Later

The coffee is still too hot, but I drink it anyway. Burns going down, sharp and bitter. Just how I need it.

It's barely dawn on Halloween morning, and the sky is that weird grayish purple that paints everything to appear haunted. Fitting, considering the absolute shit show we've got planned for today. The last few days have been filled with organizing and spending every second I can spare with my gorgeous Omega. I can't get enough of her... I'm a man obsessed.

I lean against the porch railing at the rear of our house, staring at our handiwork in the yard. The path down to the lake is lined with those tacky orange lights. Inflatable ghosts bob in the morning breeze, huge ones, at least eight feet tall. There's a skeleton bride and groom set up by the river, complete with a top hat and a veil that keeps blowing off in the wind.

It's gaudy as fuck.

Exactly what we were going for.

To our right on the grounds, the pergola structure looks like Halloween threw up on it and then came back for seconds. Orange and black streamers hang from every beam, twisting in the breeze. More inflatables crowd the corners of a giant Frankenstein, a witch on a broomstick, some kind of blow-up haunted house that Luke found on clearance. Fake cobwebs drape over the support beams, thick enough to appear almost real in the dim light. Jack-o'-lanterns line the perimeter, their faces carved into exaggerated grins and screams. There's even a fog machine tucked under one of the tables, ready to pump out that artificial mist.

The chairs by the water are set up in neat rows, which would look elegant except for the inflatable black cat, back arched like it's hissing at whoever dares walk down the aisle. Every other chair has a cheap foam pumpkin sitting on it. It's hideous. Absolutely hideous.

I fucking love it.

The back door opens, and Holt steps out. No shirt, just slack pants. His coffee mug steams in the cool air, and he's got that look on his face as if he's been up for a while but pretending he just woke up.

"You couldn't sleep either," he says. Not a question.

"Nah." I take another sip. "Wanted to make sure everything was set. You know, for this circus."

Holt moves to stand beside me, and we both stare out at the decorations.

"It's ridiculous," Holt says.

"Fucking beautiful," I agree, grinning.

We both start laughing. Can't help it. The whole thing is so over the top, so deliberately tacky, that it's almost art. Like we took every single thing Victoria would hate and crammed it into one location.

"Victoria is going to lose her goddamn mind," Holt says.

"That's the point." I smile. "She wanted a wedding and let us decorate. We're giving her one she won't forget."

Thinking of her has my jaw tightening. That woman has been pushing every button since first meeting her. Too busy for her own nephew's wedding. Too important to help with any actual planning. Just barking orders like we're her personal assistants and expecting us to jump when she snaps her fingers.

Well, we jumped. Right into the nearest Halloween store and bought out their entire fucking stock and made our own version instead of the tamed, boring version she wanted.

"I made it a thing a long time ago," I say, watching the inflatable ghosts sway. "Don't question idiots or psychos. Just let them do their thing and stay out of the blast radius."

"And Victoria falls into those categories?"

"Definitely both." I grip my mug tighter. "As long as she gets this ridiculous wedding done and leaves

Cindy alone for good, I'll play nice. But this is pushing my patience to the fucking limit."

Holt glances at me. "If she doesn't leave after today, we're fucking done with her."

"Fuck yeah, we are. After today, if she doesn't back the fuck off and leave Cindy alone, she'll be dealing with all three of us directly. No more playing nice, no more jumping through hoops. And she'll lose all access to Cindy. Completely."

"Agreed."

We sip our coffee in silence for a moment. The inflatable ghosts sway harder as the wind picks up, their faces locked in those stupid cartoon screams. One of the streamers comes loose from the pergola and flaps wildly before catching on a beam.

"The ceremony is at noon," Holt says. "Everything's ready."

"Food is prepped," I add. "Just need to cook it when we get closer to the time. I've got enough for fifty even though there's only thirty people coming. Rather have too much than run out and hear Victoria bitch about it."

"Smart."

I nod, staring out at the setup again. "I think Cindy is going to lose her shit laughing."

My thoughts drift to Cindy, still asleep upstairs. We've been taking turns sharing her bed since her heat ended. One of us each night while the other two sleep in our own rooms. Last night was my turn, and fuck, leaving her this morning was harder than I expected.

The moment I slipped out of bed, trying to be quiet, she rolled into the warm spot I'd left behind. Grabbed my pillow without even waking up, hugged it to her chest. Made this soft little sound, somewhere between a sigh and a whimper, that damn near killed me.

I stood there for a solid minute, just watching her. Wanting to climb back in. Stay there. Wake her up properly with my hands and my mouth and make her come before she even fully opened her eyes.

But we've got shit to do. A wedding to pull off. A mother to deal with.

So I left.

"She still asleep?" Holt asks, like he's reading my mind.

"Yeah." I smile despite myself, remembering. "So hard to get up and leave her."

Holt's expression softens in that way it only does when we talk about Cindy.

"Last night she told me something," I admit, watching the sky slowly lighten behind the mountains. "Said she'd love for us to start sleeping together. All of us. In the heat room, in that huge bed we set up."

Holt nods. "I think," he says finally, "that sounds fucking perfect."

"Agreed," I say.

The bond marks on Cindy's body flash through my mind. I can still remember exactly how it felt marking her, the way her skin gave under my teeth, the taste of her, the way she cried out as I bit down. The bond snapping into place like a live wire, immediate and permanent and undeniable.

Mine. Ours.

"You think she wants us to propose?" My thoughts come out as a question... something I'd been pondering recently.

Holt glances my way, eyebrows raised.

I feel uncomfortable suddenly, exposed. Not a feeling I'm used to. "I mean really propose. Not this contract bullshit we're doing today."

"What makes you think that?"

"I don't know." I stare down into my coffee. "She grew up seeing her family do weddings, right? Traditional ones. The whole formal thing. Even if her family was shit, maybe she still... I don't know. Wants the fairy tale?"

Holt is quiet again, thinking. When he speaks, his voice is careful. "She's already ours. The marks prove that. The bond is there."

"Yeah, but some Omegas want more than just the bond." I'm trying to find the right words. "They want the romance on a special day. The gesture. The down-on-one-knee bullshit with a ring and a speech."

"You think Cindy wants that?"

"I don't know," I admit. "That's why I'm asking. Her family was horrible to her. We know that. But maybe she still has this idea in her head of what a real proposal looks like? What a real wedding should be?"

Holt stares out at the lake in the distance. "We could try feeling her out today," he says finally. "See how she reacts to the wedding. If she loves it, hates it, doesn't give a shit. Might tell us what we need to know."

"Yeah." I finish my coffee in one long swallow. "That's a good idea."

"If she wants a real proposal," Holt continues, "we'll give her one. All three of us. Make it something she'll actually want to remember. And I'll fill in Luke to ensure he's on the same page as us."

The back door slams open hard enough to rattle the frame, and Luke stumbles out. He's in gray sweats and a faded T-shirt, hair sticking up in every direction. His phone is clutched in his hand, and he's got that look on his face. The one that means someone pissed him off before he even had caffeine.

"Fuck," he announces to the morning in general. "Who the hell calls this time of the morning with fucking commands?"

He holds up his phone. Even from here I can see the text message thread, long paragraphs.

"She's a damn bitch," Luke says, scrolling with his thumb. "Look at this shit."

Holt and I move closer, and Luke holds out the phone so we can actually read.

It's from Victoria. Sent just minutes ago, which means the woman has been up since before dawn planning this shit.

Good morning, Luke! So sorry for the last-minute request, but there's been a small issue with the cake. The bakery needs someone to pick it up this morning. There was a mix-up with the delivery time, and they can't bring it out to the house. They also need a final fitting for the cake topper (bride and groom figurines). I'll need someone with a van, and at least two people to help carry and hold it, as it's quite large. The address is below. Thank you so much! xx

An address follows. Some industrial area I don't recognize.

"How fucking big is a cake gonna be for thirty people?" I demand. "What, is she expecting a five-tier monstrosity?"

Luke groans, running his free hand through his already messy hair. "Right? This is fucking insane. My patience is wearing thin with her. I'm only doing this shit for Cindy."

Holt's jaw tightens. "The sooner we get rid of her, the better. So tired of being her bitch."

"I'll stay behind," I offer. "You two can handle a cake pickup."

Luke looks at me like I just suggested he jump off a bridge. "And what if it's massive? What if I can't hold it right and we destroy it on the way back? I don't want to deal with that shit. Victoria will lose her goddamn mind and blame us for ruining her precious wedding."

"Then we tell her to fuck off," I say.

"Or," Luke counters, "we just get the damn cake and avoid the drama."

I'm already shaking my head. "Fuck that. I'll make them a vanilla sponge cake myself. That's more than they deserve anyway."

Holt laughs at that.

"With some shit frosting from a can. Done." I cross my arms. "Not spending my morning playing delivery boy for that woman."

"Come on," Luke says. "It's for Cindy."

And fuck, there it is. The only argument that actually works.

I glare at him. "That's a low blow."

"But it's true." Luke's grin is smug. "We do this, grab the cake, get back before Cindy even wakes up. Then we never have to deal with Victoria's bullshit again after today."

"Fine," I bite out. "Fuck. But our fridge in the basement had better be large enough for whatever monstrosity she ordered, or I'm leaving it outside and letting the wildlife have at it."

"Deal," Luke says.

Holt is already moving toward the door. "Let's get dressed and go. Faster we leave, faster we're back."

I follow them inside, already regretting this decision. We head upstairs to change. I grab jeans that are actually clean for once, a deep blue T-shirt, and my leather jacket. Boots that have seen better days but are broken in just right. As I'm dragging everything on, I glance at Cindy, who's still sleeping.

She's curled up in bed, blankets drawn up to her chin, hair spread across the pillow. Still out cold, breathing heavily.

I linger in the doorway for a second longer than I probably should, just watching her. Even like this, flushed and half buried in blankets, she's the most beautiful thing I've ever seen.

My chest squeezes, hard. I don't know how we got lucky enough to have her, but hell if I'm ever letting her go.

I pull the door closed slowly, careful not to make a sound.

Luke appears in his doorway, pulling a shirt over his head. "Yeah. Let her have peace while she can. Once Victoria shows up, it's gonna be chaos."

We're all ready in under ten minutes. Holt grabs the keys to his truck, and we head out through the front door, closing it quietly behind us.

The truck starts with a rumble that sounds too loud in the quiet morning. Holt backs out of the drive-way, and we head toward the restaurant, where we keep the van.

I'm in the passenger seat, watching the sun finally start to crest the mountains. Halloween morning. The one day a year when everything is supposed to be spooky and fun, and here we are playing errand boys for a woman who treats her own daughter like a busi-ness transaction.

We reach the restaurant in fifteen minutes. Holt parks the truck, and we all pile out. The van is right where we left it, parked in the corner under a broken streetlight. I unlock it, and we climb in, with me driving.

The GPS directs us toward the industrial district,

and I watch the city change outside the windows. Nice neighborhoods giving way to commercial areas, then to the warehouses and storage facilities that cluster near the old factories.

"Should be coming up on the left," Luke states.

The building appears through the morning haze, with a faded sign out front: BAKED GOODS & CAKES. The front windows are dark, lights off. There's a CLOSED sign hanging crookedly on the door.

"Looks like a cheap-ass place, if you ask me," Holt says, leaning forward to get a better look.

He's not wrong. The whole building is run-down. Paint peeling off the siding, weeds growing up through cracks in the parking lot. Not exactly where I'd expect Victoria to order a wedding cake from, but maybe that's the point. Maybe she's cheaping out on this wedding.

"Go around the back," Holt says, following the GPS directions. "Loading dock."

We drive around to the alley behind the building. There's a small parking area back here, cracked asphalt. A dumpster overflowing with trash. And the loading dock door, rolled up just enough to show darkness inside.

"This feels off," I say.

"Yeah," Luke agrees, but he's already opening his door. "Let's just grab the damn cake and get out of here."

Holt and I exchange a look. Something about this

isn't sitting right with me. But we're here. Might as well get it done.

We all climb out of the van.

Holt moves to open the back doors, keeping his eyes on the quiet dock.

"I'll check it out," Luke mutters, already heading for the loading bay. His hands are stuffed in his hoodie pockets, but there's tension in his shoulders, the kind that says he doesn't trust this.

"I'll go with him," I say, falling into step beside him. Holt nods, staying back with the van, one hand resting casually on the handle of the crowbar tucked near the back doors. Just in case.

Luke and I step through the open loading dock door.

It's dark.

Not dim. Not shadowed.

Dark.

My boots scuff against concrete as my eyes adjust. This isn't a bakery.

It's a warehouse. An empty one.

Bare concrete floor stretching out in every direction, surrounded by steel walls and girders. No ovens. No cake. No racks. No lights, aside from the faint gray spill behind us.

Luke stops cold beside me. "This isn't the right place."

"Yeah," I mutter. "I don't like this."

We move farther in. The air is stale and thick with dust and a chemical tang that clings to the back of my throat.

"Anyone here?" I call out, sharp.

Silence.

Then—

Thunk.

Something whips out from the side, fast and silent, a metal pipe or a bat, I can't tell. It slams into Luke's side. He grunts, stumbles. Then drops.

Just collapses beside me like his legs gave out, crumpling to the floor with a thud.

"Luke!" I bark, diving toward him, heart kicking into overdrive.

Behind me—"Arrow, MOVE!" Holt's voice, fierce and cutting through the dark like a gunshot.

I spin around just in time to see Holt rushing in, a blur of movement as he grabs a figure that stepped from the shadows, a man in black.

Holt slams him into the wall, fists flying, teeth bared. Another man appears behind him.

He lunges.

A white cloth clamped in one gloved hand.

"Behind you!" I shout, sprinting toward them.

Holt twists just in time to elbow the guy in the throat, snarling. "You think that's enough?!"

But the second attacker is already pressing the cloth against Holt's face, dragging him down with a grip like iron.

I'm halfway to them when something crashes into my back.

I barely get my arm up before he's on me, and a cloth slams over my mouth and nose.

The scent hits instantly. It's chemical and suffocating.

I buck and twist, growling, fists swinging wild, but the bastard holds on. Military-tight.

The smell burns my nose and throat. It's fucking chloroform.

I throw my elbow back as hard as I can, feel it connect with something solid. Ribs, maybe. The man behind me grunts, his breath rushing out, but his grip doesn't loosen. If anything, it tightens. The cloth presses harder against my face, covering my nose and mouth completely.

Can't breathe without inhaling more of it.

I try to hold my breath, try to fight, but my lungs are already screaming. My body is demanding oxygen, and there's nowhere to get air except through that cloth.

Holt goes down. Just crumples, the man lowering him almost gently to the concrete like this is routine. Like he's done this before.

My vision is getting fuzzy at the edges. Everything is starting to blur, sounds becoming distant and muffled.

My legs aren't working right. Too heavy. Can't feel my feet anymore.

The warehouse tilts sideways, or maybe I'm falling. Can't tell the difference.

My last coherent thought, before the darkness swallows everything: *Fuck. How fucking stupid are we to have fallen for that bitch's trap?*

And then, as my consciousness slips away completely... *Cindy.*

28

CINDY

The pink flowy dress is too light for how heavy everything feels today. I smooth my hands down the fabric for the tenth time, staring at my reflection in the hallway mirror. Hair braided in two plaits over my shoulders, shoes that Harper helped me pick out last week when we were laughing about how ridiculous this whole wedding was going to be. If it weren't for this horrible wedding, it would be a glorious day. The sun is shining bright and warm, there's a cool breeze coming off the mountains, carrying the smell of pine and earth, and Halloween decorations are everywhere, making the whole property look like a Gothic fairy tale.

But my stomach won't stop churning.

I glance at my phone again. The screen is empty. No new messages. No missed calls. Nothing.

I sent three texts to each of them. Luke, Holt,

Arrow. Each message more desperate than the last. *Where are you? Are you okay? Please answer me.*

Nothing. Radio silence.

Luke's message from this morning is still there, sent at six fifty when I was still half asleep: *We're going on an errand. Won't be long. Still sleeping, sweetheart?*

I'd woken up at eight to find the bed empty and cold. The sheets on Arrow's side had lost all their warmth. I'd pressed my face into his pillow, breathing in his scent, figuring they'd be back by nine. Maybe ten at the latest if they stopped for breakfast.

It's past ten thirty now.

My fingers hover over the keyboard, tempted to text them again. But what good would it do? I've already sent three messages each, called them. They're not responding, and that's not normal. But now? Nothing from any of them.

Something is wrong. I can feel it in my gut, that twisting, aching sensation that won't go away no matter how much I try to rationalize it. It's the same feeling I had the night before I ran from my wedding.

I make my way to the kitchen, needing something to settle my stomach. The chamomile tea I brewed earlier sits on the counter, still warm enough to drink. I wrap my hands around the mug, letting the heat ground me, and move to the window overlooking the backyard.

Mother is out there.

Of course she is. Showed up an hour ago with what she called *the troops*. A handful of relatives. I can see the frustration on Mother's face even from here. Her lips are pressed into that thin line she gets when things aren't going according to her plan. She's gesturing at the inflatable skeleton bride and groom, her mouth moving in what I know are sharp, clipped commands. Someone is trying to deflate one of the massive pumpkins, tugging at it uselessly while it bobs in the breeze. Another person is untangling orange streamers, pulling them down from the pergola, only to have more appear. There are cobwebs everywhere, fog machine canisters stacked near the tables, jack-o'-lanterns lining every available surface.

I grin despite the anxiety clawing at my chest. The guys made this setup as un-wedding-like as possible, as gaudy and tacky and wonderful as they could manage. Every single decoration is a middle finger to Mother's vision of elegance and sophistication.

But they should be here now to see Mother's agony, to laugh about it with me, to make crude jokes about the inflatable decorations and probably add more just to piss her off further.

Where the fuck are they?

I sip my tea, the chamomile doing absolutely nothing to ease the knot in my stomach. My eyes keep going back to my phone sitting on the counter, willing it to light up with their names. With anything.

Nothing.

The marrying couple isn't even here yet either. Monica and Trevor. Mother said they're meant to appear any moment. Right now, I don't give a fuck if this wedding goes ahead or not. Mother and her troops can do whatever they want in the yard. They can deflate every decoration, replace the Halloween setup with whatever elegant nonsense she has planned.

I just want to know my men are okay.

It's not like them to not respond. In the time since my heat, we've been in constant contact. Group texts throughout the day. Individual messages when one of them thinks of something to say. Luke sending me dirty pictures when he's bored. Holt checking in to make sure I ate lunch. Arrow forwarding recipes he wants to try.

But now? Hours of silence.

My thumb hovers over the keyboard again. Maybe one more text to Holt. Just one. Just to feel like I'm doing something.

Please just let me know you're okay.

I hit Send before I can second-guess myself. Watch the message show as delivered. Wait for it to change to Read.

It doesn't.

"You okay?" a male's voice asks.

I spin around, nearly dropping my mug. Hot tea sloshes over the side, burning my hand, but I barely feel it.

Mack is standing in the doorway to the kitchen. Arrow's brother. Tall and broad-shouldered, with that same dark hair and sharp jaw, though Mack's is covered in stubble like he forgot to shave this morning. He's in dark jeans and a leather jacket, hands in his pockets, and there's something comforting about seeing him here. Solid. Real.

"Front door was unlocked," he says, nodding toward the entrance. "Figured you four might want some help today with this monstrosity of a wedding."

Relief floods through me so fast I feel lightheaded. "Mack." I set my mug down before I actually drop it. "Have you spoken to Arrow today? Or the others?"

His eyebrows draw together, and I watch concern flicker across his face. "Not since yesterday. Why? What's wrong?"

"They went on an errand this morning." My voice comes out thin, strained. "No idea what for. Luke just said they'd be back soon. But I haven't heard from them in hours."

Mack pulls out his phone immediately, already dialing. "Goes to voicemail," he says finally, and I hear the edge in his voice now. He starts typing, his thumbs moving fast across the screen. "Sending him a text now. Telling him to call me immediately."

I watch him type, my heart pounding so hard I can feel it in my throat. The marks on my neck and my upper breast are tingling, all three of them at once.

"I'm sure they'll be back soon," Mack says, but there's something in his voice that tells me he's not as confident as he's trying to sound.

I nod, but the dread won't let go. It's sinking its fangs deeper, making it hard to breathe.

"Okay." Mack pockets his phone. "Let me go check on what the fuck they're doing out there." He jerks his head toward the backyard where Mother's troops are still wrestling with decorations. "And there are some flowers at the front door. Big arrangement. I'll grab them and bring them in."

"Thanks," I manage.

He pauses in the doorway, looking back at me. "They're okay, Cindy. I can feel it. Arrow is too stubborn to let anything happen to him, and the other two are just as bad."

Then he's gone, his footsteps echoing down the hallway toward the front door.

I'm alone again with my phone and my spiraling thoughts.

What if they're hurt? What if there was an accident? The roads up here can be dangerous, especially the mountain passes. What if they went off the road, what if they're trapped somewhere, or what if they're calling for help and no one can hear them?

Stop it.

I force myself to take a breath. Then another. They're fine. They have to be fine. This is Luke, Holt, and Arrow. Three ex-bikers who've survived God knows what. They're not going to be taken down by an errand.

But then why aren't they answering?

Footsteps sound in the hallway again, and I turn, expecting Mack with an armful of flowers and maybe some reassurance.

It's not Mack.

It's Van.

The world tilts sideways. Everything goes fuzzy at the edges, like I'm looking at him through water. My vision narrows to just him, standing there in my kitchen like he has every right to be here. Like the past two years never happened. Like I never ran.

He's exactly how I remember seeing him at the Harvest Dance. Six feet tall, blond hair styled perfectly. Designer clothes. Navy suit jacket over a crisp white shirt, the top two buttons undone. No tie. Expensive watch glinting on his wrist.

But his eyes. God, his eyes.

Cold blue. Ice blue. The kind that never quite match his smile, that never show what he's really thinking. They're fixed on me now with that look I remember from every nightmare. The one that used to make me feel like prey being circled by a predator.

My hands start shaking so hard I have to grip the counter to keep from dropping to the floor.

I'm back there. In the family estate, in that room with the white walls and the locked door and the single window too high to reach. Van's voice in my ear. His hand on my arm, fingers digging in just hard enough to hurt without leaving marks visible to anyone else.

The burn scar throbs like it's fresh, like his lighter is pressed against my skin right now.

"Hold still," he said, his voice almost gentle, almost. The metallic click of the lighter echoed in the dark before the flame flared to life, hungry and bright.

"Please, don't—" I begged, jerking against the grip that held me still.

He smiled. "You did this, remember? You made me angry. You always make me angry."

Then the heat hit. White-hot, blistering pain that tore a scream straight from my throat.

He pressed harder, until I could smell my own skin burning.

"That's what happens when you forget your place," he murmured. "A good Omega knows how to submit."

I shake the memory off, sliding the cup of tea away from me on the counter.

"You owe me a wedding," Van states. His tone is smooth, pleasant even. Conversational. Like we're old friends catching up over coffee.

His hands are in his pockets, posture relaxed, leaning slightly against the doorframe.

Rage floods through me, burning away some of the fear. I'm not that Omega anymore. I'm not the scared girl who ran from the altar in a panic.

I'm marked now. Claimed. Three Alphas have bitten me, bonded with me, made me theirs in every way that matters.

I'm not weak anymore.

But my legs are still wobbling. My hands are still shaking. And that voice in my head, the one that sounds like Van, is whispering, *You'll always be weak. You'll always be mine.*

"What the fuck are you doing here?" My voice

comes out stronger than I feel, louder than I expected. "You are not welcome in my house. Get the fuck out."

He doesn't move. Just stands there, watching me with that small smile.

"Such language," he says mildly. "That's not very Omega-like, Cynthia."

My mind is spinning. Everything is happening at once, too fast, too much. My men are missing. Mother is in the backyard with her troops, taking over my home. And Van is here, in my kitchen, looking at me like I'm something he misplaced and finally found.

The pieces start clicking together in my head, each one worse than the last.

What the fuck did he do?

Is he the reason they're not here? Is he the reason they're not answering their phones?

"You speak like that to your Alpha," Van says. Still not a question. A statement of fact.

"You are nothing to me." I force the words out through gritted teeth, pushing past the fear trying to choke me. "And sure as hell not my Alpha. That's the past, and you're part of it. Dead and buried."

He scratches his chin, that calculated gesture I remember too well. The one he does when he's pretending to be thoughtful, when really he's just deciding how to manipulate the situation.

"You speak so cruelly, Cynthia. Do you have any idea the agony I went through when my first Omega rejected me?"

There it is. The victim card. The poor, wounded

Alpha whose mate ran away, leaving him heartbroken and alone and damaged.

I don't buy it. Never did.

He told me the story in the early days when he was still pretending to be someone worthy of sympathy. Before the mask came off completely.

His family was humiliated. The bride's family demanded their money back. And Van decided it was her fault. That she was defective. Broken. Too damaged to recognize a good Alpha when she had one.

He never once asked himself why she ran. What she saw in him that terrified her enough to abandon everything.

And when I came along, arranged by our families who thought we'd be perfect together, he was determined not to let it happen again.

"Get out of my house," I shout, louder this time. My voice echoes in the kitchen.

He steps closer.

I retreat immediately, instinct taking over. My hip hits the counter hard enough to bruise. My phone is still in my hand, gripped so tightly that my knuckles have gone white and my fingers are cramping.

"I really did hope we could be civilized about this," Van says. "We have a past, Cynthia. History. And I want you back."

"Like hell." The words come out as almost a snarl.

"I'm taking you back," he continues, like I didn't speak. Like my words don't matter. They never did to him. "You've had your time away. Your fun. Playing house with those bikers."

My hand is moving toward the drawer. The one with the kitchen knives. Arrow keeps them sharp, sharpens them every week. If I can just reach it, grab the biggest one, maybe I can make Van back off. Maybe I can defend myself long enough to run, to scream, to get help.

Van watches my hand move. Watches and smiles, like he knows exactly what I'm thinking.

Then he pulls something out of his pocket.

Three phones that I recognize immediately.

Luke's has a crack across the screen that he never bothered to fix. Holt's is black and pristine. Arrow's is a simple red one.

My stomach drops to the floor. The air rushes out of my lungs.

"Been watching you frantically message these guys all morning," Van says. He's holding the phones up like trophies, like prizes he won. "Sending text after text. Getting more and more worried with each passing minute."

I can't breathe. Can't think. Can't do anything but stare at those phones.

"Where did you get those?" My voice comes out as barely a whisper.

"Does it matter?" He's enjoying this. "The point is, I have them. And you don't. And neither do they."

"What did you do?" The question tears out of me. "Where are they?"

"You really think they want you as much as I do?" Van asks instead of answering. He turns one of the phones over in his hand, examining it like it's something interesting.

"Yes, they do." The words come out fierce, certain.

"They're nothing," Van says. "Not good enough for you. Not worthy of an Omega from your family."

"Fuck you." My voice breaks on the words.

He pockets the phones again, one by one, taking his time. Making a show of it. Showing me he has complete control.

"Thing is, Cynthia." He steps even closer, and I have nowhere left to go. I'm trapped between him and the counter, and my heart is pounding so hard I can hear it in my ears. "I want you. And I get what I want. Always have. You know that."

Tears start to blur my vision.

"You're going to be my Omega," he continues. "Now you'll kneel for me the way you were always meant to. You'll do your duty as my Omega."

I'm shaking my head.

"And if you want to ensure your men see another day," he adds. "You will concede. You'll take my hand in marriage. Sign the contract to be my Omega. Legally, officially, permanently."

My breath catches. "What are you saying?"

"I'm saying you have a choice. I'm not a complete monster." My skin crawls. "You refuse me, you run, you try to jeopardize anything from happening today, and those three men won't be seeing tomorrow. Simple as that."

"You fucking bastard." The words tear out of me.

My mind is whirling so fast I can't grab on to a single thought. Options flash through my head, each one worse than the last.

I could run. Scream for Mack, hope he hears me, hope he gets here in time. But even then, how do we find my men? What if Van orders them... I can't even think of the words.

Or, I could agree, sign whatever he wants, go through with this nightmare, and then escape later. Find the guys, get help, figure it out. But Van's smart. Too smart. He'll be watching every second.

Tears are streaming down my face now, hot and furious and humiliating. I can feel them dripping off my chin, can taste salt on my lips.

"You can't do this," I whisper. "Please. Please don't do this."

He just grins. "Get all that emotional stuff out now, Cynthia. Cry it out. Because everyone is going to be watching you today. All those family members. And if you so much as think you can leave, if you give me any reason to believe you're not fully committed to this, my kindness in keeping them breathing is done. Understood?"

I can't speak. Can't force words past the lump in my throat.

Van holds out his hand. "Phone. Now."

I don't move fast enough for his liking.

He crosses the space between us in two strides and rips the phone from my hand. I cry out, more from shock than pain. He pockets my phone with the others.

The back door opens.

Mother strides in from the yard, her heels clicking sharply and authoritatively on the tile floor. She takes one look at me, tear-stained and shaking and cornered, and then at Van standing too close, and her expression doesn't change. Doesn't even flicker.

She fucking knew he was here. Probably told him exactly when to come in.

"Mother." My voice cracks, breaks completely. "Did you know about this?"

She waves at Van dismissively, like he's a servant she's temporarily done with. "Give us a moment, please."

Van stares at me for a long beat. His gaze travels over my face. Then he turns and walks toward the door. He pauses in the threshold, looking back over his shoulder with that smile.

"Be sure to look beautiful for me."

Then he's gone, out into the yard.

"Mother, what have you done?" My voice is raw.

She's straightening her clothes, brushing invisible lint off her cream-colored suit. Adjusting her pearl necklace. "Maybe it's better this way, Cynthia. You're meant to be with us. Someone who understands your background, your breeding. Not some wild men who don't know what it means to be part of a proper family."

"This is insanity. I'm marked by all three of them. I chose three Alphas." I pull my braids aside roughly, showing her the bite marks on my neck. They're still visible, still healing, the skin still slightly raised. "I'm a mated Omega. You can't do this."

"Of course you would go against all our wishes. And that's easy to fix," Mother interrupts, her tone casual. Like we're discussing flower arrangements, not my life. "It's better this way. You marry Van today. Everything's already set up. The officiant is here, the guests are arriving, and the contract is prepared."

The pieces slam together in my head with sickening clarity.

"You arranged this from the beginning, didn't you?" My voice comes out hollow, echoing strangely in my own ears. "Monica and Trevor were never meant to marry. This was always supposed to be my wedding."

Mother doesn't even have the decency to look ashamed. Her expression stays perfectly composed, perfectly calm.

"Be a good girl and put on the dress I brought you," she says. "It's in the living room, hanging off the door. We're starting this union earlier than planned. I've had enough of this ghastly town and its laughable attempts at sophistication. This Halloween nonsense, these decorations." She wrinkles her nose.

I glance out the window. More people are arriving in the backyard. I recognize my father now, standing there, tall and broad and terrifying. He's talking to my cousins, people I haven't seen in over two years.

"I'm going to be sick," I whisper.

"Don't be dramatic." Mother's voice hardens. "Go now. I'll wait for you, dear. And you know what will happen if you misbehave or don't follow through. Don't be selfish. Don't let those men lose their lives because you're being stubborn."

The threat hangs in the air between us.

I stumble out of the kitchen. The room is spinning, darkness clawing at the edges of my vision. My feet carry me toward the living room on autopilot, my body moving even though my mind is screaming at me to stop, to fight, to do something.

The dress is there. Hanging off the living room door, just like she said.

It's white. Lace. High neck that would cover the bond marks, long sleeves, fitted bodice that's clearly designed to restrict movement. The kind of dress that says *pure* and *obedient* and *property*. The kind of dress that makes me feel like I'm suffocating just from looking at it.

It's hideous.

I break down. Just crumple to the floor in front of it, sobbing so hard I can't breathe, can't see, can't think. It feels like I'm back at the family estate. Back in that room, drowning, about to lose everything I am. Everything I've built. Everything I've become.

I want to run. Every instinct is screaming at me to run, to grab my keys, get in a car, and drive until I hit the ocean or Canada or anywhere that isn't here.

But fear stops me cold.

My family is vindictive. I know that from experience. I've seen what they do to people who cross them, who defy them, who don't play by their rules. And Van? Van is cruel in ways that keep me up at night sometimes, memories of what he did to me surfacing when I least expect them.

They'll hurt Arrow, Holt, and Luke. They'll make good on their threat.

I force myself to stand on shaking legs. My whole body is trembling so badly I can barely walk, but I make it to the stairs. One step. Another. My hand grips the railing like it's the only thing keeping me tethered to reality.

I'm halfway up the staircase when a voice cuts through the air behind me.

"Cindy."

I look over my shoulder.

Mack is at the bottom of the stairs, head tipped back, staring up at me. His expression is thunderous.

"I heard everything," he says softly. "Let's talk."

We both rush into my room. I practically fall through the doorway, and Mack catches my arm, steadying me. He kicks the door shut behind us, and I lock it with trembling hands.

For a second, we just stand there, both of us breathing hard.

"What the fuck is going on? Was that Van?"

I nod, unable to form words.

"Fuck!" Mack grinds his jaw. "Fuck, I should have... I heard him threatening you."

The words tumble out of me in broken fragments. Van, the arranged marriage I ran from, the day I left him at the altar. His appearance today, the phones, the ultimatum.

Mack's expression grows darker with every sentence. His hands clench into fists at his sides, and I can see him struggling to contain his rage.

"That fucking piece of shit," he snarls when I finish. "I'm gonna kill him. I'm gonna rip his fucking throat out."

"Mack—"

"No, listen to me." He grips my shoulders, forcing me to look at him. "I haven't met Van before, but the MC I wanted to join was dealing with him directly. Had some business with him."

Hope flares in my chest, painful and desperate. "They did?"

"Yeah. And I think I know how to find Arrow and the other two."

The relief that floods through me is so intense I nearly collapse. "You do? Really?"

"Van's got connections, but so do I." Mack pulls out his phone, already scrolling through contacts. "MC still has eyes everywhere. Someone saw something. Don't worry," Mack says, and his voice is steady, certain, full of conviction. "I'm going to find them. You just need to delay that wedding as long as you can. Don't do anything until we return. Can you do that?"

I want to believe him. Want to trust that he can fix this, that he can save them. So I nod.

"We got you, Cindy. All of us. This asshole picked the wrong family to fuck with. Just hold on. Buy me as much time as you can."

Then he's moving, out the door and down the stairs. I rush to the window and watch him head out the front, his stride purposeful and aggressive. He climbs onto his bike, the engine roaring to life, and then he's gone through the open gates, tearing down the driveway so fast his back tire kicks up gravel.

I sit on the edge of my bed, trying to think clearly past the panic. We have a plan. Mack is going to find them. I just need to stall. Buy time. Do whatever it takes to keep Van from hurting them.

Twenty minutes pass. I keep checking the window, watching the driveway, hoping to see Mack's bike returning with Holt's truck behind it. Hoping to see Luke's stupid grin, Holt's steady presence, Arrow's concerned frown.

Nothing.

Just more guests arriving.

A knock raps on the door. "Are you ready, Cynthia?"

Mother's voice. No patience in it. Just expectation.

The door opens before I can answer. She walks in, takes one look at me still in my pink dress, hair still braided, no makeup, and her lips press into that thin, disapproving line.

"You're not even dressed?"

"I'm not getting married, Mother."

"Oh, you are. We can do this without pain, or we can do it forced. Your choice."

"Is this how you want me married?" I stand, facing her, trying to find some strength somewhere. "Threatened? Forced? With a gun to my head?"

She actually shrugs. The gesture is so casual, so dismissive of everything I'm feeling. "Most Omegas are lucky to find someone willing to look after them. To provide for them. And here we have an Alpha ready to do exactly that, and you keep rejecting him. You're being ungrateful, Cynthia. Selfish."

"I have three men doing that already." My voice rises, getting louder despite my fear. "Three men who chose me. Who I chose back. I don't want Van. I don't want any of this."

"This isn't a discussion." Her tone goes cold, final. "Change now."

I don't move. Can't move. My body has decided to mutiny, rooting me to this spot.

In my stubbornness, in my desperate need to buy more time for Mack to find them, I blurt out, "I'm not feeling well."

I rush to the bathroom, lock myself inside, and lean over the toilet. I don't actually need to throw up, but I make the sounds anyway. Gagging, retching, anything to make it convincing. Anything to stall.

Mother is banging on the door within seconds, her fist pounding hard enough to rattle the frame. "We're heading out now. Everyone is waiting. Stop making this all about you and embarrassing us. Do the right thing, Cynthia. Think about someone other than yourself for once."

I wipe my tears with a towel, press it against my face, and take one more shuddering breath.

Then I open the door.

Father is standing behind her.

Every muscle in my body locks up.

Broad shoulders that fill the doorway, hands like hammers that I've seen break things without effort. Seen them strike Mother across the face hard enough to knock her down. Seen them grab my arm and leave bruises that lasted for weeks. He doesn't say much, never has, but he doesn't need to. His presence is enough to terrify most people into submission.

He pushes Mother aside gently, almost tenderly, and holds out one enormous hand. "Your time has run out, Cynthia. We go now as you're dressed."

I'm trembling. Every cell in my body is screaming at me to run, to fight, to do something other than just stand here. But there's nowhere to go. He's blocking the door. Mother is behind him now.

With a shaking hand, moving like I'm underwater, I slowly reach out and accept his outstretched hand.

His grip is harsh. Crushing. Then he's hauling me out of the bathroom, practically dragging me.

I'm stumbling alongside him as he pulls me toward the stairs. Tears are falling down my cheeks freely now, dripping onto my dress. His hand is practically squeezing the life out of mine, cutting off my circulation.

"We don't have to do this," I plead, trying one more

time. "Please. Father, please. I don't want this. Please don't make me do this."

He says nothing.

We're outside now. The path to the lake stretches out in front of us, winding through the yard with small bits of Halloween decorations Mother missed still in place. Father is moving fast, his long strides eating up the distance, and I'm half running to keep up. My shoes slip on the grass. I nearly fall twice, but his grip keeps me upright, keeps me moving forward.

I keep looking over my shoulder, but no one is running up to rescue me.

Just an empty driveway and the growing sound of voices ahead.

All my cousins are here. Relatives I haven't seen in over two years, maybe longer. All dressed in their formal clothes, dark suits and elegant dresses, all staring at me as I'm dragged down what should be an aisle. Some look pitying, their expressions soft with sympathy they'll never act on.

None of them do anything. None of them ever do.

They just stand there in their neat rows of chairs, watching like this is entertainment.

At the front, Van stands in his suit. Navy blue, perfectly tailored, probably custom-made to show off his physique. He's smiling that cold smile, watching me approach like I'm a prize he's about to claim. Like I'm a trophy he's worked hard to win.

Next to him is the officiant. An older Beta woman I don't recognize, dressed conservatively in gray, holding a leather-bound book that probably has my future written in it.

And on the table beside them sits the contract.

Official documentation in families like mine that shows Van has bought me, that money exchanged hands, that I legally belong to him now. Papers that strip away my autonomy and hand it over to him like a receipt, like I'm furniture being delivered.

Ice burns through my veins, cold and numbing.

I look back one more time, desperately scanning the path behind me, the driveway beyond, the gates in the distance.

Please. Please, Mack. Please hurry up. Please find them.

Van holds out his hand toward me.

Father releases my crushed, numb hand and transfers it to Van's grip without ceremony.

The touch makes my skin crawl. Van's hand is cold despite the warm day, his fingers wrapping around mine possessively, holding too tight.

"You didn't even bother changing, huh?" he murmurs, his voice low enough that only I can hear. "Bold move. The mascara streaks really pull the look together."

I want to vomit. Want to scream. Want to run.

But I don't. Because somewhere out there, Luke, Holt, and Arrow need me to be strong. Need me to buy them time.

The officiant begins speaking, her voice carrying across the assembled guests. Something about unions and destiny and the sacred bond between Alpha and Omega and duty and honor.

All I can think about is the marks on my neck, on my breast. Luke's, Holt's, Arrow's. Three bonds, three claims, three men who chose me and I chose back. Three pieces of my soul walking around in other bodies.

This isn't right. This isn't how it's supposed to be.

But Van's hand is locked around mine like a manacle, and the contract is right there on the table waiting for my signature, and I don't know what to do.

I don't know how to save myself this time.

The officiant is still talking. Van is smiling. The family is watching.

And somehow, I have to find a way to hold on until help arrives.

If it arrives at all.

29

My head is pounding like someone took a sledgehammer to it. The pain radiates from the base of my skull, sharp and vicious, making my vision blur at the edges. I try to move and can't. My hands are locked behind my back, wrists bound tight with something plastic. Zip ties, from the feel of them cutting into my skin.

I force my eyes open. Dim light. Concrete floor beneath me, cold seeping through my jeans. My back is against a wall, and when I try to shift, I realize my ankles are tied too. More zip ties.

Fuck.

The room slowly swims into focus. Not the run-down "bakery" we walked into. Definitely not. This is different. A small warehouse, from the look of it, with metal racking lining the walls. All of it empty. No boxes, no equipment, nothing. Just bare shelves and concrete and the smell of dust and motor oil.

They moved us. The fuckers who took us down moved us while we were out.

I glance to my left. Arrow is there, maybe ten feet away, also sitting with his back against the wall. His head is lolling forward, strands of blond hair covering his face, but I can see his chest rising and falling. Breathing. Alive.

Luke is on my right, closer. He's starting to stir, groaning low in his throat.

The fact that none of us have gags tells me everything I need to know. We're in the middle of fuck knows where, far enough out that no one can hear us scream.

Rage floods through me. I thrash against the zip ties, pulling hard enough that the plastic cuts deeper into my wrists. Pain flares, but I don't care. I need to get free. Need to get back to Cindy.

There's no one else in the room with us. Just the three of us and empty space. But across the warehouse, maybe thirty feet away, there's a door. Light bleeds under it, and I can see shadows moving. Legs. Someone is standing guard out there.

"Fuck," Luke croaks. "What the hell happened?"

"Chloroform," I mutter, testing the restraints again.

Arrow lifts his head, blinking hard. "How long were we out?"

"Don't know." I scan the room again, looking for anything useful. "Could be minutes. Could be hours."

"Fuck!" Arrow fights his own restraints, his face

twisting with fury. "This has to be fucking Van. That fake cake pickup, Victoria's text, all of it."

"When I get hold of them," I start, then stop. When I get hold of him, what? What am I going to do? Every violent thought I've ever had is flooding through my head right now, and none of them are enough.

Luke is cursing steadily now, a stream of profanity under his breath. "We fell for the oldest trick in the fucking book. Fake address, open door, boom. Down we go like amateurs."

"Save it," I snap. "We need to get out of here."

"No shit." Arrow is thrashing harder now, and I can see blood starting to stain his wrists. "Cindy is back there. With them. With Van and Victoria and God knows who else," he murmurs quietly.

The thought makes my vision go red. Cindy, alone, dealing with whatever nightmare they've cooked up. She's stronger than she knows, but she shouldn't have to face this alone.

We're supposed to be there, to protect her.

I force myself to think past the rage. Focus. We need to get free, and we need to do it fast.

My belt. I keep a small knife hidden on the inside of my custom belt, tucked into a pocket. It's saved my ass more times than I can count.

I shift, trying to reach behind me. The angle is awkward, my hands barely able to move. My fingers brush the leather of my belt, searching for the hidden pocket.

"They patted us down," Arrow whispers. "Took the blade I keep in my boot. Fucking thorough."

"Give me a second." I'm stretching, fingers straining. Almost there. Just a little more.

The knife falls from my grip.

"Fuck!" The word slips out of me.

I hear it hit the concrete with a tiny metallic clink, somewhere behind me and to the left.

Luke's head snaps around. "You had a knife?"

"Yeah. And I just dropped it."

"Well, pick it back up!"

"Working on it." I'm tilting sideways now, trying to feel around on the floor behind me. The zip ties dig in harder, my shoulders screaming in protest at the angle. "Just give me a damn minute."

Arrow hisses. "Van's got Cindy. You know what he's going to do to her."

"I know!" The words come out sharper than I intended. "I'm trying."

Luke is cursing again.

My fingers brush something metal. There. I stretch farther, ignoring the pain in my shoulders, and manage to get my fingertips on the knife.

"Got it," I say.

"Thank fuck." Luke shifts, angling toward me. "Hurry up, man. We're wasting time."

I'm working the blade open one-handed, which is about as easy as it sounds. The small folding knife has a thumb stud, and I'm pressing it awkwardly, trying to get leverage.

It opens. Finally.

Now comes the hard part. Cutting zip ties behind my back, blind, while my hands are numb from lack of circulation.

I angle the blade against the plastic, sawing carefully. Too much pressure and I'll cut myself. Not enough and this'll take forever.

"You got it?" Arrow asks.

"Working on it."

"Work faster."

"Helpful," I mutter.

Luke makes a frustrated sound. "We need to get back there."

The blade catches on the zip tie, biting in. "I know, just shut up and let me concentrate."

The warehouse is quiet except for our harsh breathing and the sound of the blade working against plastic. The shadows under the door haven't moved. Whoever is out there is just standing guard, probably checking their phone.

The zip tie on my right wrist gives first. The plastic snaps, and suddenly my right hand is free. Pins and needles flood my fingers as circulation returns, painful and sharp.

I bring my hands around front, flexing them to get feeling back. Then I attack the zip tie on my left wrist, cutting through it in seconds now that I can see what I'm doing.

"There." I lean forward, sawing at the ties on my ankles. "Almost free."

"Fucking finally," Luke mutters.

I get my ankles free and immediately move to Luke, cutting his restraints. He's rubbing his wrists the second they're free, red marks angry against his skin.

Arrow is next. I kneel beside him, cutting fast. "We're getting out of here. We're getting back to her."

"Damn right we are." His voice is cold. The kind that simmers beneath the surface, more lethal than any scream. "And then we're dealing with every single person who thought they could do this."

Luke is on his feet already, testing his balance. "What's the plan?"

I open my mouth—

Then we hear it.

A sound. Not from the guard's door. Somewhere deeper in the warehouse.

Metal scraping. Footsteps. Quick. Light.

We freeze.

The kind of silence that means survival.

I tighten my grip on the knife, positioning myself in front of my men on instinct. Every muscle coils, wired to strike.

Another footstep. Closer.

Closer.

Then movement. A shadow peeling out from a stack of pallets near the far corner.

Mack.

Arrow's brother, moving like a ghost, gaze sweeping the space. He spots the guard's shadow under the door, raises a finger to his lips.

"Mack," Arrow breathes. "You fucking champion. You found us."

Mack rushes over, crouched low. "To get you the fuck out," he mutters.

"How'd you find us?" I ask, already pocketing my blade.

"Long story. I'll tell you when we're not about to get shot."

We huddle close. Mack leans in, voice tight with urgency. "Listen. Your Omega is in trouble. Bad trouble."

My pulse stalls.

"What happened?" I ask, but it comes out too sharp. Like I already know I don't want the answer.

"Victoria set this whole thing up," Mack spits, pacing like his skin can't contain him. "The wedding is fake. It's not a party. It's a trap for Cindy. Van's there. The family watching, an officiant waiting, a fucking contract. He's forcing her to marry him."

Arrow makes a noise that doesn't sound human. A low, broken snarl that comes from somewhere deep in his chest. "When?"

"Right now. Or any second." Mack looks each of us in the eye, like he's making sure we understand. "I told her to stall as long as she could, and I came to find you lot. Van threatened her. Said if she didn't go through with it, you three would die."

Luke goes still. That terrifying kind of stillness that means a storm is coming. His knuckles whiten. His jaw flexes. Then he whispers, "That motherfucker."

The rage in his voice chills the air.

My heart slams against my ribs. I can't breathe past it. I can't *think* around it.

"We need to get there," I say. My voice is low. Flat. Like it's not even mine. Like it belongs to the animal inside me. The one ready to rip flesh from bone. "Now."

"Yeah." Mack nods. "But there's a problem. There's at least three guys outside. Maybe more. Van brought hired guns from Jon's gang. They're watching every exit."

Arrow's fingers are twitching like he's restraining the urge to punch through the wall. "So we go through them."

"Damn right." Mack's mouth curves into something that's not a smile. "But, Holt, you need to get out first. Get to the wedding. Stop it. We'll handle whoever is out there and be right behind you."

Arrow's eyes land on a metal pipe leaning against a shelf. He grabs it, tests the weight, spins it like muscle memory. That casual violence settles into his stance like a second skin. "We burst out. Holt goes for the bike. We'll cover the way."

"Fuck yeah," Luke adds.

Mack pulls a set of keys from his jeans and slaps them into my palm. "Black Harley. Two blocks west. Helmet's on the seat. Go full throttle and don't fucking look back."

I stare down at the keys. The weight of them is nothing. The weight of what they mean is everything.

Luke cracks his knuckles, slow and deliberate. The

sound echoes. "Time to remind these bastards why no one fucks with us."

"Ex-Savage," Arrow says, lips twitching with a fury-laced smirk.

"Still got the skills," Luke growls. "Still got the rage. Still got the *reason*."

I glance at the three of them. My brothers. Not by blood. By bond. By fire. Mack, who barely knows Cindy but still ran into the fire to warn us. Luke and Arrow, bleeding loyalty, burning alive with fury.

The same fury that's roaring through my chest.

"All right." I step toward the door. "On three?"

"Fuck three," Mack growls.

He throws his whole body into the door, slamming it open with a deafening crash. It smacks into someone outside, bone and wood colliding in a sick crunch. A shout cuts through the air.

And then—

We're moving.

Exploding out of the warehouse like a goddamn wildfire.

I don't wait to see the damage. Don't look back.

Cindy is waiting.

And I'll tear the fucking world apart before I let that bastard put a ring on her finger.

The warehouse opens onto a loading dock.

Three guys there, big, broad-shouldered, dressed in black with leather vests and the skull emblem from the Savage Sons. One of them is already on the ground from Mack's door slam, blood leaking between his fingers as he clutches his face and groans.

The other two don't hesitate. They're already moving, hands diving for weapons.

"Got company!" one of them barks, voice sharp with adrenaline.

Mack is on the closest one before he can even clear his waistband. They slam into each other, crashing down hard onto the concrete in a flurry of fists and fury.

Arrow doesn't hesitate. He swings the pipe like a bat. Bone cracks as metal meets ribs. The third guy crumples forward with a scream, clutching his side.

Luke is right there to meet him. Grabs the guy by the shirt collar, yanks him up, and drives a fist into his jaw. Once. Twice. The sick thud of impact echoes across the dock. The guy slumps, out cold.

Then footsteps.

Running.

Three more shadows burst around the corner of the warehouse. Reinforcements. Big ones.

"Fuck," Arrow mutters, already turning to face them. He plants his feet wide, pipe raised like it's just an extension of his arm. "Holt, go!" he yells, voice sharp. "Get the fuck out of here!"

Cindy needs me more.

One of the new guys lunges, trying to intercept. I sidestep, grab his arm, and use his own momentum to spin him into the wall. His skull bounces off the brick with a sickening crack. He drops like a sack of meat.

I shove past another man reaching for me. He stumbles, off-balance, and I'm through, sprinting away.

Behind me, the fight erupts in full. Grunts. Roars. The thud of bodies hitting concrete. It's a goddamn war zone back there.

And I leave them.

Because they can handle themselves.

But Cindy can't.

I hit the alley, lungs burning, muscles screaming.

Then I see it.

Mack's bike. Black Harley. Parked right where he said it'd be.

I leap on, slide the key into the ignition, twist—

The engine roars to life like it's been waiting for me.

Hold on, baby. I'm coming.

The tires screech as I tear out of the alley, engine howling. I weave through traffic like a man possessed. Cars honk. People shout. I don't register any of it.

My world is narrowed to the road ahead. To the woman I love and the bastards trying to take her from me.

I push the throttle harder. Speed climbs. The city blurs into a smear of lights and metal.

Industrial gives way to residential. Then trees. Winding hills.

Our land. Our house.

Almost there.

I rocket up the gravel driveway, barely missing a

row of parked cars. All sleek, shiny, too expensive to belong to anyone I know. My blood goes ice-cold when I see the black Mercedes at the top.

Must be Victoria's.

Then I'm moving.

Off the bike. Up the porch.

Running for the house.

"Cindy!" Her name tears out of me.

No answer.

I charge through the front door. Empty. Kitchen. Empty. Living room. Empty.

Then I hear it. Voices. Coming from the backyard. From the lake.

I sprint to the back door and see all of them. A crowd of people by the water, arranged in rows of chairs. And at the front, standing slightly curled forward, is my Omega. And the sight of her hand in Van's makes me want to burn the whole fucking world down.

Something breaks inside me.

I detour to my room. My safe. The combination spins under my fingers, muscle memory, and the door opens. My gun is there, loaded and ready. I grab it.

I'm not past using it. Not anymore. Not when it comes to her.

I charge back outside, handgun raised, and I don't hesitate. I point it at the sky and pull the trigger.

The shot cracks through the air like thunder.

Several people scream. All heads turn toward me.

Van is still holding Cindy's hand, gripping it

tightly. She turns, and I see her face. Tears streaming down her cheeks, eyes huge and terrified and so fucking relieved to see me.

"Holt!" Her voice breaks on my name.

My heart shatters and rebuilds itself in the space of a second.

"You fucking pieces of shit," I snarl, stalking forward. The weight of the gun feels good in my hand, solid, steady, an extension of my rage. I level it straight at Van's chest. "You think you can kidnap us and steal our Omega? You think you walk away breathing after that?"

Van's face drains of color. The swagger is gone; now he's just another coward with his hands on something that isn't his. He jerks Cindy in front of him like a human shield, fingers digging into her arms.

That's his first mistake.

"Cindy, baby," I say, voice low but sharp enough to cut steel. I shift my stance, feet planted, scanning the edges of the room, every shadow, every twitch of movement. "Come to me. Now."

Van tightens his grip, yanking her closer until she gasps. That sound—*her* sound—snaps something deep in my chest.

Second mistake.

Cindy's eyes flash, and before Van even realizes what's happening, she drives her heel down hard on his foot. He yelps, tries to pull her back, but she's already spinning to face him. Her knee rockets up between his legs, connects with a crack that makes *me* wince.

Van drops like a sack of bricks, clutching himself, wheezing out a pathetic, high-pitched noise.

Cindy runs.

And Victoria steps into her path.

She spreads her arms like she's saving the damn day, face twisted in that fake concern she wears like perfume.

"Sit your ass down, Victoria," I growl, voice dropping into that deep, dangerous register that used to make entire rooms go still. "You vile, manipulative witch. You lost every scrap of decency when you pulled this fucking circus."

Her face blanches. She actually *flinches*. Then she moves aside, skirts rustling.

Cindy slams into my chest, shaking. I holster the gun long enough to drag her against me, one arm banded tight around her back, the other snapping the weapon up again toward the crowd. My pulse is a war drum in my ears.

She's trembling. But she's here. She's alive. And that's all that matters.

"Everyone," I bark, my voice booming across the space. "Get over here on the lawn and on your knees. Now."

Nobody moves. Just wide eyes, frozen faces, the kind of silence that comes when people realize they're standing on a minefield.

So I fire another shot into the air.

The sound explodes like thunder. The smell of gunpowder bites the air.

"I said *now!*"

The spell breaks. Shoes scuff the grass. Chairs topple. People rush over and drop to their knees.

Except Victoria. She's trembling, but she still tries to speak, clutching her pearls like that'll save her.

"Victoria," her husband hisses from his knees. "For God's sake, get down. Do what he says."

"The police will be here soon," she snaps, her voice wobbling, ignoring her husband. "You think you can threaten us with—"

"Good," I cut her off, voice lethally calm. "And when they get here, I'll explain exactly how you kidnapped three men, forced an Omega into a marriage contract against her will, and let Van over there hire a fucking biker gang to do his dirty work."

I lower the gun just enough to point it at Van, still whimpering in the grass, sweat slicking his pale face. "Pretty sure that puts you on the wrong side of the law, *sweetheart.*"

A few people glance toward their phones. I raise the gun again, and every single one of them freezes, hands in plain sight.

"That's better," I murmur. "You're all going to stay right there on your knees. You're going to think real hard about what happens to people who touch what's mine."

The words are quiet, but they hit like an explosive. The crowd collectively holds its breath.

Part of me wants to end it here. Pull the trigger. Let them see what happens when you back an Alpha into a corner and threaten his mate.

But Cindy's hand is gripping my jacket, grounding me. Her warmth. Her scent. The tremor in her fingers.

I glance down. Her eyes are wide, wet with tears and adrenaline, but steady.

"Did they hurt you?" I ask, voice soft now.

She shakes her head, a choked sob caught between her teeth.

And in that moment, as she presses closer and my finger eases off the trigger, I know exactly how close I came to becoming the monster they think I am.

But if it means keeping her safe—

I'd become worse.

"I'm fine." Her voice is muffled against my chest, shaky and small but alive. "And fuck, I was just about to say 'I do.' Thank you so much for coming for me."

She squeezes tighter, fingers fisting in my jacket like she's afraid to let go. Something in my chest cracks wide open. She would've done it, stood up there alone, sacrificed herself just to save us. That thought cuts deeper than any blade.

Never again.

My gaze sweeps the lawn at the dozens of useless bastards still kneeling, faces pale, trembling, pretending they weren't a part of this circus. My pulse pounds, and my mind goes dark, sketching out every way I could make them *pay*. I can see it, each lesson, each scream, each reminder of what happens when you touch what's mine.

"You can't kill anyone," Cindy whispers against me, voice steady but pleading. "Please. I don't want that because of me."

I blink down at her. For a second, I almost laugh. "I hadn't planned on that."

Her eyes find mine, wide, trusting, so goddamn certain I'm going to be the good guy in this story. She has no idea how thin that line is.

"What about torture?" I ask.

She grimaces. Then her lips curve. "Maybe."

Fuck, I love her.

A flicker of movement cuts through my haze. Van is getting up, still bent over like a wounded animal but moving. And then, of course, some asshole in the crowd lifts their phone, camera aimed squarely at me.

"Kill me and everyone will see it," Van wheezes, stumbling forward, one hand clutching his groin, the other pointing like I'm on trial. "You'll rot in prison, you piece of biker trash! Cindy is mine. She's *always* been mine. Our families had an agreement. She's promised to me! You're just embarrassing yourself by taking what doesn't belong to you!"

He's still shouting when he reaches me.

I holster the gun. Don't need it for this.

The second he opens his mouth again, I swing.

My fist slams into his face with a crack that echoes off the house. Bone shatters. Van drops like a puppet with its strings cut, clutching his face and howling, blood pouring through his fingers, dripping down his tailored suit.

"You broke it!" he shrieks, his voice climbing into a pathetic whine. "You fucking broke my nose!"

I crouch beside him. My hand closes around his throat, not hard enough to crush, just enough to remind him how close he is to losing everything.

"You were saying something about *my Omega?*" My voice is a low rumble, calm and cold.

Van gurgles, eyes watering, face turning red as my fingers tighten a fraction more. He tries to shake his head, to talk, though nothing comes out but a wheeze.

"That's what I thought." I shove him back into the dirt, let him suck in a ragged breath that sounds like it hurts. Then I'm on my feet and stride over to Cindy, dragging her into my arms.

Gravel crunches behind me. Heavy boots.

I glance back, still keeping one arm around Cindy, and the sight that greets me nearly leaves me smiling.

Arrow, Luke, and Mack are storming across the lawn. Behind them, broad shoulders, black leather, grim faces, come some of the Savage Sons. The new cut of the old club. The ones who rose from the ashes after we burned it down.

And at the front of the pack is Jon.

He hasn't changed much, just hardened around the edges. Long, dark hair pulled back, beard thick and streaked with gray, eyes like sharpened glass. The kind of man who doesn't need to shout to make people listen. His presence rolls across the yard like thunder, steady, heavy, impossible to ignore.

He stops a few feet away, arms crossed over his chest, the Sons fanning out behind him in a half circle.

"Holt." His voice is gravelly, deep, calm, the kind that carries authority without effort. "Heard you had some trouble."

I can't help the grin that cracks my face. "You could say that."

Jon glances at Van, still bleeding and whimpering in the grass, then at Victoria, frozen near the group, not kneeling. His jaw flexes once.

"Some of my boys went rogue," he admits. There's steel under the calm, a weight that makes the words feel final. "Helped this asshole set you up. That's on me." He steps closer. "I'm here to make it right. Whatever you need."

Cindy slips out from under my arm before I can stop her, bolting straight toward Arrow and Luke. They catch her together, Luke's arms first, Arrow's next, pulling her in tight. Relief breaks across their faces like dawn after a storm.

I nod once at Jon, every muscle in me finally starting to unclench. "Appreciate that."

He nods back, slowly. "Wouldn't expect less from one of mine." His gaze sweeps the scene, the broken groom, the cowering guests, the kneeling chaos. "You handled this clean, considering."

I glance down at Van. Blood everywhere. My knuckles split. Cindy safe.

"Clean enough," I mutter.

Jon's mouth twitches into something that might be a smile, or maybe it's just approval. Hard to tell with him.

Either way, the storm has passed. But if any of these bastards move again, I'll make sure it's the last mistake they ever make.

"You cannot keep us prisoner," Victoria's voice cuts through. "We've done nothing wrong, and you're going to be very sorry when—"

"When what?" I turn to face her slowly. "When your lawyers show up? That shit doesn't work on me, Victoria. Not anymore."

Cindy's father gets to his feet. Tall. Barrel shaped. The kind of man who's built a life on making people flinch when he enters a room.

"How much can we pay you for her?" he says, like we're negotiating over a damn car. "Name your price."

Silence crashes over the crowd like a bomb.

I blink at him. "Are you fucking shitting me?"

"Everything has a price," he replies, calm as anything. Like he didn't just try to buy back the daughter he threw away.

My jaw clenches. "Get back on your knees."

He hesitates, only for a second, but then kneels.

"Here's what's going to happen," I say, voice razor-sharp. "You're all leaving town. Right now. Not stopping to get your stuff, not making calls, nothing. You get in your cars and you go. You come back, and between me and Jon's team, you'll never leave this town. You understand?"

I glance at Cindy, wrapped in Arrow's and Luke's arms, protected between them like the damn treasure she is.

"Cindy is no longer part of your family," I say, loud enough for every single one of them to hear. "She's mine. She's Arrow's. She's Luke's. Our mate. And if you dare to so much as speak with her again, if you threaten her, if you even *think* about coming back, you'll have me on your doorstep."

I turn to Jon. "Can your boys escort some of these people personally? Make sure they actually leave?"

"Absolutely." Jon is already scanning the crowd. "Which ones?"

I lift a hand and point. "Victoria. Her husband. And Van."

"On it." Jon gestures to his men. "And if they give us any trouble?"

"Do your thing," I say.

Three bikers move forward. Big men, covered in ink and muscle, with the kind of cold, dead eyes that make smart people nervous.

Victoria starts protesting the second one of them grabs her arm, not gently. "How dare you handle me like that! Do you know who I am?"

The biker doesn't even blink. He just drags her toward the driveway.

She throws one last look over her shoulder at

Cindy. "Is this how you enjoy seeing your mother treated?"

Cindy doesn't flinch. Doesn't cry. Doesn't beg.

"After how you treated me, you're lucky this is all you get."

Victoria's face drains of color.

Another biker has Van by the hair, dragging him to his feet. He's a bloody mess, whining about his nose, nothing left of the arrogant Alpha who strutted closer earlier. His suit is torn, mouth slack with pain. He looks pathetic. And it's exactly what he deserves.

Cindy's father stumbles beside them, red-faced and humiliated, head ducked as a third biker marches him toward the driveaway. The man won't even look at his daughter. Good. He shouldn't.

Guests scatter in every direction. Running for their cars, dresses tangled, heels kicked off, fear stamped across their faces. They just witnessed something real, and they're desperate to pretend it didn't happen. Cowards.

Mack stands at the edge of the chaos, arms folded, chin raised as he watches them go. "I'll make sure they all actually leave town," he says. His eyes cut to us. "Make sure no one gets any ideas about coming back."

"Thanks, brother," Arrow says, voice low and grateful.

And then it's quiet.

Just us.

Me. Arrow. Luke. Cindy. And the ghost of everything that just happened still clinging to the breeze.

She's between us now, trembling. I wipe her tears with the rough pad of my thumbs, gentle as I can be. Her eyes are swollen, red. But her scent, God, her scent is love.

"No more crying," I whisper. "You're home now. You're ours. And your family will never touch you again. We'll make sure of that."

She nods, swallowing thickly. "I still can't believe what she planned..." Her voice trembles. "My own mother." She shakes her head. "But having them gone is enough. I don't want revenge. I just want... peace."

I draw her against me, bury my face in her hair. Then I press a kiss to her forehead. Her nose. Her lips. I take my time. Because this is what matters.

Arrow steps in, fingers trailing down her spine. Luke brushes his knuckles over her cheek. We surround her again. We breathe her in. And for the first time all day, she lets out a real laugh. Broken, soft, but real.

"This day turned out so much worse than I imagined," she says, giggling through the tears.

"But it ends better," Arrow murmurs. "Because we're still here. And we'd do anything for you. You know that, right?"

She looks between us. "I do."

Luke glances at me and then at Arrow. "So... what now?"

We don't speak.

We don't have to.

My eyes meet Arrow's first. Then Luke's.

No words. Just a look. A silent command wrapped in something raw and certain.

It's time.

They know it.

Arrow gives a faint, almost imperceptible nod. Luke exhales slowly, like he's been holding it in since the moment everything went to hell.

I glance at Cindy—fuck, she's everything—and then back at them. Just to make sure they feel it too.

They smile.

And then, in sync, all three of us drop to our knees in the grass in front of her.

She freezes. Eyes wide, lips parted, skin still blotchy from crying, but goddamn beautiful.

More than I deserve. More than any of us do.

But I'll fight to keep her every damn day.

Cindy gasps, lips parting. "What... what are you doing?"

I reach for her hand. My heart is pounding, but my voice is steady.

"Cindy," I say, rough and low. "Will you marry us? All three of us. I love you so damn much."

Her eyes go glassy again, but this time, not with grief.

With joy.

Hope.

Love.

Arrow shifts forward on his knee, grinning like a damn idiot, eyes wet. "I love you, sunshine. You're everything I didn't know I needed."

Luke brushes his thumb along the back of her other hand, his voice deep and steady. "I love you, Omega. You're my heart."

She lets out a shaky laugh that breaks into a sob, covering her mouth like she can't believe any of this is real.

"Oh my God. I love you all so much." Her lips tremble. "Are you... are you serious?"

I squeeze her hand, leaning in closer.

"As a fucking heart attack," I respond.

"Dead serious," Arrow says, taking her other hand.

Luke grins, wide. "We don't have rings. Not yet. But we're getting them. This? This is just the start."

"You're making us sweat here, baby, waiting for an answer," I add, nudging her with a crooked smile.

She laughs through the tears. Nods her head. "Yes. Yes. Of course yes. A million times yes."

And then she's on us, arms flung around our necks, clinging like she'll never let go, and we don't plan to let her.

The Halloween decorations flutter in the wind behind her. And for the first time in my life, something clicks into place.

This is it.

She's it.

And with her in our arms, nothing else matters.

30

CINDY

Later In The Evening

I'm standing in my bedroom, in my underwear, staring at Harper like she's lost her mind.

"You just happened to have a wedding dress at your apartment?" I ask.

Harper is grinning, holding up the most gorgeous white dress I've ever seen. "Okay, so technically, it was for a themed party I never went to. But look at it! It's perfect!"

She's not wrong. The dress is stunning. Off-the-shoulder with delicate lace sleeves. The bodice is fitted, with intricate beading that catches the light. The skirt flows down in soft layers of tulle and silk, not too poofy, not too plain. Just right. And there's a slit up one side that's definitely more sexy than traditional.

"Come on, try it on," Harper demands, already moving toward me with it.

I slip into the dress, and Harper zips me up. When I turn to look in the mirror, I barely recognize myself.

"Holy shit," I breathe.

"Right?" Harper is beaming as she hands me a bobby pin she probably stole from someone's gym bag. "I can't believe you're getting married, Cindy. Like, actually getting married. Today. Right now."

"Me either." I stare at my reflection, touching the fabric of the dress like it might vanish under my fingers. "This feels like the weirdest day in the world."

"And the best ever too," Harper adds quickly.

I laugh, but it comes out with this high-pitched edge that sounds suspiciously like panic. "Yeah. That too. Weirdest and best. Like a fever dream but with appetizers."

She keeps working on my hair, pulling it into something vaguely elegant, and maybe a little sexy too. Her purple-tipped black hair falls in her face, and she blows it away in annoyed little huffs that keep making me giggle.

"They didn't even hesitate," I say, voice soft. "I said, 'Let's get married today,' and all three of them just said yes. Immediately. Like I asked if they wanted takeout, not a legally binding scent-bonding ceremony."

"That's because they're obsessed with you." Harper's nose wrinkles as she concentrates on pinning another section. "It's honestly rude. I used to think love was dramatic. Now I think it's clingy. Disgusting. I want some."

I smile into the mirror, heart doing that fluttery

thing again. "Speaking of obsessed." I catch her eye. "You and Mack seemed pretty cozy recently."

Harper pauses, blush blooming across her cheeks like she's been caught stealing cookies and kissing boys. "Shut up."

I tilt my head just enough to be annoying. "He saved them, Harper. Went to the warehouse. Fought off Van's guys. Helped get them all out. That's, like, Alpha-hero level five."

"He really proved himself," she admits, quiet now. "I knew he was Arrow's brother, but today? Seeing him show up like that? Fuck, Cindy. I think I'm in trouble."

I raise an eyebrow. "Good trouble?"

"The best kind." She grins, then smacks my shoulder lightly. "Now hold still. I'm going to do your makeup, and if you keep making me laugh, I'm going to stab your eyeball with this mascara wand."

I snort but freeze obediently. "Eyeballs are sacred on your wedding day. Got it."

She starts brushing on foundation, then concealer, then something glittery that feels like I've been kissed by a fairy. Her fingers are fast and gentle, and despite the war zone in my chest, I start to relax. A little.

Maybe.

"Okay, so." Harper's voice has that tone that means she's about to take charge of my soul. "Do you have something old?"

"What?"

"You know." She waves the mascara wand like a conductor. "Something old, something new, something borrowed, something blue. It's a thing. You can't tempt fate without armor."

"I have no idea." I glance down at the dress. "This is borrowed?"

"Check." She nods. "New?"

"The rings?" I gesture vaguely toward the door. "The guys rushed out to get them earlier. Unless they got distracted and came back with donuts and a new puppy."

"Also valid. But yes. Check." She leans in with a tiny brush. "Old?"

I blink. "Uh... my trauma?"

Harper cackles, nearly poking me in the eye anyway. "Cindy."

"I don't know! I wasn't planning to wake up and get married today. But now I'm here. In a white dress."

She grabs my hand, squeezing. "You're doing amazing. Seriously. I've never seen you look so happy."

"I feel like I'm about to barf glitter," I whisper.

"That's the dream, baby." She grins. "Now hurry up and pick something old before I give you my old hoodie as a joke."

I gasp. "I swear to God, Harper." And I break out laughing.

"Then find something else! Come on. There's gotta be something around here." Harper is digging through my bag like a woman possessed.

I blink, then point to the nightstand. "That bracelet. The cheap one. In the bowl."

She grabs it and lets out a soft laugh. "This? The one Holt won you at the ring toss booth?"

"Yeah."

"The plastic white one with a crooked heart charm?"

"It was a terrible game, but they wouldn't stop until I picked a prize."

Harper slides it onto my wrist, her voice soft now. "Then it's perfect for 'old.'"

I smile, chest tight. "They were so smug about it. Like I'd just been crowned festival queen."

"You kind of were," she murmurs, adjusting it so the charm sits right.

I laugh through the sudden pressure in my chest. "Good enough."

Outside, the sound of tires on gravel.

"They're home," I whisper.

Harper pulls back, grinning.

"Almost time to go marry the hell out of your feral Alpha boyfriends."

Harper sets down the mascara. "Now blue."

"I don't have any blue jewelry."

Harper is already digging through my drawers. She pulls out a pair of lacy blue thongs, the kind that's more decoration than function. "Here."

"Are you serious?"

"Dead serious. Go put them on."

I take the underwear into the bathroom and change, laughing the whole time. When I come out, Harper is waiting with her hands on her hips.

"Well?"

"I'm wearing blue lace underwear to my wedding," I announce.

"Damn right you are." She high-fives me. "Your Alphas are gonna lose their minds later."

"Harper!"

"What? I'm just saying." She's grinning wickedly. "Three Alphas, one Omega, fancy underwear. That's a recipe for a very fun wedding night."

I'm blushing so hard my face feels like it's on fire. "You're terrible."

"You love me."

"I really do."

There's a knock on the door.

Mack's voice comes through, muffled but unmistakably amused. "You decent?"

"Come in!" Harper says.

The door creaks open, and Mack steps in. He's cleaned up from the earlier chaos, no blood, no bruises, and somehow looking halfway presentable in dark jeans and a button-down shirt. The sleeves are rolled to his forearms, like even he knew full sleeves would be pushing it.

He stops dead when he sees me. "Wow."

I blink. "Good wow?"

His grin is slow and sure. "Really good wow. Like, 'holy shit, you're about to ruin every man's standards for the rest of his life' kind of wow."

I flush all the way to my ears. "That's... a lot of wow."

Harper winks at him. "Try not to cry, Mack. You'll ruin your street cred."

He rolls his eyes. "I'm not crying. You're crying. And also, are we seriously going to ignore the fact that you look like a literal goddess to me?"

"Flattery will get you everywhere," Harper mutters, swooning on the spot.

I'm smiling now, my nerves momentarily forgotten.

"You ready?" he asks, softer this time. "Everyone is waiting."

My stomach does a full somersault. "I think so."

He nods toward the backyard. "The entire town might have turned up after we called everyone. It's standing room only out there."

Harper snorts.

"I can't believe this is happening," I whisper for maybe the hundredth time.

Harper grabs my hand and squeezes. "Believe it. You're about to marry three gorgeous, possessive men who adore you. This is real."

"Come on, future Mrs. Chaos. Let's go cause a scene."

We step outside, and I nearly stop breathing.

The backyard has been transformed. The chairs that were set up by the lake have been moved closer to the house, arranged in neat rows facing the mountains. White flower petals scatter across the aisle between the chairs. Flaming torches line the path. And, oh God, the sky is perfect. Orange and pink streaked across the horizon, the sun setting behind the mountains. The trees around us are copper and gold in the fading light, and the whole scene resembles a postcard.

And the chairs are full. Every single one. Plus people standing around the edges, all of them turning to look at me, just as Mack said.

I recognize so many faces. People from work. Ruby and Lily, owners of the brewery and the bakery in town. Staff from the festival, where we had our first real date. Friends I've made since moving to Whispering Grove, people who smiled at me when I was new and scared and didn't know where I belonged.

They're all here. For me.

My emotions are overwhelming. Excitement and joy and disbelief all tangled together.

Harper squeezes my hand again. "You ready?"

"I think so."

Mack offers me his arm, and Harper carefully hands me over to him. She leans in close, her voice soft in my ear. "You deserve this. All of it. Don't you dare doubt yourself. Go get your happy ending."

Tears prick at my eyes. "Thank you."

Harper disappears to the side, and Mack starts walking me down the aisle.

The white petals are soft under my shoes. Someone is playing music, something instrumental and beautiful. People are smiling at me, some of them wiping their damp cheeks.

But I only have eyes for the three men waiting at the end.

Luke is on the left, and he's wearing a suit. Dark gray, fitted perfectly, with a black shirt underneath and no tie, because of course no tie. His hair is slicked back, and he's grinning at me like I'm the best thing he's ever seen.

Arrow is in the middle, also in a suit. Charcoal gray with a burgundy shirt that brings out his dark eyes. His hair is styled. He looks like he could be on the cover of a magazine, except for the way he's staring at me with so much emotion I can barely breathe.

Holt is on the right. Black suit, white shirt, actually wearing a tie. His hair is pushed back, his expression serious, but his eyes—God, his eyes are so full of love it causes an ache in my chest.

They're all staring at me like I hung the moon.

The officiant is there too, the same older woman from earlier. We called her back, and when we asked if she'd marry us for real, she agreed immediately, even if she was confused and probably traumatized.

Mack walks me all the way to my men. He leans down, his voice low enough that only I can hear. "Welcome to the family, Cindy. Officially." Then louder, for everyone: "Take care of her, or I'll kick all your asses."

"Noted," Luke says.

Mack steps back, and suddenly I'm standing in front of them.

My three men.

My Alphas.

My mates.

Luke reaches for my hand first. His fingers are

warm, steady, grounding me like always. His eyes roam over me slowly, like he's seeing me for the first time and memorizing every inch.

"You look fucking incredible."

"Language," the officiant chides gently.

Luke shrugs, grinning without apology. "She looks really fucking incredible."

I laugh, and just like that, the nerves unravel a little. Luke has always been able to do that—cut through the noise and center me.

Arrow takes my other hand, his thumb brushing across my knuckles with a kind of awe that leaves me catching my breath. His gaze is soft and shining, and I can tell he's struggling to find words.

"You're beautiful," he says finally. "So beautiful I can't think straight."

Luke smirks. "That's just your default state."

"Shut up," Arrow mutters, but he's smiling too.

Then Holt steps in behind me. He doesn't say anything at first. He just presses a hand to the small of my waist, firm and possessive, and kisses the top of my head.

"You ready?" he asks quietly.

Releasing my men's hands, I turn to look at all of them, Luke's steady love, Arrow's open heart, Holt's fierce protectiveness, and I don't hesitate.

I take Luke's and Arrow's hands in mine again. "Yeah," I whisper. "I'm ready."

The officiant clears her throat as she begins. "We

are gathered here today to witness the joining of these souls."

She pauses, glancing at me, and her smile grows warmer. "Today, we celebrate a bond forged not just in biology or fate, but in choice. In trust. In devotion freely given."

My hands tremble in Luke's and Arrow's grasps. Holt hasn't let go of my waist. I'm aware of every breath they take, every bit of heat rolling off them and grounding me.

The officiant turns her attention to me. "Cindy," she says, and my name sounds different here, formal and full of meaning. "You stand before three Alphas who have chosen you. Who have marked you. Who wish to bind themselves to you in every way that matters."

She pauses again, waiting. But I can't take my eyes off the three of them.

My chest tightens.

"Do you accept them?" The officiant's voice softens.

"I do," I say, my voice catching just slightly. I swallow and lift my chin. "I accept all three of them. Always."

A soft murmur of emotion stirs through me.

Then she turns to the guys. "Luke, Arrow, Holt," she says, and they straighten as one. "You stand before an Omega who has already given herself to you through the bond. Do you now pledge yourselves to her in the eyes of this community? To honor her, protect her, and cherish her for as long as you all shall live?"

"We do."

My knees wobble. Holt's arm braces me without needing to be asked.

The officiant exhales gently. "The rings?"

Luke pulls the small box from his jacket and opens it, revealing the four rings they chose.

Three dark metal bands for them, simple, rugged, but etched with a tiny pattern only someone paying attention would notice. A braided design, like rope. Like strength woven from many threads.

And mine.

A single band made from three metals—gold, silver, and rose gold—twisted into an unbreakable knot.

Holy shit.

My breath hitches, but this time from awe.

Arrow catches my look and whispers, "Like it?"

"I love it," I whisper back, eyes stinging.

The officiant nods toward us, giving us space to continue.

I take the first ring with unsteady fingers and turn to Holt. His hand is already waiting, palm down, like he's been ready for this since the day he met me.

"You were the first one who made me feel safe," I say, voice thick. "The first one who made me believe I was worth loving."

He presses his forehead to mine, just briefly. "Love you too, beautiful."

I turn to Arrow, placing the next band onto his finger. "You made me laugh again. Trust again. Breathe again."

His jaw clenches. "You saved me too," he murmurs.

Then I turn to Luke. His hand dwarfs mine as I slide the ring on, and I blink fast to keep the tears from falling.

"You gave me a home when I didn't believe I deserved one. You gave me yourself."

His voice is rough and low. "And I'll give you everything else too."

They gather close then, all three of them, and together, hands overlapping, they guide the intertwined ring onto my finger.

Our bond. Our love. All of it, sealed here.

And I'm shaking, but I've never felt steadier.

It's not just a ring.

It's a promise.

A vow.

A forever.

And I've never felt more loved. More seen. More *home.*

I'm trying so hard not to cry, but the tears are coming anyway. Happy tears that I can't stop even if I wanted to.

"By the power vested in me," the officiant says, smiling, "I now pronounce you bonded mates. You may kiss your bride."

They don't need to be told twice.

Luke kisses me first, deep and claiming. Then

Arrow, soft and sweet. Then Holt, possessive and perfect.

Everyone erupts into applause. People are standing, cheering, and I can hear Harper whooping somewhere in the crowd.

"I love you three so much," I say, barely able to get the words out past the emotion.

"We love you too," Arrow adds. "More than anything."

"Always," Holt finishes.

My breath catches. I swear the world tilts a little. If they weren't already holding me, I'd probably melt straight through the ground.

"Okay, well." I take a shaky breath, trying to steady the flutter in my chest. "Now it's time for me to show you how we dance. Because I've kept this from you, but... I'm dreadful at it."

Luke chuckles, brushing a thumb over my cheek. "Can't be worse than Arrow."

"Hey!" Arrow protests.

"It's true," Luke fires back, and Holt snorts beside them.

We start down the aisle together, hearts pounding in sync. Someone cheers, and laughter ripples through the crowd. I catch sight of twinkling string lights strung between the trees. When did those go up? They spill golden light over everything, warm and dreamlike. The sun has dipped low, painting the lake in molten orange, and for a second, I can't tell if this is real or some fever dream spun out of happiness.

The photographer, a woman I don't even recognize, is snapping away, camera clicking.

We reach the pergola, where tables are set with flickering candles and food is laid out perfectly. Someone has rigged up a bar, and the faint scent of bonfire smoke drifts through the air.

"Join us!" I call, throwing my arms wide to our guests. "Let's make this a night we'll never forget!"

Cheers answer back, and music swells. Harper appears from nowhere, throws her arms around me, and spins me once before hugging me tight.

"You did it," she says against my shoulder, her voice half laugh, half sob. "You actually did it."

"I did," I whisper, breathless with disbelief. "I'm married."

"It's perfect," she says, grinning.

Luke doesn't even give me time to recover before he grabs my hand and twirls me onto the dance floor, the other two following.

"This is the best day of my life," I say.

They glance over at me. "Mine too," they answer in unison.

For one perfect moment, surrounded by golden light, music, and the men I love, I realize something I never thought I'd believe again—

I'm not just loved.

I've finally found my true home.

EPILOGUE
CINDY

The boat lurches to the left, and I grab the railing with both hands, laughing so hard I can barely breathe.

"Luke!" I shout over the motor and the wind. "You're gonna kill us!"

"I got it!" he yells back, overcorrecting that we swing right.

Arrow's beer sloshes over the side of his cup. "You clearly don't got it!"

Holt is gripping the bench. "And we've almost hit three other boats."

"They were in my way," Luke argues, spinning the wheel again.

We zigzag across the water like drunk dolphins, leaving a wake that probably violates several maritime laws. Other boats are giving us a wide berth, and I swear I see someone on a yacht shaking their head at us.

"We are one hundred percent getting banned from this marina," I manage between laughs.

"Worth it!" Arrow raises his beer in a toast, then nearly drops it when Luke takes another sharp turn.

I'm sitting on the waters of Waikiki in O'ahu, Hawaii, life jacket strapped on tight, sundress billowing around my thighs. The sun is blazing overhead, hot and bright, and the ocean stretches out in every direction. Deep blue fading to turquoise near the shore, so clear I can see straight to the bottom in the shallow parts.

We left the hotel three hours ago. Luke insisted he knew what he was doing. Seeing as it's the first day of our honeymoon, the rental guy had looked increasingly concerned, yet all of us were piling into this tiny boat with a cooler full of drinks and zero actual plans.

It's been the best three hours of my life.

"Okay, new rule," Holt says, standing carefully. "I'm driving."

"I'm fine!"

I'm still laughing, wiping tears from my eyes.

Holt physically moves Luke away from the wheel. There's some shoving, but eventually Luke gives up and flops down beside me on the bench.

"Mutiny," he mutters.

I lean into him, and his arm comes around me automatically. "I'd like to survive my honeymoon, thanks."

"Where's your sense of adventure?"

"I left it back on the dock where we almost hit that piling."

Arrow is laughing now too, standing at the front of the boat with his arms spread wide. The turquoise Hawaiian shirt he's wearing is flapping in the breeze, and his blond hair is wild. "This is amazing! And exactly what honeymoons should be!"

"Chaotic and near fatal?" Holt asks dryly, but he's smiling as he steers us into smoother waters.

"Exactly!"

The boat settles now that Holt is at the helm. We're still moving fast, but it's intentional. The motor hums steadily, and the water stretches out around us.

I tilt my head back, closing my eyes, letting the sun warm my face. The breeze smells like salt and sunshine. The sound of the waves, Luke's breathing beside me, Arrow's whooping from the front. It all blends together into something perfect.

"I can't believe we're actually here," I say.

Luke draws me closer. "Where else would we be?"

"I don't know. Home? At the mansion?"

I stare up at the blue sky. Not a single cloud. Just endless sunshine and warmth.

"Four weeks ago, I was standing in our backyard, in a borrowed dress, getting married," I say. "And now I'm in Hawaii. On a boat. With you three. It doesn't feel real."

"It's real." Luke presses a kiss to my temple. "You're stuck with us now."

"Good."

Arrow turns from the front, grinning. The water color shifts to that brilliant turquoise that's incredible. I spot fish darting below us, colorful flashes of yellow and blue.

"There!" Arrow shouts suddenly, pointing.

I follow his gaze and nearly scream.

Dolphins.

A whole pod of them, surfacing beside our boat. Sleek gray bodies arcing through the water, so close I could reach out and touch them if I leaned over the railing. They're swimming alongside us, keeping pace, and I can hear them making sounds. Clicks and whistles that carry over the motor noise.

"Oh my God," I whisper, frozen. "They're right there."

Luke grins beside me. "Told you boats were a good idea."

The dolphins stay with us for what feels like forever but is probably only a few minutes. They dive and surface, playing in our wake, and I'm completely transfixed. One of them does a full breach, launching itself out of the water, and I scream with joy.

"Did you see that?" I'm gripping Luke's arm so hard I'm probably leaving marks. "Did you see?"

"We all saw, gorgeous."

"I'm never leaving. I'm staying here with the dolphins forever."

"What about us?" Arrow calls.

"You can visit. On weekends."

The dolphins eventually dive deep and disappear,

but I'm still buzzing with adrenaline and joy. My face hurts from smiling.

Holt slows the boat, letting us drift.

"This is insane," I say for maybe the twentieth time today.

"You keep saying that," Holt observes.

"Because it keeps being true!"

Arrow moves to the back of the boat, opening the cooler and pulling out... wait.

"Is that a portable grill?" I ask.

"Yep." He's already setting it up on the flattest part of the boat, like this is completely normal.

"When did you pack a portable grill?"

"I rented it when we got the boat."

Luke is pulling things out of the cooler now. A big fish wrapped in paper with its tail sticking out, vegetables, aluminum foil. "Freshly caught."

Holt anchors us, doing something complicated with ropes and chains. The boat settles, rocking gently with the waves.

"We're cooking on the boat," I say slowly. "In the middle of the ocean." This whole day is absurd. We've been in Hawaii for less than twenty-four hours, and this is my life now.

Holt finishes with the anchor and moves to help Arrow with the grill. Luke is seasoning the fish.

I sit on my towel on the bench and just watch them.

Luke's Hawaiian shirt is bright red with huge yellow flowers, unbuttoned halfway down his chest because he claims it's too hot to button it properly. His sunglasses keep slipping down his nose. He's barefoot, swim trunks riding low on his hips, and he's gesturing wildly while arguing with Arrow about seasoning.

Arrow's turquoise shirt is still buttoned all the way up despite the heat. His blond hair is getting curly from the salt air and humidity. He has his serious cooking face on, the one he gets when he's focused on making something perfect. Spatula in one hand, the other hand shooing Luke away from the grill.

Holt's purple shirt with the neon parrots should look ridiculous, but somehow he makes it work. His aviators are still on, hair pushed back, and he's watching Arrow and Luke with that small smile he gets when he's amused but trying not to show it.

The grill gets lit without incident, which feels like a miracle. Soon the smell of cooking fish mixes with the salt air, and my stomach growls loudly enough that Luke hears it from across the boat.

"Hungry?" he calls.

"Starving."

Holt comes to sit beside me, his thigh pressing against mine.

I lean into him. "I keep waiting to wake up. For this to be a dream."

"It's not a dream."

"I know. But months ago, I was terrified. Running. And now I'm here. In Hawaii. With you three. Married. Happy." My voice catches slightly. "I never thought I'd get this."

His arm comes around me, pulling me closer. "You deserve this. All of it."

"We all do," Luke adds, apparently listening. "We all fought like hell to get here."

Arrow flips the fish with more force than necessary. The fish is done eventually, plated on paper plates that Arrow somehow also packed. We eat sitting on the benches, feet dangling over the side, the boat rocking gently beneath us.

It's the best meal I've ever had. The fish is perfectly cooked, flaky and seasoned just right. The vegetables are charred and delicious. Even the cheap beer from the cooler tastes like luxury out here with the sun warming my skin and the ocean stretching endlessly around us.

"Hey, Cindy," Luke says after we've all eaten our fill. "How about a dip before we head back?"

He's already standing, pulling off his Hawaiian shirt and tossing it on the bench. His swim trunks are black with tiny white skulls on them.

"The water is probably cold," I say.

"Only one way to find out."

Holt is already kicking off his shorts, revealing pineapple-covered swim trunks, and I'm giggling. Arrow sets down his plate and looks at me with a challenge in his eyes.

"You coming or not?"

I stand, suddenly decisive. The sundress comes off easily. Underneath, I'm wearing the magenta bikini I bought specifically for this trip, with little white ties on the sides and more coverage than Harper wanted me to get but less than I'm used to.

All three of them are staring.

"What?" I ask, suddenly self-conscious.

"Nothing," Luke manages. "Just... damn."

"Eyes up here, boys."

"Nope," Arrow says cheerfully. "Not happening."

Holt recovers first, shaking his head. "You're trying to kill us."

"I'm wearing a normal bathing suit!"

"There's nothing normal about that," Holt says.

Before I can respond, Arrow runs and cannonballs off the side of the boat. The splash is enormous, soaking the deck, and he surfaces, laughing and sputtering.

"It's perfect!" he shouts. "Get in here!"

Luke goes next, diving smoothly off the side. Holt follows with barely a splash.

They're all treading water, looking up at me expectantly.

I take a breath and jump.

The water is cool but not cold, perfect against my sun-warmed skin. I surface, gasping and laughing, and immediately they're all around me.

Luke's hands find my waist, pulling me close. "There she is."

Holt is behind me, steadying me in the current. Arrow is floating nearby, grinning like an idiot.

"This is insane," I say again.

"You love it," Luke counters.

"I really do."

We float there, the four of us, held by the ocean and each other. The boat bobs nearby, abandoned. The beach is close enough to see clearly, palm trees swaying in the breeze. The sun is starting to lower, still hours from sunset but casting golden light over everything.

I'm weightless here. Surrounded by water and warmth and the three men who somehow became my entire world.

"I love you," I say suddenly. To all of them. "I love you all so much."

"Love you too," they say, voices overlapping.

Luke kisses me, salt water on his lips and sunshine in his smile. Holt's hand finds mine underwater, squeezing gently. Arrow splashes us all, breaking the moment with laughter.

This is my future now.

Not running. Not hiding. Not terrified of what comes next.

Just here. Floating in the Pacific Ocean on my honeymoon with three Alphas who would follow me anywhere.

Who did follow me. Through everything. Through fear and danger and chaos and somehow came out the other side with me.

Into this.

Into floating and laughing and being completely, utterly, impossibly happy.

And I wouldn't trade a single second of it.

Because it led me here.

To them.

To this moment.

To everything I never knew I needed.

And I'm never letting it go.

Make sure to grab your BONUS Scene...

BONUS SCENE
CINDY

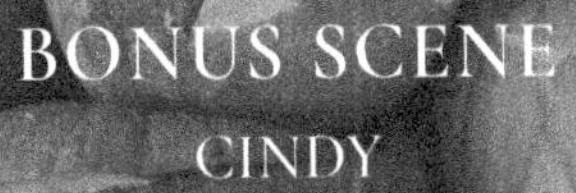

A Few Days Before Halloween

The dining table is a war zone.

Not of arguments or awkward dinners, but of pumpkin carnage. Layers of old newspaper blanket every inch of the wood like a crime scene cleanup, soaked with stringy orange pulp and rogue seeds that squish under our elbows. Four monstrous pumpkins sit like bloated sentinels in front of us, their tops decapitated, their guts spilling out. The whole room smells like autumn.

Classic rock is rolling from Luke's Bluetooth speaker, and the crackle of the fire in the living room adds a golden flicker to the walls.

I'm elbow-deep in cold, slimy pumpkin guts, fingers dripping as I yank out another hunk of stringy innards.

"This is *disgusting*," I declare, flicking a seed at Arrow. It bounces off his arm and sticks. Ha!

"And yet you volunteered," he says, unbothered, delicately extracting seeds like he's performing a transplant. "Try not to contaminate my work, please."

"You're *gutting a pumpkin*, not building a nuclear reactor."

He sniffs. "Precision is the difference between art and... whatever your triangle-eyed disaster is about to be."

"Rude," I mutter, trying to wipe my hand on a piece of newspaper, only to smear it further.

Luke grins from across the table, already deep into carving. He has that same laser focus he uses when he's fixing a busted carburetor, only now it's aimed at a poor, defenseless gourd. "You just gotta commit to the vision," he says, not looking up. "Pumpkins can smell fear."

"Or maybe you're just too competitive," I say.

He lifts a brow without pausing his carving. "Jealousy is not a good look on you, Miss Can't Carve A Straight Line."

"*Excuse* me—"

"Focus," Holt says, deadpan. He's already halfway through his own carving, of course. Probably freehanding something ridiculous like a perfectly proportioned skull. The man sharpens knives for fun; this is foreplay for him.

"You're awfully smug for someone who refused to

wear the matching 'Let's Get Smashed' pumpkin shirt," I shoot back at Holt.

His mouth twitches. Barely. But it's there. "It was orange."

"It's for Halloween."

"I don't wear orange."

"You wore it last week."

"That was rust."

Arrow groans like he's in pain. "I'm *begging* you two to focus. I can't be dethroned by Pumpkin Picasso."

I throw a pumpkin seed directly at his forehead.

Luke peers over, finally done. "You're making a basic jack-o'-lantern? Babe. That's like carving a smiley face into a loaf of bread."

"It's *classic*," I insist.

Holt sets down his knife with a quiet finality. "Done."

I glance up. "Already? What, did you carve the Mona Lisa?"

He doesn't answer. Just sits back with that secret smile that says we're *all* about to be humbled.

Luke finishes next, dropping his knife like he just completed a Michelin-star dish. "Behold," he says, gesturing dramatically. "A masterpiece in three dimensions."

Arrow is still bent over his pumpkin, surgical gloves on. His tongue pokes out slightly at the corner of his mouth, brow furrowed.

I lean toward him. "Need a magnifying glass, Doctor?"

He doesn't even blink. "Some of us believe in craftsmanship. You wouldn't understand."

"Oh, I *understand*. I just know I'm gonna win on charm points alone."

He smirks. "From your pumpkin? Or your little smirk?"

"Both," I say, sticking my tongue out at him.

The mansion feels different tonight. Not like the intimidating, echoey beast it was when I first arrived, but like *our* place. Warm light. Too much laughter. Seeds in our hair. Knife handles sticky with pumpkin. The smell of cinnamon tea, soot, and satisfaction.

It's a mess.

It's perfect.

And it feels like home.

I rush through the last few cuts on mine, trying to make the teeth even. They're not, but it's got character.

"Okay, I'm done too," I say, brushing pumpkin pulp off my hands onto my jeans.

Arrow makes one final cut, flicks a seed off his cheek, and leans back. "Finished."

Luke rubs his hands together. "All right. Show-and-tell time. Cindy, you're up first."

I turn my pumpkin around with a proud little flourish. The face is lopsided, one eye bigger than the other, and the grin is crooked like it's had a few too many drinks.

"It's cute," Arrow says, tipping his head.

"It's drunk," Luke corrects. "Your pumpkin is wasted."

"It's happy!" I protest.

"Drunkenly happy," Holt agrees.

I lob a sticky pumpkin seed at his chest. "Your turn, Grim Reaper."

Holt doesn't flinch. Just reaches down, rotates his pumpkin with both hands, and reveals his creation.

And I burst out laughing.

He's carved a detailed skull face into the pumpkin. Not a cartoon. Not silly. An actual, anatomically correct skull with hollow eye sockets and disturbingly realistic teeth.

"Okay, that's terrifying," I say, shivering dramatically.

"That's the point."

Arrow goes next, placing his pumpkin down. He's carved an intricate geometric pattern, interlocking triangles, sharp diamonds, and crisscrossed lines that shimmer where the light catches.

"Show-off," Luke mutters, squinting at it.

"It's beautiful," I say, genuinely impressed. "How did you even do that?"

"Very carefully." Arrow is grinning.

Luke is last. He grabs his pumpkin. We all lean in.

It takes me a second, and then—

"Oh my God."

He's carved a perfect, painfully detailed middle finger. Like, knuckle ridges and all. Anatomically accurate, just... flipped off.

"Seriously?" Holt says, one brow raised.

"What?" Luke looks way too proud. "It's art."

"It's juvenile," Holt mutters.

"It's perfect," I say through my laughter, wiping a tear from my cheek. "Mother's gonna see this and spontaneously combust."

"That's the plan," Luke adds.

We sit in the quiet presence of the jack-o'-lanterns, surrounded by bits of pumpkin rind, discarded tools, and seed slime.

"We should put these outside," Arrow says, stretching his arms above his head. "Line them up on the porch."

"Agreed," Holt states. "But first… we have a surprise."

I blink, looking at them. "What kind?"

All three of them are grinning now. That kind of grin that says I'm in trouble. The mischievous, we-planned-something kind of grin.

"Should I be worried?" I ask warily, narrowing my eyes.

They don't answer, just exchange glances like they're enjoying dragging this out way too much.

Luke stands first, dusting off his jeans. "Time to find out. Stay here. We'll be right back."

They all head upstairs, leaving me alone with the pumpkins.

"Is this something I should know about?" I call after them. "Should I be doing something? Hello?"

Laughter echoes from upstairs.

"Just wait!" Arrow shouts back.

I hear them talking up there, laughing hysterically, and I know that whatever this is, it's going to be insane.

Minutes pass. More laughing. Some thumping sounds. A crash followed by "I'm okay!"

"What are you doing up there?" I yell.

"You'll see!" Luke calls back.

Finally, I hear footsteps on the stairs. All three of them are coming down.

They appear before me wearing nothing but towels around their waists. Bare chests, bare feet.

"Okay, are we going swimming?" I ask, completely perplexed.

"Remember that conversation we had at breakfast the other day?" Luke's grin is wicked.

I think back and shake my head. "We talked about many things."

They all look at each other, some silent communication passing between them.

Then, in unison, they drop their towels.

I'm not sure what I was expecting, but it definitely wasn't this.

Arrow is wearing an elephant thong. Bright pink with a long trunk that dangles down, complete with little tusks on either side. The elephant's face is positioned right at his groin, and the trunk is moving as he shifts his weight.

Luke is wearing a python. Neon green and black stripes spiraling around, the snake's head positioned strategically with its tongue sticking out. The body wraps around, and the tail disappears around the back.

And Holt's is a rhino. Gray with a massive horn jutting out from the front, so realistic and absurd at the same time. The horn is positioned exactly where you'd expect, and there are little ears on either side.

"Oh my God!" The words burst out of me along with uncontrollable laughter.

They're all just standing there, letting me take it in, and I can't stop laughing. Tears are streaming down my face. My stomach hurts.

But also, I can't stop staring.

The thongs fit them way too well. After my heat, after days of being with them, I know exactly how well-endowed all three of them are. And these ridiculous animal thongs are doing absolutely nothing to hide that fact. If anything, they're emphasizing it.

The elephant trunk is swaying. The python looks like it's about to strike. The rhino horn is definitely pointing at me.

"You guys are insane," I manage between laughs.

"We're committed to the bit," Arrow says, starting to wiggle his hips. The elephant trunk swings wildly.

Luke joins in, doing some kind of snake-charmer move that makes the python writhe.

Holt just stands there, but the rhino horn bobs up and down as he shifts his stance.

I'm clapping now, doubled over with laughter. "This is the best thing I've ever seen!"

They take a bow, all three of them, and the animals dangle and swing, and I'm going to die from laughing.

Luke reaches behind the couch and pulls out a wrapped parcel. "Your turn."

"You got me one?" I take the package, suddenly nervous.

"Obviously." Arrow grins. "Can't let us have all the fun."

"Go put it on," Holt says.

They all usher me toward the stairs, and I'm clutching the parcel, half excited and half terrified about what's inside.

I get to my room and unwrap the package carefully.

It's a cat costume. And I'm using the word *costume* generously here, because this thing looks like it lost a fight with a pair of scissors and some double-sided tape.

There's a bra, or what might've once been one. Two black velvet circles connected by a wisp of string. Cat ears on a headband, a tail, and little whisker stickers. And the bottoms... well, calling them bottoms is ambitious. It's basically a thong with a single triangle of fabric that might—*might*—cover my dignity if I hold very still and pray.

Everything is black. Everything is tiny. Everything screams *This will end badly... and also, possibly, loudly.*

I hold up the thong. "This is insane."

And yet, I'm already stripping. Because they wore ridiculous animal thongs for me, so the least I can do is return the favor with a purr.

I slide the bottoms on first, tugging them gently into place, not that there's much *place* to work with. The strap disappears between my cheeks like it was designed by a sadist. The triangle of fabric in front rides high, exposing a dangerous amount of hip bone and curve. One wrong move and I'm flashing someone. Then I attach the tail to the back of the thong. A long black piece.

Then the nipple covers pretending to be a bra. I adjust the velvet circles until they line up just right.

I glance at myself in the mirror. And yep.

"Oh, hell," I whisper.

But damn if it doesn't look *good*.

Somehow my waist appears smaller. My legs are longer. I arch a brow at my reflection, striking a pose. "Who's a bad kitty?"

My cheeks flush, and I grin.

Okay. I look like trouble. Time to act like it.

I wrap a towel around myself for modesty's sake, not that the guys are expecting modesty tonight, and head downstairs, already hearing their low voices rumbling from the living room.

The moment I hit the last step, all three heads snap up.

They're still in those damn animal thongs. The fire is crackling behind them. Pumpkins on the table leer with carved faces.

And, oh, yes. All three of them are definitely already... *rising to the occasion.*

I smirk. "Be careful with those," I say, nodding

toward their very obvious situations. "You poke some-one's eye out like that, we're gonna need a first-aid kit."

"Show us," Luke growls, voice deep with hunger.

Arrow whistles low. "Come on, kitty. Drop the towel."

Holt doesn't say a word. He just crosses his arms, gaze locked on me like he's picturing all the ways he's going to ruin me.

I turn slowly, my back to them, making sure they get the *full* view.

Then I let the towel fall.

The silence that follows is *glorious*.

I hear a sharp inhale. Someone mutters a curse.

I shift my hips slightly, giving them a better look. The string of the thong disappears between my cheeks, leaving almost nothing to the imagination. My back arches just a little. I glance over my shoulder and purr, "Still breathing?"

Arrow fans himself with a throw pillow. "Barely."

Holt's voice is a low rasp. "Turn around."

So I do, slowly, letting them see the full picture, and wriggle my tail.

The tiny circles barely cling to my breasts. The straps press into my skin, emphasizing how soft I look. The thong sits high on my hips, baring everything else.

Luke's mouth drops open. "You can't just wear that and expect us to function."

"I was told there'd be pumpkins and snacks," I say sweetly, walking toward them with a little extra sway in my hips. "No one said anything about being hunted by jungle animals. Meow."

Arrow reaches for me, eyes glazed. "Correction, kitten. We're the ones being hunted."

"Good," I say, stopping in front of them with a wicked smile. "Because this kitty bites."

Luke sweeps me into his embrace like he's claiming his prize, his grip possessive, careful, and strong. Holt's lips are at my shoulder now, teeth grazing my skin, while Arrow trails behind us like a wolf circling, his eyes hungry and fixed on me like I'm his next obsession.

I'm carried up the stairs like some kind of decadent offering, laughter still bubbling from my chest, even as my body tightens in anticipation.

"This tail is going to be tugged later," Holt murmurs, voice thick with promise.

"Oh no!" I say dramatically, looping an arm around Luke's neck. "Not the tail. That's my only weapon of self-defense."

Once they set me on my feet, I flick my tail and give Holt my best mock pout. "This kitty needs some milk," I purr.

Luke's hand tightens on my hip. "You keep talking like that, and you'll get more than milk."

Arrow snorts, shaking his head. "She practically begged for it."

"I've got all the milk you want," Holt says, reaching down and groping his rhino horn.

I'm breathless again with arousal.

Holt swoops me into his arms and lays me on the bed, but Arrow is already crawling in from the other side, palms braced as he stalks over to me. Luke moves closer too.

I'm surrounded.

Admired.

Wanted.

"You've got no idea what you just started," Arrow says as he kneels beside me, trailing a finger down the strap of my bra-dot. "This barely counts as clothing."

I smirk. "You're one to talk, elephant boy."

He growls and leans in, nipping at my throat, and my breath stutters.

Luke slips a hand under the strap at my hip. "I could snap this string with a thought."

"So don't think," I whisper.

His eyes flash. "Dangerous thing to say to a man with a python in his pants."

"You say that like it's not half the reason I wore this."

Their laughter is low, dark, feral.

And then they move.

Hands glide up my thighs, across my stomach, everywhere at once. My tiny costume is peeled away piece by piece, headband tossed across the room, one whisker sticker licked clean off my cheek. Holt takes his time with the bra-dots, his tongue flicking against a nipple before he tugs the fabric off entirely.

"I don't think cats purr like this," he mutters, voice muffled against my skin.

"They do if they're properly stroked," I quip, and then moan when Arrow nips at my hip.

The room smells like musk and something distinctly *us*. Warm, wild, intimate.

This isn't just sex. Not just teasing.

This is ours.

My body is lit up like a live wire. Every touch makes me arch. Every whisper leaves me whimpering. I'm laughing and panting and gasping all in the same breath.

And then—

They pause.

Just for a second. Long enough for me to open my eyes and see all three of them staring down at me.

"You okay?" Luke asks, and I hear the real question in his voice.

Do you still want this?

Do you trust us?

Are you ours?

"Yes," I whisper. "I'm so okay it should be illegal."

And that's all it takes.

The teasing is gone.

The pretending, the costumes, the jokes, all fade into something hotter, rawer. *Real*.

I'm laid bare under their hands and mouths, and they worship me like they've waited a lifetime.

And maybe they have.

Because I realize that something cracks open in my chest like a firework.

I'm not scared anymore.

Not of being too much. Not of loving them too hard. Not of this future we're stumbling into together.

I want it all.

The ridiculousness, the chaos, the affection, the animal thongs, the puns, the insane chemistry.

I want *them*.

And I want *me*, this version of me they bring out. Fierce and free and laughing at the edge of ruin.

ABOUT HARLEY KNIGHT

Hi, I'm Harley Knight! I'm a romance author who's absolutely obsessed with books, writing, and happily-ever-afters. I love creating stories filled with emotion, passion, and unforgettable characters that stick with you long after the last page. When I'm not writing, you'll find me lost in a good book or dreaming up my next big adventure. For me, there's nothing better than crafting love stories that remind us all why love is worth fighting for.